THE STORYTELLER

ALSO BY TRACI CHEE

The Reader

The Speaker

THE STORYTELLER

BOOK THREE OF THE READER TRILOGY

TRACI CHEE

G. P. PUTNAM'S SONS

G. P. PUTNAM'S SONS
an imprint of Penguin Random House LLC
375 Hudson Street
New York, NY 10014

Library of Congress Cataloging-in-Publication Data is available upon request.

Printed in the United States of America.
ISBN 9780399176791
1 3 5 7 9 10 8 6 4 2

Photographic elements (or images) courtesy of Shutterstock.
Text set in News Plantin MT Std.

THIS IS A BOOK.
THERE ARE HIDDEN ELEMENTS AND CODES WITHIN ITS DESIGN.
LOOK CLOSER AND HAVE FUN.

For Dad
I hope you would have been proud of me

The NORTHERN REACH

GORMAN

NORTHERN OCEAN

SHAOVINH

UMLAAN

Umlari

CANDARAN OCEAN

LICCARO

EPHYGIAN BAY

CAI

VRITHI

To the EASTERN EDGE

HYE

QIN

Karak

HAVEN

BRANDAAL

Anarra

Dead Man's Rock

ANARRAN SEA

JIHON

CHAIGON

CHAIGON OCEAN

INNER CHAIGON SEA

MASERIN

AKAPÉ

EVERICA

ZHUELIN BAY

Mae

KELANNA

Ian Schoenherr © 2016

Once

Once there was, but it would not always be. This is the ending of every story.

Once there was a world called Kelanna, a wonderful and terrible world of water and ships and magic. The people of Kelanna were like you in many ways—they spoke and worked and loved and died—but they were different in one very important respect: they couldn't read. They had never developed the written word, never inscribed the names of the dead in bronze or stone. They remembered the dead with their voices and bodies, repeating names and deeds and dizzying loves in the desperate hope that the dead would not disappear from the world altogether.

For in Kelanna, when you died, when the rhythms of your heart and lungs stuttered and failed at last, you would be gone. They'd put your body on a floating barge. They'd place you on a pile of logs and blackrock, dry brush and kindling, and they'd send you burning onto the ocean.

And that would be the end of you. In Kelanna, they didn't believe in souls or ghosts or calming spirits that walked by your side after your friend or your sister or your father had died. They didn't believe you got messages from the dead. The dead could not speak. The dead no longer existed.

Except in story.

Every life in Kelanna was a story—a tale to be lived and remembered and repeated.

Some stories were modest in scale, existing in a single family or a small community of believers who whispered among themselves so their loved ones would not be forgotten.

Others were so powerful they would transform the very fabric of the world.

Once there was a reader. She would be the daughter of an assassin and the most powerful sorcerer the world had seen in years, and she'd grow up to surpass them both in greatness.

She would be young, only five when her mother died and nine when her father was murdered, and her childhood would be steeped in violence. She'd grow up to be a formidable force in a formidable world, and one day she would be responsible for turning the tide in the deadliest war Kelanna had ever seen. She would demolish her enemies with a wave of her hand. She would watch men burn on the sea.

And she would lose everything.

Her parents. Her friends. Her allies.

The boy she loved.

Once there was a boy with a scar like a collar. He would lead an army so great they would mow down every foe they came across. He and his forces would be unstoppable, and they would conquer all Five Islands in a bloody altercation known as the Red War.

He'd be young when he did it, and he'd die soon after his last campaign . . . alone.

Once there was a storyteller, a chipped-toothed outlaw, who said he'd do anything to be part of a tale with such greatness and scope. But after the Red War, he'd regret every word.

CHAPTER 1

Fine as Gossamer, Hard as Iron

Sefia sat up in the shadows of the sick bay, startled out of some half-remembered dream.

The ship rocked and plunged beneath her, making the jars of ointment and bottles of tonic rattle on their shelves. Outside, rain spattered the portholes, blurring her view of the waves, high as rolling hills.

A storm. They must have come upon it in the night.

Sefia shivered, hugging her knees to her chest. In the four days since she'd returned to the *Current* with Archer, she'd had the same dream again and again. She was back in the house on the hill, and ink was seeping—no, *flooding*—from the secret room in the basement where her parents had kept the Book, the dark waves reaching across the floor to grasp them by the ankles and crawl up their calves. In the dream, Lon and Mareah scooped her up. In the dream, they shoved her out the door. But they were always too slow to save themselves, always too slow to escape the growing pool of ink that drew them, screaming, into its black depths.

Destiny. Her parents had been destined to die young, their futures recorded in the Book with everything that had ever been or would ever be, from the flicker of a mayfly's wings to the life spans of the stars overhead.

Somewhere in the Book was the passage where her mother got sick.

Somewhere were the paragraphs that described her father being tortured.

It had been written, so it had come to pass.

But they'd fought it. They'd betrayed the Guard, the secret society of readers to which they'd sworn their undying allegiance. They'd stolen the Book, the Guard's most powerful weapon, to protect their daughter from her own future. They'd run.

They'd lost, in the end, but oh, how they'd *fought*.

As Sefia had to fight now. Fight and *win*, or she'd lose Archer to destiny too.

Beside her, he lay curled beneath the blankets, hair tousled, fingers twitching in his sleep. He always slept so little, his dreams haunted by memories of the people he'd killed.

He felt *fractured*, he'd told her. At all times, he was the same small-town boy he'd been before the Guard's impressors took him, and yet, at all times, he was an animal, he was a victim, he was a killer, he was loud as thunder, he was the boy from the legends, with a bloodlust that could not be slaked.

Lightning forked in the distance, pulsing like veins in the restless sky.

As if in response, Archer's body spasmed. He let out a wordless gasp.

Sefia shifted out of his way. "Archer. It's okay. You're safe."

His eyes opened. For a moment, he seemed to have trouble emerging from his dreams, seemed to have trouble recognizing where he was, *who* he was.

But the moment would pass. It always did. And then—

The smile. It spread across his face like dawn racing over water—his lips, his cheeks, his golden eyes. Every time, it was like he was seeing her for the first time, his expression full of such hope that she longed to see it again and again for the rest of her days.

For a second, the storm abated. For a second, the ship was still. For a second, Sefia's whole world was light and soft and warm.

"Sefia," he whispered, tucking her hair behind her ear.

She bent closer, drawn to him as a hummingbird is drawn to a flower, her mouth gently landing on his.

He leaned into her kiss, responding to her lips and wandering hands as if her very touch was magic, making him moan and arch and yearn for more.

He laced his fingers in her hair, like he needed to be closer to her, like he couldn't get enough of her, but as he tried to sit up, he let out a sudden hiss of pain and reached for his injured side.

"I'm sorry," she said.

"Don't be." Propping himself up on his elbows, he grinned. "I'm not."

Her cheeks warmed as she pulled aside the blanket to examine his bandages. Doc had stitched and dressed the wound twice now: first when he'd arrived, half-conscious, with the gash below his ribs black and nauseatingly deep, and a second time when Archer had torn his sutures trying to help Cooky dump a pot of potato peels overboard. Sefia would never hear the end of it if Doc had to redo the stitches again.

"I'm fine." Archer tried batting her away.

"You almost died."

"Only almost." He shrugged. He'd told her about the fight with Serakeen. There had been the smell of cordite and blood. A gust of magic that had swept Archer's lieutenants, Frey and Aljan, into the wall of the alley before dropping them, unconscious, onto the cobbles. The resistance of bone as Archer severed Serakeen's hand at the wrist.

"I should've been there," Sefia said, not for the first time. If she'd been there, she could have protected him. She had the same magic as Serakeen—a magic the Guard called Illumination— she might have even matched him in a fight. *After all,* she thought bitterly, *I'm the daughter of an assassin and the most powerful sorcerer the world has seen in years.*

No. She didn't want to believe in that future. She wouldn't become a weapon in some war for control of the Five Kingdoms. She wouldn't lose Archer, the boy she loved.

"You're here now. That's what matters," Archer said quietly. "Without you, we wouldn't be able to rescue Frey and Aljan."

His bloodletters, his *friends*, had followed him into the fight with Serakeen, and Serakeen still had them. The Guard's Apprentice Soldier, known to Sefia's parents as Rajar, had once been Lon and Mareah's friend and collaborator. Together, they'd orchestrated the war that was supposed to claim Archer's life.

7

How many of her parents' mistakes would Sefia have to fix? She'd loved them, but they'd made *so many*.

"Frey and Aljan will be all right," Sefia said.

"You really think so?"

She trailed her fingers down his arm, over the fifteen burns that marked his kills in the impressors' fighting rings, and took his hand. "Yes," she said.

The plan was to return to the bloodletters, organize a rescue, and meet up with the *Current of Faith* again at Haven, an island in the unexplored reaches of the Central Sea—one of those places you could get to only if you were told how to get there. Reed had set it up months ago to take in outlaws on the run from the widening scope of the war. If Sefia and Archer got there with the bloodletters, they would all have a place to wait while the fighting—and destiny—passed them by. If they got to Haven, Archer would live.

But first, they needed the Book. Sefia couldn't teleport to the bloodletters without a clear image of where they were, and only the Book, with its infinite pages of history, could provide that.

She'd hidden it in the safest place she could think of: the Jaharan messengers' post. The messengers' guild dealt in all kinds of secrets—delicate packages, incriminating information— and they never broke their trust. They were respected and powerful, and while it was with them, no one could touch the Book.

Not even the Guard. She hoped.

The *Current of Faith* was on its way to Jahara now; they were only a few days away. A few days, and she'd have the Book back.

A few days, and she'd be able to find the bloodletters and mount a rescue. A few days. Frey and Aljan just had to hold on a few more days.

Archer lifted Sefia's hand to his lips. "What would I do without you?"

"You'll never have to find out." She kissed him again, and the kiss was a promise. A promise of high winds and open waters, of lying, legs tangled, on a white beach with nothing but the firmament for a coverlet, of succulent days and hot breath and damp skin and years rich as wine and endless as the sea.

When she drew back, she had the satisfaction of seeing his gold eyes darken with want, with *yes*—he licked his lips—with *forever*. He reached for her again.

"You'll be sorry if you tear your stitches."

"If I tear them doing what I want to do to you, it'll be worth it." He pulled her, grinning, onto the bunk beside him, smothering her laughter with kisses until she was delirious with them.

Then the alarm began to sound.

Archer grumbled and rolled onto his side, pinning Sefia between him and the wall.

"That's the bell for all hands!" she protested.

He nipped at her collarbone. "I'm injured, remember?"

"I'm not!"

Before he could reply, the door opened, and Sefia let out a yelp as Marmalade, the new chanty leader of the larboard watch, stuck her head into the sick bay. She was in her rain gear, hood pulled over her honey-colored hair.

"Ugh!" she cried as Sefia peered around Archer's naked shoulder. "Do your canoodlin' on your own time!"

"I'm trying!" Sefia gestured to Archer, who grinned unapologetically.

Marmalade rolled her eyes. They'd all become friends playing Ship of Fools with Horse and Meeks, and the girl had consistently fleeced all of them but Archer, who at least broke even. "Yeah, you're tryin' *real* hard. Just get out of bed before the mate comes to fetch you, or you'll be scourin' pots till we reach Jahara."

"Fine, fine. I'm getting up."

"Oh, and Archer?" The chanty leader's gaze roved along his body, from his chest to his waist, where his pajamas hung low on his hips. *"Nice."*

Sefia hurled a pillow across the room as Marmalade ducked back into the corridor and slammed the door, laughing.

As Sefia scrambled from beneath the blankets, scooping up her clothes, Archer followed.

"You're injured, remember?" she said with a touch of sarcasm.

"I'm not." He stuffed his feet through the legs of his trousers, wincing as the abrupt movement pained him. "At least, I'm not too injured to help."

"Yeah, right." Blinking, Sefia summoned her magic, and in an instant, Archer's body, the bunk beneath him, the well-worn walls of the sick bay, even the portholes and the rough water outside were overlaid with spiraling golden torrents.

The Illuminated world.

If the Book was a written compendium of past, present, and future, the Illuminated world was the living embodiment of it—an ocean of light in constant motion beneath the world of touch and smell and taste. With enough time and training, Illuminators like Sefia could sift through the shimmering specks to see the events of the past or move objects through the air.

Once, long ago, the rarest of talents could rewrite the fabric of the world itself. But skilled as Sefia was, that power was beyond her.

As she wound her fingers into the fine golden threads, the fibers of the Illuminated world bent and rippled, cascading toward Archer and nudging him gently back onto the bunk.

"Hey!" he cried.

For good measure, she also flung the blanket over his head.

"Stay here." Shrugging into her oilskin coat, she glanced up and opened her arms wide. Under her hands, the waves of light parted as if they were curtains. Details of her surroundings whirled past as she used her magic to peer through the ceiling to the main deck, the outlaws racing across the ship, the downpour streaming out of the sky, the sails flapping madly in the storm. But she ignored these. For Teleportation, she needed to locate a place she knew so well it had been burned into her memory.

Ah, yes, there—the edge of the quarterdeck, where she used to read the Book on their first voyage with the *Current*.

With that image fixed in her mind, she waved her hands and transported herself through the Illuminated world—out of the sick bay, through the timbers of the ship—appearing on deck to the rain on her face, her feet skidding on the slick planks.

Marmalade caught her by the arm. "Seven out of ten for the entrance," she said.

"Just need to stick the landing." Blinking, Sefia allowed the world of light to ebb from her vision, leaving her in the dark of the storm with the other sailors. Overhead, long trails of water dripped from the sails like icicles.

The alarm bell went silent as Captain Cannek Reed appeared on deck, looking wild as the sea with his coat flaring behind him and his eyes glinting like sapphires in the shadow of his wide-brimmed hat. As if on cue, lightning lanced through the clouds behind him, crackling as it dissipated.

"Ten out of ten for dramatic lighting," Sefia muttered.

Marmalade let out a peal of laughter, which she stifled when the chief mate glared in their direction with his dead gray eyes.

"I sensed this wreck in the water during the night," the captain began in his weatherworn voice. "Thought they might be outlaws, so we came to investigate."

According to legend, Captain Reed was the only man alive who could talk to the water. It told him all sorts of things about its tides, its currents, its deep-sea creatures. Some people said it had even told him how he was going to die—with one last breath of salty wet air, a black gun in his hand, and a white dandelion floating above the deck.

Sefia glanced over the rail. The water was full of splintered crates and kegs emptied of their contents, scraps of sails, and corpses, their hair rising and falling around their heads like kelp. In the dark seas, their crimson uniforms appeared the same bruised mulberry as Archer's stained bandages. Among the wreckage were two narrow longboats crammed with survivors.

Redcoats—soldiers of the Oxscinian Navy—there were redcoats in the water.

Once, crouching on the edge of the forest with her aunt Nin,

Sefia had been afraid of the Red Navy soldiers. But that was back when she could imagine nothing worse than being apprehended by the authorities. Now she knew there were worse things than redcoats out there—Serakeen, the Guard, war.

"They ain't outlaws," continued Reed, "but we ain't leavin' 'em out here to die."

"What of the *Crux*?" someone asked.

Sefia glanced around, but the great golden pirate ship that had been accompanying them was nowhere to be seen.

"The *Crux* went on to Jahara to arrange for provisions," Captain Reed answered. Then, with a nod, he dismissed them. "Go on, do some good out there."

There was no cheering, no chorus of huzzahs, but Sefia felt a wave of determination go through them as Meeks and the chief mate began sending the crew into the rescue boats.

She ended up on the first boat with Reed and the doc. The oar was slippery in her hands as the waves brought the corpses crashing into the hull.

She wanted to teleport; it would have been faster. But she needed a clear referent—a strong memory or an unobstructed view—and she couldn't see through the rain and the waves to get a good look.

As they pulled up, one of the redcoats tossed her a line and she hauled them in, lashing the boats together. Brusquely motioning Sefia aside, Doc climbed in among the wounded, bearing her black bag.

The Red Navy soldiers were festering and damp, the smell of sickness clinging to them like a fungus. They must have been out there for days.

"Rotten hulls," exclaimed the one who'd thrown her the rope. "It *is* you, isn't it?"

Surprised, Sefia blinked water from her eyelashes. The redcoat was easily one of the prettiest boys she'd ever seen, with green eyes, a handsome jaw, a curling forelock of hair wet with rain. His features were so striking, he might have even given Scarza, Archer's silver-haired second-in-command, a run for his money, but for the flabbergasted expression on his perfectly symmetrical face.

"Do I know you?" she asked doubtfully. She would've remembered a face like his.

A round-headed boy with narrow eyes popped up beside him. He appeared so suddenly, so comically, it almost made her laugh. Almost. "Don't think so," he said. "You were unconscious at the time."

"I was *what*?"

"Out cold," the second boy explained matter-of-factly. "On Black Boar Pier."

She'd only been at Black Boar Pier, in Epidram, a city on the northeast coast of Oxscini, once in her life. She and Archer had stumbled into a trap. There'd been a fight, and she'd lost consciousness. Later, Archer had told her how Reed and the outlaws had shown up to save them. Had these redcoats been there too?

"Petty Officer," said the captain from behind her.

Still bewildered, Sefia watched Captain Reed clasp hands with the boys. All their paths must have crossed three months ago, like shooting stars in the night. What a coincidence that all of them would meet again.

Except there *were* no coincidences, as the Guard was fond of saying.

This meeting wasn't happenstance—it was *destiny*. And it was a net, fine as gossamer and hard as iron, closing in on her and Archer with every passing second.

"It's midshipman now, sir," said the first redcoat, who managed a handsome, waterlogged smile. "Midshipman Haldon Lac."

CHAPTER 2

The Second Adventure of Haldon Lac

For as long as anyone could remember, the Five Islands had been at war. Provinces fought. Colonies revolted. Even the most stable kingdoms had long histories of blood feuds and political assassinations that lent interest to otherwise dull pastoral chronicles of more peaceful times.

For red-blooded, battle-loving Oxscinians like Midshipman Haldon Lac, war was a source of pride. War brought glory to the Forest Kingdom and Her Majesty Queen Heccata—long may she reign. Expansion, conflict, competition. This had been their way of life for more generations than he could count.

They had been at war with the kingdom of Everica for five years when the enemy, King Darion Stonegold, made an unprecedented move: he convinced Liccaro, the weaker, impoverished kingdom to the north, to join him in the battle against Oxscini. He turned a legion of pirates into privateers.

He formed the Alliance, the first union between kingdoms in Kelannan history.

To combat the combined force of the two eastern kingdoms, Queen Heccata had commissioned a new fleet of ships. Most of the personnel stationed at Epidram, in northeast Oxscini, were shipped out, among them Haldon Lac, Indira Fox, and Olly Hobs, a trio who had been inseparable since almost apprehending Hatchet and his impressors at Black Boar Pier. They were assigned to the *Fire-Eater* and tasked with scouring the Central Sea for Alliance vessels.

The day the fleet left port had been the happiest day of Midshipman Lac's life. There was a parade, a crowd waving crimson Oxscinian flags embroidered with gold. Though his frigate was easily dwarfed by the bigger ships of the line, Haldon Lac was certain he'd never seen a more majestic ship than the *Fire-Eater*: her scarlet hull, her crisp white sails, her cannons black as ebony. He puffed out his chest as he stood at the rail, watching as brokenhearted boys and girls waved him off under a sunset red as romance.

But the rest of Lac's maiden voyage had fallen woefully short of his expectations.

They did not tell you, for example, how *dirty* it would be, how *dull*, with long, tedious watches interrupted only now and again by the sighting of a sail on the horizon.

Nor did they tell you that when you did finally spy an enemy ship, the chase could take *hours*, and more often than not, your quarry would escape as soon as night fell, dousing their lamps and slipping away into the darkness.

Or perhaps they did tell you, but Midshipman Haldon Lac had chosen only to hear the stories of grand exploits and magnificent naval battles.

At any rate, one night Lac was roused from sleep by the clanging of the ship's bell. They had been tailing an Alliance vessel, and, to his surprise, their quarry had *not* bolted into the night. In fact, the *Fire-Eater* had almost caught up to their target.

Soon they would be near enough to engage.

The crew cleared away their hammocks and chests, secured the shutters, loosed the great twenty-four-pound cannons, and laid out cases of shot. They dampened the decks to prevent stray sparks from catching the tarred timbers and filled tubs with seawater in case of fire.

Exchanging conspiratorial grins with Fox and Hobs, Lac skipped about his duties filled with a sparkling mixture of excitement and fear. This was what he had been waiting for: adventure, purpose, glory.

He and Fox were in command of the fighting tops on the fore- and mainmasts. Since their time in Epidram, Fox had caught up to him in rank, and now she was the most trusted of the midshipmen. She deserved it, he admitted freely. She worked harder than he did. She was quicker and smarter and braver. She'd make lieutenant in no time, at the rate she was going.

Lac found her at the base of the mainmast before she climbed to her position. "Our first engagement!" he declared, somewhat obviously.

Fox punched him lightly in the shoulder. "Not our *first*."

"You mean that failed ambush on Black Boar Pier?" He rubbed the old bullet wound, a reminder of his foolish attempt to apprehend Hatchet and his criminal crew. "I was so stupid."

She grinned at him with that wild coyote smile he'd come to love so much. "Stupid *brave*, you mean. It's like your own personal brand of courage."

"Or my own personal brand of cologne."

Fox laughed. "If we make it through the war, you can bottle it. It'll smell like starched collars and gunpowder."

"What do you mean, 'if' we make it?" Lac asked.

In the low light, her gray eyes flashed like smoky quartz, and she arched one of her naturally perfect brows. He didn't like to admit it, but he was envious of her brows.

"Nothing's for certain," she said.

The activity on deck flurried around him—the rattle of cannons being locked into place, the *click* of bullets being loaded into chambers, the anxious thrum of voices and murmured words of encouragement.

Bravely, stupidly, he placed a hand on her shoulder. "This is. *We are*."

"How do you figure?"

"Because we're the heroes, aren't we?" he said with a wink. "The heroes always live in the stories."

"That's stupid." She gripped his arm. "But nice stupid."

"That's my other cologne."

With a laugh, Fox swung up into the rigging with such lithe grace that Haldon Lac was momentarily dumbstruck by how lucky he was to know her. She'd be a lieutenant by the end of the voyage. He was certain of it.

He watched her until she was safely in the fighting top, where she leaned over the side, still wearing that coyote smile, and waved at him.

"Our turn, sir," said Hobs, appearing suddenly beside him.

Lac started, clutching his chest dramatically. But the midshipman was glad of the company. If he was being honest with himself, which he certainly was not, he hated the climb to the fighting top. Hated the way the deck seemed to drop away beneath him, hated the way he had to pause and shut his eyes, hooking his arms through the ropes like they'd come undone at any second.

By some miracle Lac made it, shaking, to the platform where his men were waiting. He must have looked more anxious than he realized, because Hobs patted him on the shoulder, a broad smile on his round face. "Don't worry, sir."

"I'm not worried!" Lac protested. Too loudly.

Some of the men cackled, and he had the good sense to blush.

"It's okay," Hobs said. "Everyone's worried. Everyone's got something to fear."

The topmen agreed as they loaded rounds into their rifles.

"Death, capture, drowning . . ." Hobs ticked off each word on his fingers.

"Enemy fire," one of the sailors added.

"Shrapnel," said another.

"Impalement."

"Falling," Lac ventured, with a glance down at the swaying decks.

Hobs nodded his nearly spherical head. "That's the spirit, sir."

With a sigh, Lac looked over to the mainmast, where Fox was gathered with her own topmen. He doubted *she* was afraid of anything.

There was a deep breath of calm.

Then the Alliance vessel came about to meet them, flying blue-and-gold flags from the yardarms. Fire shot from the mouths of her cannons.

"Brace yourselves!" the captain of the *Fire-Eater* yelled.

A shot struck their frigate's bow, splintering their red hull, and there came a great roar from the crew—a sound Midshipman Haldon Lac had only ever heard about in stories—full of blood and rage and pride.

The great guns flashed. Cannonballs sailed through the smoke. Men screamed. The *Fire-Eater* plunged up and down in the swells as they fired broadside after broadside. On the fighting tops, the sailors manned the swivel guns, sending iron into the enemy ranks. They took up their rifles, the muzzle flashes brightening the air. In the smoke, the Alliance soldiers crumpled to the fire of Lac and his topmen.

For over an hour it went on like this: the gunfire, the shrieking of the wounded, the ships circling each other like sharks.

Then a series of cannon fire erupted from the Alliance ship.

"Incoming!" someone shouted.

The *Fire-Eater* shuddered. Timbers fractured. The mainmast

shook. A great *crack!* rent the air as the base of the mainmast splintered. Frightened cries went up around the ship as the main topsail quivered, losing wind. The mast was going to fall.

"Fox is over there," Lac said in a horrified whisper.

Beside him, Hobs nodded. "I know, sir."

But from the foremast, there was nothing they could do for their friend. They watched helplessly as the sailors scrambled into the rigging. Racks of guns toppled.

As if in slow motion, the length of timber began to fall. The sails wavered in midair.

Then *she* appeared—between the rippling canvas, running across the yardarm as the mast tipped toward them.

"Fox!" Lac cried. He dashed to the edge of the foretop, clinging to the rigging as he leaned out over the chaos below.

Fox reached the end of the yard. She leapt, arms and legs pumping, hand outstretched.

Her palm struck his. Her fingers dug into his skin. Locking his hand, he held fast as she dangled beneath him. Below, tiny redcoats screamed and scrambled back and forth like ants.

Lac managed what he hoped was a rakish smile. "What'd I tell you?" he asked. "Heroes."

Fox grinned up at him.

But then there was a burst of blood at her chest. A stain. The report of a distant rifle.

And Fox went limp in his hand.

He couldn't understand it at first, couldn't fathom why she was so heavy all of a sudden, why she didn't lift herself up.

It wasn't until Hobs helped him drag her body onto the platform that Lac realized Fox was dead.

No.

It wasn't supposed to happen this way. He was supposed to heave her safely onto the foretop. She was supposed to stand, testing her wrenched shoulder, and smile that wild coyote smile.

There was another round of fire from the gun deck, and the explosions lit them from below. Across the sea, the rudder of the Alliance ship snapped. Glass shattered at the stern. The enemy was dead in the water.

In other circumstances, the redcoats would have cheered.

But they had not won.

Behind their broken enemy, the towering, monstrous forms of three-decker ships appeared out of the night—blue hulls, bristling with guns, their rails outlined with lanterns like hundreds of flaming eyes.

The Alliance. The collective might of Stonegold's Everican Navy and Serakeen's pirates from Liccaro.

Lac fell to his knees, cradling Fox's body in his arms. This wasn't how it was supposed to be. She was supposed to live. She was supposed to have captained her own ship, one day—she'd been quick enough, smart enough, brave enough—with Lac and Hobs as her lieutenants.

They were supposed to have lived long and happy lives together, and told this story—the story of their second adventure—over and over, so many times it became legend, not belonging to them at all but to the lives of some far-off heroes.

But Fox was dead.

And the Alliance fleet loomed over them.

Below, the captain of the *Fire-Eater* was shouting, her

voice desperate and defiant. The crew was stamping their feet, pounding the butts of their rifles and the hammers of their fists, as the massive Alliance warships loosed their broadsides like blue dragons breathing fire in the night.

In the foretop, Midshipman Haldon Lac pressed his lips to Fox's temple.

Y ou miss a man so much," someone said.

Blinking, Lac looked up from his mug of bourbon-laced tea and found Horse, the *Current*'s carpenter, watching him with sad, wide-set eyes across the crowded great cabin, where he'd squeezed his broad form between the black-haired girl and the scarred boy from Black Boar Pier, whom Lac now knew as Sefia and Archer.

That they were here, on the *Current of Faith*, with Lac and Hobs, was a quirk of happenstance that Fox would have found both curious and amusing.

If Fox had been here.

The rain continued its deluge outside as the *Current*'s cook and steward wound through the tangle of legs and elbows, re-filling mugs. Cooky was a slim man, all skin and muscle, with a bald head and cascades of silver earrings spangling the rims of his ears. Aly, the steward, dwarfed him in height, but something about her demeanor almost made it easy to overlook her, though Lac had no idea how anyone could miss the magnificent blond hair she wore in long braids down her back. The two of them seemed to have found the perfect working rhythm, following and leading in turns, seamlessly weaving in and out of each other's paths even in the cramped space.

It reminded Lac of working with Fox.

"Then what happened?" asked Meeks. Lac recognized him, too, from Black Boar Pier and from the legends—the second mate was a renowned storyteller, one of those people who could string you along for hours on nothing but his words. To think that such a man was listening to lowly, humble Midshipman Haldon Lac—

Fox would have told Lac not to let it go to his head.

He swallowed a few times before speaking again. "The foremast snapped as soon as the Alliance fired on us. Half my topmen fell immediately, and I—I couldn't . . . the force was so great, I—" His gaze found Hobs, whose eyes were glistening faintly in the lamplight. "I lost my hold on Fox's body, and she fell into the sea."

"We both lost her," said Hobs.

Draining the last of his tea, Lac described how the *Fire-Eater* had fought back as long as they were able, but ultimately they'd been forced to run up the white flag.

Surrender had been painful enough. In Lac's mind, Oxscinians *never* surrendered. It was a disgrace to his kingdom, his queen, the far-reaching legacy of all the redcoats who'd come before him. But the Alliance had ignored the rules of combat; they'd continued to fire on the *Fire-Eater*.

"Even under the bombardment," Lac continued, dashing angry tears from his eyes, "the captain kept her head. She gave Hobs and me command of the boats and ordered us to abandon ship. We shouldn't have—*I* shouldn't have run—but it was an order, wasn't it? We obey orders, don't we? We took the injured and piled in. With the *Fire-Eater* blocking us from

25

view, we escaped while the Alliance battered her again and again.

"Then there was an explosion so bright it was like the ocean itself was aflame. The *Fire-Eater* went up like a tinderbox. The captain had taken a lantern down to the magazine and detonated what was left of our powder kegs. Better to destroy the *Fire-Eater* than let those bonesuckers have her. *She* was no coward, the captain."

And her sacrifice had worked. The boats had gotten away, and they'd been trying to make their way back to the Royal Navy ever since.

"But I had no idea where we were," Haldon Lac admitted.

"Terrible sense of direction, see," Hobs explained. "Not one of his talents."

Lac chewed his lip. Fox had possessed an impeccable sense of direction.

"We're four days from Jahara," said Captain Reed from where he'd been leaning against the back windows, listening attentively. "Lucky for you, we're headed that way now."

Jahara was a mostly neutral island off the southern coast of Deliene, Oxscini's northern neighbor. If Lac got them to the Oxscinian embassy, the redcoats would be clothed, fed, and sent back to the Royal Navy, where they'd all be given new posts, or perhaps promotions.

Well, not *all* of them.

Lac's eyes felt so full they burned. He must have been making an unbearably unattractive face, because the captain straightened.

"What's the matter, kid?"

"I—I told Fox we'd be heroes."

"You think that leap she made wasn't heroic?" Captain Reed laughed, but not unkindly. "Meeks, tell me that leap wasn't heroic."

The second mate's face broke into a fetching chipped-toothed smile. "Nah, Cap. That's the stuff stories are made of."

"But she *died.*" Lac's voice broke, embarrassingly.

"That's the thing, kid." With enviable grace, the captain made his way through the crowded cabin, and even in his grief, Haldon Lac could not help but notice how ruggedly handsome he was, how self-assured and at home in his own skin. The man refilled Lac's empty mug from a crystal decanter. "Heroes die all the time."

Lac found himself staring at Reed's tattoos—skulls, sea serpents, a man with a black gun, and a maelstrom spinning in the crook of his left elbow, for the time he snatched the Thunder Gong from under the nose of his rival, Captain Dimarion.

"What's more important," Captain Reed continued, "is that *you* survived."

"Why?"

The captain poured himself a finger of liquor and clinked their glasses. "Because survivors get to decide who the heroes are. And the villains."

As the night wore on, they laid out a map on the dining table, and Reed and the others gathered around. To the west was Oxscini, Lac's beloved Forest Kingdom, with its smaller islands to the south. Those islands were the reason Oxscini had never been conquered—no one had ever possessed the naval prowess to breach the heart of the kingdom.

To the east were Everica and Liccaro, the two kingdoms that comprised the Alliance.

And between the two halves of the map, closer to Oxscini than Lac wanted to believe, Hobs pointed out a spot on the Central Sea. "That's where we encountered the Alliance line, sir."

The Alliance was sailing west, spreading across Kelanna like a stain.

"That's what the Guard wants," said Sefia. "First Everica, then Liccaro and Deliene, and Oxscini and Roku last. If all goes according to their plans, it won't be long before they've conquered all Five Kingdoms."

"But why?" Lac asked.

"Stability and peace." Her voice dripped scorn. "They think with all of Kelanna under their thumb, it'll be a better world."

"Peace through war," Hobs said. "Seems a funny way to go about it, if you ask me."

"Oxscini will give 'em a fight. But Roku"—Reed tapped the smallest of the kingdoms, a cluster of islands that, like much of Kelanna, had once belonged to Oxscini's sprawling empire—"won't be much of a challenge."

"What's the Guard?" Lac asked.

Sefia eyed him suspiciously. At that moment, she reminded him of Fox, who'd looked at him in precisely that way at the beginning of their friendship.

But it was Archer, the boy with the burned throat, who answered. His golden eyes flashed in the lamplight like a cat's. "The real villains," he said.

CHAPTER 3

Close to the Heart

The *Current of Faith* reached Jahara long after midnight, when even the seedier taverns and gambling dens of the Central Port were shutting their doors, but Archer and Sefia remained awake in the great cabin, planning their next moves with Captain Reed.

"In the morning, I'll take you to the messengers' post to get the Book," Reed said, pacing in front of the glass cases that lined the walls. "The chief mate will see to the resupplyin' of the ship, and Meeks will get a guide for the redcoats."

Archer was a little disappointed. Over the past four days, he'd become friends with the Royal Navy soldiers, Lac and Hobs in particular, and he'd hoped to see them to the Oxscinian embassy himself.

But his priority was the Book. His priority was Frey and Aljan and his bloodletters, who, like him, had once been kidnapped and groomed for killing by the Guard. He was the one who'd rescued them. He was the one who'd given them purpose. They'd all come together so brilliantly, so beautifully deadly, as they'd hunted down impressors in Deliene. Then he'd abandoned them as soon as they reached Epigloss, only returning for the promise of more revenge, more bloodshed. And he'd gotten Frey and Aljan captured by Serakeen.

He owed it to them to fix his mistakes. To protect them, the way he should have all along.

"Then you're heading out?" Sefia asked, interrupting Archer's thoughts.

Captain Reed tapped an eight-beat rhythm on an empty glass case. "Yep." The *Current* and the *Crux* would load up and set sail for the Trove of the King, the greatest treasure hoard in Kelannan history. Hundreds of years ago, King Fieldspar of Liccaro had collected all his people's amassed wealth and buried it somewhere in the caverns beneath his kingdom. For generations, treasure hunters had told tales of the Trove's labyrinthine tunnels, the pyramids of gold and silver ingots, the halls overflowing with gems. The contents of just one of the caves would have been enough to satiate even the greediest of appetites.

But Archer knew that deep hunger in Reed's blue eyes was for one treasure and one treasure only: the Resurrection Amulet, a magical object that allowed you to cheat death. It had been lost for generations, buried somewhere in the maze-like tunnels of the Trove, but if he found it, it would at last give him the immortality he'd craved for years.

If you wanted something that badly, for that long, you wouldn't let anything stop you. Not even a war.

"Wish you were comin' with us," the captain said, taking

a slip of paper from his pocket, "in case we need you to read something else for us."

Like the rest of the crew, Archer had memorized the paper's contents—it was a copy of the poem they'd found inscribed on the bell of King Fieldspar's ship. He had been a Guardian, they surmised. That was the only way he could have written out their only clue to the location of the Trove:

> *The brave and the bold may find Liccarine gold*
> *Where the stallions charge into the spray.*
> *Where the sidewinder waits, the heart lowers its gates,*
> *And the water will show you the way.*

Reed believed that the riddle would lead them to four different landmarks—starting with Steeds, a headland of rock shaped like two wild mustangs on the far side of Liccaro—that would reveal the way to the Trove of the King.

But Archer and Sefia would not be there to see it.

"I've been teaching Meeks and Theo to read," she said.

Reed scoffed. "Meeks and Theo are smart, but they ain't you."

She shrugged. "I can't leave Archer, Cap."

Under the table, Archer found her hand. She laced her fingers in his. "And I can't leave the bloodletters," he said.

His bloodletters. His responsibility.

"I know, kid." Reed sighed. "They're your crew."

Once Archer and Sefia had the Book, she would teleport them to the bloodletters, in Epigloss, Epidram's sister city in northwest Oxscini, where they'd rescue Frey and Aljan. After that, they'd sail the bloodletters' ship, the *Brother*, to Haven, where they'd wait for the *Current* and the *Crux* to return from the Trove.

The hidden outlaw sanctuary was run by the only two people to whom every thief and cutthroat in the Central Sea would listen: Adeline, the Lady of Mercy, who'd given Reed's old silver-and-ivory revolver its name, and Isabella, the gunsmith who'd made it for her. The women were living legends.

"Haven's here." Captain Reed pointed on the map of Kelanna, still spread out on the dining table, to a spot in the Central Sea surrounded by the Five Islands.

The Five Islands Archer was supposed to conquer.

Right before he died.

No, he thought. He was going to bring the bloodletters to Haven, where they were going to swim and till the earth in the shadow of the island's old volcano. He was going to listen to Sefia's stories and kiss her in the mornings and build her a house in the trees. They were, all of them, going to let the war pass around them like water around a pylon. And they were, all of them, going to live.

There was a sudden knock. Startled, Archer jumped to his feet, grimacing at the pain in his side. He hadn't popped his stitches in days, but the occasional twinge was a reminder that, for the moment, thread was still the only thing keeping him together.

Gingerly, he touched his bandage as Dimarion, captain of the *Crux*, entered the great cabin. He was like a king, Archer thought. A tyrant who believed he owned everything he saw simply because he'd seen it.

Dimarion leveled his ruby-handled cane at Captain Reed, who had stopped his restless movement. "I arrange for re-supplying your ship with the best provisions Jahara has to offer—graciously, I even pay for some of it out of my own pocket—and you can't even be bothered to let me know you've arrived?"

Reed leaned against the edge of the table, smirking. "Didn't want to disturb your beauty rest."

Dimarion laughed. "My dear captain, there's no rest for the wicked." Then, seeing Archer standing at the table, he crossed the room in a few quick strides.

For a big man with a cane, he was surprisingly light on his feet. No wonder none of them had heard him approach. Archer stepped over the bench to meet him.

"Sefia." The pirate captain gave her a little bow.

Archer had been too wounded to see anyone when he and Sefia had first teleported to the *Current*, but Dimarion had demanded an audience with Sefia. She'd been on the *Crux* for hours, telling him their story, from her parents' betrayal of the Guard to Archer forming the bloodletters to learning the magic of the Book.

"Captain," she said coolly. She didn't return the bow.

Then the pirate turned to Archer. He looked down at him like a jeweler examining a diamond, his gaze lingering on the knotted scar that encircled Archer's neck—the scar the impressors had given him, the same one each of the bloodletters had, the same one given to all of the Guard's "candidates"—the scar that made him the boy from the legends.

The boy with the unstoppable army.

"I've been wanting a look at you," Dimarion said. "But Captain Reed insisted on keeping you caged away like one of his prizes."

Archer could feel Sefia bristling beside him. Had she summoned the Sight? He wouldn't put it past her to fling the man across the room if she thought he was a threat.

Or if he annoyed her.

"And now that you've had a look?" Archer asked.

Captain Dimarion sniffed. "You don't look like a born killer to me."

Born killer. That was what the impressors had called Archer. But he hadn't been born this way—he hadn't even been born *Archer*—he'd been made, chiseled and chipped away at until he was no longer the little lighthouse keeper he used to be, but *Archer*, chief of the bloodletters, a legend for what he'd done to the impressors in Deliene, with stories of his brutality and efficiency in battle quickly spreading to the other kingdoms.

And he'd chosen it. Maybe not at first, maybe not intentionally. But yes, in the end, he'd sought out the fights, he'd wanted the kills, he'd shaped himself into whatever he was now.

Trapped, he thought. He was trapped by destiny. Unless he and Sefia could escape it.

Dimarion was still watching him, as if waiting for the bloodlust to overtake Archer like a red haze.

Archer already knew how he'd incapacitate the pirate. Captain Dimarion's brute strength and his cane were worth considering, but Archer was faster, even with his bandaged side, and in the back of his mind he'd already been devising ways to strike Dimarion's weak joints, his old wounds ripe for reinjury. But violence was not a party trick Archer unveiled for curious spectators.

To him, violence was something ugly, something to be ashamed of.

And at the same time, something precious, to be carried close to the heart.

When Archer didn't respond, Dimarion pivoted to Reed. "You could offer me a drink, you know, but I suppose such hospitality is beyond you." Picking up a crystal decanter from a side table, Dimarion poured himself three fingers of liquor and settled in one of the armchairs as if it were a bejeweled throne instead of threadbare velvet. "I have information for you."

He paused. He seemed to be waiting for them to applaud, or perhaps bow.

Archer sat.

Sefia yawned.

Sighing, the pirate captain took a sip of his drink, licking his lips before declaring that the Lonely King, Eduoar Corabelli II, was dead. "Poison," Dimarion explained. "He took his own life, same as his father, in the same room as his father."

Deliene, the Northern Kingdom to which Jahara ultimately owed its allegiance, was without a monarch for the first time in generations. Conveniently, the nobility from the four Delienean provinces had already decided upon a regent to replace him. "Arcadimon Detano," said Dimarion. "An adviser and friend to the late king, apparently."

"And no one protested?" Sefia asked.

"The decision was unanimous." The pirate tapped one ringed pinkie on the edge of his glass. "Does that surprise you?"

"It surprises me," Reed said. "Gorman shoulda put up a fight for the crown."

Gorman was the northernmost of Deliene's territories. Kaito, Archer's second-in-command, his brother in arms, had been Gormani.

Kaito. Archer closed his eyes. Sometimes, the boy still came to him in his dreams: He'd be sketching battle plans in the dirt. He'd be leaping into a frigid river, whooping with joy. He'd be bloody and snarling. He'd be dead on the ground, with Archer's bullet between his eyes. Sometimes they'd talk. Sometimes Kaito would forgive him. Sometimes not, and Kaito would say Archer was so broken inside he'd never be whole again, no matter how many lives he saved.

Or took.

Sefia squeezed his hand, her touch firm, as if to reassure him that she was there. She was with him.

He opened his eyes again, his vision blurry with tears.

Kaito Kemura, the son of a Gormani chief, had been the most belligerent person Archer had ever met. If the people of Gorman were anything like him, they would rather have seceded from Deliene than bow to a regent.

"I suppose this is the doing of the Guard you were telling me about," Dimarion said to Sefia.

She nodded.

The Guard. The name made Archer's fists burn. The Guard was responsible for his kidnapping, for his disfigurement, for setting him on the path that would lead him to his fate. If he could have, he would have killed them all. And gladly.

But fighting the Guard meant fighting the Alliance, and fighting the Alliance meant joining the war. And his own death.

"Is Arcadimon Detano one of 'em?" Reed asked.

"I knew they had an agent in Deliene," Sefia said, her voice sounding smaller than usual, "but I never heard them speak his name."

Archer wiped his eyes. "So the Guard controls three kingdoms now."

"Yes," she whispered.

That left only two kingdoms for the Guard to defeat, and they planned to conquer both in a conflict Sefia's parents had called the Red War.

The war Archer was supposed to win. The war that preceded Archer's death.

Haven, he reminded himself. He would be at Haven. With Sefia and the bloodletters.

"Well then." Draining his glass, Dimarion stood. All of a sudden, there seemed to be less room in the cabin. "It won't be a surprise to hear Arcadimon Detano is making an announcement tomorrow. Here, in Jahara, at noon."

"Noon?" Reed muttered a curse.

The pirate captain smirked at him. "You'd have known this if you'd come to see me as soon as you arrived."

"He's going to join the Alliance," Archer said. That was what he would do, if he— No, he couldn't think like that. He may have been a murderer. He may have been a legend before he'd reached the age of nineteen. But he wasn't a commander. He wasn't a conqueror. And he didn't want to die.

"Course he is." Uncrossing his arms, Reed turned to Dimarion. "Think we can load up and get outta here before the announcement?"

The pirate captain shrugged delicately. "If we don't, we're not getting out of here at all."

They turned in a short while later, and after a few hours of restless dreaming, Archer and Sefia joined the others on the deck of the *Current*. It was before dawn, the sun still simmering below the horizon. At the early hour, this part of the Central Port was mostly deserted, the houseboats and sailing ships silent but for the creak of their timbers.

The dozen redcoats they'd rescued were nervously stuffing their uniforms into burlap sacks. Sure as they were of what the regent would say, they didn't want to attract undue attention.

They had a tense energy about them that reminded Archer of the bloodletters before battle.

But if all went according to plan, he'd never lead anyone into battle again.

"How come *you* don't need a guide?" Haldon Lac asked as he straightened his cuffs.

"We're with Captain Reed. He doesn't need one." Archer exchanged a knowing look with Sefia. Meeks had said the same thing to them the first time they were in Jahara, sauntering into the fighting ring at the Cage like they could've brought down the impressors simply by demanding they stop.

"I heard he can tell where to go from the sound of the water against the pilings," Sefia added.

Lac's perfect mouth fell open in shock. "You don't say!"

She rolled her eyes.

Archer patted him on the shoulder. Haldon Lac was dumb as a brick, which irritated Sefia, but Archer found the boy's stupidity endearing.

"But how does the water know where he wants to go in the first place?" Hobs asked. He was an odd fellow, always asking funny but bizarrely logical questions about why birds never lost their way at sea and whether the chief mate could hear *every* splinter from the timbers that composed the *Current* or if he needed a twig of respectable size.

Archer liked him too.

"He must communicate with it in his mind," Lac declared. "I've heard of such things."

"Did you hear them in your mind?" Sefia asked.

The boy looked puzzled. Archer almost felt bad for him, but sometimes his comments were an open invitation for mockery.

"Actually," Reed said, coming up behind them in his walking coat and wide-brimmed hat, "I whistle to it."

"Captain!" With a little bow, Haldon Lac tried to make a farewell speech, but Captain Reed ushered him quickly down the gangplank while the other redcoats followed, laughing quietly. On the docks, Meeks's guide sized them up dubiously and sighed.

Archer, Sefia, and Reed watched them disappear into the maze of the Central Port.

"Good riddance," Sefia muttered.

"I liked them."

"You're nicer than me."

"You're nicer than you give yourself credit for." Archer took her hand as they wound into Jahara, their footfalls echoing on the wooden walkways.

Soon, they'd have the Book back. They'd teleport to the bloodletters and rescue Frey and Aljan. And once they were all back together again, they'd sail to Haven. And he'd be free.

• • •

Sefia and Archer followed Captain Reed as he led them unerringly among the crumbling piers, past glass buoys tied with twine, and sunken carracks, their decks submerged and only their masts peeping above the waves, until they reached an immense warehouse with the black wings of the messengers' guild insignia flying over the entrance.

Sefia had been here only once before, but she'd been intimidated by the sheer size and frenetic energy of it then too. Inside, it was packed with messengers hurrying about their business, guild enforcers with bronze wings embroidered on their clothes, nervous customers whispering rumors as they milled about like chickens in an overcrowded henhouse.

Speculation about the regent's announcement was on everyone's lips as Sefia, Archer, and Reed took their places at the end of a line.

Warships had been spotted to the southeast. Deliene was going to join the Alliance. It was going to be a war of three kingdoms against Oxscini alone. Against the redcoats.

The war on the reds, they were already calling it.

The Red War.

The generations-in-the-making, world-altering endgame of the Guard.

"Next," someone called, and they stepped up to the counter, where the messenger Sefia had left the Book with sat behind a barred window.

"Name?" the woman asked perfunctorily.

"Cannek Reed," said the captain.

With a nod, the messenger looked toward the ceiling, drawing on her extensive memory. Both messages and packages were transferred via simple question-and-answer. If you could answer the question, you could pick up whatever someone had left for you.

After a moment, the woman looked down and asked, "After the maelstrom, why didn't you choose to stay on land, if you knew you'd die at sea?"

The black gun. The white dandelion. The explosion of the ship.

Reed glanced at Sefia. A wry smile touched his lips. "I had a choice. Control my future, or let my future control me."

They were the words he'd told her when she learned the truth about the Book—that it was a record of everything that had ever been or would ever be.

Somehow, the words had taken on new meaning, now that she knew she had to change fate itself.

Satisfied with Reed's answer, the messenger nodded and retreated to one of the back rooms where the packages were kept.

"Do you still believe that, Cap?" Sefia asked.

"I better." He chuckled. "I'm goin' right back onto the water after this, ain't I?"

Within minutes, the messenger returned with a rectangular parcel wrapped in paper and twine.

Sliding a coin across the counter, Sefia scooped up the package, pressing the Book to her chest. It felt so familiar, like a piece of her had been missing all this time and only now was she complete again.

But as she stuffed the Book into her rucksack, she caught sight of a familiar figure on the warehouse floor.

The boy was around Archer's age, with floppy curls and large eyes that seemed almost owlish behind his round spectacles— Tolem, the Apprentice Administrator. She'd seen him only once during her time with the Guard, but she hadn't forgotten the way his glasses kept slipping down the bridge of his nose, the way he kept pushing them up again.

And she hadn't forgotten his Master, walking beside the boy with unnatural grace. The man was slender as a rail, with eerily symmetrical features, except for a milky scar in his right eye. In perfectly tailored clothes, with a tiepin through his cravat, he looked as unreal as a painting among the scruffy messengers and worried customers.

"Dotan," Sefia whispered. What was he doing here? Had the Guard figured out where she'd hidden the Book?

She wasn't afraid of much, but the sight of the Master Administrator sent a chill through her veins. The man tasked with poisons, torture, and the Guard's dungeons *hated* her. Hated her so intensely that when she was at the Main Branch, she could feel him watching her, his malice so strong it was like a foul odor.

And now he was looking straight at her.

"A Guardian?" Captain Reed asked, narrowing his eyes. He flung back the tails of his walking coat, drew his long blue revolver—the new one called the Singer, after their old chanty leader, Jules—and fired.

People screamed. Beside Dotan, Tolem ducked.

The Master Administrator, however, barely lifted his hand and the bullet halted in midair, dropping harmlessly to the warehouse floor.

Reed cursed. He hadn't fought a Guardian yet. He didn't know what they could do.

Dotan lifted a slim finger and, in a voice more penetrating than any Sefia had ever heard, called, "Enforcers, protect your guild!"

Enforcers? Sefia blinked, bewildered. Only the guild could command its enforcers. *Unless . . . the Guard controls the guild?* In Deliene alone? Or all of Kelanna?

Even as she thought it, large guards with bronze wings embroidered on their clothes shoved through the thinning crowd. Archer met one of them, disarming her and hurling her flat onto her back. Picking up the woman's truncheon, he knocked another senseless in two quick strikes.

But he wasn't quick enough to dodge as Dotan swiped his hand through the air. The magic caught Archer at the ankles, slamming him to the floor.

That brought Sefia back. Seeing Archer in danger brought Sefia back. *"Run!"* she cried, pulling him to his feet. Blinking, she summoned her magic and flung aside enforcer after enforcer as she and Archer raced for the exit.

43

Risking a glance behind her, she saw the Master Administrator crossing the warehouse as if he were floating on a cloud, with Tolem trotting along beside him.

And Captain Reed was standing before them, firing the Singer again and again, emptying the chambers as Dotan deflected each shot.

"Cap! What are you doing?" Sefia palmed the air, sending a blast of magic at the Administrators.

Dotan shoved his Apprentice out of the way, taking the full force of her magic. The Administrators had never been fighters. He flew backward into the wall, where he dropped, groaning.

Beside her, Archer had grabbed a second truncheon and was fighting off enforcers twice his size. His injured side was dark with blood—he must have ripped his stitches in the fight—but he seemed not to feel it as he twisted and parried and attacked, a savage light in his eyes.

As Reed refilled his cylinder, Sefia seized his arm. "Come on! What if he recognizes you from the legends and figures out the *Current* is in Jahara?"

If the Guard controlled the messengers, they were more powerful in Jahara than Sefia had thought. Dotan could ground the *Current*. Worse, as soon as he figured out where she was moored, he could sink her.

At that, the captain snapped into action. Turning for the exit, he struck an enforcer across the face with the Singer as Sefia shoved another aside.

Something flew into her from behind, and she slammed to the floor. Blood filled her mouth as her teeth caught her lip.

Glancing over her shoulder, she saw Tolem, hands raised. On his frightened face, his glasses were askew.

Behind him, Dotan was on his feet again. A glass vial gleamed in his hand.

Master of poisons.

She didn't know what the contents of the vial would do, but she knew it wouldn't be good.

Scrambling up, Sefia grabbed Archer by the waist. His shirt was damp and hot with blood.

"Cap, hold on to me!" she cried.

The vial was leaving Dotan's fingers. It was sailing across the warehouse, propelled by the force of his magic. Inside, a thick black liquid pressed against the glass, as if willing it to shatter.

Then Sefia felt Reed's arm go around her, and she opened her hands wide.

The Illuminated world flashed past her—the web of piers and boats that formed the floating Central Port, catwalks, brigs, barges, the shapes of masts and sails all outlined in sparkling gold—until she found the only place in Kelanna she could run to, time and again—and then she, Archer, and Reed were gone, winking out of the messengers' post and reappearing less than a second later on the deck of the *Current*.

Chapter 4

Not a King

Ed could not help but worry the spot on his middle finger where he used to wear the signet ring that marked him as Eduoar Corabelli II, King of Deliene. But the only part of that life that remained to him now was this pale circle of skin, quickly going as brown as the rest of him.

Still, he kept trying to turn the ring.

Still, he kept having to remind himself that he was no longer a Corabelli.

He was no longer a king.

Instead, he sat anonymously along the upper tier of the Jaharan amphitheater, overlooking the lapis ribbon of the Callidian Strait and the dark stripe of the Delienean mainland beyond. Along the crowded stone tiers, soldiers in black-and-white Delienean uniforms were posted at regular intervals.

It was almost noon.

Arcadimon would be making his announcement soon.

Ed would see him soon. It had only been a week since they'd parted, since Arc had saved Ed's life by faking his death, but every day had felt like an age. Ed had lost count of the times he'd considered sailing back to Corabel and flinging open the castle doors, rushing into Arc's arms and kissing him senseless.

He shifted aside as a group of a dozen sat in the spaces next to him.

"I don't see why we're here," said one. "We could have been at the Oxscinian embassy by now."

Oxscini? Ed gave them a second look. In the past few days, he'd heard rumors of Oxscinian leaders being rounded up for questioning by Jaharan authorities. He'd heard some of them hadn't returned. He'd seen Oxscinian merchant ships quietly departing for the south or changing their flags to avoid notice. The embassy had been taking people in, but if tensions continued, they wouldn't be able to get out again.

"It's because *someone* lost our guide," said another.

"I may have *misplaced* our guide," said the one they all seemed to be upset with. He had endearing good looks, with green eyes and a strong jaw he'd grow into in a few years, with a bluster that Ed found both admirable and hilarious. "But certainly it was a happy accident. The Royal Navy may appreciate our eyewitness accounts."

They weren't just Oxscinians, then; they were soldiers, redcoats. And clueless ones, at that.

There was a rumble of excitement as a line of heralds lifted their horns and blew a series of bright notes into the crisp winter air.

Someone announced the arrival of the regent.

47

The crowd cheered.

And Arcadimon Detano strode to the center of the amphitheater, looking as if he belonged in the night sky in his black-and-silver uniform, with the ivory crown of the regent like a crescent moon upon his brow.

"He's so handsome," said the green-eyed redcoat, his gaze glued to Arc, who commanded the attention of the entire audience as he silenced their applause with a wave of his gloved hand.

Then Arcadimon opened his mouth, his strong voice carrying to Ed as if they were face-to-face instead of separated by a hundred yards. Ed shivered. He'd almost forgotten the rich, intoxicating timbre of Arc's voice.

"It is no accident that I am here today, in the most glorious center of trade in Kelanna," Arcadimon began. "Although it is technically part of Deliene, Jahara is an island ruled not by one voice but by many, and has for years been an experiment both in neutrality and in unity. It will be of no surprise to anyone here when I declare that the experiment has been a rousing success."

His words were greeted by riotous applause. Arc had always been a marvelous speaker. Even with all that had happened in the past—Arc revealing that he'd been sent to take Ed's throne, Arc deciding to spare Ed's life, Ed's exile from Deliene, the kingdom his family had ruled for generations—Ed was comforted to know that some things didn't change.

When the cheering had subsided, Arcadimon continued, "Jahara is prosperous. Jahara is stable. Jahara is at peace. Jahara is what the rest of the world must aspire to become. Gone are the days of blood feuds and civil war. Gone are the years of Oxscinian imperialism, under which both Jahara and Deliene have suffered. Gone are the days of division and discord."

The redcoats bristled at the mention of Oxscinian imperialism, their faces stony as the Jaharan audience grew more enthusiastic in their applause.

"For too long, Deliene has remained indifferent to the Oxscinian conflict. It is not, as some would have you believe, a dispute over old Oxscinian colonies in Everica, but a struggle for the very future of the Five Islands . . ."

"No," Ed whispered. "Arc, don't do it."

Don't send my kingdom to war.

"Queen Heccata is a barbarian . . ."

A roar of protest from the redcoats made Arcadimon's next words inaudible.

". . . Oxscini will continue its reign of terror and violence, as it has always done . . ."

The green-eyed boy leapt to his feet. "I can't believe I called you handsome!"

The boy beside him, who had a shaved, curiously round head, booed.

Some people in front of them turned, hissing at them to shut up.

Below, Arcadimon was still speaking. "The Alliance aspires to a new future, a better future. We are all approaching a new era—open, unified, and at peace for the first time in thousands of years. This is the vision of King Darion Stonegold. This is the mission of the Alliance. Neither Deliene nor Jahara will stand in the way of progress and peace. Today, we join King Darion Stonegold's Alliance."

No. Ed put his hands over his eyes. He would have been a fool to ignore the signs, but he hadn't wanted to believe Arcadimon would really do it. Just like he hadn't wanted to believe Arcadimon would murder Ed's younger cousin, Roco, to eliminate all blood claims to the throne. The Arcadimon Ed knew would never . . . but how much did he know about Arc, really?

"Today, we are greater than we were before. We are not one kingdom, but three. We are unified. We are strong. And together, we will defeat Queen Heccata and the Oxscinian menace that threatens us all."

When Ed looked up, all the redcoats were on their feet, the first two leading them in the Oxscinian anthem.

> *Red hearts can't be broken.*
> *Red fire fills our veins.*
> *We fight, cannons smoking.*
> *Forever shall the red flag wave.*

Everyone in their vicinity was staring now. Uniformed guards had begun making their way toward them.

"Didn't you hear?" Ed said, grabbing the first redcoat's hand. "You're at war now. You're going to get yourselves thrown into prison."

The boy looked aghast. The words of the anthem died on his lips. "What do I do?" he asked.

Ed looked around. He knew the amphitheater's secret tunnels from his days as king, when Ignani, the captain of his guard, had drilled him until she was confident he could escape in the event of an attack.

The Delienean guards had drawn their swords.

Aiding and abetting the redcoats' escape was as good a use for those tunnels as any.

"Follow me!" Ed said, yanking the first redcoat after him. He hoped the others were behind. They dashed through the crowd, pushing audience members into the guards. People cried out in alarm as they scrambled out of the way.

"This is a war," Arcadimon was saying below. "A war on the old ways. A war to end the generations of violence that have preceded us. A war on Queen Heccata and her redcoats."

As Ed ushered the redcoats into a stairwell, he glanced over his shoulder. In the center of the amphitheater, Arcadimon looked up.

Their gazes met.

Ed almost gasped aloud, the intensity of his yearning was so great. He could go running down there right now, crashing into Arc with such force that they'd never be parted again.

But then Arcadimon spoke the words that made Ed turn, dashing down the steps with the redcoats. "The Red War," he said hollowly.

E d's mind spun as he led the redcoats through the black amphitheater passageways, feeling their way down rusted ladders and tunnels so narrow they had to squeeze sideways, cobwebs brushing their faces.

Arc had seen him. Arc knew he was here.

But he didn't think Arcadimon would give him away. *If they find out you're alive,* Arc had told him, *they'll have both our heads.*

"Say, are you certain we're going the right way?" one of the redcoats asked. "I swear we've passed this lumpy bit of wall before." Ed recognized the voice as belonging to Lac, the posturing green-eyed one.

"I'm sure," Ed replied.

"But how do you know?"

"Maybe he can see in the dark." That was Hobs, the one with the round head.

The suggestion was so absurd Ed found himself caught between a smile and a frown. "I memorized these tunnels when I was a child," he said. And now he was using them to smuggle Deliene's enemies out of danger.

Ed shook his head. Deliene had *enemies.* Deliene was at *war.*

"Whatever for?" Lac asked.

"You're not afraid of the dark, are you?" Ed countered. He was surprised at himself; it wasn't a comment King Eduoar Corabelli II would have made.

But he wasn't Eduoar Corabelli anymore, was he? The thought gave him a little thrill of delight.

"Certainly not!" Lac exclaimed.

"He's afraid of the dirt," Hobs added.

There was a soft chorus of laughter from the others.

"Hobs, as the ranking officer here, I'd like to maintain a *little* of my authority, and you're not helping."

"It's not the dirt that will get you," Ed said, nearly joining in their laughter. "It's the spiders."

He was rewarded with a gasp of horror.

He chuckled aloud this time.

It surprised him, sometimes, how much lighter his steps felt since he'd given up his name. How it felt to exist without a curse hanging over your head like the executioner's ax.

Free.

And . . . empty, lacking purpose. He had no court to hold, no disputes to mediate, no trade agreements to negotiate. It had left him feeling scooped out, a shell of his former self wandering aimlessly through the Central Port.

For a time, they continued palming their way along the walls, shuffling through the darkness, until Ed reached the exit. Lac stumbled into him from behind.

"Are we here?" the boy asked. "At the Oxscinian embassy?"

"The wha—" Ed shook his head, though the redcoats couldn't see. "The tunnels don't go to the embassy. What made you think—? Never mind. We're at the amphitheater's west gate." He pressed his palm to the wall, searching for the lever he was sure was there.

"And then you'll take us to the embassy?"

Ed paused. He'd been to the embassy many times before. Given his past week of exploring the city, he could probably get them there without hiring a guide.

But in wartime, things changed.

Deliene hadn't been to war since before the White Plague, when his fourth great-grandfather became king—at the cost of thousands of lives and a curse upon his bloodline—but Arcadimon had ended their peaceful history.

They have a plan for Deliene, he'd said, *and that plan doesn't include you.*

Ed could have revealed himself during the announcement.

He could have stood up and reclaimed his throne and prevented Deliene from going to war. A part of him still thought he should.

But he'd simply stood by while the new flag of the Alliance—with three stripes of blue, gold, and white to signify the three allied kingdoms—was unfurled before his very eyes.

He told himself he loved Arcadimon, the boy who'd taken his crown and his heart. He trusted Arcadimon. He had to believe Arc had the best interests of his kingdom at heart.

No, not *his* kingdom. Not anymore.

He was no longer Eduoar Corabelli. He was no longer a king. And it had to remain that way, if he wanted Arc to survive.

In the darkness, Ed found the lever, cold in his palm. "Jahara is at war with Oxscini now," he said. "They won't be letting anyone enter or leave the embassy."

"Then how do we get home?"

He pushed the lever. Deep in the stones, there was a rumbling as the door cracked open. He couldn't prevent Deliene from going to war. But he could do this. He could rescue a dozen redcoats, though they weren't his own subjects—*because you don't* have *subjects anymore,* he reminded himself. "I'm going to get you on a ship to Oxscini," he said.

Unfortunately, saying he was going to get them all out of Jahara was easier than actually getting them all out of Jahara.

As Ed had predicted, the Oxscinian embassy had been closed. All vessels flying red flags had been grounded. All other ships with upcoming voyages to the Forest Kingdom were being temporarily held until their captains and crews could be questioned.

But little by little, Ed found the redcoats ways off the island.

He had money left from selling the dinghy he'd used to escape Corabel, and he blew most of it bribing port officials to allow small fishing boats with Oxscinian crews to depart, overpaying guides to learn which yachts and cutters were flying false colors.

As king, he'd never done anything so underhanded.

But he wasn't a king, and he liked it. For the first time in a week, he felt useful. He had a *purpose* again, however minor, however temporary.

One by one, he secured a place for each of the redcoats. They took work as deckhands in exchange for passage. They paid for hammock space between cargo crates. They were smuggled into hidden compartments.

Until at last it was sunset, he was out of gold, and two redcoats still remained: Haldon Lac, who didn't possess even the most basic common sense, and Olly Hobs, who had a seemingly endless supply of strange questions.

The other redcoats had offered up their places many times throughout the day, but both Lac and Hobs had repeatedly refused—Lac claiming loudly that it was his duty as ranking officer to see them all home safely, and Hobs giving no explanation but a shrug.

As a pair of lamplighters passed them, setting flame to the lanterns that lined the docks, Lac flopped down on a tangle of fishing nets, throwing his arm theatrically over his eyes. "*Now* what are we going to do?" he moaned.

Hobs plopped down beside him. "We'll do what we always do," he said.

"And what's that?" asked Ed, sitting between them.

Hobs paused for a moment. "I'm not sure, exactly. But if I know us, and I think I do, Lac will do something dramatic, I'll make an astute observation, and Fox . . . well, Fox would have criticized both of us and come along for the ride anyway."

Lac dropped his arm, and in the dusk light his features were lined with sadness. "Ah," he said, his voice stripped of its usual extravagance. "Fox."

"Who's Fox?" Ed asked.

"She was our friend," said Hobs.

"We lost her," added Lac simply.

"I'm sorry." Ed knew about losing people. Because of the curse on his family, he'd lost aunts, uncles, his mother and father, his little cousin, Roco—*to a weak heart,* he told himself—until only he remained.

There was a short silence.

"You know, this is the longest I've gone without thinking of her?" Lac asked. "Just a week ago I couldn't go an hour without wanting to ask her for help, or wanting to show her something that would make her smile . . ."

"She had a good smile, sir," Hobs added when Lac trailed off.

"One of the best," Lac agreed. "But I don't think she's crossed my mind since this morning."

Hobs shook his head. "Me either."

"It almost feels like a betrayal, doesn't it? Like we're being disloyal to her memory."

Thoughtfully, Ed looked north. From this southern sector of the Central Port, he couldn't see the Delienean coast, but he could imagine the lights coming on in Corabel. He wondered if Arc had returned to the castle, if he was removing his gloves and striding across the courtyard with the first stars just beginning to appear overhead.

"Fox would say disloyalty would be not making it back to the Royal Navy," said Hobs, interrupting Ed's thoughts.

"Hobs, you've never spoken truer words." With athletic grace, Lac sprang to his feet, managing to strike a dashing pose despite one of his boots getting caught in the nets. "We shall not give up. We shall make it home. We shall honor Fox's memory by returning to our kingdom and our queen."

"Very dramatic," said Hobs. "I already made an astute observation. Now we need someone to criticize us."

As one, both redcoats turned expectantly to Ed.

"Me?" he asked.

"Glare at him," Hobs said helpfully.

"Tell him to shut up," said Lac.

"You can berate us any way that feels comfortable to you."

Ed shook his head. "I'm not going to berate you—"

"Oh," Hobs interrupted, sounding almost disappointed. "I suppose that's different."

"But I'll say you won't get home just talking about it." Ed stood, digging into his pocket for his last copper coins. There were seedier parts of the Central Port they hadn't yet tried, more disreputable captains they hadn't yet spoken to. He wouldn't give up yet. "Come on, I have an idea."

"Spectacular!" Haldon Lac flashed him a smile of such unabashed joy that Ed couldn't help but smile back. The redcoat didn't know if the plan would work—he didn't even know what the plan was—but it seemed that hope was enough for him. Maybe Ed could learn something from him, about joy and hope.

With the last of his copper zens, Ed hired a guide to take them through the twilit catwalks. They passed rooster fights, high-stakes games of chance, shady figures making shadier deals.

"We're not going to end up dead in some alley, are we?" Lac said in a stage whisper.

Ahead of them, their guide snickered. A wrought-iron sign above a tavern door creaked ominously in the evening breeze.

"I hope not," Ed muttered back.

"If we end up dead in some alley, it's a good thing we wouldn't be in charge of locating the bodies, or we'd never be found," Hobs said.

"Another astute observation, Hobs," Ed said, testing the words. They were snappier than he was used to, but at Lac's approving smile, he decided he wouldn't mind trying it again.

"Points for sarcasm," Hobs replied. "I think you're getting better at this."

Their guide brought them to a gray ship she claimed was from Epidram, on the north coast of Oxscini, though the splintery old tub was now flying the new Alliance flags of blue, gold, and white.

Ed hoped the guide's information was good. They might all be arrested otherwise.

Someone would surely recognize him if that happened. And Arc would forfeit his life.

"The captain's a former redcoat," the guide said as Ed dropped the second half of her payment into her open palm. That left him a couple zens and a pocketful of lint. "They go by Neeram, and don't 'sir' or 'ma'am' them either. It's 'captain,' or keep your mouth shut."

"Sir," said Hobs, tugging needlessly on Lac's sleeve. "Do you recognize that ship?"

Haldon Lac squinted. "Uh, if by *recognize*, you mean *not recognize at all*—"

"It's the *Tin Bucket*. From Black Boar Pier."

"She's called the *Hustle* now." Their guide stuffed her payment into a threadbare coin purse and strode down the dock, disappearing quickly into the shadows.

Ed glanced at the gray ship again. He didn't know what significance Black Boar Pier had for the redcoats, but that they were familiar with the ship was a surprising moment of serendipity.

"What a happy accident this is!" Lac cried.

"Is it an accident?" Hobs asked, narrowing his eyes. "Or is it on purpose?"

"Whose purpose could it possibly be?"

"I'm just saying . . ."

As the redcoats fell to bickering about the nature of luck and coincidence, Ed sighed. Though he'd known them less than a day, he'd miss the redcoats when they were gone. But he'd done them a good turn. And done something to oppose Arcadimon's choices, though Arc would never know.

"Well," Ed said, "I've got two coins to rub together, but that's about it. Do you think you can wheedle your way aboard with nothing but your good looks and charm? I'm sure they'll take on two able-bodied sailors for a sympathetic cause."

"I have no doubt," Haldon Lac declared with one of his dazzling smiles. "But I'm hoping they'll take three."

"Three?" Ed almost retreated. *Leave Jahara?*

"Come with us, Ed."

"I can't." What about Arcadimon? What about Deliene? He couldn't abandon them, not now, when they needed him.

"I think you can," Lac said, clasping Ed's hand. "I think you need this."

"Almost as much as we need you," Hobs added. "For the sarcasm and such."

Ed looked down at his hand, which Lac still held. In the lamplight, he could see the tan line from his missing signet ring.

He was no longer a Corabelli. He was no longer a king. He wasn't capable of extricating Deliene from the Red War. Or of saving Arcadimon. They didn't *need* him.

But these ridiculous, hapless, good-natured redcoats did.

And he needed them, he realized. They were giving him a chance to reinvent himself, and for the first time in a long time, he actually liked who he was—and who he was becoming. Helpful. Capable. With a touch of sardonic humor that Arc would have appreciated.

"Look," Lac said. "I happen to have a nose for important

situations, and I believe this, unlikely as it may seem now, is an important situation. If you come with us, I promise you won't be disappointed . . . although, for the time being, all we can offer is friendship."

"And banter," Hobs added helpfully.

"And later, perhaps even a bit of glory fighting the Alliance, if that interests you."

Knowing he wouldn't see the lights of Corabel on the horizon, Ed didn't bother looking north. Instead, he shook Lac's hand. "Glory is for more important people than me." Then, with a grin, he added, "But I'll take the friendship. And the banter."

CHAPTER 5

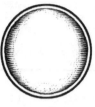

Epigloss

The *Current of Faith* was a vortex of activity as the outlaws flew into action, loading sacks of rice and bricks of butter wrapped in paper, amphorae of oil, boxes of bullets and barrels of gunpowder, glass bottles of vinegar stoppered with wax, bundles of bamboo, bolts of sailcloth, kegs of water, and all the other provisions Dimarion had arranged to be delivered that morning. They had to leave for the Trove before Dotan and the Guard found them.

Marmalade, their fastest runner now that Jules was gone, raced over to the next berth to tell the *Crux* what had happened at the messengers' post, while Doc spirited Archer belowdecks to the sick bay to see to his wounds.

Without a moment to lose, Sefia said her good-byes to Reed and the crew. Meeks told her to come back with a good story. With a wide, dimpled smile that always gave her heart, Horse slipped her a new packet of lock picks to replace the ones she'd lost and lifted her off the ground in a rib-cracking hug. "Take care of yourself, Sef."

Climbing down the hatchway, she dug her hand into her rucksack, pressing her palm to the hard surface of the Book.

A part of her knew she couldn't rely on it as she used to. The Book may have been a record of all time, from the beginning of the world to its distant end, but it had manipulated the truth before—manipulated *her*—promising safety and protection, and delivering only heartache.

Because of the Book, they'd lost Versil—Aljan's loud, laughing brother—to the impressors.

And Kaito shortly after.

Because of the Book, she'd abandoned Archer and the bloodletters, thinking that it would stop him from becoming the boy from the legends. Thinking that it would save him.

But that had gotten Archer injured and Frey and Aljan captured, and now, with the Red War closing in on them and the Guard on her heels, it felt like they were nearer to destiny than ever.

But she couldn't give it up either. The Book had been the only constant in her life for nearly eight years. It had been there when she lost her father. It had been there when she lost Nin. It had been a source of comfort and knowledge and power. For all it had betrayed her, she couldn't help but treasure it.

In the corridor, she halted when she heard Archer's voice from the sick bay: "But, Doc—"

"No, Archer." The surgeon's voice was firm. "I know you.

If you go, you'll end up leading that rescue, and in your state, you'll end up getting yourself or someone else killed. Is that what you want?"

"You know it's not."

"Then stop acting like it, and sit this one out."

Clutching the strap of her rucksack, Sefia pressed herself against the wall as Doc swept into the hallway. Tall and severe, she looked over the rims of her spectacles, leveling Sefia with a stare, and snapped her black bag closed with a crisp *click*.

"I'm confining him to the sick bay until his stitches are removed. If you want him to remain in one piece, you'll leave him here when you go."

"Yes, ma'am."

"I mean it, Sefia."

"Do you think I'd do anything to hurt him?" Sefia asked. "I'd give up the world for him."

Doc's expression softened. "I know. And he'd do the same for you. Sometimes I think the two of you are competing to see who will sacrifice the most to save the other." Squeezing Sefia's shoulder with one of her slim brown hands, she strode down the hallway and climbed up to the deck to finish cataloguing supplies.

Archer was sitting on the end of the bunk when Sefia entered the sick bay. He was shirtless, his side swaddled in a clean bandage. "Did Doc tell you?" he asked.

"Yes." She began loading her rucksack with her knives and the new lock picks. "I'm sorry."

"We were all going to go to Haven together." He toyed with the piece of quartz at his neck. "Me, you, the bloodletters."

"And we will. But we can't wait for you to get better. The Guard has had Frey and Aljan for over a week already."

Archer continued fretting with the worry stone. "What if they need me?"

"*I* need you. In one piece. That's why you need to stay here." She laid her hands on his shoulders. "Once we've rescued them, I'll come back to get you, and soon we'll be at Haven with nothing to do but lie on the beach until the war is over."

Swiftly, he caught her by the waist and pulled her into his arms, murmuring, "I hope we have more to do than that."

She inhaled his smell—like trail dust and thundershowers—and let him kiss her from the open collar of her shirt to her chin, his hands roving up her back and into her hair.

"We'll have as long as we want to do whatever we want," she said. "We could probably stay at Haven forever, if the outlaws would let us."

Archer's hands stilled. "Say that again."

"If the outlaws would let us?"

"*Forever,*" he breathed, like the word was a magic spell.

"Forever," Sefia repeated and, as if they were in a bedtime story, sealed the incantation by pressing her lips to his.

Then they parted, and she pulled the Book from her rucksack, folding back the waterproof casing. Bit by bit, she exposed the gilt-edged pages, the burnished gold clasps, and the ⊖ on the cracked leather cover.

The symbol of their enemy.

The symbol that had led her to Archer.

And Archer to the bloodletters.

She sank onto the bunk beside him. The worst and best

things in her life were inextricably linked to that symbol. To the Book. And to destiny.

She ran her hands along the edges of the cover, whispering, "Show me where the bloodletters are now."

The gold clasps clicked as she popped them open, spreading the Book in her lap. The pages seemed to stick together, almost uncooperatively, as if the Book knew she no longer trusted it.

Looking down, Sefia skimmed the paragraphs, searching for the bloodletters' location among the black sentences. The ink seemed to swirl under her gaze, re-forming into pointed masts, hard decks, a red ship with white trim—the *Brother*.

"Found them," she whispered.

And with a deep breath, she closed the Book. She had what she needed. She couldn't risk reading on, couldn't risk the Book showing her something that might make her want to keep reading, couldn't risk getting trapped again.

She traced the ⊜ once. Two curves for Frey and Aljan, a curve for the bloodletters. The straight line for herself. The circle for what she had to do: Beat the Book. Beat fate. The way her parents had never been able to.

Because destiny was conditional. If Archer amassed a following and conquered the Five Islands during the Red War, he would die.

If he didn't do either of those things, he'd live.

"Time to go," she said.

As she stuffed the Book back into her rucksack, just in case, Archer kissed her. "Come back," he said.

"Always," she replied.

Then, standing, she blinked. The Illuminated world came

surging up around her as she lifted her arms, making a path through the sea of light, and with a wave of her hands, she teleported from the sick bay and onto the deck of the *Brother* . . . where she found herself standing in a downpour.

It was torrential. It was apocalyptic. A monumental twisting of the skies until they were wrung dry again. She was definitely back in Oxscini; only the Forest Kingdom had rains like this.

As the water soaked into her clothing, she wondered sourly if the Book would have warned her if she'd read on a little longer.

She wondered if *not* warning her was a sort of revenge for distrusting it.

Blinking water from her eyelashes, she studied the shoreline of brightly colored buildings. This had to be Epigloss, Epidram's twin city on the northwestern tip of Oxscini, a month's voyage from Jahara. That she'd traveled so far in less than a breath was still a marvel to her.

"Sorcerer?"

Sefia turned to find a boy peering at her from beneath his hood. His red curls were damp, clinging to the edges of his pale, freckled face. "Hi, Griegi," she said.

She'd given them no warning when she left—she'd just left. For Archer. To save Archer. Two months on the road with them, and she hadn't given them an explanation, hadn't even said good-bye. Would they forgive her for that?

"You're really here!" He pulled her into a large, wet hug. "Where'd you come from?"

With a relieved grin, Sefia threw her arms around him. Griegi gave the best hugs—he'd wrap you up and wouldn't let go even when you thought you should lean away, and for a full minute it would be like you were the only person who existed to him.

Griegi drew back suddenly, his hazel eyes wide. "Archer's gone! He—"

But before he could finish, the other bloodletters surrounded them, descending from their watch posts or emerging from belowdecks. Like Griegi, some of them seemed glad to see her, touching her arm or squeezing her hand, but others hung back, glowering at her from beneath their rain gear.

"What are *you* doing here?"

"Where have you been?"

Why had she come back, after all these weeks? *How* had she come back?

"Sefia." Scarza's soft voice reached her over the noise, and a hush fell over the bloodletters as they let him pass. With the rain trailing out of his short silver hair and down the handsome lines of his face, he seemed tired, older than his twenty-odd years, but his weariness seemed to melt away when he smiled, dimpling the corners of his mouth. "We've got a lot to catch up on."

S oon they were all ensconced in the great cabin, which had become a workshop of sorts, crammed with scraps of leather and paper, spools of thread and bottles of glue. Griegi doled out steaming cups that filled the room with the scents of coffee, cardamom, and cinnamon. Some of the boys were muttering to each other. Others watched her warily from their seats. Closing her eyes, Sefia inhaled deeply; the smell of Griegi's coffee and the sounds of the boys' voices made her think of smoky mornings around the campfire, with the mist rising from the hills of the Delienean Heartland.

Home's what you make it, Nin had told her once. For a long time, Sefia had thought home was lost to her—a house on a hill overlooking the sea, a woman with hands like miracles—but looking around the great cabin, she realized now that she had not one home but many.

Archer. The *Current.* The bloodletters.

She hoped they'd forgive her, eventually.

While they took seats around the cast-iron stove, she asked if they still had the wand that had been among Archer's things. The chief mate had given it to her a season ago, to contact the *Current of Faith* if she ever needed. Magic bound the mate to the trees that made up the *Current,* and he could use the timbers as his eyes, though he was blind, and as his ears. The wand had come from the same trees, and with it, she could speak to him as if he were right beside her.

At Scarza's command, Keon, the skinny boy from the south coast of Deliene, ducked out to fetch it, though not before shooting a glare in Sefia's direction.

In Archer's absence, Scarza had clearly become their leader. The silver-haired boy had always been self-possessed and level-headed, but quiet, outshone by Archer's skill in combat and Kaito's brash personality. Watching him lead the bloodletters now, Sefia wondered if all this time Scarza should have been their chief. If he'd been the one leading them, maybe Archer wouldn't have been consumed by his desire to hunt impressors. Maybe Kaito would've still been alive.

When Keon returned, he bowed before her, extending

the wand as if on a satin pillow instead of his callused hands. *"Sorcerer."* He made the title sound like an insult.

"Stop that," Griegi said, tugging him back.

"She left us."

"But she came back."

Begrudgingly, Keon allowed himself to be pulled down next to Griegi, but he continued scowling at Sefia as he put his arm protectively around the curly-haired cook.

In her fingers, the smooth length of wood felt familiar, still smelling of mint and medicine. Feeling the bloodletters' eyes on her, she lifted the wand and whispered, "I hope you can hear me. Please tell Archer I made it to the bloodletters, and we'll all be together again soon."

She half-expected the wand to warm in her hands. To shiver. Something. But it gave no sign that the chief mate had received her message.

With a shrug, Sefia handed the wand to Scarza, who laid it carefully in his lap. "So," he said, nodding at her, "start at the beginning."

She told them everything: how she'd left to save Archer, how she'd bargained with Tanin to keep him out of the war, how her parents had betrayed the Guard to change her destiny, how she'd teleported to Archer and fought off his captors—

"So that's what happened," said Scarza, rubbing his left arm where he was missing his left hand and the lower part of his forearm. "When Frey and Aljan didn't return, we organized an assault on the tavern."

They'd seen evidence of a fight—a splintered door, clay floors soaked with blood, the sour scent of spilled wine.

70

"Yeah," Sefia said. They must have arrived after she'd taken Archer. "That was me."

"But you left Frey and Aljan?" Keon snapped.

"Shh." Griegi took his hand. "Let her tell her side of the story."

Flexing her fingers around her mug, she explained that she didn't know Frey and Aljan had been captured until it was too late. She couldn't teleport back without the Book to guide her, just like she'd needed the Book to teleport to the bloodletters. But now she was back. She wanted to help them rescue Frey and Aljan. Then she'd get Archer from the *Current*, and they could all sail to Haven, the hidden island in the Central Sea, home to over seventy outlaw ships that had been driven off the ocean by the Alliance.

"The chief," someone whispered. "We'd have our chief back."

"We can all live there," she said, "while the Red War passes us by."

The bloodletters were silent.

"What?" she asked.

"There's a problem. The tavern was deserted when we got there, but we found a note." Scarza handed her a scrap of paper. "Keon deciphered it for us."

The skinny boy nodded. "Aljan was teaching me, after you abandoned us."

Guiltily, she bit her lip. She'd taught all of the bloodletters something about reading—every one of them could recognize the mantras tattooed on their forearms—but Aljan had been her most diligent student. And now he'd been captured.

71

The parchment crinkled under her fingers as she unfolded it.

The Book for the bloodletters.

Viridian Shipyard. Half-moon. Midnight.

—2

Two—the Second Assassin—Tanin's new title.

Tanin, who'd promised Sefia that Archer would remain untouched. Tanin, who'd *lied*. Despite her assurances, the Guard had gone after Archer anyway.

But it was Sefia who'd trusted her, who'd wanted to believe that Tanin respected her—loved her, even—enough to keep her word.

"Half-moon is tomorrow night," Sefia said.

Scarza rubbed his eyes. "We know."

They'd already scouted Viridian Shipyard, hoping to break out their friends before the exchange, but they could find no trace of their fellow bloodletters anywhere.

Sefia folded the note again. "Tanin will probably teleport them in at the last second, if she brings them at all."

Sheepishly, Keon brought out the decoy book he'd been constructing in his makeshift workshop, but the leather wasn't quite the right color, the stains weren't in quite the right places, the metal they'd used to cap the corners wasn't quite the same tarnished gold. It might have fooled Tanin for a minute, in the dark, but a minute wouldn't have been enough for them to escape.

"The whole thing will be a trap anyway," Sefia said, shaking her head.

"A trap within a trap," Scarza agreed. "But without you, without the Book, what could we do?"

She fingered the strap of her rucksack, which sat on the floor beside her, dripping water. Giving up the Book would mean giving up Archer—with the Book, the Guard would be able to find him, no matter where he was, and drag him into their war. *Not* giving it up would mean giving up Frey and Aljan.

But Sefia could use the Book. With it, she could find Frey and Aljan, wherever Tanin was keeping them, and evade all the snares the woman must have set for her.

The problem was that the Book was a trap too, and Sefia had already failed many times trying to escape it. Even now, she felt like she'd been trapped again . . . but a small part of her was glad for the excuse to open it again.

"Well," she said, "you have me now, and we have the Book. We'll get them back."

The shadow of a smile touched Scarza's lips. Some of the others cheered.

"And then we'll go to Haven?" Keon asked warily. "All of us?"

Sefia looked from him to the rest of the bloodletters. "All of us."

Before he departed with the others, Keon took her aside. Through the fringe of his wavy, sun-streaked hair, his eyes were hard. "He'd never tell you, but you broke Griegi's heart when you left. Don't get his hopes up if you're just going to leave again."

She swallowed. "I won't."

He left her in the cabin with the Book as she tried to figure out the safest way to get the information they needed, tried to foresee the tricks that were surely in store for her.

Questions about the future were perilous. She'd learned that the hard way, when they'd lost Versil and Kaito.

But a location would be innocuous enough. She hoped.

Outside, the downpour continued.

Taking a breath, she traced the edges of the cover, as she did every time she opened the Book. "Where is Tanin holding Frey and Aljan now?"

Then, taking another sip of Griegi's coffee to sharpen her wits, she opened the Book and began to read.

Twice Betrayed

Tanin moved languidly along the fine wood-paneled corridor, her fingers trailing over the carved friezes of wild horses, hooves sharp and teeth exposed, manes and tails flying in a nonexistent wind. At either end of the short hallway stood a guard, each one alert and well-armed, their weight shifting easily with the gentle rocking of the ship.

"There's an additional guard in each of the rooms," said her lieutenant, Escalia, walking beside her. The woman was so tall and broad she seemed to strain the confines of the narrow corridor. Others might have shrunk from her presence, but Tanin had been forced to kneel before Stonegold, that pompous, overstuffed excuse for a king—for a *Director*—and she'd sworn she'd cut out her own spleen before she cowered in front of anyone again.

"One for each prisoner," Escalia finished.

Wordlessly, Tanin opened the door to the nearest cabin and looked in. Already cramped with its bunk, wardrobe, and small basin for washing, the room seemed even smaller with the prisoner chained to a chair in the center of the floor and the guard standing behind him, blocking the light from the single porthole.

Face hidden beneath his black hood, the prisoner turned toward her. His chains clinked faintly.

Since his head was covered, even Tanin couldn't tell if this was one of the two bloodletters or one of her decoys.

Perfect.

The guard flicked Tanin a salute, and she said nothing as she closed the door again.

"Satisfied?" Escalia asked. The woman's gold teeth gleamed in the dim light filtering from the hatchway at one end of the hall.

"Hardly," Tanin whispered. Hearing her ruined voice, she lifted her fingers to the scarf at her throat, the one that hid the scar Sefia had given her the first time they'd met.

She wouldn't be satisfied until she had the Book in her possession.

Until she'd killed Stonegold, the bloated snake who'd displaced her.

Until she was Director of the Guard again.

"Now give them all the same clothing," she said. "So they'll look identical too."

"Will do, ma'am."

With the Book, Sefia was at an advantage. If she was clever—and she *was* clever, as clever as her father, if she'd mastered Teleportation, the highest tier of Illumination, simply by observing Tanin—she'd see the shipyard for the ambush it was. She'd detect Tanin's tricks and see through her deceptions.

A flicker of admiration—or was that pride?—sputtered in Tanin's chest, but she quashed it instantly.

Twice, she'd been betrayed by the girl and her family.

She would not be caught out again.

Sefia was her enemy—and her target—nothing more.

And for all her talents, she had a weakness that her parents didn't. Lon and Mareah would never have gone back to rescue their captured friends. Lon and Mareah would have cut their losses and run.

But not Sefia. Sefia had come for the Locksmith. Sefia had come for the boy.

She was a girl of sentiment. She would come for her friends too.

Tanin checked on the next prisoner, heard the rattle of his chains, and smiled. She hadn't held her own as Director of the Guard for over twenty years without cleverness and talent of her own.

She would outmaneuver both Sefia *and* the Book.

And then they would both be hers.

CHAPTER 6

The Shell Game

Sefia had never been more convinced that the Book had motives of its own. As Scarza had said, Tanin had laid a trap within a trap, but Tanin was not the only one trying to trap her.

The Book was an instrument of destiny. It wanted her to become the reader from the legends, destroyer of armies. It wanted Archer to become the boy who conquered all of Kelanna and died soon after. It would do anything to make that future come to pass.

And, she realized, it had been doing so for years. It hadn't merely foretold her parents' deaths—it had given them the exact information that would make them betray the Guard, so the Guard would, when Sefia was nine years old, torture and murder her father, leaving his body on the kitchen floor for her to find.

It hadn't merely warned her about Archer's future, either. It had led her to believe that if she left him, he'd return to his hometown, to his family, to a girl he used to love, and he'd be safe. But leaving him had led her here . . . to *these* traps.

It wanted something else now, something that would nudge her closer to destiny. She just didn't know what.

And she didn't have long to figure it out.

She wished she didn't have to risk going, but she was the only hope Frey and Aljan had. The bloodletters couldn't come with her. Tanin wasn't in Epigloss—there'd been no sounds of rain outside her ship—and Sefia couldn't teleport them all in and back out again without taking more time than they had.

On the table in the great cabin, she sketched out a rough diagram of the corridor for the others to study: closed doors, hooded prisoners, heavily armed guards.

"It's a shell game," Scarza said, tapping each of the six cabins—three on the port side, three on the starboard. "If I were her, I'd shuffle them every few hours."

"It'll be total guesswork if they're gagged," said Keon as he placed a set of sleeping darts into a cuff for Sefia to hide up her sleeve.

"Not *total* guesswork." She slid a sharpened knife into a sheath at her waist. "I'll have Illumination."

"You'd better hope they're gagged, sorcerer," Griegi added as he brought them a plate of fried, sugared dough, "or, if you guess wrong, they'll bring the whole ship down on you."

While they tried to predict what other traps Tanin had laid for her, Keon cobbled together a rig from bottles of acid and a revolver's firing pin—for destroying the Book if Sefia was caught.

Whatever happened, the Guard could not get the Book.

Tanin couldn't get the Book. Carefully, Sefia packed the Book and the bottles of acid into her rucksack, nestling them in wads of cotton batting so they wouldn't break by accident.

Taking Scarza aside, she told him Captain Reed's directions to Haven—the positions of the sun and stars, the colors of the water, the signs that would show them the way. If something went wrong, they still had to get to safety.

Outside, the sky darkened. Rain continued to hammer the ship.

When Sefia was finally ready, Scarza bowed his head and crossed his forearms—the bloodletter salute. It had been Kaito's idea, originally, copied from his old Gormani customs.

The others mirrored him.

The words inked on their arms seemed to taunt her now: *We were dead, but now we rise*—the way they described themselves, having survived the impressors' training and fighting rings. *What is written comes to pass*—the way they used to throw themselves into battle, believing the Book guided their blades.

Which it did, Sefia thought. Only it was also guiding them toward something else—the Red War, Archer's death.

"Come back safe," said Scarza.

"Come back," Keon added meaningfully. Griegi elbowed him, but the skinny boy just shrugged. "With Frey and Aljan."

Sefia didn't respond. She and Scarza had already discussed the possibility that Frey and Aljan were dead, and the whole shell game was only to support the illusion that they were still alive.

She blinked, and the Illuminated world sprang to life before her eyes—a sparkling, ever-shifting landscape of light and time and power. Narrowing her eyes, she swept her hands through the golden particles, which curled and eddied around her fingers like motes of dust.

Where was the corridor she had seen in the Book?

Ships, oceans, jungle fronds, and night-blooming flowers seemed to fly past her . . . and then she saw it: a narrow, darkened hall, its walls carved with wild horses, with six doors and two guards at either end.

"Good-bye," she whispered to the bloodletters, and, lifting her arms, she teleported herself from the *Brother* and into the corridor.

She landed in a crouch, flinging two sleeping darts from her sleeve.

The barbs made no sound as they flew through the air.

For a startling moment, she felt like her mother, the Assassin.

One struck the guard in the hatchway. The second embedded itself in the other guard's calf.

They fell immediately, so quick, Sefia almost didn't throw out her magic in time to catch them before they hit the ground.

She paused, listening for sounds from above.

Nothing. The ship was quiet but for the footsteps of the watch.

Now for the shell game. Inhaling deeply, Sefia stood and faced the doors: three on one side of the corridor, three on the other.

As the Illuminated world ebbed and flowed around her, time appeared to run in reverse, the prisoners shuffling backward out of their cabins and into others, again and again, their paths crossing and re-crossing so many times in the past day she couldn't track even one of them, much less all six.

The seconds she hesitated felt like eons. Maybe Frey and Aljan weren't here at all.

No, wait. There.

Two days ago, one of the prisoners had made an escape attempt, bowling into the guards, his hood pulled up to his chin.

Brown skin and a neck blistered with burns.

Aljan.

Sefia grinned.

The ocean of light washed through the hall as she tracked him over the next two days, being prodded from one room to another.

At last she blinked again, dismissing her magic. He was in the middle port-side cabin.

Cracking the door, she sent a dart flying into the room, where it struck the woman standing behind the chair. She slumped.

Behind her, in the porthole, Sefia caught a glimpse of moonlight on turquoise waters, a nearly perfect crescent of white sand, and the old cone of a volcano rising in the distance. She allowed herself a smile. She'd been right—Tanin's ship *wasn't* in Epigloss.

Creeping forward with the soundless stalking steps she'd cultivated as a hunter, Sefia approached the chair.

"Aljan?" she whispered.

He didn't speak. Perhaps he was gagged after all.

Gingerly, she lifted the hood from the prisoner's face. "Aljan, it's m—"

But it was not Aljan.

He was a boy, yes. He was branded, yes.

But he launched himself at her so fast she barely had time to dodge out of the way. He caught her by the leg, slamming her to the floor.

She winced, thinking of the Book in her rucksack. Was the padding enough to keep the bottles of acid from breaking?

She lashed out with her knife, cutting his sleeve, the scarred skin beneath.

His arm had fifteen parallel burns, like Archer's. He'd killed fifteen other boys for the impressors, like Archer. He'd made it to the Cage, like Archer.

Unlike Archer, he'd been taken by the Guard.

The boy was a candidate.

Her stomach twisted. How many did the Guard have?

He wrenched her ankle so viciously she cried out in pain. Her grip on the knife loosened, and the boy tore it from her grasp, slashing her across the hand before she blinked, throwing him back with a sweep of her arm.

He struck the edge of the bunk. There was a sharp *crack* and a grunt.

"Who's out there?" someone cried from the next cabin over. "What's going on?"

Sefia scrambled to her feet. She knew that voice.

It was Frey.

Standing, the boy lunged at her again. She tried to send him flying, but he ducked her magic and came at her, her own blade flashing in his hand.

She threw a dart from her sleeve.

The candidate dodged. It didn't even come close to him, he was so fast. Almost as fast as Archer.

But the dart distracted him long enough for her to dash from the cabin into the corridor, slamming the door behind her.

Footsteps pounded on the deck above as she ran to Frey's cabin. The guard inside was already opening the door, but Sefia hurled him back, into the tiny wardrobe, and rammed his head against the wall.

"Frey?"

"Sefia!"

Sefia ran to the chair, pulling off Frey's hood as she swept the guard's unconscious body in front of the door seconds before someone else struck it from the other side.

"There's a lock on my chains," said Frey, nodding over her shoulder. Her high-cheekboned face was stubbled and bruised, and her black hair was coming loose from its braids.

"Did they hurt you?" Sefia asked quickly.

"A few cuts and bruises." The girl's brown eyes gleamed, showing she hadn't been defeated. Not by a long shot. "Honestly, the worst thing was not being able to shave, but look at me and tell me this face isn't as pretty with stubble as it is without."

That brought a smile to Sefia's lips. Drawing her picks from the inner pocket of her vest, she knelt behind her friend and took hold of the padlock. "Do you know where Aljan is?"

The iron felt tacky in her palm, as if it had been slathered with tar. But it was a simple contraption, easy enough for her to undo.

"No, they've kept us separate. And Archer—"

"Archer's fine. I'm sorry I didn't come sooner. I—"

"You came." As the lock popped and the chains loosened, Frey stood, squeezing Sefia's hands once. "That's what matters."

Another *thud* sounded on the door as Sefia pressed two bone-handled knives into Frey's hands. "I'm sorry they're not switchblades," she said.

With a wicked grin, the girl spun them in her hands. "They'll do."

"There's a candidate out there," Sefia said. "Maybe more."

"A candidate?" The bloodletters never used that word to refer to themselves.

"He has the brand, but he's not one of ours. I think the Guard got him before we—"

Frey's eyes narrowed. "Leave him to me."

The door buckled inward, pushing the guard's unconscious body farther into the room.

Sefia blinked, readying her magic. But there was something wrong with her vision. The currents of gold seemed to halt and stutter, winking in and out as if they were electric bulbs about to burn out.

What did Tanin do to that lock?

"Ready?" Frey asked.

Sefia nodded and swept open the door moments before the candidate rammed through it. Frey was on him in an instant, the knives wicked and deadly in her hands. Behind him, more boys with scarred throats were in the corridor, the doors of the shell game all thrown open.

Sefia ducked into the hall as Frey and the first candidate fought, slamming into the cabin walls, their blades finding bare patches of skin. Sefia closed her fists, catching two of the guards in her magical grip.

She could kill them.

They'd kill *her*, if they got the chance.

While she hesitated, her Illumination weakened. The candidates slipped from her grasp and sprang at her.

She caught them again, mid-leap, and this time she didn't hesitate.

She snapped their necks.

Behind her, Frey jammed one of her knives into the first boy's side and hit him so hard in the jaw he dropped.

For a moment, her expression was tinged with regret.

Then she retrieved her blade and joined Sefia in the hall with the rest of their enemies. "Aljan!" Frey cried.

"Frey!" Aljan's voice reached them from the middle starboard cabin.

More guards were crowding in from the hatchway at the opposite end of the corridor. With one heave, Sefia flung them all away.

Then her magic winked out entirely. The world, once alight with tides of gold, went dark.

Sefia blinked, trying to summon her sense of the Illuminated world. It flickered to life just long enough for her to send another batch of guards flying out of their way.

Then it went black again.

She and Frey raced into Aljan's cabin, where Frey quickly dispatched the guard and began barricading the door as Sefia whipped off Aljan's hood. He squinted up at her—a gash, deep and wide, had bled down the left side of his face, over the flaking white paint he applied to the corners of his eyebrows in honor of his dead brother.

"Sorcerer," he said. "Where's Fr—"

"Here," said Frey, leaving the barricade to cup his cheek with her palm. Closing his eyes, he leaned into her touch and kissed her hand.

Behind him, Sefia examined the lock on his chains. The metal glistened slickly in the light from the porthole. *Poisoned.* Something that would interfere with Sefia's ability to use Illumination . . . and her ability to escape.

A trap within a trap.

Shots burst through the door. Frey cursed as one of them took a chunk of her ear.

Ripping the blanket from the bunk, Sefia used it to hold the lock while she tinkered with it. A few seconds later, it clicked, releasing Aljan from his restraints.

He stood as Frey tossed him a knife.

"How are we going to get out of here?" Frey asked, retreating from the door, which was beginning to bow inward under the onslaught from the corridor.

But before anyone could answer, the door flew off its hinges. Sefia and the bloodletters ducked as wooden shards exploded into the room.

There, in the doorway, was Tanin.

She was a vision, with her silver-streaked black hair cascading around her shoulders.

She was a monster, rising from the depths of the sea, her skin pale as sun-bleached bones.

"Kill them," she rasped.

Sefia's mind raced. She had to do *something*. At her side, the rucksack was heavy with the weight of the Book and the bottles of acid.

There was the *click* of hammers being drawn back.

In a single movement, Sefia leapt in front of Frey and Aljan, raising the rucksack like a shield.

"Wait!" Tanin cried.

At her command, the candidates stopped. Sefia let out a breath. But she still had to get Frey and Aljan away.

"Is the Book really in there?" Tanin asked, her ragged voice almost sweet. "Have you brought it to me after all?"

"What do you think?"

"Sefia, what are we going to do?" Frey whispered behind her.

She didn't know. Without her magic, she didn't stand a chance. She blinked, but the lights of the Illuminated world were faint and fading even quicker as she skimmed through the currents, searching for a way out.

She *had* to get them out. She had to get them somewhere safe.

"I think I could kill you all without damaging whatever's in that bag of yours." Tanin lifted her hand.

For a second, Sefia pictured Nin's death all over again. A twitch of Tanin's fingers. A broken neck. An empty body.

Not again.

"Hold on to me!" Sefia cried. She felt Frey grasp her around the waist and pull Aljan toward them. He stumbled, grabbing Sefia's leg as she waved her arms.

The candidates fired their weapons. They flung their knives. Flame and steel flashed in the darkness of the cabin.

The walls of the room flickered. The floor seemed to drop from under Sefia's feet. For a second, she could feel a fresh breeze on her cheeks.

But her magic faltered again, and she, Frey, and Aljan were back in the cabin with Tanin.

Long enough for Sefia to see Tanin's gray eyes widen with surprise and triumph.

Long enough for the bullets to strike them.

Pain lanced through her shoulder, her thigh, the side of her scalp.

No! Sefia thought, wrenching them back through the Illuminated world.

They appeared on the *Current of Faith*, under clouds like smoke in the black night. Aljan collapsed beside her, clutching his chest as blood seeped through his slender artist's fingers. Frey flung herself down beside him, crying for help.

Sefia staggered back, her wounded leg going out from under her. She struck the deck as the crew of the *Current* gathered around them.

"Sefia? Sefia, you're hit."

"Is that Frey and Aljan?"

"Doc! *Doc!*"

Ignoring them, she blinked. The Illuminated world sputtered once and left her. She blinked again, tried to summon the golden world that had once come so easily to her.

But her magic was gone.

CHAPTER 7

Powerless

Sefia spent hours cleansing her hands of Tanin's poison, rinsing them, washing them, scrubbing them until the stitches in her shoulder pulled and she began to bleed through her bandages. But the poison had done its work. The Illuminated world was closed to her. For the first time in years, she was in the dark.

Pale and sweating with exhaustion, she flexed her fingers, staring at her bleeding cuticles, the raw patches on her palms. She couldn't stop bullets. She couldn't teleport.

"Scarza and the bloodletters will be waiting for us," she whispered. They'd be on the *Brother*, listening to the sounds of the rain, waiting for her to appear with Frey and Aljan. They'd think she'd failed. They'd think she'd abandoned them again. Keon would never forgive her now. "But we won't come."

"Then they'll come to us," Archer said, climbing onto the bunk beside her. "You told them where Haven was."

"But we have over a month until we reach the Trove. Who knows when we'll head back for Haven? And what if . . . what if something else happens?"

The Alliance could attack. Already today, as they sped northeast toward Liccaro, the *Current* and the *Crux* had been forced to run at the sight of blue ships on the horizon.

The bloodletters might be caught.

Who knew what fate had in store for any of them?

Sefia still had the Book—it lay in her rucksack across the room, the acid rig dismantled and the bottles tucked into well-packed boxes—but the Book hadn't warned her about the poison. The Book had *wanted* her to lose her powers.

Which meant this was part of her destiny. She'd always thought her fate was contingent on magic—that was why her father had forbidden her from learning it—but maybe *demolishing her enemies with a wave of her hand* didn't refer to Illumination but to a command. A flick of her fingers and a word of attack.

Kill them.

Sefia shuddered, remembering the chill in Tanin's voice.

She had *known* Tanin was her enemy. Tanin had tortured and murdered her father. Tanin had killed Nin. Tanin had betrayed her to get at Archer. But she had only ever wanted Sefia for an ally, for a friend, for family, and deep down, Sefia hadn't thought Tanin would really try to hurt her.

Eyes burning, she turned her face to Archer's shoulder and cried silently into his sleeve.

"It's okay," he murmured, stroking her hair. "You did it. You rescued them."

"Did I?" Sefia looked up at him. His face was a blur through her tears. "Will Aljan make it?"

There had been so much blood—*so much blood*—as Horse scooped up the boy in his massive arms.

"Doc says the bullet missed his heart."

"But will he make it?"

Archer said nothing. The bloodletter still hadn't awoken. Frey was with him now, in the sick bay.

"If he dies—" Sefia choked on the words. It was like she was back in Tanin's office beneath Corabel again.

Nin was yelling at her to run.

Tanin was lifting her hand.

Nin's neck was breaking.

Nin's eyes were wide. Nin's eyes were unseeing. She was falling to the floor. She was dead. She was dead.

And Sefia was screaming. Small. Weak. Powerless.

She clenched her red, swollen hands, relishing the sting. "He can't die. I can't let someone else die because I couldn't—because I wasn't strong enough to—because I—"

Because I'm not enough. She wasn't enough to save Nin. She might not have been enough to save Aljan. What if she wasn't enough to save Archer?

He drew her gently against his side. "I didn't follow you because you were strong. I followed you because you were brave and smart and kind. I didn't believe in you because you had magic. I believed in you because you were compassionate and resourceful and too stubborn to give up." He kissed her hair. "I don't love you because you're powerful. I love you because you're a good friend and a better partner and by far the best person I have ever met." He tilted her chin toward him. "Sefia, you are *more* than enough."

She burst into sobs.

He believed in her. He loved her. He saw so many great things in her, and without her powers, she knew she would let him down.

• • •

After Sefia had cried herself to sleep, Archer slipped into the corridor to peer into the sick bay. He couldn't see Aljan except for the shapes his legs made beneath the blanket, but Frey was in the chair by the bedside, dozing. She'd shaved, though bruises still shadowed her jaw, and her ear had been bandaged. She looked worried, even in sleep.

But as Archer began to close the door, she started up, blinking.

"I'm sorry," Archer whispered. "I didn't mean to wake you."

Her brown eyes focused on him, and for a second he was afraid she'd strike him. It was his fault, after all, that they'd been captured. It was his need for revenge, his bloodlust.

But when she got to her feet, she embraced him. "I'm glad you're all right, chief."

Chief. He smiled.

"Same," he said. "How's Aljan?"

With a sigh, Frey released Archer and sank back into the chair. "No change."

Archer stepped into the sick bay. Beneath the sheets, Aljan looked ashen, like his twin brother the day they'd wrapped him in linen and placed his body on a funeral pyre. There were fresh spots of white at the corners of Aljan's closed eyes. Frey must have asked for paint.

"I'm sorry," Archer said again, and this time he wasn't talking about waking her.

Frey glanced up, giving him a little shrug. "I know."

For a time, they were silent, listening to Aljan's labored breathing. Frey began to braid her hair, plaiting it and unplaiting it and plaiting it again as she watched Aljan for signs of waking.

At last, she spoke again: "Doc said we aren't turning around."

Archer nodded. He'd wanted to go to Reed, wanted to ask him to return to Jahara, to sail to Epigloss and the bloodletters. But the Red War had begun. If the *Current* sailed back to Jahara now, or to Oxscini, they might never make it to the Trove.

And Aljan wouldn't survive if he didn't have rest and proper medical care.

So they continued sailing toward Liccaro, hurtling farther away from the bloodletters with every passing minute.

Archer's bloodletters. He knew now that he couldn't lead them into battle without rekindling that deep desire for violence that was always smoldering inside him like an ember, but he'd hoped he could lead them to safety.

Now he'd just have to hope they'd make it to Haven without him.

"Archer," Frey said quietly, interrupting his thoughts. "On Tanin's ship . . . there were candidates."

He stiffened. *Candidates* were what the Guard called the

branded boys they bought from the impressors, the ones they were grooming to become soldiers, the ones they'd hoped would win the Red War, before Archer surfaced as chief of the bloodletters.

But Archer was going to Haven. They were all going to Haven.

The boys he'd gotten to in time, anyway.

"I fought one," Frey continued.

Archer pictured the cage matches he'd been forced to participate in. The boys he'd murdered—skewered, decapitated, beaten to death with rocks or his bare fists.

And Kaito. He saw them racing horses across the Delienean Heartland, with the sound of Kaito's riotous laughter whipping past him. He saw them fighting in the rain. He saw himself shooting Kaito between the eyes like a dog.

He flinched at the memory. "How many were there?"

"At least a dozen that I could see, but it was dark, and the hall was too narrow to fit more than that. Who knows how many more the Guard has?"

Sefia said the Guard had been looking for the boy from the legends since her father first conceived of the impressors nearly thirty years ago. They might have forty candidates. Or over a hundred. To think that they were out there, fighting for the Guard . . . Archer clenched his fists.

Frey traced the words that spiraled up her left forearm: *We were dead, but now we rise.* The bloodletters' battle cry.

"Even as we were fighting," she said, "I kept thinking, *That could've been me.* That could've been Aljan. That could've been any of us, if you and Sefia hadn't found us first."

Archer's fingers went to his throat, tracing the rough tissue of his scar.

The candidates were like him. They could've been bloodletters. They could've been brothers. But he hadn't been able to rescue them.

"I know it's too late," said Frey, "but I wish there was something we could do."

Archer nodded.

But what could they do? The candidates belonged to the Guard. And he was bound for the Trove. He was bound for Haven. He couldn't save them.

And he couldn't stop them.

• • •

Over the next few days, they saw signs of the Alliance again and again. In her bunk, Sefia would hear someone cry, "Alliance! Alliance!" There'd be a furor of activity—the drumming of footsteps, the creaking of the ship—and the *Current* and the *Crux* would quickly scramble out of sight.

During that time, Aljan awoke, and Archer sneaked Sefia out of her room to see him.

The boy beamed when they entered. His lanky body barely fit in the bunk, but he still seemed so small lying there, his mottled bruises slowly healing.

Setting aside the bowl of Cooky's seaweed, mushroom, and bone broth she'd been spoon-feeding to Aljan, Frey offered Sefia the chair while Archer knelt at his bedside.

"I'm sorry," Archer said softly.

"Don't be."

"It's my fault you—"

"I wanted Hatchet too." Aljan coughed weakly, and Frey gave him a few sips of water from a wooden cup. Before she stood back, she went to kiss his forehead, but at the last second, he lifted his chin, catching her mouth with his own.

She pulled away, rolling her eyes, but her cheeks were pink with pleasure.

Sefia grinned up at her, and Frey let out a flustered little sigh. Then, with deft hands, she turned Sefia's face away from her and began combing through her hair, fingers twisting and plaiting the black strands.

Aljan settled back on the pillow with a self-satisfied chuckle, but he sobered again as he continued to speak. "Maybe I didn't want him as much as you did, but I wanted him. After Versil died, I—I wanted all of them, every single one, and you couldn't have stopped me even if you'd wanted to."

"But—"

"And if I'd gone without you, I would've died. Don't apologize for keeping me alive."

Sefia saw Archer swallow a few times. After a pause, he said, "Hatchet's dead."

Another smile, this one bitter, appeared and disappeared on Aljan's lips. "Good."

The boy fell asleep quickly after that, and Archer helped Sefia back to her own bunk.

With the bullet wounds in her shoulder and thigh still healing, she'd been confined to her room. She spent the days there, listening to the activity on the main deck, trying not to think of the Book in her rucksack.

The Book could tell her how to get her powers back.

If she could get her powers back.

"I never knew how much I relied on it," she said to the chief mate when he came to visit one day, "how much I was *counting* on it to—"

He shrugged, feeling along the wall for cracks in the timbers. "You didn't have much magic when we met," he said. "You don't need it now."

"When we first met, I didn't know I'd be fighting fate itself."

Finding a split in one of the boards, he slathered a mixture of wood dust and linseed oil into the fissure, smoothing it gently with a putty knife. "You've still got your wits, girl. Or did you lose those too, since you came back?"

Sefia made a sour face.

The mate wiped his knife and, without turning, said, "Don't look at me like that."

She smiled sheepishly. No matter how much time she spent with the mate, she always forgot he could sense things that were happening all over the ship. "Sorry, sir."

Giving the timbers a pat, he crossed to the door. "You have a good plan. It'll just take you more time to execute it."

She bit her lip. "That's what I'm afraid of. The Red War's already here. I feel like I'm running out of time to get Archer to Haven."

"No one on this ship wants anything to do with that war. Besides Haven, there's no safer place for him."

Still, she wondered.

As Aljan healed, Archer began to spend more and more time with him and Frey. Sefia could hear them laughing in the sick bay down the corridor. Had the Book wanted to strand them on the *Current* together?

It was the Book that had steered Archer toward the blood-letters in the first place, had given him fighters who would follow him into battle, and though they were only twenty in number, they were so skilled, so feared already, that tales of their strength and brutality had already spread from kingdom to kingdom.

A great army, like the legends said.

If a small one.

Would Frey and Aljan convince him to lead the bloodletters again? Into what? They had no reason to join the war and all the reason in the world to go to Haven.

The Book could tell her.

Or the Book could trap her again.

She tried to put it out of her mind.

Two weeks passed, and they scurried away like rats at every hint of an Alliance ship on the horizon. Archer's stitches were removed, and he and Frey were assigned to a watch as the *Current* doubled their lookouts, cloaked in furs to protect them from the dropping temperatures. Reaching the northern curve of Liccaro, they raced eastward past deserted beaches and crooked coastlines of red sandstone Sefia could only see through the frosted portholes.

She spent most of her hours stewing in her bunk as she recovered from her gunshot wounds. She'd spend hours eyeing the outlines of the Book, where it hung in her rucksack from a hook on the wall.

All knowledge. All history. All the answers she wanted.

They were still weeks from Steeds, the first landmark in the riddle for the Trove, when Sefia heard shouts from above.

"Archer!"

Her gaze snapped away from the rucksack. She saw a body go falling past the portholes.

"Man overboard!"

She bolted upright in bed.

Archer. In the freezing water.

She didn't care that Doc had forbidden her from leaving the room. She didn't care that her injuries were still healing.

She was out of bed. She was running down the corridor. She was racing up the hatchway. She was almost to the main deck when pain lanced through her wounded leg. She collapsed, banging her forehead on the steps.

Her vision swam, but that didn't stop her.

"Archer!" she cried, clambering onto the deck. She blinked, but her magic did not come.

She needed her powers. She needed to get to him. She needed to lift him out of the water. She stumbled toward the edge of the ship, blinking over and over as her vision grew bright with tears.

But not with the Illuminated world.

"Archer!"

Someone caught her around the waist. Someone was carrying her away from the rail—Horse. "Frey's got him, Sef." His voice rumbled through her. "Frey's got him, and we've got Frey."

With gentleness unexpected for someone his size, the big carpenter dried her cheeks with the yellow bandanna he usually wore around his forehead as the other sailors hauled up Frey's dripping, shivering form and, with her, Archer. He was looped to her with rope, and he was soaked, teeth chattering, ice already forming on his eyelashes.

But he was alive. Gloriously alive.

For now.

While the others brought Frey and Archer to the great cabin, plying them with new furs, hot stones wrapped in blankets, and one of Cooky's restorative draughts, Sefia struggled out of Horse's arms.

"Sef?"

She shook her head, staggering back down the hatchway. A part of her knew destiny would not have let him die. A part of her knew destiny had greater plans for him. A part of her knew she shouldn't give in.

But she'd come too close to losing him.

Back in her cabin, she dug the Book out of her rucksack and flung the waterproof wrapping aside. The curves of the ⊜ on the cover seemed to smile.

She caressed the edges of the Book, whispering, "How do I get my magic back?" As she sank onto the bed, the pages parted willingly under her fingers.

And the Book answered her.

The poison was called *nightmaker*, for the darkness you experienced when the Illuminated world winked out, and it was one of Dotan's concoctions. He made it in small batches, where it fermented for six months in the apothecary, deep in the mountain of the Main Branch. Since Tanin had used the last of it trying to trap Sefia, he was brewing another mixture now, in case they needed it again.

There was no cure. Either the damage the poison had done to your system would heal, with time, and your magic would return. Or, if the dose had been high enough, you'd be powerless forever.

Wait, the Book told her. *Wait and see.*

But she couldn't wait. She needed to know if there was a way—any way—to recover her powers. She needed a mentor. Someone who could show her what to do.

She shut the Book, thumbing the gilt-edged pages, and closed her eyes.

She needed her father. Rule-breaking, destiny-defying Lon. Lon would never have let a little poison stop him. Lon would never have let his magic slip from his grasp.

Opening her eyes, she leaned in to the Book again. "What would my father do, if he were me?"

Laws of the Dead

Once there was a world called Kelanna, a smooth plane of ocean dotted with islands and little boats that left wakes like scrawling sentences in the water. It was a wonderful and terrible world, filled with creatures as large and ancient as the mountains; unruly, ever-changing jungles that bloomed and wilted and bloomed again; and people, like you in many ways, who lived their lives beneath a curved sky that encased their whole world like a glass dome.

Most Kelannans believed this was all there was. This little life. For a short time—such a tragically short time—they spoke and worked and loved and died, and when they died, that was the end. Their bodies were burned; their names, in time, forgotten.

But some of them, a sad and courageous few, wondered what lay beyond the edge of their world, beyond the dome of their sky.

The answer—as you know, as Captain Reed and the crew of the *Current* discovered when they journeyed to the far west, to the wild waters beyond all the known currents—was darkness.

Infinite black waters.

It was the place of the fleshless, the world of the dead, where all the souls that had ever left Kelanna collected and merged, heaving against the invisible barrier that forever divided them from the vibrant, living world they so loved and grieved and craved.

In Kelanna, death was permanent. Your body was burned, and your soul was cast out into the endless dark, never to return.

This, however, did not stop people from trying to subvert death in whatever way they could.

Terrified of the abyss, a jeweler crafted a diamond necklace that would keep her heart pumping, her organs from decaying, her hair from thinning, and her skin from growing loose, though it also cursed her to a life of misery.

To tether his love to the living world, a blacksmith forged the Resurrection Amulet.

An outlaw turned his own life into a story so grand, so worth repeating, that his name would never fade from memory.

Kelanna may have been a world rife with magic, inconsistencies, exceptions, but no one could break the laws of the dead, not in the way they most desperately wanted.

Once someone died, they could never return, no matter how much you missed them, no matter how much you wanted to see or hold or speak with them again.

You didn't get messages from the dead.

CHAPTER 8

Dangerous Wants

Captain Reed found her poring over the same pages, tracing each word as if it were a code she had to decipher. "Should you be doin' that?" he asked.

Sefia looked up, startled, guilty. "No."

He sat in the chair by her bedside, elbows on his knees. "The way I see it, the Book's a weapon, like the Executioner." He gestured to the black revolver at his side. People said the gun was cursed, crafted of steel and ill intent, for it took a life every time it was removed from its holster, and if you didn't choose your target, it would choose one for you. "It'll cut you as easily as it'll cut your enemy, if you ain't careful."

"I am careful," she said.

He lifted an eyebrow. "How many people have you lost 'cause of that thing?"

Versil—run through by a sword.

Kaito—dropped by a bullet between the eyes.

She'd almost lost Aljan. She could still lose Archer.

"Two," she said quietly.

"That careful enough for you?" His words were harsh, but his tone was not.

"No."

The captain shrugged and sat back.

"I just wanted to see my father again," Sefia said, fingering the corner of the page. It glinted in the light like a knife. "I wanted to know what he would have done."

"And? The Book answer you?"

She shook her head. "It told me I don't get to hear what my father would have done," she said bitterly, "because *you don't get answers from the dead.*"

It wasn't fair. It wasn't fair that he was gone. It wasn't fair that the Book, which had willingly—even gladly—shown her her father before, wouldn't let her see him now, when she needed him most.

"But . . . ," she said slowly, "it told me what you and the *Current* found at the edge of the world."

Nothing but death. No wonder neither he nor his crew spoke of it.

Captain Reed looked at her sharply. "It told you that?"

"Yes."

Cursing, he stood and began to pace the tiny cabin. He circled the room once, twice . . . eight times. Eight was his favorite number. He liked the sound of it, he said, and the length of time it took you to count it out. Enough time to think through a choice but not so much you started second-guessing yourself.

With a sigh, he sat down again and, touching his arm, trailed a finger down the tattoos that told the story of his journey to the world of the dead: the maelstrom where he'd found the Thunder Gong and learned how he was going to die, the skull gnawing its own ulnas for Captain Cat and her cannibal crew, the turtle island where they'd lost Jigo and where Harison had picked up his red lory—now Theo's, since Harison was gone— the rent in the sky with the light pouring through, and then . . . nothing. An empty circle of skin at his wrist where their time at the place of the fleshless should have been.

The sun had been a gateway, he told her. They'd passed through as it sank into the waves and passed back through when it returned a day later.

"How?" she asked. "The Book said you can't return."

"We were still alive." The captain shook his head. "We left our dead out there with the rest of 'em."

The Book had said the laws of the dead could not be broken.

It had also told her Kelanna was a world rife with inconsistencies and exceptions. And it had fed her information about the Resurrection Amulet: *to tether his love to the living world.*

Was there another way to beat the Book, besides outlasting the war?

Was there another way to cheat fate?

Or subvert it?

Would the Resurrection Amulet save Archer?

"I want it, Sef," Reed said when she told him the Book had mentioned it. "I want it so bad I can feel it in my *teeth*. You know how many things I've tried so I could live forever?"

He kept them in the great cabin, in those polished glass cases—the Cursed Diamonds of Lady Delune, the hunk of gold that would make him immortal if only he could figure out how to swallow it whole, the lamp that burned so brightly death couldn't find you, all the magical objects and legendary talismans that were said to make you immortal. But none of them had worked. Not really.

"I'd just about given up when Tan told me the Resurrection Amulet was buried in the Trove," he continued.

Tan was the captain of the *Black Beauty*, the quickest ship in the southeast. When Sefia was younger, listening to snippets from market storytellers until Nin dragged her away, she'd loved tales of Tan's bravery and brazenness. She was eager to finally meet her at Haven.

"Did she tell you how it worked?" Sefia asked.

Reed nodded, licking his lips. "D'you know the story of the great whale?"

It was a myth. It was a bedtime story. It was the tale Lon had told Mareah the night she killed her own parents to earn her bloodsword.

There are no coincidences.

"Not the part about the whale hunter," Captain Reed continued. "The part about *why* the great whale swims across the sky each night. Tan told me a story when I saw her. She said when you die, something splits from your body—she called it a *soul*. It's all the parts of you that make you *you*—except your skin and bones, of course—your thoughts, your feelings, your memories."

Sefia nodded. The Book had mentioned *souls* too.

"When you die, the great whale summons your soul and guides you to the edge of the world, where you pass into the place of the fleshless. But if you're wearin' the Amulet when your soul takes off, the Amulet draws you back. You never join the great whale. You never cross the invisible wall that separates the living from the dead. You go right back into your body. And you live."

She bit her lip. "Do you think it'll work if it's missing a piece?"

Unconsciously, Reed rubbed his chest. He'd inked over it since, but once upon a time, her parents had tattooed a page of the Book into his skin.

It had described the location of the last piece of the Resurrection Amulet. When Sefia still had the Sight, she'd seen them do it: her mother lifting the page to the light, her father dipping the needle into the ink. Did they know why they'd done it? Or had they simply done it because it was written that they would? She didn't think she'd ever find out.

"Doubt it," the captain said wryly. "It'd be too easy otherwise."

Sefia twisted the sharp silver ring she wore on her finger—her mother's ring, with a hidden compartment and a spring-loaded blade for poisoning her enemies. "I think . . . ," she began. "I think the Book *wants* me to want the Amulet. It wouldn't have given me that information otherwise. I think I'm *supposed* to think it'll save Archer. And if that's what it wants, maybe it's better if it stays lost at the bottom of the Trove."

"Better?" Captain Reed looked at her the same way he had the night he discovered her on his ship—the same way he looked at Dimarion, who might turn on him the second it suited his needs. "That mean you don't think I should have it either? You think my wantin' it is part of some trap?"

Placing a bookmark between the pages, she closed the Book again. "I don't know. I know I could find it, if I wanted to. I just . . . don't think I should."

"Would you help me find it, if I asked you to?"

She looked up suddenly—hurt and betrayed. "Would you ask me to, if you knew it might lead to Archer's death?"

Reed didn't answer, but the fact that he didn't say no convinced her of what she had to do next.

She had to leave. Archer had to leave.

She didn't know exactly how, she didn't know exactly when, but she knew the *Current* was full of people they loved, people for whom they would do anything, and that meant every one— Frey or Aljan or Captain Reed or the chief mate or any of the crew—was a lever destiny could push at any time, forcing Sefia and Archer to act, forcing them closer to the Red War.

And Archer's death.

They couldn't stay. They couldn't meet the bloodletters at Haven.

Without her powers, she couldn't protect Archer. So they had to run. As soon as possible. Somewhere without their loved ones.

Y ou read the Book?" Archer asked when she told him.

"I'm sorry. I know we can't trust it. I just—"

I just need to save you.

"After all that's happened, I just wish I could see them again," she finished. While it wasn't the whole truth, it was true. It had been true ever since Mareah died, and it had only grown truer every time Sefia lost someone else.

She wished she could see her mother more clearly than in her muddled memories.

She wished she could talk to her father, who would have known what to do.

She even wished Nin would yell at her and tell her to snap out of whatever spell the Book had her under.

Archer sat on the bed next to her. "I can't blame you," he said, sighing. "I think I would've done the same thing."

She smiled, reached for his hand, paused when he shook his head.

"But we can't leave just because Cap *might* want us to help find the one thing he's wanted for years."

"That's not—" Sefia frowned. "Don't you get it? The Book *wants* us to get the Amulet, or try to. That means you shouldn't be anywhere near it."

"C'mon." He nudged her uninjured shoulder. "Give us a little credit. We'd be finding it for the captain. The only way we could get it would be to steal it from him, and we'd never do that. Even *if* he asked us to help him, which he hasn't."

She shook her head. "But—"

"Let's just stick to the plan, okay? You, me, the bloodletters, Haven." He leaned in as he spoke, his voice lowering until it was just a whisper against her neck. She closed her eyes as he kissed her throat, his lips finding their way down her shoulder as his hands found their way to her waist. "Forever."

She blinked up at the ceiling, gasping softly as his fingers splayed over her ribs. *Forever.*

B ut she would not give up. For the next two weeks, as they neared Steeds, she tried all the ways she could think of to convince him to leave the *Current* as soon as they made landfall.

She tried to tell him what their lives could be like in the Liccarine desert, riding horses across the shifting sands, exploring the abandoned gem mines of Shaovinh, visiting the old cottonwood tree like other runaway lovers, sampling foods in the open-air markets, their faces swathed in scarves to conceal their identities.

She tried to tell him Frey and Aljan were safe on the *Current*. That the bloodletters were already on their way to Haven. That they didn't need him anymore.

She tried. And tried. And tried.

Archer was patient at first. But when she persisted, their conversations turned into arguments, voices low and tense, and he refused to budge.

The night before they reached Steeds, she even went to Frey and Aljan to ask them to push Archer to leave with her.

Frey looked up from a wax slate Horse had fashioned for her to practice her lettering. "He's our chief, Sefia," she said. "We want to protect him too."

"But?"

In the bunk, Aljan looked up from the ink and paper he was using to write out exercises for Meeks, Theo, and now Marmalade, who'd gotten the idea to record the lyrics to Jules's old songs. The boy blinked his gentle hazel eyes. "But we can't protect him if he's not here."

Sefia stormed out, slamming the sick bay door behind her, and stopped cold.

Captain Reed was waiting in the corridor, his face in shadow beneath his wide-brimmed hat. She was surprised; he hadn't spoken more than a few sentences to her in weeks, since their conversation about the Amulet, which, in truth, she'd been glad of.

Because if he'd asked her to help him locate the Amulet, she would have refused, and she didn't think he'd forgive her for that.

Silently, he handed her a cloak and jerked his head toward the hatchway.

Taking the furs, she followed him up onto the main deck, where the cold bit into her cheeks and exposed hands. Shivering, she pulled the cloak around her shoulders as snowflakes drifted from the sky, covering the *Current* in a thin veil of white.

The captain stopped at the rail, where he stared out at the black water for a moment. "So," he said finally, "you want to leave."

She nodded.

The captain rubbed the back of his neck. "I wish you wouldn't go, kid. But it ain't my place to stop you."

Sefia shrugged. "I'm not going anywhere, though. I can't get Archer to leave."

Reed wouldn't look at her. She could feel him counting. *One, two, three, four* . . . "Well." He sighed. "I think I've got a way for both of us to get what we want."

CHAPTER 9

The Trove of the King

If the legends about the labyrinthine caves of the Trove of the King were true, Captain Reed could have spent the rest of his life searching for the Resurrection Amulet, climbing echoing shafts, excavating tunnels, long collapsed, exhausting the remainder of his days in the cold dark of the earth.

But Sefia had the Book, and the Book could lead her directly to the Amulet, sparing him years of searching. The thought had haunted Reed for weeks.

> *The brave and the bold may find Liccarine gold*
> *Where the stallions charge into the spray.*
> *Where the sidewinder waits, the heart lowers its gates,*
> *And the water will show you the way.*

Every night, he would lie in his bunk, repeating the words of King Fieldspar's riddle and tapping out counts of eight on his chest. With every passing second, they were closing in on Steeds, the first landmark. With every passing second, he was closing in on a dream that had consumed his every waking moment for years, driving him to greater and greater exploits in the attempt to live a life too epic to be forgotten, to make his name too memorable to ever die.

But if he had the Amulet, he wouldn't need adventures or a collection of tattoos and treasures to prove that he'd lived.

He'd simply *live*. Forever.

He wanted it so bad he could feel his own want pulsing like an ember in his chest, smoking in the morning when ice spiked the running lines and the frosted sails sparkled in the first light of dawn. The sea, the spray, the ship skimming the water, this could all be his for the rest of time.

But if the Amulet was meant to lure Archer into fulfilling his destiny, could Reed live with the fact that getting the Amulet might cost Archer his life? Could he live with it *forever*?

Then he heard Sefia wanted to leave the *Current*. She wanted to take the boy and go running into the dunes as soon as they dropped anchor.

He'd be sorry to see them go. He remembered the night he'd discovered them on his ship: the Assassin leaping from the rails; the Executioner hot in his palm; Archer, breathing hard and bleeding from a dozen knife wounds; and Sefia, clutching the Book, telling him a story about magic and answers and revenge. They'd been good additions to the crew.

But if Archer was gone, the Amulet would be no danger to him.

"If you get me the Resurrection Amulet," Captain Reed said,

his breath clouding in the black night, "I'll make sure Archer doesn't set foot on this ship again. The crew will get their treasure. I'll get the Amulet. And when we leave here, neither of you will be with us."

Sefia blinked. "You'd strand Archer with me?"

Reed swallowed and nodded, rubbing the blank space at his wrist. "And I'd take the Amulet far away from both of you."

"But you haven't told him this."

He scoffed. "You think he'd agree? It's a mean, underhanded trick to pull on someone you love."

She was silent, still as a stone as the snow sugared her hair.

Was Reed going to have to beg? He hadn't begged for anything since he'd begged the former captain of the *Current* to let Jules, the runaway pearl diver with the voice like velvet, join their crew. Jules, who'd look at him now and tell him he was wrong to ask this. Jules, who was dead. Jules, whom the Amulet could've saved.

"All right," Sefia said finally, extending her hand. "He might hate me for this. But at least he'll be alive."

Her fingers were ice cold when Reed gripped them.

"Guess we got a deal, then," he said, and the words did not give him the satisfaction he thought they would.

The next morning, they reached Steeds. The oddly shaped headland was part of a series of capes and coves that dotted the Liccarine coast, the waters riddled with shallow channels and submerged rock formations that would rip holes in unsuspecting vessels. To complicate matters, the ebb and flow of the tide would change the landscape, allowing ships to pass into sheltered inlets at high tide and stranding them when the tide ran out, revealing and concealing cave entrances that dotted the sandstone cliffs.

But the Trove was here somewhere. And in it, the Resurrection Amulet.

Anchored in the deeper waters off the nose of Steeds, the outlaws surveyed the changing coastline. It would be dangerous to sail closer, but the ships could remain here while the sailors set off in the longboats, searching for the "sidewinder" from Fieldspar's poem.

Sefia and Archer began to pack for the solo expedition they would take into the Trove while Reed and the outlaws excavated the main caverns. Horse equipped them with rock hammers and a collapsible boat made from bamboo and sailcloth. Cooky plied them with provisions, including cakes for Sefia and packets of Archer's favorite spiced nuts.

"I'm glad you changed your mind," Archer said, coiling one of their ropes.

Reed caught Sefia's eye, their plan unspoken between them, invisible and heavy as lead. "You were right," she said, her voice a touch too light. "We stick to the plan. Haven's just around the corner now."

Archer kissed her on the cheek.

From the great cabin, the captain brought out an ebony box inlaid with stars of diamond and ivory. Lifting the lid, he took out a round rock, smooth as a pearl and slightly smaller than his palm. Through his fingers, the stone glowed with pale silver light.

"The moonstone?" Sefia asked.

"This is the first treasure I ever collected. I was sixteen, and the *Current* had just fished me out of the water, after . . ." He scratched his chest.

"After my parents tattooed you with a page from the Book," Sefia finished for him.

"The moonstone will light your way when you're in there."

Archer took the stone and slipped it deep into his pack. "Thanks, Cap."

The captain looked at him sadly. Poor kid. He didn't deserve to be tricked.

But, selfish as it was, Reed wanted that Amulet. And he wanted Archer to live.

The captain tossed him another bundle of warm woolen clothing. "Be careful. You get wet and you'll die of cold. Ain't no way to warm up in there."

They were just organizing search crews when Aly leaned out from the crow's nest, blond braids dangling over her shoulders. "Alliance ships, two points off the port bow!"

"Aly!" Captain Reed lifted a hand.

Drawing her arm back, she flung him the spyglass. It smacked into his palm, and he lifted it to his eye.

Four blue vessels were sailing up from the south.

He cursed. They were too exposed out here beyond Steeds— they'd be spotted as soon as the Alliance was close enough to see their sails against the sandstone cliffs. They couldn't run, not this time. Their only hope was to sail for one of the protected coves and hope that neither the *Current* nor the *Crux* ran aground.

As he gave the orders, the crew leapt into action, pulling up the anchor, unfurling the sails.

"There," Reed said to Jaunty, pointing out a shallow channel between two arms of an inlet. "Can we get through without hullin' ourselves?"

The passage would be dangerous. But Jaunty was the best helmsman in the Central Sea. If anyone could get them through it, he could.

Squinting at the water, Jaunty removed his hat and ran a hand through his dry, straw-colored hair. Then, with a non-committal grunt, he turned the helm.

The captain clapped him on the shoulder. "Good enough."

Killian of the larboard watch ran up a signal flag to tell the *Crux* to follow them, and then they were sailing past Steeds for the shelter of the cove, narrowly avoiding the stone columns that jutted through the waves and the underwater peaks that nearly scraped the bottom of their ship.

Reed spared a glance behind them. The *Crux* was sailing gamely after them, with the Alliance vessels still approaching from the open water.

Had the outlaws been spotted? Reed couldn't tell. They'd be fish in a barrel if the Alliance wanted to attack them in the inlet.

"Cap, in the water!" Meeks cried from the bow. "It's the *sidewinder*!"

Reed's attention snapped forward again, but he could see nothing but the sandstone walls and turquoise water of the cove.

"Below us!" The second mate pointed.

The captain raced to the bowsprit, where he climbed into the branches, leaning out over the water. A meandering ridge of stone lay beneath them, sinuous and green in the blue water.

At the end, a spade-shaped head seemed to sway from side to side under the waves.

He grinned.

The entrance to the Trove must be somewhere in the inlet. And they had only one more landmark to go.

As they entered the cove, he ordered the crew to drop anchor and haul in the sails. His sailors clambered up onto the yards. The enormous squares of white canvas were furled, making the masts less visible to searching Alliance eyes.

The *Crux* followed them, her hull scraping against the sidewinder's uneven spine.

Reed winced, imagining the hustle belowdecks as Dimarion's crew raced to patch their ship.

He could see the Alliance vessels out past Steeds, closer now. They weren't headed inland, for the *Current* and the *Crux*. They were sailing north toward a small fleet both he and Aly had missed.

He expected the ships to keep running. But they turned. They were fighting back.

The outlaws were too far to hear the cannons, but they were close enough to see the smoke.

Reed couldn't believe it. Who was left in these waters to resist Stonegold and the Alliance?

They watched the strange ships blast the Alliance until the winds shifted and the battle disappeared over the horizon.

That night, Captain Reed and the outlaws drank to the resistance ships, whoever they were, and all their sailors, dead or alive.

"You know," he said to the chief mate when they'd retired to the great cabin, "since we left Jahara, I'd almost fooled myself into thinkin' things were the same as they used to be."

The mate laughed harshly. "What voyage have you been on? Because the rest of us have been dodging Alliance patrols for a month."

Reed's gaze flitted from one glass case to another, counting each of his treasures—the Thunder Gong, which was supposed to be able to summon and dispel a storm, only he'd never gotten it to work; the tooth of a sea serpent; the black box, now empty of the moonstone. "I know, but in between, it was easy to forget that the seas ain't wild anymore. That we ain't free as we used to be."

"Haven's free."

"Haven's a small island in a big ocean."

Wearily, the chief mate drew his square-fingered hand down his lined face. "Will that be enough for you, if the Alliance wins the war?"

Reed didn't answer as he finished counting the treasures and began again.

There was a pall hanging over them the next morning as they piled into the longboats to scour the cliffs for the "heart" from Fieldspar's riddle. The currents were perilous and the stone pillars seemed to rear up beneath them when they least expected it. More than once, they were almost dashed to bits against the rocky coast.

Sefia had refused to use the Book to find the Trove's entrance. "It's dangerous enough using the Book at all, when it can manipulate us into doing whatever it wants," she said. "Please don't ask me for more." But she and Archer joined them in the boats all the same, with their packs ready to go.

The crews searched until their hands were blistered and their shoulders ached from rowing. They searched until night fell. And the next morning, they got in the boats and began their search again.

It was Goro, the oldest sailor on the *Current*, who spotted the cave—a dark entrance shaped exactly like a human heart, with great cracks like arteries branching into the stone above.

As the tide ran out, more and more of the entrance became visible, as if the heart were revealing itself to them, *lowering its gates*, just as the riddle had said.

Reed's pulse skipped. This was the way to the Trove of the King. This was the way he got the Amulet. This was the way he lived forever.

"We got till mid-tide before that cave floods again," he shouted, gripping his oars. "Let's get that treasure!"

Through the heart they rowed, into the vaulted cavern beyond.

Inside, the water seemed to glow aquamarine beneath the high shadowed ceilings. At the back, there was a sort of stone dock with conical stalagmites, perfect for mooring boats, and beyond it rose a flat wall more than thrice Reed's height.

The crews of the *Crux* and the *Current* pulled up and disembarked, leaving one boat outside to watch the tide. Captain Reed ran to the wall, fanning his hands over its smooth surface, searching for seams.

"You reckon this is the way in?" Meeks asked while Sefia, Archer, and Dimarion's own group of treasure hunters unloaded their packs onto the shore. *No matter,* Reed thought. With so much other treasure to distract them, they wouldn't get the Amulet. Not when Sefia had the Book.

Dimarion shook his head. "Fieldspar said, 'the water will show you the way.' We must be looking for an underwater channel of some sort."

Reed pressed his palms to the wall. "No way the king squirreled away all his treasure through an underwater tunnel."

The pirate captain rolled his eyes. "By all means, continue hugging the wall. I'm sure we'll find the Trove that way."

While Dimarion's sailors began to strip off their shirts and boots, and others lit lanterns to illuminate the cavern, Frey knelt at the base of the wall, where the stone was still damp.

Reed crouched beside her. "What's that, kid?"

Frey tucked a loose strand of hair behind her scarred ear and pointed. "Look, Captain."

Parts of the rock were the same burnt red as the rest of the chamber, but here and there were veins of gold that seemed to sprout from the floor like new shoots of grass.

Reed grinned at her. *The water will show you the way.*

Sefia, Archer, and Meeks were already dipping bailing buckets into the water and carrying them to the wall, where they emptied their contents onto the rocks.

Wherever the water touched, the gold lines appeared, forming trellises and exquisite patterns in the stone.

Captain Reed clapped Frey on the shoulder proudly. "Good job, kid!"

She beamed at the praise.

All of them, even Dimarion, flocked to the wall, flinging

bucket after bucket of water onto the rock, until they had revealed a golden archway that nearly touched the ceiling.

"Well, this seems promising," the pirate captain said, wiping his brow with his silk scarf. "But how do we open it?"

"Here." Meeks wet his hand and smeared it across the center of the wall. Beneath his fingers, the golden curves glistened more brightly:

FOR THE WEALTH OF THE KING,

THE BLOOD OF THE KINGDOM.

Reed crossed his arms. They were so close, and King Fieldspar still had one more riddle for them. Again, he wondered if the man had been a Guardian and, if he was, why he would have hidden all that treasure from the Guard.

The second mate sounded out the words silently while Sefia read them aloud. "Blood?" she wondered. "Is anyone here Liccarine?"

Old Goro offered his weathered palm. "My mother was Liccarine." Drawing his knife, he cut his hand. Blood welled along his lifeline, and he pressed it over the words.

Nothing happened.

Meeks shrugged. "Maybe we need someone who's *all* Liccarine."

"Or perhaps," Dimarion said thoughtfully, fingering a chain at his neck, "we need the true blood of the kingdom." Light glinted off his necklace as he removed it.

"Right." Reed started forward eagerly, a tug in his chest drawing him toward the door and what lay beyond it. "The blood of the kingdom ain't blood."

The pirate captain grinned at him. "The blood of Liccaro

has always been gold." With a flourish, he pressed the chain to the wall.

With a groan, the golden arch split down the center, the two halves swinging inward, dislodging bits of dust and stone. Reed laughed as the shadows yawned before him, the lamplight touching on flashes of metal and precious gems.

They'd opened the Trove of the King.

CHAPTER 10

The Crystal Globe

The first cavern of the Trove was not only filled with gold and jewels, but also with huge stalagmites, evenly spaced in widening semicircles on the stone floor. Decades of water dripping from above had left streams of hardened sediment on their domes and curving sides, and to Sefia, they looked almost human, with helmets and sightless eyes, feet fused to the floor.

The legends said King Fieldspar had locked his soldiers inside the Trove after they'd finished unloading his treasure. Were these his soldiers, somehow turned to stone?

She shuddered.

At the entrance, the crews of the *Current* and the *Crux* were making plans to excavate the Trove. Dimarion's treasure hunters were checking their equipment. Like Sefia and Archer, they would be exploring the tunnels, seeking out the rarest prizes for their captain.

"A week is all you need?" Reed asked, coming to stand beside her while she stood alone at the edge of the darkness.

She nodded. The Book had told her it would take seven days to retrieve the Resurrection Amulet, so they'd packed only seven days' worth of food and water.

"By the time you get back, we'll have loaded the ships and we'll be ready to go."

The timing had to be right so that Captain Reed would be the only one at the entrance when she and Archer showed up with the Amulet. She'd hand it over. He'd leave them there, rowing out of the cave on his own.

And the *Current* would sail off with Frey, Aljan, and all the crew.

"I'm sorry it has to be like this, kid," the captain said.

"Me too."

He tipped his hat at her. "Maybe we'll meet again when the war's over?"

Sefia hiked her pack higher on her shoulders and nodded. "I'd like that, Cap."

One by one, she embraced the crew of the *Current*, wishing she could say good-bye to the chief mate and the others who had remained on the ship. It could be years before she saw them again, if ever.

She hugged Frey, who laughed. "Find me something pretty, will you? And something sharp."

Sefia blinked back tears before she released her. "Of course."

"Ready?" Archer asked, shouldering the pack with the collapsible boat strapped to it.

To betray you? she thought. *No.* But she *was* ready to save him.

Leaving the others among the stalagmites, they wandered into the Trove.

She'd memorized the beginning of their road to the Amulet. Their path was easy at first, as they wound through cavern after cavern of treasures: rooms of chalices and polished plates, grottoes of painted porcelain urns, halls piled with gemstones that glittered like waves under the light of the moonstone, menageries of statuary so lifelike Sefia could have sworn the fantastical creatures moved when she wasn't looking.

The first galleries were well organized, with paths twisting through the towers of crowns, stacked pyramids of scepters, crates of rotting silk and velvet, toy chests of exquisitely detailed automatons that, when their keys were turned, performed sweet songs and eerie, stuttering walks.

Everywhere was treasure. You could have fed and clothed the entire kingdom of Liccaro for a year on the wealth of just one of the vaulted halls.

It wasn't long before Dimarion's treasure hunters caught up to them, and they all stopped to *ooh* and *aah* at sapphires carved into the shapes of sea creatures and collections of pearls larger than human skulls. They ran their hands along tapestries of golden thread and tortoise shells that seemed to have grown crystals from their carapaces, laughing incredulously as they stuffed their hands into barrels brimming with millions of beads of chrysoprase and topaz, lapis and corundum that trickled through their fingers like grains of sand.

Later, after they and the pirates wished one another luck and took diverging paths on their quests for greater and greater treasure, Sefia and Archer plowed deeper into the labyrinth with the moonstone to light their way.

They spent the first night—or what they assumed was the first night; they couldn't be sure—camped beside an enormous bronze elk, at least twice the size of a real animal, its antlers festooned with garlands of rubies. They lay in a clamshell big enough to fit them both and covered the moonstone, dousing them in darkness.

"I know you still want to leave," Archer said, his voice seeming small in the dripping cave. "I'm sorry."

A faint wisp of gold seemed to glimmer in the black.

Light?

Sefia rubbed her face. No, not light. In the pitch-darkness, her eyes were playing tricks on her.

She curled up against him. "Do you know what scares me most?" she whispered. When he didn't answer, she continued, "I'd do anything to keep you alive."

He kissed her hair. "I know. I would too."

"No. I mean *anything*." She let out a breath, feeling it, warm, on the back of her hand. "Captain Reed wants the Amulet so badly he'll sacrifice you to get it."

"He's not—"

"And I'd do the same to him, if it meant saving you. I'd let him, and anyone on the *Current* or the *Brother*, die, if it meant saving you. If we stay, and it comes down to choosing you or them, I'm going to choose you. And I don't want to have to make that choice."

In the dark, Archer squeezed her tighter. "It won't come down to that."

She buried her face in his clothing, feeling the tears on her cheeks. She'd already chosen, after all. She was leaving the people she loved, all the people she loved in the world, except for him. To keep him alive.

A s they continued deeper into the Trove, the way became more treacherous. They climbed up slippery rock faces beside waterfalls that left their coats and cheeks starry with spray. They knotted ropes to stone columns and descended into echoing black pits.

In every new cavern, at each new intersection, Sefia consulted the Book on which fork to take or which narrow passage to excavate. And as she'd expected, the Book did what she asked, revealing to her, paragraph by paragraph, the path of King Fieldspar himself as he hid the Resurrection Amulet from the world so many decades ago.

Archer kept finding gifts for their friends—an ornamented rifle for Scarza, a jewel-encrusted fiddle case for Theo, a diamond bangle and a pair of switchblades for Frey—setting the treasures along the path so he could pick them up on their way back to the entrance. As she passed, Sefia brushed her fingers over the presents their friends would never receive and hoped that Archer would forgive her.

The Book led them to the edge of an underground lake. Among a gallery of giant slanting crystals, milky white and wide as catwalks, the pool was still and clear, revealing an underwater chasm spiked with submerged crystals.

Lifting the moonstone, Archer let out a low whistle. The lake was both deep and wide, so wide they couldn't see the far shore. But the Amulet lay somewhere in the dark tunnels beyond, and to get it, they had to cross.

They unpacked their collapsible boat and fastened the sailcloth over the frame. Placing the paddles inside, Archer tested its buoyancy. Sefia bit her lip, remembering Reed's warning about the cold and the wet. But the boat held. Ripples spread from the hull, washing lightly against the pale crystals that pierced the surface.

They set out across the water, their shadows sliding eerily over the enormous sunken gems below.

When they could no longer see the shore behind them, Archer tapped her on the shoulder, whispering, "Sefia, look up."

The ceiling was a chandelier—no, an entire *sky*—of crystals. Hundreds of thousands of them winking in the light of the moonstone. It was as if she and Archer were caught in the center of a sparkling globe—the glassy surface of the lake mirroring the glittering facets above—and sitting there, with the water lapping against their boat, it was like their world was shrinking.

There was no shore behind them. No outlaws waiting at the entrance. No past. No war. No destiny.

There was only the boat, the water, the sphere of crystal.

And Archer.

Sefia didn't know how long they sat there, silent and still, but when they set off across the lake again, something had changed.

They moved slowly, almost languidly, as if the urgency to reach the Amulet had been leached from them like a toxin.

As they disembarked on the far shore, Sefia found herself focused less on the dismantling of their boat than on Archer—his scarred, well-muscled arms; his feet and calves and thighs; his temples; his hair, waving ever so slightly in the breeze.

A breeze? Sefia straightened, searching the crystal cavern. On the surface of the water, ripples appeared and disappeared like scribbles of magical ink.

"Do you feel that wind?" she asked.

Archer licked a finger. As if in response, the wind picked up, whirling around them, teasing their arms and legs. Goose bumps rose on the backs of Sefia's arms.

"Fresh air," Archer said. "There must be an exit around here somewhere. Should we try to find it?"

"Nah." She began removing supplies from her pack. "It could be little more than a crack, for all we know. We might not be able to fit through, even if we found it. Let's make camp and continue on when we've rested."

Beneath two towering crystals that had grown together at the apex, forming a sort of tent, they made a nest of bedrolls and blankets and ate and talked and watched the light of the moonstone play across the ceiling like real moonlight on a field of ice.

"Tell me something," Archer said at one point. "Something new."

Sefia curled up against him and laid her head on his shoulder. "New?"

"We've only known each other six months. That's a fraction of our lives." His fingers slid through her hair. "There's still so much I don't know about you. Sometimes I'm afraid I'll never have enough time to know it all."

"What do you want to know?"

"Anything," he answered immediately. "Everything."

She closed her eyes. There were parts of her life she'd locked away for years because they were too painful to remember— memories of Lon and Mareah and Nin. But sitting here with Archer, she wondered if it would be safe to crack open those memories again. Maybe it would be okay to remember the past, because once they left the Trove, she'd have a future to look forward to.

"My parents used to sing me songs and tell me stories every night before I went to sleep. My father hated repeating him- self, but my mother would sing the same song at least once a week . . ." Sefia described the warmth of the blankets, the soft cloth of her toy crocodile against her cheek, the shadows in the corners of her basement bedroom, the pressure of Mareah's body on the edge of the bed, dimpling the mattress, and the way she'd brush back Sefia's hair and kiss her on the forehead before she began.

"Will you sing it for me?" Archer asked.

She hesitated. She hadn't heard it in so long, she wondered if she could remember all the words. But even as she questioned her memory, the words came back to her. In a small, faltering voice, she began:

Little hawk, little hawk, don't fly away.
For you're a mighty huntress with claws to catch your
  prey.
Little lark, little lark, don't waste your voice.
The songs that come from your beak will always be your
  choice.

Little owl, little owl, don't be afraid.
Your right wing is a cudgel; your left wing is a blade.
Little bat, little bat, don't close your eyes.
I know the world is frightening, but I am by your side.

Larks, lift your right wings.
Hawks, raise your chins.
Bats, lift your left wings.
Owls, dig your talons in.

Sefia, Sefia, listen to my song.
Follow every movement and you cannot go wrong.

As her voice died away, it was like she and Archer were both being dropped, one after the other like marbles, out of the cloudy world of her memory and back into the cave, with the crystal columns and the darkness beyond.

"What does the last line mean?" he asked.

To demonstrate, Sefia hooked her fingers. "On the word *claws*, we'd do this. Or on *eyes*, we'd point, like this. It was part of the game. Sometimes she'd sing it three or four times a week, if my father wasn't there." She sat up, frowning. "She only ever sang it when he wasn't there."

"Why?"

"She must have wanted to tell me something . . . and only me." Her mother had been the one to teach her the alphabet, spelling out words with wooden blocks while Lon was out of the house. What else had Mareah been trying to teach her? Something about Illumination?

Sefia settled back against Archer's shoulder. She'd never know now—you don't get messages from the dead.

O n their third day, near the halfway point of their week in the Trove, the Book led them to a small cave. Its walls were veined with metal so bright, it looked as if they'd been clawed by some enormous creature.

Atop a pedestal in the center of the room stood a man carved from marble. He'd lifted a hand as if to shield himself from some assailant seen only with his unblinking eyes.

The statue was so lifelike, it was as if he'd once been alive and had somehow been trapped in stone, his face forever frozen in an expression of horror, like he had seen a thing too terrible to ever unsee.

From a chain around his neck dangled a ring of dull metal embedded with red stones the likes of which Sefia had never seen before.

She leaned closer. The disc was engraved with symbols arrayed in concentric circles, though she couldn't decipher them.

"What does it say?" Archer whispered.

"I don't know."

So this was the Resurrection Amulet. Along the inner rim there were evenly spaced notches, as if a wheel or cog should fit inside. That must have been the missing piece, its location tattooed on Reed's chest by Sefia's parents.

"Can we touch it?" Archer asked, interrupting her thoughts. He extended a finger toward the Amulet.

"No!" She didn't know how it worked. She didn't know if you had to find the last piece first. But she knew she had to keep Archer away from it. Using one of Horse's bandannas to protect her hand, she took hold of the dull disc, lifting it carefully from the marble man's head.

The chain clinked softly in the silence of the cave. Did the statue's features soften, or was that her imagination?

Sefia wrapped the Amulet and placed it in her pocket, where it lay heavy and cold against her thigh. "Well, we got what Reed wanted. Let's go back."

Archer grinned at her. "And sail to Haven."

Guilt gripped her throat, and she had to swallow a few times before she could smile back. "Yeah," she said. "Haven."

Back in the crystal gallery, they packed their belongings into the collapsible boat, and as Sefia was climbing in, taking up her paddle, there was a splash.

She didn't see the Amulet fall from her pocket, only heard the hollow sound of it striking the water, and as she whirled around, she saw the bandanna unfurling like a sail as the Amulet began to sink.

She hadn't meant to drop it. It was an accident. Or was it fate? Maybe destiny didn't want Archer—or anyone—to have the Amulet after all.

But Archer was pulling off his boots. Archer was going to go after it, into the frigid water.

Risking himself for Reed. For his friend. Just like she'd known he would.

But she had to keep the Amulet out of his hands. Before he could finish stripping off his outer layers, she grabbed the moonstone from the center of the boat and dove into the lake.

The water was so cold it sucked the breath from her lungs and the strength from her limbs. She almost dropped the moonstone, paralyzed by the cold.

For a moment, she flailed in the water as Reed's words floated past her: *You get wet and you'll die of cold. Ain't no way to warm up in there.*

Below, the Amulet was sinking to the bottom of the lake, drifting inexorably toward the sunken crystals.

Gripping the moonstone as hard as she could, Sefia kicked, lunged, fought, pushing at the water, trying not to gasp as the cold hit her again and again.

At last, her fingers closed over the Amulet. It fit perfectly in her palm, almost as if it belonged there.

She turned, lungs burning, for the surface.

Above her, Archer waited, his figure distorted by the play of light from the water, scarred and chipped and cracked and perfect, with the dark cavern echoing behind him. But the closer she got, the more the shadows seemed to close about him, creeping over his shoulders, up his neck, over his jaw, until they had eclipsed everything but his golden eyes.

She was three feet from the surface when even his eyes disappeared, and there was nothing left of him at all.

And then . . . *light*. A million glorious golden motes washing over the world, gliding over every crystal in the cave, illuminating black crevices at the bottom of the lake, glimmers of lost treasure.

She sobbed, choking.

Her system must have finally healed. Her magic had returned.

SOMETHING CHANGES WHEN SHE SEIZES THE AMULET. OR IS IT WI

HER POWERS REEMERGE?

DARKNESS IS COMING.

AN END. *THE* END?

ENI

BUT HOW CAN AN INFINITE STORY

WHAT, SEFIA, HAVE YOU STARTED?

ENDED?

CHAPTER 11

The Thwarted Adventure of Haldon Lac

The more Haldon Lac got to know his new friend Ed, the more he liked him. First, though not most important, the boy was the kind of beautiful you only saw in paintings, totally unattainable, with thick curls and a clear gaze that Lac felt as if he could drop into like an endless well, falling so long it would feel like flying.

Second, Ed had a way about him that could elevate even the most lowly of circumstances. With a tilt of his head or a wave of his hand, he could make beckoning you to join him for your daily cup of grog seem like he was asking you to recline beside him on a chaise while you drank rice wine and ate sweet cakes from a silver tray.

Perhaps it was his elegance that also made Ed a wonder to watch. He had such an otherworldly grace that despite being given tedious, ungainly jobs like emptying the bilge or swabbing the deck—and having to be instructed, moreover, on how to use a mop, as if he'd never had to clean a floor in his life—he seemed to be floating over the surfaces of things, barely touching them with his toes or fingertips.

Fox had been graceful too, but she'd had a different sort of grace—alive and bodily, like she was fully in her skin at all times.

Ed was the opposite, and that was the thing that Lac wondered at most. The boy was so sad sometimes, it was as if he were disappearing, even when he was surrounded by the other sailors, chanting in unison as they reefed sails or hauled up the anchor. You might not have noticed if you weren't looking for it, but Ed was Lac's friend, and Lac noticed.

He wanted to cheer Ed up, but they were trapped on the *Hustle* with Captain Neeram and their disreputable crew, working like dogs for meals of hardtack and beans, so sometimes he borrowed a few young chicks from the henhouse and brought them to Ed, where he was crying quietly in his hammock, to sit on his chest and peep softly. Sometimes Lac and Hobs would just be with him in the crow's nest, staring out over the indigo seas and talking until their next grueling watch.

Sometimes Hobs told jokes—or Hobs's versions of jokes, which Lac had to admit he never quite understood.

"What's it called when you sit between two desert sorcerers?"

"What?"

"A sand witch sandwich."

Or: "There are two sand witches with two sandwiches. Which sandwich did the first sand witch wish for when her sister sand witch wished away her first sandwich?"

142

"A fish sandwich," Ed replied.

"Yes, but what kind of fish?"

"Does it matter?"

"Yes. Tuna!"

In fact, with little better to eat than some sort of beige glop that the cook tried to pass off as porridge, they often spoke of food. Lac and Hobs would talk of the street food they planned on making Ed try when they reached Epidram: skewered eel, plantains fried in oil, roasted nuts they'd pluck out of steaming shells. And Ed would lean back on his hands and describe in wistful tones the richness of Delienean wines, the supple flesh of persimmons harvested from bare winter branches, warm cheeses made with milk from black-faced Heartland sheep.

Beyond this, however, Ed would say nothing of his past, and the mystery made him even more interesting. Hobs was convinced he'd been a kitchen boy in one of the provincial castles and, when the *Hustle*'s cook wasn't looking, planned on sneaking him into the galley to whip up something delectable out of their dwindling stores of salted meat and eggs.

Whoever Ed was, both Lac and Hobs liked him, and to make sure he fit in, they taught him to care for the chickens and the pigs, which seemed to bring him out of his sadness even when it was heaviest upon him, and to sing bawdy redcoat drinking songs so he could join in with the rest of the crew during the dogwatches.

Like Lac, most of the other sailors were anxious to return to their kingdom. Some had family. Many, like Captain Neeram themself, were former redcoats—dishonorably discharged, perhaps, but former redcoats nonetheless.

Everyone was jumpy, on high alert for the slightest sign of the Alliance. With their false colors, Neeram didn't think the *Hustle* would run into much trouble, but their forged identities wouldn't hold up under close scrutiny—or any scrutiny, truthfully—and without armaments more powerful than pistols, rifles, and a single swivel gun, they wanted to avoid a confrontation at all costs.

So they fled when they saw other ships on the horizon, even when Lac protested that they could be Royal Navy vessels. The lonely weeks passed, and the chill northern winds were slowly replaced by long afternoon downpours.

But every day, they drew nearer to Oxscini. To Epidram. To home.

They were only a day out when they spotted lights on the horizon. In the east, the great whale was rising out of the sea, drawing the curtain of night over the sky, and all across the southern horizon, lanterns were flickering to life like a field of fireflies on the water.

Ships. There had to be at least fifty of them.

The Royal Navy? Lac almost wept with joy. What a grand welcome after their two long weeks at sea!

"Light the lamps!" he cried. "Raise our true colors!"

No one listened but Hobs, who ran for the trunk where they kept their signal flags. Even Ed didn't move from the rail.

"Belay that," Captain Neeram snapped.

With the scarlet Oxscinian flag clutched to his chest, Hobs looked to Lac, who looked to Neeram, confused. "But, Captain, they need to see we aren't the enemy."

Neeram flicked their fingers, and someone relieved Hobs of

the flag, stuffing it unceremoniously back into the trunk. "*We need to see they aren't the enemy*," they said, lifting a spyglass to their eye.

Lac smiled at their foolishness. "There's no way the Alliance could have gotten here so quickly." Jahara and Deliene had joined the Alliance the day the *Hustle* had left port. The Alliance would need another three weeks *minimum* to muster a fleet before they could set sail from Deliene.

Gently, Ed laid a hand on Lac's arm. "Let's wait for confirmation."

Haldon Lac smirked. His smirks were perhaps the least attractive of his smiles, but he could already picture the consternation on Neeram's face when they saw what he already knew, and he felt he could afford to look a little less than his best when the captain was proven wrong.

But they remained grim as they lowered the spyglass.

"What colors are they flying?" someone asked.

Red and gold.

Lac was already opening his mouth to laugh triumphantly when Neeram shook their head. "They're Alliance. Flying blue, gold, and white," they said.

Haldon Lac's jaw dropped in a most unattractive fashion. Alliance colors? The Alliance had reached Oxscini?

Ed's hand fell from Lac's arm as the boy drifted to the rail, his brow furrowed in thought.

"It can't be!" Lac cried. Calculations had never been a strength of his, but it was patently, *mathematically* impossible for the enemy to have reached Oxscini before them.

"It is."

"But *how*? Even if the Alliance left Jahara the same day we did, we're smaller and faster. We should have beaten them here."

"There is one explanation," Hobs ventured, "but you won't like it."

"What?" Lac looked, bewildered, from Hobs to Neeram.

But it was Ed who answered. He looked over his shoulder with those infinitely sad eyes. "Deliene must have been planning the attack for months, long before they joined the war. Before the king was even gone. Arcadimon just had to—to wait for him to die before sending the fleet south."

"We have to warn Epidram, then!" Lac said immediately.

Captain Neeram leveled him with a withering glare. "We don't have to do anything," they said coolly.

But he was too stupid or too brave to back down. "But all those people—"

"Are not my responsibility."

"But you're one of us!" Lac cried, his voice breaking in a most embarrassing fashion, though even his mortification couldn't stop him now. "You have a duty—"

"I *was* one of you. I was even part of a fleet like that once. You know what a fleet that size is for, boy? It's only got one purpose." When Lac didn't reply, they continued, "Destroying cities. Battering them until no one is left to man the ramparts. That's what *we* did. That's what *they're* going to do. And when they're done, they're going to walk in and take Epidram for themselves. That's not just an attack—that's an invasion. And if you think the city has even a shred of hope of surviving it, you're an even bigger fool than I thought you were."

Lac blinked angry tears from his eyes. They were right, though he didn't want to admit it. Couldn't admit it. If he admitted it, he'd be admitting the city would fall. He had friends, senior officers, lovers there. They'd die if they weren't warned. He couldn't admit that.

Instead he said, stubbornly, "There's got to be something we can do!"

"There's no moon tonight," Hobs offered helpfully.

"Yes! We can douse our lamps and sneak past—"

Neeram's eyes went cold. "No."

As if of their own accord, Lac's feet carried him forward. He caught their arm. "Please, Captain, if we could just let them know the Alliance is here . . ." He attempted one of his most dazzling smiles. No one refused him when he smiled like that.

But they jerked out of his grasp so suddenly he stumbled forward. "Stupid boy. Do you know how close we are to Epidram? The invasion will be there by dawn. If we go in now, we'll never come out."

Hobs bit his lip. Ed, still at the rail, seemed to have left his body, his mind drifting somewhere far away.

Lac, however, squared his shoulders. He lifted his chin. "Then you're a coward."

There was a pain in his jaw—

—and he was on his back, the deck hard beneath him, staring dazedly up at the darkening sky.

Hobs tried to leap forward, but the second mate, a burly, barrel-chested man with a braided beard, caught him by the arm and jerked him back like a rag doll.

Lac tried to stand, but he'd only gotten to his knees when there was a sharp pain in his stomach.

Captain Neeram had kicked him! Rotten hulls, it *hurt*.

"*I'm* a coward?" they snarled.

Lac wanted to vomit. Oh, he dearly hoped he wouldn't vomit.

"Would you have me sacrifice my crew?" Neeram demanded, punctuating the last word with another blow from their pointed boot.

Lac doubled over, clutching his stomach while the captain kicked him again and again.

"We ain't redcoats anymore. We don't owe our lives to queen and kingdom."

Lac felt something in his side crack. He curled up on the deck, hands over his head. Somewhere in his haze of pain, he could hear Hobs wrestling with the second mate. There was a *thud*, and he heard Hobs's rough breathing near him.

Lac coughed. Blood sprayed from his lips. Dimly, he wondered if he'd be able to clean it from his clothing. As the blows continued, Hobs tried to put himself between Lac and Neeram's boot, but Lac shoved him unceremoniously out of harm's way.

Things were going dark. Lac was going to faint, he was fairly certain. For a brief moment, he hoped he would faint elegantly so Ed, if he'd come back to his body by now, wouldn't think less of him. But as Neeram kicked him again, Lac realized belatedly that he was already past the point of looking good. He tried to get up, but his body was no longer obeying him.

Stupid body! There were people to save. *His* people. He

couldn't just lie here while they were in danger. *Not again,* a voice inside him whispered.

Suddenly, the blows stopped. He peered up through the shelter of his arms and the first thing he saw was Ed—tall and dark and slender—drawing Neeram aside with the unobtrusive courtesy only Ed possessed.

"Sir?" Someone shook Lac—Hobs, with a bloody nose and a cut lip. Good old Hobs.

What was Ed saying to Neeram? His lips were moving. But no sound was coming out. No, Lac could hear a ringing. A definite high-pitched whine. But there was no earthly way Ed could be making that sound.

Neeram's lip curled. They said something to Ed, their words slowly becoming more distinct. ". . . more trouble than you're worth."

"We can change that," Ed said quickly. "We'll work for half rations. I don't know what your plan is, but you might need the extra hands in the days to come."

"Sir?" Hobs shook him again.

"I'm all right," Lac burbled through a mouthful of blood. He wasn't even sure his words were intelligible. "Help me up, will you?"

Captain Neeram must have finished negotiations with Ed, because they shook their head. "Fine. But if he makes trouble again, I'm taking it out of *your* hide." They looked around for other dissenters. "We're sailing south."

South?

In his befuddlement, Lac tried to picture the Oxscinian coastline. The eastern edge of the Forest Kingdom was a mountainous maze, impervious to large-scale invasions. The next logical point of attack was Broken Crown, where the kingdom broke up into smaller islands.

"If we're lucky, we make it to Broken Crown in time to warn them that the Alliance is coming. We still get to be heroes, but we get to be heroes who live." For good measure, it seemed, they kicked Lac once more. "That all right with you, pretty boy?"

Pretty? Lac mouthed, torn between laughing and sobbing. *Heroes?*

They weren't heroes.

Heroes didn't let hundreds of people—people they were sworn to protect—die.

Did that make him a villain?

Or worse, a coward?

Stupid brave, Fox had called him. But he didn't deserve to be called that now.

He felt Ed and Hobs lift him up by the armpits as the captain rattled off their orders. They were running again. Like he'd run from the *Fire-Eater*. Overhead, wind filled the sails, and they sped away, the lights of the Alliance fleet disappearing into the night as they left Epidram and all its people to their fate.

CHAPTER 12

How We Fail

Archer dashed to the edge of the lake. He had to get to her. Shedding his coat, he thrust his hand into the water, hoisting Sefia onto the shore. She spit, coughing, gasping. She was soaked—and *freezing*—shivering in a fit to shake her bones apart.

Ignoring her protests, Archer pried the Amulet and the moonstone from her grip, setting them securely in a depression among the rocks. He began pulling off her shoes, her coat, the waterproof trousers, all her sodden layers, peeling them back and tossing them into a dripping heap until she was in nothing but her underthings. Then he took those off too.

He'd never seen her naked before, but he didn't stop to look as he wrapped a blanket around her, tucking it over her trembling shoulders, her exposed toes.

It was happening again. He was going to lose her again. And this time, it would be permanent. If she didn't get warm, she'd die.

As he yanked a bedroll from the packs, he heard Sefia's voice. "F-fire."

"We're in a cave. There's no fuel."

"The breeze."

Stupid. He could have kicked himself. The wind was getting into the crystal gallery somehow. He just had to find where, and hope there'd be kindling outside.

"There." She pointed over his shoulder as he wrapped the bedroll around her. "The exit."

"How do you know?"

Her voice was fading. "My magic came back."

So the poison had finally left her system. Archer took her chin in his hand. She wasn't shivering anymore—was that a good sign?—but her skin had gone pale and cold as snow. "Don't die on me."

With painful sluggishness, she nodded, and in a voice so soft he barely heard it, she whispered, "Never."

Handing her the moonstone, he hoisted her up and carried her over the crystals until he reached an opening no bigger than a crawlspace, blocked from view by a crystal point as large as his torso.

Sefia wasn't doing well. He helped her through the exit, cringing as she whimpered, trying to get her uncooperative limbs to move. Outside, she lay in the sand, curled into a ball with the blankets and bedrolls heaped around her, as he gathered thorny shrubs and dry branches.

Then, with flint and tinder, he lit a nest of withered grasses and lifted it to his lips, blowing gently, just as Sefia had taught him half a year ago, in the jungle.

Smoke bloomed in his hands, followed by flame. He shoved the tinder bundle under his pile of sticks, where the dry desert scrub quickly caught fire.

Nearly sobbing, Sefia tried to crawl toward it, but her arms and legs no longer seemed to be working.

Archer swept her up again, positioning her closer to the flames. "I've got you," he murmured. "I'm here."

He fed the fire, he dried her hair, he collected their belongings from the cave and dressed her in the warmest clothing they had, crawling under the blankets beside her and wrapping his arms around her like he'd never let go.

Slowly, her body seemed to thaw. Slowly, Archer's heart stopped racing.

He'd almost lost her. He'd almost let her slip away, into the water, the cold, the impenetrable dark.

He could stand loss. He knew it well, like a familiar touch.

But he couldn't stand to lose Sefia.

Closing his eyes, he buried his face in her hair, and when she mumbled a sleepy response, her body uncurling in his embrace like a new leaf, he held her closer—precious and alive.

He must have slept, because when he awoke, Sefia was watching him, her face a hand-span from his, her eyes dark and serious.

"How are you feeling?" he asked.

"Better."

He cupped her cheek in his palm, brushing his thumb across her lower lip. "You went into that water for me? So I wouldn't touch the Amulet?"

She nodded. Tears glimmered in her eyes. "But you did anyway, didn't you? When you pulled me out of the water?"

"Nothing happened, though." After he'd built the fire, he'd stowed it safely among their things. "It was you who—who almost died. To save me. Because you always save me. You always choose me."

She bit her lip. "Archer—"

He kissed her on the forehead, on each of her cheeks. "Now that we have the Amulet," he murmured, "we're only days from leaving the Trove. We're one step closer to Haven . . . and the rest of our lives."

With a small sob, she buried her face in his chest.

He stroked her hair, surprised. "What's wrong?"

She shook her head, but when she looked up at him again, her eyes were still bright with tears. "I just . . . It's so hard to believe. We're almost free, aren't we?"

He nodded. Free of fate. Free of the future. Free to do whatever they wished.

"Tell me about it," she said in a soft voice. "Haven."

With a grin, he described leisurely days of eating what they caught from the sea and scavenged from the jungle, and nights spent in hammocks dangling from the trees, hundreds of thousands of hours talking and cooking and arguing and laughing and sitting, quietly, watching the lagoon with steaming cups clasped in their hands.

"We can do anything," he said, "as long as we do it toge—"

But he couldn't finish. She grabbed him by the back of the neck and pressed her mouth to his. Burrowing his fingers into her hair, he ran his tongue lightly along the edge of her teeth and was rewarded by a soft groan. Her hands found the hem of his shirt, pulling it over his head and tossing it into the sand beside the embers of their fire. He fumbled with her buttons, removing every layer until she was lying naked beside him.

His gaze roved over her—every curve, this time, every exquisite shadow—as his hands explored her body: the hills, the dips, the smooth planes of her arms and back and thighs.

She rose up to meet him, murmuring *yes* against his neck.

He touched her in ways that left her gasping. Kissed her in places that made her murmur and moan and scream.

It was a second. It was an hour. It was the whole night or the whole day or maybe it was forever, the two of them pressed chest to chest, sweating and breathing hard and whispering each other's names in the dark.

They were here. They were together. And they had their whole future ahead of them.

They awoke at dawn, while the sun skimmed the horizon like a caress. They kissed and washed on the shore of the underground lake, where, for a moment, Archer marveled at her legs, her exposed hips, her hair trailing down her back in tangled waves, before she flung her shirt over the moonstone and doused them both in darkness.

They still had three days to meet Reed at the Trove's entrance, so they took their time on the return journey, stopping often to drink and talk and test new places on each other's bodies with their tongues and teeth.

Leaving the crystal gallery, they meandered through the halls, stopping to uncover trinkets and shiny things. Archer found Sefia an emerald pin, which he placed in her hair, and held up a tarnished silver mirror for her to study her reflection.

She touched the vivid green gems. "I'm sorry, Archer."

"For burning the feather?"

Her reflection seemed to waver, as if through water. "Yeah," she said at last.

"This is better." He set the mirror aside. "This lasts."

They continued through the Trove all through the fourth day. With her magic back, Sefia could see the history of every piece of treasure, and as they walked, she told him stories about ancient jewelers and weaponsmiths, gem cutters and sculptors with a touch of magic themselves.

They found chests of weapons—rifles and bayonets and beautiful revolvers—and sometime during the morning on the fifth day, Sefia presented Archer with a six-gun. The grip was inlaid with feathers of ivory and gold.

"A real Behn revolver," she said. "You know Isabella, the gunsmith who made the Lady of Mercy? This was made by one of her ancestors."

He ran his thumb over the cylinder. "I hope I won't need it."

For the first time in months—in years, maybe—there was no taste of violence on his tongue, no craving for blood, no tingling in his fingers and knuckles. All he wanted now was to listen to the sound of Sefia's voice—he could have made a whole occupation out of listening to her tell stories, of keeping her warm and safe and happy.

As they neared the entrance, the caverns grew larger. They saw no sign of Dimarion's treasure hunters, and Archer was glad. Desperate to use every last second of their time in the Trove, they found reasons to delay.

"Look at this!"

"Over here!"

Once, Archer climbed onto the back of an obsidian winged horse and refused to come down until Sefia joined him, and for what seemed like hours, they lay in the curve between the horse's black wings, dropping clothes onto the glinting coins below and giggling in the dark.

Another time, they discovered a room packed with royal regalia from each of the Five Islands. Tiaras and orbs, rings, moldering gloves, bejeweled mantles, swords, mirrors, robes and sashes, long decayed, all arrayed around six oversize thrones.

Sefia stared at them for a moment before she whispered, "These belonged to the six original divisions of the Guard."

"The Guard?" At the name, he waited for the rush of anger and hurt.

It didn't come. Was this what it was like not to be haunted all the time? Not to be looking for a fight?

"Almost a thousand years before the Last Scribe eradicated writing from the world."

Archer took another look at the tarnished metals, the rotten fabrics, and reached for Sefia's hand. "That was a long time ago."

But they couldn't loiter in the Trove forever, and on the

seventh day, they found their way, begrudgingly, back to the entrance halls. The floors were bare of treasure now, the stalagmite soldiers standing guard over nothing but rock.

Archer's pack was heavy with gifts for their friends, but his heart was light; his head filled with dreams of the future.

They clasped hands as the doors began to swing inward. A vein of light touched their twined fingers and opened wide as fresh air swept into the cavern.

"Ready?" he asked.

She looked away. "Yeah."

The daylight soared over them, so bright it made Archer's head ache.

"Sef!"

"Cap?" she called, shielding her eyes. "What's the matter? What's going on?"

Reed dashed through the opening doors, his coat flying out behind him. "There's been news," he said. "The Alliance has taken Epigloss."

All the warmth left Archer's body. The bloodletters were in Epigloss. *His* bloodletters.

"Probably Epidram too," the captain continued.

Sefia's grip tightened on Archer's hand. "How do you know?"

"The chief mate heard through the wand. Your lieutenant, Scarza, said the bloodletters escaped with six other ships—a mix of outlaws and merchants—but they're on the run from the Alliance and can't find their bearings to get to Haven. The crew's already decided to help them." Captain Reed looked from Archer to Sefia and back again. "But they're asking for *you*."

Sefia's dark eyes were glazed with fear. She was squeezing Archer's hand so hard the tips of his fingers were starting to tingle.

Or maybe he just wanted to fight.

• • •

Y ou were going to strand me here with you?" Archer demanded. "Without giving me a say in it?"

"I thought it was the only way to keep you safe!" Sefia cried. She wished Captain Reed hadn't told them any of this. She wished he'd just gone along with the plan. But he hadn't, and she'd been trapped by fate again. Seven days—the exact amount of time they'd needed to find the Amulet, the exact amount of time the Alliance had needed to attack Epigloss and send the bloodletters on the run, asking for help.

Archer whirled on Reed. "And you agreed to this?"

The captain shrugged. "It was my idea. I ain't proud of it, kid, but if it kept you alive . . ."

Archer's eyes narrowed. "You mean, if it got you the Amulet."

Reed said nothing.

"Why'd you change your mind now?" Archer asked.

"It's your crew out there. I'd wanna know, if it was mine."

"Don't you get it?" Sefia snapped. "This is exactly what I was afraid of. This is how we fail. This is how you *die*."

"We *have* to help them." Archer glared at her. "This is the bloodletters we're talking about."

"Wasn't that what I told you in the Trove? We try to leave. We try to escape. We get drawn back in again and again and again until we're in too deep to save ourselves. Unless we leave. Together. Right now."

"We're gonna fetch 'em anyway," Captain Reed added. "We don't need you for that."

"But *I need* to go." Archer looked to Sefia. "They're *my* bloodletters. My responsibility."

She stared at him for a moment, searching his face for signs of relenting, but his jaw was set, his gold eyes resolute.

He was going to get himself killed, and he didn't care.

Shaking her head, she turned away, placing the Amulet in Reed's hands. "Here. I'm holding up my end of the deal."

There was a pause as she stalked to the edge of the stone dock, where the tide thrashed against the stalagmites, spraying her shins with water.

"What do these marks mean?"

"We don't know," Archer answered.

From behind her, she heard the captain murmur, "Thank you."

She twisted her pack straps. She'd tried to leave, and destiny had beaten her again. Archer was right. Now that she knew the bloodletters were out there, that her *friends* were out there, asking for her help, she couldn't abandon them.

"Don't worry," Archer said, coming up behind her. "We'll go get them and we'll take them to Haven. That was the plan all along, anyway. We'll all be safe at Haven."

That was the plan all along.

Sefia straightened. She spun around, feeling the weight of the

Book heavy in her pack. "You're right. It was always supposed to be Haven. Get to Haven. Let the war pass us by at Haven."

"See? It's per—"

"What if we were wrong, though? What if Haven wasn't where we were supposed to go to escape destiny, but where we were supposed to go to fulfill it?"

Archer frowned. "Then why wouldn't fate have let us go after you saved Frey and Aljan?"

Reed ran his thumb along the edge of the Amulet. "Maybe you had to get this first . . ."

Sefia shut her eyes, grasping for the rest of her idea, her new plan, trying to make it come together. "What if, all this time, we thought we were running from our future, when really we've been running *toward* it?"

Archer shook his head. "I get what you're saying, Sefia, but how do we beat fate if everything we do, everything we try to avoid it, has already been written?"

That was why they hadn't been able to escape.

Everything they did had already been written. And what was written always came to pass.

To beat the Book, they had to change what was written. But how?

As she opened her eyes, the Illuminated world flooded her vision. A million drops of light rained down on the cave, cascading over the walls, the boat, the water, until she, Archer, and Reed were soaked in gold.

They were so bright, the threads that connected them, twisting and joining—her parents giving Reed his first tattoo, the Book, the ⊜, the day Lon decided to form the impressors, the invisible crate, the Second Assassin—the innumerable ways their lives were linked.

And she was reminded of the first time she'd seen this magnificent tapestry of fate, in all its interwoven glory—the first time she'd killed a man, in the Oxscinian jungle.

Palo Kanta. That had been his name. She remembered the scar on his lower lip, the bullet she'd turned back on him. He wasn't supposed to have died in the forest with her. She'd seen his future—he was supposed to have made it to Jahara with the other impressors; he was supposed to have died of a knife wound, stabbed outside of a bar in Epidram.

But Sefia had changed his fate. She had rewritten his future.

Because she possessed a power no one had used for thousands of years. The power of the Scribes. She'd used it once, without even knowing it. And she would use it again to rewrite what was written and save Archer from destiny, once and for all.

Look Closer

Books are curious objects. They have the power to trap, transport, and even transform you if you are lucky. But in the end, books—even magic ones—are only objects pieced together from paper and glue and thread. That was the fundamental truth the readers forgot. How vulnerable the *book* really was.

But not only to fire, or the damp, or the passage of time.

To misinterpretation.

A woman with a burned page assumes that once she gets what she wants, she also gets to keep it.

But she doesn't understand the story goes on beyond the page, and she doesn't see it coming when her throat is slit.

A girl with a flicker of magic believes she sees a man's death—knifed outside of a bar, past midnight with no witnesses—and has the audacity to believe she can change the future.

But she doesn't understand that a life is more than a few isolated scenes. He's been a kidnapper, an abuser, and a murderer for much longer than she knows. He's already been to that bar with the birdcage above its door. He's already been stabbed between the ribs and left for dead.

If you're reading this, by now you know you ought to read *everything*.

By now you know you ought to read deeply.

Because there's witchery in these words and spellwork in the spine.

And nothing is what it seems.

Which is why, for a long time, Lon and Mareah didn't know how it would happen. They couldn't get enough information from the Book or the Illuminated world to give them the answer. Would it be an accident? A fall? An aneurysm, sudden as a summer storm? Maybe the Guard would find them, and Mareah would fight them off, sacrificing herself so Lon and their little girl could escape.

All they knew was that she had five years. Five years after their daughter was born.

And then she would die.

Every week, Lon would study her with the Sight, searching for anomalies, endings, signals in the smoke and secrets in the sea.

Look closer, his Master had told him once.

So he looked closer. He looked deeper. He saw more.

The sickness was in her lungs.

She'd contracted it years ago, on one of her missions, long before they'd even conceived of abandoning the Guard.

She'd dug in the sword, gleaming copper as it entered her target's chest. The blade had soaked up whatever blood it touched, but it didn't touch all of it.

She remembered the red liquid seeping through the gaps in his teeth. Then the cough. The spray, warm and wet, speckling her face.

It had taken this long to manifest, but now that it had, she and Lon finally knew. This was how it ended.

Unless Lon could prevent it.

As Apprentice Librarian, he'd used Transformation, the third tier of Illumination, to extract strains of mold from ancient books. He'd made cracked leather covers new again. With Transformation, you could augment and change all sorts of physical objects, from pieces of parchment to weapons.

But you couldn't change the human body. Only one branch of the Guard had ever had power like that, had had the ability to rewrite the world however they wished.

The Scribes.

So with the Book, he studied them. He learned of all the failed experiments they'd tried at the nascence of their craft—cutting paragraphs from the Book with the point of a knife, burning pages, blacking out whole chapters with the broad strokes of a brush, removing ink from the parchment with solutions of acid and alcohol, leaving behind passages empty as deserts. But you could not change the future by changing the Book.

No, you changed the future by changing the Illuminated world, with the power of the Scribes, a power that had once been called Alteration.

Lon read and studied and realized, to his dismay, that for all the years he'd devoted to mastering Illumination, he was not skilled enough, not powerful enough, to be a Scribe.

He was a mere Librarian, and he struggled to grasp the Scribes' most basic theories. He had little hope of mastering the full force of their magic.

But he'd always had a healthy dose of arrogance, and he did not give up.

All he had to do was harness the first tier of Alteration, a skill the Scribes had called *excision*. They'd used it to remove parts of history like organs from a body—he could use it to remove Mareah's illness, one diseased cell at a time.

He'd eradicate every last trace of her sickness from her past, her present, her future. And it would be as if the disease had never existed in her body at all.

CHAPTER 13

Our Past Lives

*A*udacity. That was what the Book called it. She had the *audacity* to believe she'd changed Palo Kanta's future, even though she'd been wrong. She hadn't tapped into the power of the Scribes; she'd just used Manipulation, like she'd done countless times now.

But despite her failures, despite her misinterpretations, she still had the audacity to believe she could change *Archer's* future. She was her father's daughter, after all.

Of course Lon had tried to master Alteration, the power of the Scribes. Of course the fact that they'd erased themselves and all their magic from history hadn't deterred him.

Of course he'd tried to save Mareah.

Just like Sefia was trying to save Archer.

Laden with treasure, the *Current* and the *Crux* sailed past Steeds and began the voyage back to the Central Sea to rendezvous with the bloodletters and the other refugees from the attack on Epigloss while Sefia began to study Lon's efforts. With the Book open before her, she researched his breakthroughs, his techniques, following his progress up and down the pages of the Book as he pursued Alteration with a single-mindedness Sefia recognized in herself.

Using the Book was a risk, she knew, but she had to believe she could defeat it before it defeated her.

As the days passed and they skirted the northern coast of Liccaro, she began to see the Illuminated world as the Scribes must have seen it—as her father must have seen it.

The lower levels of Illumination—the Sight, Manipulation, Transformation, even Teleportation—dealt only with the currents and tides of the Illuminated world. For that magic, Sefia could draw her hands through the light and it would respond like streams of water or threads in an endless tapestry, flowing and bending around her fingers in constant movement, but there were limits to that power, physical laws she could not break.

But the Scribes had also understood and controlled the most fundamental components of the Illuminated world, not the great cascades and shifting tides but the individual motes of light, linked together in fine strands that, in turn, joined and changed and split apart again like swallows in flight.

"Erastis said the Book was a living story, but he was wrong," she told Archer excitedly as they sat across from each other on the bunk one night. "The Scribes knew that. Nothing you do to the Book changes the real world. The *Illuminated world* is the living story. The Illuminated world is where you can make a difference. Every second, it's changing, the way the sea changes with rain or glacier runoff or the passage of a minnow."

"And you think the power of the Scribes can change our future?"

"It already changed the future once, when they erased themselves and the written word. They created this future."

Archer's fingers went to his throat, grazing the scar that marked him as the boy from the legends. "But you said they killed millions of people to do that."

"That was different. They were altering the entire *world*. I just want to change *one thing*." Sefia looked up at him, and she couldn't help the tremor in her voice when she said the next words. "You live."

His expression softened, and he crawled across the bed, taking her in his arms. "I will."

"I know," she said into his chest. "I'll make sure of it."

Her access to the Illuminated world was still weak, sputtering out when she least expected it, so she started small, at first, with grains of rice.

Placing one in her palm, she'd summon the Sight, and the Illuminated world would come flooding over her, bringing visions of glassy green fields, the *swish* of rice stalks in the wind, the rhythmic movements of human hands plunging beneath the surface, planting new shoots.

But she'd try to ignore all this. Instead, she'd focus on all the light contained in a single grain of rice, all the coiled filaments, branching and crossing, and then she'd look closer—she'd look *deeper*—until she could see each particle of light, distinct as drops of water on a black slate.

Her father had taken months to master this deep form of seeing.

Sefia did it in a week.

Soon she could stand on deck while the snow came down, watching the sparkling motes of the Illuminated world shift and dance around her with every flurry.

She was certain that if only she could look closer, if only she could sharpen her Sight, she'd see something else, something more, in each brilliant particle.

But not yet.

Until her Illumination strengthened again and she could attempt the Scribes' actual powers, she could only practice honing her vision.

And she practiced on Archer. At night, she studied him, *all* of him—the hard muscles, the fading scars, the memories he bared to her like wounds—and in the Illuminated world he was *brilliant*, beautiful, an entire ocean of gold blazing before her eyes.

She saw the abuse he'd endured. She saw the pain he'd inflicted. She saw the day the messenger arrived to tell the family his father had died in service to the Royal Navy. She saw him make love to another girl for the first time. And she saw Kaito Kemura—over and over—fighting, drinking, talking, dying.

She kissed the nicks on his knuckles and ran the tip of her tongue along the scars on his shoulders. She held him and watched him and waited for the opportunity to rewrite his destiny and change the trajectory of his future.

・ ・ ・

A little over two weeks after they left the Trove, Archer finally saw the *Brother* again, in the icy waters off the Gorman Islands, battling the Alliance.

The bloodletters and the two outlaw brigs had closed ranks around the four Oxscinian merchant vessels, protecting the civilians as six blue warships circled them like sharks, their cannons taking bite after bite out of the refugees from Epigloss.

The bloodletters were in trouble.

His bloodletters.

As the *Current* and the *Crux* barreled down on them, Archer watched an Alliance vessel with a vulture for a figurehead draw up alongside the *Brother*. He saw the boarding ladders go slamming into the bloodletters' rails and the soldiers in blue uniforms flood from one ship to the other. In the distance, he could see Scarza's silver hair in the melee, the bloodletters obeying his every order.

Buckling on his new revolver, Archer turned to Sefia, touching his temple. *Can you get me there?*

She shook her head. "My magic isn't strong enough to teleport yet."

There was a distant battle cry: *We were dead*—Archer's heart thundered in response—*but now we rise.* He had to get to them. With a frustrated growl, he ripped his gaze from the *Brother*. "Can you get us to the bloodletters, Cap?" he called.

"Nah, kid." Reed pointed to the Alliance ship locked to the *Brother*'s decks by the boarding ladders. "But we can get you there."

Archer grinned as Sefia strapped on her knives and sleeping darts. "Good enough."

While the crew of the *Current* manned their rifles and loaded their cannons, Frey dashed toward them with two grapples slung over her shoulders.

"Aljan?" Sefia asked. The boy had had his sutures removed, but Doc hadn't cleared him for battle yet.

Frey handed Archer a length of rope. "He told us to make those bonesuckers pay."

Yes. Yes. At last, an enemy he could fight. Not like fate. Not like the future. This was an enemy he could feel *bleed*.

He, Sefia, and Frey raced to the rail as the *Current* neared the Alliance ship. The outlaws' great guns boomed. The blue vessel splintered. The vulture figurehead screamed.

"Sefia, can you—" Archer began, gesturing to the Alliance's rigging.

She blinked; her pupils constricted to points of darkness in her brown eyes. "Already ahead of you."

The *Current of Faith* plunged into the troughs. Archer and Frey flung their grapples, ropes uncoiling in their hands.

Lifting her arms, Sefia steered the hooks into the rigging of the Alliance ship. Around them, the crew of the *Current* cheered.

Mounting the rail, Archer grabbed Sefia by the waist. Her hands locked around his neck.

"Ready?" he murmured.

She nodded.

Then they jumped. They were soaring through the air,

clutching their grappling lines, over the smoke and shrapnel, dropping lightly onto the Alliance decks.

Archer leapt in among the soldiers, shooting, as Sefia thrust them back like leaves before the wind. Frey was with them, agile as a cat with her new switchblades flashing in her hands. Archer picked up a fallen sword, and together they carved their way through the enemy.

Across the boarding ladders.

Onto the deck of the *Brother*, where Scarza and the other bloodletters closed in around him in perfect formation, as if no time or distance had ever come between them.

He was home.

With his bloodletters.

Their opponents fell, one after another—gutted, hamstrung, with broken arms and shattered kneecaps. Blood splashed the tips of his boots.

Around him, the cannons thundered. Smoke billowed across the decks. The Alliance soldiers were many, but they were no match for the deadly skill of his bloodletters.

Over the din of battle, he heard Keon's voice, full of relief and joy: "I can't believe you really came!"

And Sefia's: "I couldn't abandon you again."

As Archer glanced toward them, grinning, he saw it—an Alliance ship was sailing toward them at full sail, picking up speed every second.

It was going to ram them. The *Brother* was going to buckle.

"Sefia!" Archer shouted, pointing. "The boarding ladders!"

With a nod, she lifted her hands. One after another, the

boarding ladders popped into the air and fell, splintering, into the sea.

The *Brother* was free.

"Griegi, Keon, the helm!" The boys raced to the wheel, hauling the ship to starboard. Groaning, they began to turn.

But the oncoming Alliance vessel was too fast.

With the wind in her hair, Sefia braced herself against the bow, facing down the big blue ship. Her hands clenched at the air. Sweat glistened at her temples. Every muscle in her body seemed to go taut.

The foremast of the Alliance ship shuddered. The sails trembled.

But they were still coming.

"Bloodletters, to Sefia!" Archer shouted, dashing toward her.

At his command, Frey and the boys surrounded their sorcerer in a protective ring—parrying, stabbing, firing as the blue-uniformed soldiers converged on them. Archer felt his blade slide through ligaments and tendons, saw his bullets burst through flesh and bones. Alliance bodies fell around them like moths falling to flame.

Then, with a great scream, Sefia pulled, yanking at the air, and the mast of the Alliance ship came toppling down, yards snapping, sails deflating, crashing into the water as the Alliance soldiers scrambled for cover.

The *Brother* turned. The oncoming ship slowed, missing their hull by mere feet, and floundered into the open water.

With the Alliance ship out of the way, Archer saw that a fleet of strange white-hulled ships had joined the *Crux* and the *Current* in battle against the enemy. Black-and-white flags flew from their yardarms, displaying ravens, whales, bears, and all other manner of northern creatures.

Gormani? Archer wondered. Maybe Kaito's old province hadn't joined the Alliance with the rest of Deliene after all.

Aboard the *Brother*, Archer and the bloodletters continued fighting. They killed and maimed and fought until the soldiers, seeing the new white ships chase off three Alliance vessels and take the others captive, laid down their weapons and laced their hands behind their heads.

"Did you find your peace, brother?" Scarza asked, clasping his arm in welcome.

Archer swallowed. "Not yet."

He had Scarza see to the prisoners as he went to Sefia, shaking and exhausted at the bow. "Are you okay?" he asked as he helped her sit.

"Didn't think I'd topple that mast in time. Not something I can do every day." She looked up at him with red-veined eyes and wiped a trail of blood from her nose. All of a sudden he was aware of the stickiness of his hands. The blood spatter on his face and clothing. "Are *you* okay?"

Yes.

No. He was different. He was hungry again, hungrier than he'd been since the fight with Serakeen, for battle, for slaughter, for *more*.

But before he could answer, Frey and the boys took up a chant. "Chief! Chief! Chief!" Turning, he saluted them with a grin.

While they broke out kegs of ale and washcloths for the worst of the blood on their faces and hands, the new white ships sent boats to the *Current* for a meeting. Archer supposed he could have joined them, as leader of the bloodletters, but he wanted nothing more than to sit with Sefia, Frey, and the boys and listen to stories of what had happened since they were separated.

They were all on their second or third drinks—with the exception of Griegi and Keon, who were asleep in each other's arms—when a boat pulled up to the *Brother* and a woman with loose black curls and green eyes climbed over the rail, followed by a contingent of what appeared to be officers in thick black cloaks.

Captain Reed was up last, his blue eyes finding Archer as he introduced the woman: "Chief Oshka Kemura."

But Archer hadn't needed to be told. He knew that broad face. He knew those eyes, like slivers of glass. He knew that posture, so full of pride it bordered on arrogance.

Kaito's mother. Chief of her clan.

The bloodletters stood, shifting uneasily as she raked them with her gaze. Out of the corner of his eye, Archer saw Sefia stagger to her feet.

"Which one of you is in charge?" Chief Kemura said.

Archer stepped forward, keenly aware of being drenched in other people's blood.

She was fast—fast as her son had been and just as deadly. In less than a second, she slammed Archer to the deck and had her knife at his throat, digging into his scar.

"Archer." Her voice was a growl. "Chief of the bloodletters."

It took everything he had not to fight back. Not to take

her blade and snap her wrist. Not to kill her in half a dozen different ways.

Sefia raised her hand. The bloodletters leapt forward to haul the woman off him. Chief Kemura's officers went for their weapons.

Reed drew the Singer, the revolver cold and blue in the winter sun. "Chief," he said, "you told me you'd play nice."

Archer stayed them all with a shake of his head. He felt the edge of Oshka Kemura's knife draw blood. With a shrug, Captain Reed holstered his weapon again.

"Is it true?" Kaito's mother asked, ignoring the others. "You killed my son?"

Archer closed his eyes. The legends must have reached her in Gorman, then.

Archer, chief of the bloodletters, had fought his own lieutenant, a Gormani boy with green eyes, on the shores of a flooded quarry.

Archer, chief of the bloodletters, had *killed* his own lieutenant, his friend, his brother, in a flooded quarry, far from the north.

He opened his eyes. "Yes," he whispered.

Did she know about the gun, the rain, the regret and resignation on Kaito's bruised face? The burst of blood as Archer's bullet struck him between the eyes?

Did she know he'd loved him?

Did it matter?

He'd taken her boy.

"I'm sorry." The words felt thick in his throat.

"You're sorry?" She laughed in his face. Her tears struck his cheeks. "You're sorry? You're *sorry*?"

Archer swallowed. He could let her slit his throat right now. He could let her take all his nightmares away, and Kaito would never again visit him in the dead of night, telling him how ruined he was.

But Archer didn't want to die.

He grabbed her knife hand and twisted, flipping her off him. He was on his feet before anyone else could react, slipping the blade from her grasp and holding it to the back of her neck as he forced her to her knees.

He could kill her. A little pressure and he'd sever her spine.

"I loved him," Archer said. He could feel Sefia, Reed, the bloodletters, and the Gormani officers all watching him, ready to act. But no one moved.

Chief Kemura was laughing, each breath strained, as she fought his grip. "You've got a lot to learn, Archer, chief of the bloodletters. Your love? Your remorse? Your good intentions? *They don't matter* if your actions do more harm than good."

Archer blinked. His fingers loosened on her wrist, and she rolled to her feet, where her officers closed around her.

What was he doing? Threatening Kaito's mother? How—?

He stumbled back, shaking his head. It was happening again. He was becoming that boy again—the one who'd killed Kaito, the one who'd gotten Frey and Aljan captured—hungry for violence, for victory, for the kill.

For months, he'd been fine. He'd been fine, even after fighting the enforcers in Jahara. Why was this different?

You weren't leading anyone, he thought. *You weren't a commander, a chief.*

But his bloodletters had been in trouble. And he hadn't been able to stop himself.

He hadn't *wanted* to stop himself. Because he *wanted* to be their chief. Besides being loved by Sefia, being their chief was the greatest honor he'd ever experienced.

It also made him someone he didn't want to be.

The boy who killed his friends.

The boy who would conquer a world.

In a flash, all the faces of his victims flickered before his eyes: Oriyah, Argo, the candidates from the cage fights, the impressors, the robbers, the rancher girl, Versil, Kaito, the boys whose names he hadn't even known when they were killed under his command.

Shaking, he extended Chief Kemura's knife to her, handle first. "I'm sorry," he said again. "If I could, I would bring him back."

She took the blade, glaring up at him with those familiar eyes. "There are many things you cannot take back, Archer, chief of the bloodletters. Death is only one of them."

CHAPTER 14

The Breaking of Broken Crown

Everywhere the *Hustle* went, she found the Alliance. More ships seemed to be converging on Oxscini every day, and it took all of Captain Neeram's savvy to elude the fleets that crowded the horizon, the scouts like sharks seeking prey.

As they sailed south to Broken Crown, Ed kept a rough tally of the Alliance vessels they saw. Twenty-three. Forty-two. Forty-nine. The numbers kept climbing, each one heavier than the last.

He'd been to Broken Crown once, before his mother and father died. The girdle of islets separated the Oxscinian mainland from the Sister Islands and Their Kin, the large cluster of islands to the south. While Broken Crown was a bustling point of access for trade and commerce, it was also the weakest point in the Oxscinian defenses, with wide, deep channels through which any number of warships could enter the Bay of Batteram on their way to the capital, Kelebrandt.

Fifty-one. Fifty-seven. Sixty.

How many ships would it take for the Alliance to breach Broken Crown? Had Queen Heccata had the foresight to fortify her defenses there?

Ed had no way of knowing, and no way of sending her a warning.

He'd gotten a dozen redcoats out of Jahara. He might have prevented Lac from being killed. But he kept thinking of the invasion fleet they'd seen at Epidram. He kept thinking of Delienean soldiers storming the ramparts, flooding the city, killing and conquering—all for the Alliance.

He never should have given up his crown. But he had. And that was a mistake he wasn't sure he could ever fix, no matter how many redcoats he rescued.

Sometimes, in his hammock at night, he cried. He cried for his uselessness. He cried for Arc. He cried for Deliene, in the grip of the Alliance and a shadow organization Lac and Hobs called the Guard. He cried for his dead days, when all he wanted to do was sleep, though those days grew fewer and farther between the longer he was away from the Northern Kingdom.

Lac would wake—the boy had become such a light sleeper since his beating, startling awake at every little sound—and sit silently with him, patting his shoulder. Sometimes Lac would suggest they see to the animals, and the slow, measured motions of cleaning the pens and refilling the water troughs as the pigs snuffled at his pockets for treats would calm Ed again.

Ed did what he could, when he could. He worked faster and harder for Neeram, despite their violence, because they kept the crew alive and out of Alliance hands. He picked up extra chores for Lac, whose broken ribs made him slow. He even thought of riddles for Hobs: "If you sandwich a sandwich in sandwich sandwiches, how many sandwiches do you get?"

Dropping the lines he was trying to weave together, Hobs stroked his chin. "If you sandwich a sand witch in sandwiches, and witches . . . wait, which kind of witches?"

"Belay that chatter!" the first mate bellowed.

Stifling their laughter, they returned to repairing the rigging. In the silence, Ed could hear Lac's labored breathing. He sneaked a glance at the boy's face. Neeram had broken his perfectly symmetrical nose, and bruises and cuts marred the skin he'd taken so much pride in. He was quieter now. Ed missed his braggadocio.

"Seven!" Hobs cried suddenly.

Ed patted him on the shoulder. "Nope."

Three weeks after abandoning Epidram to the Alliance, they got their first glimpse of Broken Crown . . . and immediately ran in the other direction.

They were too late. Too late to warn Queen Heccata and the Royal Navy. Too late for Lac and Hobs to rejoin the redcoats.

The island cities of Broken Crown were on fire. A wall of noxious black smoke rose into the sky. Ash dusted the decks of the *Hustle* like snow. A horrid red light hugged the southern horizon.

This was where all those vessels had been headed, arrayed across the sea in perfect formation: hundreds of warships, thousands of cannons, hundreds of thousands of soldiers from the three kingdoms of the Alliance.

Ed watched them disappear behind the *Hustle* as they raced north again. It was an invasion force that could have swallowed the fleet at Epidram and still been hungry. It was a kingdom-killer.

Broken Crown hadn't stood a chance.

"Anyone in pursuit?" Captain Neeram called across the ship.

"No one, Captain," Ed called back. With the blaze still raging at Broken Crown, their little ship seemed to have escaped notice.

Beside him, Hobs was crying. Lac was not. Lac looked sick, his pallor almost as green as his eyes. As they sailed off, he leaned over the rail and emptied the contents of his stomach.

"We ran for nothing. We saved our own hides . . . for nothing," he said. "We should have stayed at Epidram. At least there, we would have been able to—"

"Where to, Captain?" the first mate asked.

Neeram ran a hand down their face. "We need provisions. I was hoping to resupply at Broken Crown, but . . . we'll have to find somewhere else."

"All that's between us and Epidram are fishing villages."

Their jaw clenched. "Then we'll hit one of them."

"Hit?" Hobs muttered, glancing sideways at Ed. "That's an ominous word choice."

Ed shook his head as Lac began dry heaving. He rubbed the boy's back. "Let's hope not."

They found a tiny village a half-day's sail from Broken Crown, almost invisible at the feet of the steep forested mountains rising from the shoreline. The docks were deserted; the streets in chaos. Animals were running, bleating, on the muddy streets. Urns and other crockery lay smashed on the roadsides among trampled bundles of vegetables and discarded items of clothing. People ran in and out of their houses, stuffing belongings into crates, settling infants onto carts.

As the sailors of the *Hustle* disembarked, a man paused on the docks in front of them. "What are you doing? Haven't you heard?" In his arms, he held a box of what looked like medical supplies. "The Alliance is marching north from Broken Crown, burning villages as they go."

"Where are you headed?" Ed asked him.

"Into the Cloud Pillars. If we leave the coast, we might have a chance."

The Cloud Pillars were the deep canyons and tottering columns of rock that lay beyond the mountains to the west. Mist swirled up from the ancient riverbeds and through the trees, mingling with the low-hanging clouds that obscured the peaks, giving the landscape its name. People said seers lived at the tops of the pillars, subsisting on nothing but the incense that stimulated their visions, but for everyone else, the Cloud Pillars were a place to be avoided, a maze of slippery rocks and passes too steep to climb.

"Do you know a way through?"

The man shook his head, already running off. "I'm sorry, I have to go!"

For a moment, Captain Neeram watched his retreating form with narrowed eyes. Then, taking a breath, they turned to the crew of the *Hustle*. "All right, you've got an hour to get us re-supplied and get back on the boats. If you're late, we leave you. No exceptions." They began rattling off a list of provisions—fresh water, lamp oil, dry stores . . .

As soon as they'd finished, the sailors began running into buildings. There was the sound of wood breaking, glass shattering.

"Looting?" Lac blinked, dumbfounded. "We're looters now? Captain, we can't—"

"If they left this shit behind, they don't need it. We do." Neeram hefted a coil of rope onto their shoulder. "You want to be a hero, you can die with the saps you're trying to save. Cowards may be the bonesucking scum of the sea, but at least we live." Without another word, they grabbed a second length of rope and turned away.

Lac looked miserable.

"What are we going to do, Ed?" Hobs asked.

A mule ran past, trailing a rope from its halter. A girl ran after it, crying, "No, no! Stop!"

Without a second thought, Ed took off after the mule, dragging Lac and Hobs with him. "Come with me."

Together, the four of them corralled the animal. Ed took the mule by its halter, stroking its nose while the fright ebbed from its large, intelligent eyes. Not for the first time, he missed his gray mare, whom he'd left behind in Corabel along with his dogs. He hoped Arcadimon was looking after them. He hoped they were looking after Arc.

"Thank you," the girl said.

Ed gave a little shrug. "What else can we do?"

"Please," Lac added, taking her hands. "Allow us to do *something*."

They stacked water kegs on wagons. They carried chests of heirlooms. They caught chickens and stuffed them into wooden cages for the journey.

Once, Ed looked to the docks and saw the *Hustle* leaving the harbor. "Well," he said, "there goes our ride."

"Do you think they'll make it?" Hobs wondered.

"They'll make it," Lac answered. "Neeram will make sure of it."

"What about us?" Hobs asked. "We can't reunite with the Royal Navy now."

Ed looked toward the smoky skies above Broken Crown, toward the war front, toward the Delienean ships, which had been painted Alliance blue, and the soldiers that Arcadimon had forced to join them.

Briefly, Ed wondered if he could march south, directly into the oncoming Alliance forces, and announce himself. He was the Delienean king, returned from the dead, and he would be removing the Northern Kingdom from this ludicrous war.

Could he really do it, though? These past weeks with Lac and Hobs and the animals aboard the *Hustle*, he'd finally started feeling well. The melancholia still reached him sometimes, but now that he'd left his kingdom and his title, he wondered if he was becoming the boy he could have been if he hadn't been born under the Corabelli Curse, if he hadn't watched so many of his loved ones die, if he hadn't been poisoned, for years, by his best friend.

And if the Alliance was, as Lac and Hobs believed, under the control of the Guard, the Guard wouldn't blink twice before executing Ed on the spot. Even if he managed to sneak past the Alliance foot soldiers to the Delienean generals who were surely among them, he wondered how long it would take King Darion Stonegold to send an invasion like this to the Northern Kingdom. He wondered what his beloved cliffs and White Plains would look like strewn with Delienean bodies.

And he wondered if, perhaps, Arc had had the best interests of the kingdom at heart after all.

But what had he done to get there? Ed swallowed, thinking of his cousin's body on the funeral bier. Whom had Arcadimon sacrificed?

Ed turned back to Lac and Hobs, who needed him now. "We can help these people," he said, "while we have the strength to help them."

They lugged and dragged, they packed and carted, they worked without complaint until almost the entire village had evacuated, winding up the narrow paths into the mountains.

Finally, there was only one wagon left, and two women who were wrapping a pair of ornamental shutters that had been in their family for hundreds of years.

"You look familiar," one of them said as Ed gave her a hand up onto the front of the cart. She squinted at him, and he wondered how much he resembled his likeness on Delienean coins. He'd put on muscle, he knew that. His hair had grown longer. "Who *are* you?" she asked.

But it was Lac who spoke up. "We're redcoats," he said, and smiled for what seemed like the first time in a week.

Ed frowned. He may not have been the King of Deliene anymore, but he wasn't a redcoat. He was no one, with no last name and no home.

The second woman leaned over her partner. "You boys survivors from Broken Crown?"

"No," Ed said, "we came from up north."

"We had a messenger two days ago who said the Alliance razed Epidram to the ground," she said, reaching out with a soft hand. "We're sorry."

Gently, Ed squeezed her fingers. The pale band of skin where he'd worn his signet ring was completely gone now, the same tanned brown as the rest of him.

"You boys need a lift?" asked the first woman. She jerked her head at the back of the wagon, where their goat was lying among some dry fronds.

"In the back?" Lac said. "With the *goat*?"

Ed wandered to the wagon bed, where he let the goat nuzzle his palm. "Where are you going?"

"Kelebrandt. Queen Heccata will protect us."

Ed hadn't been to Kelebrandt in five years. It had the natural protection of Tsumasai Bay, which had only four entrances, in addition to the stone forts the Oxscinian monarchs had built over the years. Lac and Hobs would finally be back with the Royal Navy. And Ed? Well, he'd find another way to be of service, somehow.

CHAPTER 15

Chief of the Bloodletters

L ater, Sefia found out that most of the Gormani clans had refused to join the Alliance with the rest of Deliene. Since Arcadimon Detano had sent the bulk of the kingdom's navy to invade Oxscini, Oshka Kemura and her allies had been causing all sorts of trouble up north, preying on Alliance patrols like the one the *Current* and the *Crux* had seen at the Trove of the King.

"Kaito would have loved that," Sefia said.

Thumbing the worry stone, Archer nodded. After his confrontation with Chief Kemura, she and the other Gormani captains had departed for the north, taking the Oxscinian merchants with them, and the *Brother* had begun sailing south for Haven with the *Current*, the *Crux*, and the other two outlaw ships from Epigloss.

Sefia, Archer, Frey, and Aljan moved their belongings from the *Current* to the *Brother*, where Keon excitedly ushered them to the great cabin. It was in even greater disarray than Sefia remembered it: great swaths of leather slung over the chairs, jars of glue sticking to the tabletop, knots of thread mixed up with scraps of paper, and dozens of books stacked on chairs, in corners, and crammed between sofa cushions.

"I kinda got carried away," the skinny boy said sheepishly, jamming his hands in his pockets. Even though they hadn't needed the decoy Book, he'd found he enjoyed the work, and with nothing better to do when he wasn't on watch, he'd begun making other books: palm-size books, large books, books that could fit easily in a satchel or on a shelf . . .

"And they're all blank?" Aljan asked, reverently leafing through one of the bigger codices.

"Grieg took one for his recipes," Keon said with a shrug. "But all the rest are, yeah."

"Got a story to write?" Frey asked, looping her arm through Aljan's.

He nodded.

He took over writing lessons aboard the *Brother*, teaching Frey, Keon, Griegi, and a couple others, while Sefia continued her study of Alteration.

Objects that had been excised didn't just disappear, she learned. Once you'd eliminated every trace of them, it was as if they'd never existed at all. Once, the Scribes had used this power to erase entire armies—all those people, all those stories—*gone*, as if they'd never been.

Sefia returned to studying grains of rice. In the Illuminated world, she would examine every particle of light. Then, as if her fingers were tipped with blades, she'd slice through each golden flake, and one by one, they would melt into darkness.

In her hand, the grain of rice would disappear.

Excision.

But the Illuminated world was a painstakingly connected web. Some streams of light were dim, like the faintest constellations in the sky, and others were so bright they seemed to pulse with the strength of their connections, forming a complex system of rivers and brooks and many-armed deltas.

And she soon learned it was these she had to treat with care.

Once, she was going too quickly—she was getting overconfident—and as she was eliminating particles, her hand slipped. Entire strands of gold started disappearing, faster and faster, farther and farther away from her, burning out like candles in the wind.

Around her, the tides of the Illuminated world shifted. Somewhere across the years, she saw a stalk of rice wink out of existence. She saw a sickle. A flash of red. A scar.

She reeled, blinking. Her palm was empty. She'd excised the grain of rice successfully, but she'd also taken the entire plant— somewhere, in burlap sacks and earthen pots, every piece of rice that plant had produced had also disappeared—and that one change had caused permanent injury to a person she'd never met.

She was more careful, from then on, but she was not deterred.

She didn't yet know how this power could alter the course of Archer's future, but she would make sure he would no longer be the boy from the legends. She would make sure he lived.

• • •

Archer had expected to be relieved, being back with the bloodletters, but his run-in with Chief Kemura had unsettled him, and he could not help wondering if he'd made a mistake, not leaving with Sefia after the Trove.

But he loved the bloodletters. They were his family—sometimes they felt more like family than his own flesh and blood back in Jocoxa, on the northwest tip of Oxscini. No one else knew what he'd been through with the impressors. No one else could really understand.

One day, as he sat with Scarza in the great cabin, he asked, "We've done some good together, haven't we? The bloodletters?"

They'd stopped the impressors in Deliene. They'd freed dozens of boys.

Looking up from the rifle he'd been cleaning, Scarza watched him with his gray sharpshooter's eyes. "Is this about what Chief Kemura said?"

You've done more harm than good.

Archer nodded. "Even after Versil, and Kaito, and the others we've lost, I still think the good we've done outweighs the bad . . . but the longer I'm your chief, the more battles I lead you into, the more I'm afraid I'm tipping the scales the other way. It's not the fighting . . . or not just the fighting. It's the leading. When I'm leading you, I can feel myself becoming a different person."

The commander. The conqueror. The boy from the legends.

"A worse person," he added. "If I keep leading you into

battle, it's only a matter of time before I *am* him, and I won't be able to come back from that."

"But we're not going into battle anymore," Scarza said, deftly snapping pieces of his rifle back into place with his one hand.

No, they were going to Haven. And if Sefia was right, they were going exactly where the Book wanted them to. A stay at Haven, however, would at least buy them a little time to figure out exactly how to use the power of the Scribes to rewrite the future.

Scarza gripped his shoulder kindly. "I'll lead us if I have to. But I don't think I'll have to."

And for two and a half weeks, things were fine. Archer remained chief of the bloodletters, but they didn't fight or train as they used to. They had no one to fight.

Instead, they sailed. They took turns on watch. They ate and gambled and told stories. Aljan taught them to write. He was a patient, gentle teacher, certainly more patient than Sefia had been with him, weaving between the bloodletters and Meeks, Theo, and Marmalade, who came over from the *Current*, offering a word of advice here or a kind adjustment there. During her lessons, Frey began drawing trees in one of Keon's books—a gift for her lumberjack brothers back in Deliene—filling it with enormous Oxscinian hardwoods, banyans dripping aerial roots, other Forest Kingdom trees she must have seen in her short time in Epigloss, each neatly labeled with Aljan's help.

Theo, in particular, was impressed with Frey's catalogue. The *Current*'s starboard chanty leader and an aspiring biologist, he kept pushing up his spectacles and gesticulating wildly over her detailed drawings of leaves and seed pods, making the red lory on his shoulder spread her wings and chirp in alarm.

At the back of the class, Sefia continued studying the Book in her pursuit of excision.

It was all the good parts of being back with the bloodletters, and none of the fear, the violence, the bloodlust. It was exactly what Archer wanted.

But it was too good to last.

Because when they finally arrived at Haven, they found it on fire.

All around the island were the sinking wrecks of ships, the cries of the wounded in the water. Nearby, half a dozen ships bearing the blue, gold, and white flags of the Alliance were battling what remained of the outlaws.

Reed had said Haven boasted seventy-seven ships.

Only thirteen were left.

The thunder of cannon fire echoed off the rock pillars that guarded the island, peppered with the sharp reports of rifles and revolvers.

Archer's hands gripped the rail, his fingers hot with the urge to fight. To rip. To kill. "I thought Haven was unfindable," he said.

Except, somehow, the Alliance had found Haven. Somehow, the Red War had found *him*. He couldn't escape it.

Scarza slung his rifle over his shoulder. "Do you think one of the outlaws betrayed them?"

Archer watched the *Current* run up their battle flag, followed by the *Crux* and the two outlaw ships that had come from

Epigloss. "I don't know," he said, "but they'll have to answer to Captain Reed."

"Archer," Scarza said, "what do you want to do?"

Archer's pulse roared in his veins. He wanted to fight. He wanted to lead. He wanted to hit the Guard so hard they'd think twice about coming at him again.

And that was exactly why he shouldn't.

He took the boy by the shoulders. "I can't stay," he said. "Will you lead them? Will you be their chief?"

Scarza's gray eyes were solemn when he nodded. They embraced. "I'll take care of them for you."

"Better than I ever did," Archer murmured into his shoulder.

"What will you do?"

"I may not be able to lead, but I can still fight. I'm going to get Sefia to take me somewhere I'll do some good."

On Scarza's orders, the bloodletters began preparing the *Brother* for confrontation. Aljan raised a battle flag of their own—a boy with bowed head and crossed forearms.

The bloodletters cheered.

A part of Archer ached to fight with them. But he couldn't.

"Once they get us close enough to an Alliance ship, I can teleport us," Sefia said, checking her cuff of sleeping darts.

"Okay," Archer whispered.

They turned the *Brother* into the fray, letting off broadsides. Cannonballs went smashing into the hulls of their enemy.

The Alliance returned in kind.

While Archer waited miserably by the foremast, Sefia joined the riflemen at the prow, deflecting bullets and spheres of iron into the waves. Curls of smoke blew past them as they sped through the water.

The *Current of Faith* surged ahead of them, firing their chase guns.

One of the outlaw ships, with a scrappy little dog for a figurehead, had been boarded by the Alliance. Archer could see blue uniforms swarming the decks.

The *Brother* pulled up on the ship's other side, and the bloodletters leapt across the rails, swords flashing as they cut down Alliance soldiers, six-guns cracking like fireworks.

Sefia ran to Archer's side. "Ready?"

No.

On the outlaw ship, Griegi cursed as a bullet skimmed the side of his head.

Archer nodded. His arms went around Sefia's waist.

The last thing he saw before he felt the deck go out from under him was Scarza and the bloodletters pressing the Alliance soldiers back onto their own ship.

When they touched down again, they were hundreds of yards from the *Brother*. Sefia had taken them to the farthest ship out.

It was just the two of them against a vessel full of Alliance soldiers.

Archer grinned at her. His weapons were heavy as death in his hands.

"You're welcome," she said, flinging out her hand as the soldiers attacked. Bullets were thrown back. There were spurts of blood and startled cries among the enemy.

He and Sefia ducked behind the mainmast as the soldiers

charged. Beside him, Sefia was a blur of movement, shoving enemies aside, redirecting shots into the Alliance ranks. Archer's rounds found their own targets, one after another, bullets striking bone.

"In there!" Sefia cried, pushing him toward the door of the great cabin.

They tumbled inside just as the soldiers rushed them, and Archer glanced back to get his first good look at his enemy.

Boys.

Some younger than him. Some a little older. But all of them boys. All of them with the blistered ring of scar tissue around their necks.

Candidates.

His stomach turned as he pressed himself against the door, trying to close it.

From behind him, a gust of air slammed the door shut. The lock clicked. "Get back!" Sefia cried.

He stumbled away as bullets punctured the wood around him, and Sefia slid a wardrobe in front of the door. Hands trembling, he fed bullets into the cylinder of his revolver. One dropped, striking the floor with a *ping!*

"What's wrong?" Sefia asked.

He scooped up the bullet and managed to get it into the last empty chamber. "They're candidates," he whispered. "All of them. The Guard must have brought them out here to annihilate the outlaws at Haven—"

"I'll teleport us out of here," she said immediately, sweeping her arms wide.

He caught her hand. "No."

"Why not?"

He touched the scar at his throat. Because they were like him. They were his brothers, in a twisted way—they were all victims of the impressors, of the Guard—even if they were brothers on opposite sides of the war.

He flicked the cylinder closed. "I can't save them," he said, "but right now, I can stop them. Some of them, anyway."

Grimly, Sefia nodded. She flexed her fingers. "Ready?"

He shoved a table onto its side and crouched behind it. Lifting his fingers to his neck, he gave the worry stone a swipe with his thumb.

Behind her own barricade by the windows, Sefia lifted her hands. He could almost feel the air shift beneath her fingers.

The wardrobe slid away from the door.

In rushed the candidates. Archer popped out from under cover and let off a round. The bullet struck one of them square between the eyes.

Except they weren't a stranger's eyes.

They were Kaito's eyes.

Archer ducked as gunfire drove him under cover again. He stared at the carpet beneath his boots.

Carpet. Not loose stone.

He wasn't back there anymore. He wasn't chief of the bloodletters. He wasn't killing his best friend.

He forced himself up again, firing quick shots that found eye sockets and scarred necks. The boys collapsed on the threshold as their brothers ducked behind the door frame.

Brothers.

He shut his eyes. *No, no, no.* He could do this. He had to do this. They were his responsibility.

He heard Sefia calling as if from a distance. "Archer! *Get under cover!*" He felt the force of her magic on his back, thrusting him down again.

His cheek struck wet rock. Kaito was leaning over him, grinning, with blood between his teeth and the black sky beyond.

Then—the *crack* of thunder—no, gunfire. Archer was back in the great cabin. He was fighting candidates. He leapt up, found his next target, a dark boy with striking blue eyes.

He pulled the trigger.

But it was Kaito now—black hair plastered to his forehead, face lined with regret.

The bullet went wide, puncturing the wall behind the candidate.

They tossed a grenade into the cabin. Archer watched the smoking fuse, the glowing ember, but it was as if he wasn't seeing it at all.

He was seeing the rain on the rocks. He was seeing lightning flash in the puddled water. He was seeing Kaito.

Archer felt for the worry stone as a gust of air shot past him and Sefia flung the grenade out the door, where it exploded.

Thunder.

Lightning.

Kaito.

CHAPTER 16

The Myth of the *Black Beauty*

O ver his shoulder, Reed watched the bloodletters board the *One Bad Eye*, the ship he'd once stranded in the Ephygian Bay and later found and brought to Haven, and begin battling back the Alliance alongside Captain Bee's crew.

Those bloodletters could *fight*. They weren't as good with the great guns as the *Current* or the *Crux*, which was trading broadsides with two Alliance warships, but get them face-to-face with the enemy and the enemy was as good as dead.

The secret entrance to Haven loomed ahead of him. Black smoke billowed from between the stone columns. Fear gripped his chest. Were Adeline and Isabella all right? Were there any other survivors?

Thirteen ships. Thirteen out of seventy-seven.

That couldn't be all.

Then, as if from the walls of Haven itself, a black ship with black sails appeared—a shadow—a wraith, trailing mist and smoke from her yardarms.

Reed let out a whistle.

She'd made it. Captain Tan and the *Black Beauty*.

"The Alliance better turn tail now." Meeks laughed. "Tan ain't gonna be happy if she was in the lagoon when they attacked."

Reed grinned down at him.

But their smiles faded as they watched the *Beauty* approach one of the outlaw ships from Epigloss and open fire.

Flames spewed from the mouths of her cannons.

The outlaw hull buckled. Bodies and timber went up in the explosion. A mast fell. Even at this distance, Reed could hear the screaming.

"That was one of ours," Meeks whispered. "What's Tan thinkin'?"

Captain Reed let out a growl.

No one but the outlaws knew where Haven was. No one but an outlaw could have led the Alliance here.

He'd trusted Tan. He'd even loved her, in a way. Loved what she stood for. Loved the myth of her: her wildness, her chaos, her fierceness and independence, uncatchable as the wind. A woman who promised herself to nothing but the sea.

"All hands!" he roared. "Full sail!"

"Cap?" Meeks asked.

"Tan's our traitor. She must have forgotten what it means to be an outlaw." He pointed at the black ship. "Let's remind her what our justice looks like."

With a cry, the crew leapt into the rigging, loosing the sails, which gathered the wind. They shot across the water, leaving the *Brother*, the *Crux*, the *Bad Eye*, and the outlaw refugees from Epigloss.

They were an arrow.

They were a bullet.

They were a cannonball.

And they had one target. With Jaunty at the helm, they could not miss.

But the *Black Beauty* was the quickest ship in the southeast, the only ship that could outstrip the *Current* in a flat-out race.

And the *Current* was laden with treasure from the Trove of the King. Heavy and sluggish, she floundered in the water as the *Beauty* began to outpace her.

But the *Black Beauty* did not have Captain Cannek Reed. He and Jaunty worked in concert, catching the wind, finding a current.

The wind screamed. The waves carried them. They skimmed the surface like a bird, barely touching each crest before taking off again, lunging forward with each wave.

They were speed incarnate.

They were the water and the wind in motion.

They were the *Current of Faith*.

And they were gaining.

The distance closed.

Reed could see carvings of horses with gold eyes adorning the stern, the gleam of the windows.

The *Current*'s chase guns thundered. Behind the gunwale, the cook and steward crouched, reloading their rifles. On the

Beauty's quarterdeck, Captain Tan's officers ducked and cursed. Squinting down her sights, Aly clipped a lieutenant's shoulder. Whooping, Cooky and Aly smacked hands and pumped fists in a special handshake.

The lieutenant turned and snarled, baring gold teeth. That must have been Escalia, Tan's most trusted officer.

But where was Tan?

As he searched the *Beauty*'s decks for her silver-streaked hair, her white blouse and leather vest, she appeared on the deck of the *Current* in a rush of wind.

Her gray eyes. Her sickle scar. Her arms lowering, as if they'd carried her here.

Just like Sefia's did when she teleported.

On the main deck, Reed's sailors shouted. There was the chittering of dozens of hammers being pulled back.

Reed held out his hand to stop them. "Tan?" His voice seemed thin in the wind. "You—"

She looked him up and down, haughty as ever. "Hello, Cannek." The drawl had dropped from her damaged voice, and though she spoke in a whisper, her words had the clipped precision of a chisel. "I wish you hadn't seen this. You arrived quicker than we thought."

"We— You're—"

She lifted an eyebrow, perfectly arched.

"Tanin." The word twisted as it left his lips. "Director of the Guard."

Her brow creased. "*Former* Director."

"All this time?" he asked. All the things he'd heard about the captain of the *Black Beauty*? All the legends? All the rough-

203

and-tumble stories of tavern brawls and underhanded deals and races against the rain?

Were any of them true?

"All this time."

"Why?"

"The Amulet." She shrugged delicately. "I needed to be a treasure hunter, because I wanted a treasure. Because I wanted answers from the people who'd betrayed me . . . the only two people I'd loved, and they were dead. The rest was . . ." For a moment, she looked not like the proud, cold Guardian but like the outlaw he used to know, who kicked up her feet on tables and threw sucker punches. "Well, the rest was just for fun."

He felt sucker-punched himself. "You did all this for the Resurrection Amulet?"

"Do you have it?" She raked him with a glance, like she knew the Amulet was around his neck, resting over his heart. "The *Current*'s heavier than she should be. You must have found the Trove."

"Why send me and Dimarion on this treasure hunt in the first place? Why didn't you just get it yourself, if Fieldspar was one of you?"

At the mention of Fieldspar's name, Tanin went still as a statue. "How did you know?" Her gray eyes narrowed. "*Sefia.* Is she here? Does she have the Book?"

Without waiting for an answer, she flung out her hand.

The magic hit him like a battering ram. All across the ship, his crew toppled, thrown to the decks. In a split second, she scanned the ship.

"Where is she?"

The Singer was in Reed's hand, blue as the sea. "Gone."

The bullet went spiraling from the chamber just as Tanin raised her arms like a black-and-white bird lifting her wings. She was disappearing from sight when the bullet struck her between the ribs.

He heard a faint curse, and then she was gone, leaving a trail of blood and the bullet, striking the mast behind her.

CHAPTER 17

The Real Villains

Archer tried to fight. Sefia knew he *tried*. But from the second she let the door open, allowing the candidates to flood into the room, he began to sweat. He began to shake. After the first three boys, he'd emptied his chambers and hit nothing.

Again and again, she shoved the candidates back. Breaking bones. Wrenching limbs from their sockets. Deflecting bullets meant for Archer.

But after the first grenade took out the door, there were too many for her to wrestle back out of the cabin. She had to get Archer out of there, but the candidates had pinned her behind the bullet-pitted sofa she'd been using as a barricade. When she knocked one boy down, another took his place, pressing forward inch by inch. They were relentless.

They were like him.

Fighters.

Killers.

They were like the bloodletters a dozen times over—organized, deadly.

Standing, she shoved the wardrobe at the open doorway, crushing a body against the wall. The candidates quickly assembled behind it, using it for cover as they bombarded her with gunfire.

She piled on a liquor cabinet—the bottles smashing, spilling pungent liquid onto the floor—a leather settee, anything to halt the candidates' advance, to give her enough time to get to Archer.

The doorway was almost blocked again. Lifting her arms, she heaved the table Archer had been using for cover over the last gap and held it fast with her magic.

He was curled tightly on the floor, hands over his head.

She dashed out from behind the sofa, but a *whoosh* of air stopped her in her tracks—she smelled gun smoke—and Tanin appeared between her and Archer.

Sefia's mind churned. Tanin, here? Why? With one hand still holding the barricade over the door, she watched the woman warily.

Tanin grimaced, touching her ribs. Blood stained her palm, her silk shirt. She was injured.

A disadvantage.

But was it enough of a disadvantage for Sefia to get to Archer and teleport him away without losing her hold on the door? The candidates were banging on the barricade—she could feel them pounding against her magic.

Tanin's gaze darted across the floor. "You don't have the Book to hide behind this time," she whispered.

"I'm done with hiding." Sefia glanced at Archer. She was only seven steps away. Could she make it past Tanin without letting the candidates in?

"Your whole life, all you've done is hide." Tanin smiled. "From us. From *me*. What did you think you were doing, running to your precious Hav—"

Sefia attacked, palming the air with her free hand. Tanin tried to deflect, but her injury must have made her slow, because Sefia's magic caught her in the shoulder. She stumbled.

Sefia was already drawing a knife from its sheath at her waist. It was already singing through the air.

Regaining her balance, Tanin narrowed her eyes. She flicked her wrist, sending the blade point-first into the floorboards at her feet, and put her hands together, summoning a wave of force.

Wide-eyed, Sefia saw the sofa come rushing at her, huge and heavy. She leapt aside, rolling, as Tanin hurled a broken lantern at her. She felt her ribs bruise.

She hit the floor, winded, as Tanin's magic caught her again, flinging her back.

Her grip on the barricade loosened. The wardrobe splintered.

Wrenching a leg from the table, Sefia sent it flying at Tanin.

The woman brushed it aside easily, but the momentary distraction gave Sefia enough time to stand, firming up her hold on the door.

Grimly, Tanin grabbed Sefia's knife from the floor and reached for the windows at the rear of the cabin. She flung the blade. She flexed her fingers. The glass shattered, shards soaring toward Archer, where he lay curled on the floor.

Sefia didn't have enough hands. The knife, the glass, the candidates. Which would she stop?

She chose the glass. She chose to save Archer.

Whipping her free hand through the air, she sent the points of glass quivering into the wall.

The knife sank into the arm holding the door. Crying out, she dropped her hand. In the barricade, the table split. The wardrobe cracked. Bullets whizzed into the room, sending both her and Tanin under cover.

With the blade still in her arm, Sefia shoved the sofa at the door, plugging the holes in the barricade, and ripped the glass shards from the wall.

Tanin was getting up.

But Tanin was too slow. The glass struck her in the back. She let out a cry.

Pulling the knife from her arm, Sefia leapt across the room and knocked Tanin to the floor.

Her foot was on Tanin's neck.

Her blade was in her hand.

This close, she could not miss.

And Kelanna would be rid of another Guardian.

That's it. In a flash, Sefia understood what she had to do, how to use the power of the Scribes to beat every enemy she had— the war, the Alliance, the Guard, fate, the future, the Book.

But while she hesitated, Tanin thrust upward with the heel of her hand. Magic like a battering ram slammed into Sefia's chin. Her head went back. For a second, her vision went dark.

That second was enough for her power to falter. The barricade shattered. More liquor bottles came crashing to the floor as gunshots burst into the cabin.

Staggering to her feet, Sefia shook her head and summoned her magic. She ran to Archer's side. He was hot. His breath was coming too fast. It was like he couldn't get enough air.

"I've got you," she whispered, putting his arms around her neck. He buried his head against her, hands holding her tight. "You're safe."

Tanin groaned, trying to get up, with spikes of glass sticking out of her back as the candidates rushed into the cabin. Sefia and Archer teleported to the *Current of Faith,* where the battle r Haven was roaring around them. There was the smell of smoke and gunpowder, salty air and blood.

"Sefia?" In her arms, Archer was clutching the worry stone, rubbing his thumb across its smooth facets over and over, his face streaked with tears.

Ignoring her bruised ribs and wounded arm, Sefia clutched him tightly. "Don't worry," she whispered. "I know what to do. I know how we can save you."

Even with the power of the Scribes, they couldn't fight the Red War as it raged across the Central Sea on Oxscinian shores.

Nor could they fight the combined strength of the Alliance, with its three kingdoms' worth of ships and soldiers.

But the *Guard* that controlled the Alliance was only ten people—Librarians, Politicians, Administrators, Soldiers, Assassins. If they stopped those ten people, the Guard would be finished. The Alliance would dissolve. The Red War would end.

And without a war to win, Archer would not fulfill his destiny.

Archer would live.

He'd said it two and a half months ago, to that cotton-headed ninny Haldon Lac.

The *Guardians* were the real villains. The *Guard* was the real target. Not fate, not the future, not the war. The *Guard*.

A Threat to Roku

Facedown on the bed, Tanin could see little beyond the crisp white pillow and the carved headboard, but she could hear the *snip, snip* of the scissors under the distant rumble of cannon fire, and she could feel every lance of pain as her clothes were cut from the glass shards embedded in her back.

"My Apprentice's daughter did this to you?" The First's voice was faint and dry as smoke. *Snip.*

Tanin couldn't see him, but she could smell the scent of his bloodsword filling the cabin with its distinctive metallic odor. The smell still reminded her of Mareah, who'd earned her bloodsword after using it to murder her own parents.

To fulfill their grisly duties, Assassins could have no compassion, no mercy, no ties to anyone other than the Guard. They couldn't even have names. Which was why they were only referred to as the First and the Second.

Snip. "How I would have liked to train her." The First began peeling Tanin's clothing from her skin. The Master Assassin had taken on another Apprentice after Mareah betrayed him—the Second, with pockmarked skin and muddy gray eyes, who'd been killed on the *Current of Faith*. And he had another Apprentice now—*Tanin*. But after all these years, he still spoke of Mareah as if she were the only one who mattered.

Isn't she, though? Tanin thought before she could stop herself. She'd loved Mareah and Lon like they were her siblings. She'd almost let herself love their daughter.

But because of her love, she'd lost the Book. She'd lost her position. She'd been stripped of her name. She would never let love do that to her again. Sentiment was for the weak. That was the one thing Stonegold had taught her.

"Unfortunate that you didn't kill her," someone said in an indolent voice, "but you did well at Haven, my little dog." A heavy hand patted the back of Tanin's head, jarring her whole body. She could feel every fragment of glass in her skin.

Biting her lip, Tanin closed her eyes to hide her revulsion. *Stonegold.* The King of Everica was the Guard's Master Politician—and now their Director. He'd forced her out. He'd made her *beg.* It was all Tanin could do to keep from leaping up and slicing each of his jowls from his face.

Forbearance, she reminded herself. If she murdered him in front of all these witnesses, the other Guardians would turn on her immediately. And that wouldn't do.

"Really, Director," she whispered, "it's my pleasure to serve."

In the dead of night, she and the candidates had slipped from the *Black Beauty* to sink every ship in Haven's protected lagoon and slit the throat of every person they came across. They'd detonated bombs in Adeline and Isabella's compound and torched the jungle. By the time the outlaws knew what was happening, the Alliance had opened fire on the ships patrolling the currents beyond the islet.

She'd counted thirteen of the original outlaw vessels, plus a stray from Oxscini, the *Crux*, and the *Current*.

Only, the outlaws could not make a difference now, not when the Alliance had hundreds of ships ready to go.

Like a wisp of fog, the First's raspy voice reached her again: "The pain may cause some nausea."

Tanin set her jaw and said nothing as he began removing bits of glass from her flesh. She'd done this dozens of times for Mareah, plucking shrapnel from her arms and legs, sewing up gashes, smoothing salve on welts the First had inflicted on her. Assassins had to be trained to take wounds as well as inflict them, or they'd be of little use.

"You've proven your loyalty, but you failed to do what I asked." Stonegold's hot breath skimmed the bare skin of Tanin's back. "You failed to kill the traitors' daughter. That's twice she's escaped you since I allowed you to live. Once more, and I'm afraid you won't be able to be our Second Assassin after all."

"My apologies, Director, but she has an advantage. She has the—"

Stonegold interrupted her with a long, drawn-out sigh.

Tanin paused. "I have no excuse, Director." The words made her mouth pucker with distaste. To quell her gag reflex, she imagined the look in his dying eyes when he realized she was the one who'd killed him.

Somewhere behind him, she could hear pen nibs racing across parchment. Tolem, the Apprentice Administrator, and June, the Apprentice Librarian who'd replaced Lon, had been summoned to take notes and report back to their Masters at the Main Branch.

Once, the two Apprentices had been frightened of her. Now they were witness to her humiliation.

Tanin turned her face away.

They were in the captain's quarters of Braca's prize flagship, the *Barbaro*. The cabin was roomier than most, with friezes of battles from the Everican Rock-and-River Wars carved into the doors of the built-in wardrobes and walls decorated with the military awards the Master Soldier had racked up during her lifetime—gold bars, multicolored ribbons, shields—under frames of glass. Among these simple, martial adornments, the only item that appeared out of place was a full-length mirror, its frame a lavish carving of the Library—a portal for Guardians like the Apprentices and Stonegold, who hadn't mastered Teleportation and needed a way to access her ship.

By the cabin windows, the Master Soldier herself, Braca Terezina III, military leader of the Alliance, stood with her hands crossed behind her back, watching distant explosions light up the night sky.

After the attack on Broken Crown, she and her forces had pushed into the Bay of Batteram, the Oxscinians' next line of defense. Now they were battling the Royal Navy and a complement of Black Navy ships Roku had sent to the Forest Kingdom's aid.

Braca's Apprentice, Serakeen—Rajar—was out there somewhere, in the darkness, leading the attack in his flagship, the *Amalthea*, a former pirate vessel with a winged horse flying at her bowsprit.

The lantern light touched Braca's blue suede coat, her gold-tipped guns, the edge of her burned face. Her name wasn't even Braca—at least, it hadn't been to begin with. When she was an Apprentice, the Guard had required her to take on the identity of a soldier who'd died in a fire, to legitimize her place in Stonegold's army, so she'd submitted to the facial disfigurement, later appearing out of the ashes as Braca Terezina III, soon to climb the ranks.

They all made sacrifices for the greater good.

"I'm reassigning you, my little dog," Stonegold said, interrupting Tanin's thoughts. "You won't be returning to the *Black Beauty* and the candidates."

Tanin gritted her teeth. The *Beauty* was *her* ship. The

candidates were *Lon's* brainchild. Both should be under *her* command. But her voice was level when she spoke. "What's to happen to them?"

"They'll sail south for the invasion of Roku."

In Lon's original plan for the Red War, the fifth and final kingdom had been an afterthought. A former territory of the Oxscinian empire, the littlest kingdom was a cluster of rugged volcanic islands near the Everlasting Ice, useful for mining the materials necessary for making weapons, but the high cold winds, the stench of the geysers, and the periodic eruptions of lava, ash, and mudflows made Roku so inhospitable that no one went there unless they were forced to.

Now, however, half of the Black Navy was here, in the Bay of Batteram, leaving Roku ripe for the taking.

An Alliance invasion fleet was already on its way. In three weeks, they would batter the Rokuine defenses; capture Braska, the capital; and compel Sovereign Ianai to bow to the Alliance or be executed.

The Alliance would be four kingdoms strong. And it would not be long after that Oxscini, the last holdout, would fall.

"What of me, Director?" Tanin asked.

It wasn't Stonegold who answered but the First. "You're to stay with me, in Kelebrandt," he whispered. His low rasping voice sent a chill down her injured back. "It's time to begin your training so when you face my Apprentice's daughter again, you won't lose."

Chapter 18

Enough

Sefia closed the Book, wondering how fate wanted to trap her this time. Did it want her to teleport to the *Barbaro*? If only she were strong enough, she could take out half of the Guardians right now . . .

And what? Kill them? She'd taken a lot of lives in her sixteen years, but she'd never set out with murder in her heart. Besides, Tolem wasn't much older than her and Archer. She hadn't seen much of him during her time at the Main Branch, but she suspected he might have even been their friend, if circumstances had been different.

No, the Book must have been manipulating her another way, with the knowledge of the attack on Roku, maybe.

Sighing, she brushed a lock of hair from Archer's face as he slept. After his fit of panic during the fight with the candidates, he'd fallen into a deep sleep while the remaining outlaw captains had convened in Haven's compound with Scarza, representing the bloodletters, and Adeline and Isabella, who'd fled into the jungle during the attack, taking with them dozens of outlaws who never would have survived otherwise. Sefia had been invited to join them, but she wanted to be at Archer's side when he awoke.

So while Haven's leaders argued over their next course of action, she watched his sleeping form. And she planned.

She had to take out the Guard some other way, but she wasn't skilled enough to erase the entire organization from history, and excising individual Guardians would be as good as killing them. There was, however, another option . . .

Her father's plan for the Red War. She'd seen it in the Book—a scrap of paper scribbled over many times in different hands, describing the Guard's plans for conquest. Tanin used to keep it in her room, under glass. If Sefia excised that plan from the world, if Lon never conceived of it, maybe she could create a series of reactions like the ones she'd made when she'd erased an entire plant instead of a single grain of rice: The Guard would never plan for the war. They'd never hire the impressors to kidnap and mutilate children. Archer would live.

She shook her head.

Excising a single plant had given someone a scar they'd carry the rest of their life. If she took something as important as Lon's plan for the Red War and allowed that erasure to cascade? She could have been born into the Guard. She could have been shaped into a weapon. She couldn't even guarantee that Archer would live, because even if he was never captured by the impressors, that didn't mean he wouldn't die another way.

Whatever she did, she had to *control* her magic.

No, she thought suddenly, *I have to control* theirs. What made the Guardians so formidable now was Illumination. The most powerful Illuminators—Tanin, the First, the Soldiers, Erastis, maybe even his Apprentice, June, if she'd gotten that far in her studies—would be able to teleport from any prison Sefia put them in. But without their powers, they were just like anyone else—able to be contained by cell walls and locked doors.

If there'd been any nightmaker left in Dotan's laboratories, she could have stripped them of their Illumination now, but the Master Administrator was still in the process of making his next batch.

She would have to use excision to take their powers. And with excision, she would be rewriting the future, doing something fate could not control.

Sefia stroked the Book's cover thoughtfully. Had the Book given her this idea? Was her plan part of some elaborate trap meant to drive her and Archer toward their destinies?

No, she'd first thought of it while fighting Tanin. And what she'd read in the Book hadn't influenced her thinking.

Except . . . the attack on Roku. The *Black Beauty* and the candidates were sailing south with an invasion fleet. It wasn't a coincidence that the Book had revealed this information to her. It wanted her to go south.

The question was, would she? Would she refuse to play into the Book's traps and let the attack happen? Would she sacrifice Roku to spare Archer and herself? Would she choose the many or the few?

• • •

Archer slept, and when he slept, he dreamed of killing boys. In the fighting rings. On the deck of an Alliance ship. In a flooded quarry, while the dead tried to drag him into the black waves. He dreamed of killing boys he knew and boys without names, and most of all, he dreamed of killing Kaito.

No matter how many times Archer put him down, the boy would not stop coming for him.

You don't get to walk away from this, he said. He was standing bare-chested on a stony shore, with snowflakes like dandelion seeds drifting in the chill air. *You don't get to walk away from* us.

Archer had been here before, on this icy beach, he was sure of it. He tried to run. *I wanted to help people!* he said as he stumbled away. *I wanted to do something* good—

But wherever he went, Kaito followed. *You wanted to kill people, same as me.*

There was a revolver in Archer's hand. Had it always been there? *Leave me alone.* He pressed the gun to Kaito's forehead. *I'm* done *with you.*

Kaito didn't move. The black ink on his forearms was spreading over his skin, up his elbows and over his shoulders and chest, until it had eclipsed everything but his eyes, glowing red. *I know what you are, Archer. You* can't *be done with us.*

Archer pulled the trigger.

The gunshot startled him awake, panting.

"Archer."

Kaito? Coming back so I can kill him again?

No. There had been no gunshot; the gunshot had been a

dream. There had been no Kaito; Kaito was dead. The words had been real, though—Kaito had said them all, the night the bloodletters tattooed their arms with words that now sent shivers down Archer's spine.

We were dead, but now we rise.

What is written comes to pass.

"You're safe, Archer."

"Sefia?" he whispered.

As she peered down at him with dark eyes, the previous day's events came rushing back to him. The appearance of the candidates. The black, all-consuming panic. Vaguely, he remembered Sefia fighting with Tanin, being teleported to the *Current*, the departure of the Alliance.

"The Guard is planning an attack on Roku," Sefia said, tucking the Book under her arm. "And I think I know how to stop them."

Nodding shakily, Archer drew back the covers and began pulling on his clothes as she explained her plan.

"But it's the Book," he said. "If it wants us to go to Roku, doesn't that mean we shouldn't?"

"And let all those people die?"

He said nothing. She'd been right, back at the Trove. They were being drawn into the war again and again and again . . .

She shook her head. "If I pull this off, what is written *won't* come to pass, because I'll be rewriting the future. If the Book doesn't know what's coming, it can't trap us, no matter what information it reveals or withholds."

She was going to fight. She was going to fight the Guard. And he—

He would fight, yes. He would kill, one Alliance soldier at a time. He would make more corpses, the memories of the dead would continue to haunt his dreams, and he would never be able to rest.

But he had to do something, didn't he? The Guard was still out there. The candidates were still out there. He couldn't rest, either, if he didn't try to stop them.

But what if the panic came for him again?

He followed Sefia through the burned-out remains of Haven's compound, avoiding logs and blackened furniture where buildings must have once stood. Passing the collapsed wreck of the barn, he covered his nose to stifle the smell of charred fur and bone.

Haven's leaders were gathered around a table in the middle of the trampled garden. A woman was seated at the head of the table, one of her legs elevated, her brace gleaming among her voluminous skirts. She was Isabella Behn, Archer realized, the legendary gunsmith who'd made the Lady of Mercy. She wasn't saying much, but she would cock her head toward whoever was speaking, smoothing her thundercloud of hair behind her ear. With strong, plump hands, she placed stones on a map of Kelanna laid out in front of her: one for the western front of the war in Oxscini, one for the Gormani Resistance in the north, the smallest for the outlaws at Haven.

Beside her stood another woman who could only be Adeline Osono, the Lady of Mercy. With her shock of thinning white hair and liver-spotted hands, the slender old woman looked frail compared to Captain Dimarion, who loomed over her shoulder as he peered down at the map, but by all accounts, she was still the quickest gun in Kelanna—quicker, even, than Captain Reed—and Archer didn't miss how the others kept looking to her for opinions as they discussed their next moves.

Some wanted to go north to join the Gormani Resistance.

Others wanted to disperse. Haven was a failed experiment. The outlaws should take their chances with the sea, as they'd always done.

"I have another idea," Sefia said, marching up to the table.

The outlaws parted for her. Scarza slung his arm over Archer's shoulder, pressing their foreheads together. As was the rifleman's way, he said nothing, but he didn't need to. He'd probably already heard what had happened aboard the *Black Beauty*. He, of all people, would understand why Archer had fallen to pieces.

Quickly, Sefia explained what she'd read in the Book: In three weeks, the Alliance was going to invade Roku. If they succeeded, they would control four of the Five Islands. After that, it would only be a matter of time before Oxscini fell, and the Alliance—the Guard—conquered all of Kelanna.

For a moment, the group was silent.

Then, crossing her arms, Adeline spoke: "Well, you're a bright little ray of sunshine, ain't you, kid? Who wants to spend their last months drunk? There's got to be a cache on this island that Tan and her boys didn't touch."

At the mention of the candidates, Archer flinched. Though he only closed his eyes for a second, he saw the dead in his mind—red-eyed and led by Kaito. He reached for the worry stone hanging at his throat.

Scarza squeezed his arm.

"Addie, hush." Isabella patted the Lady's hand. "Let the girl finish."

With a grateful nod, Sefia continued, "Archer and I can teleport to Braska to warn Roku about the invasion. If we leave today, that gives them three weeks to fortify their defenses."

Scarza ran a hand over his silver hair. "If the invasion fleet is anything like what we saw at Epigloss, fortifying the defenses won't be enough."

"And you said half the Black Navy's in Oxscini," said one of the outlaws, a short woman with scars flecking her face. "Sovereign Ianai won't have the ships."

"That's where we come in," Sefia said.

She'd go to Roku like the Book wanted, and she'd have three weeks to master excision, the first tier of the Scribes' powers. If she did it right, she could erase some of the Alliance ships right out from under their sailors, dropping them and their cannons into the water before they even reached the capital of Braska. It'd be dangerous, toeing the edge of destiny's plans, but in the end, she'd rewrite destiny itself.

And she'd be ready to begin the work of capturing Guardians and taking their powers.

"Can you really do that, dear?" asked Isabella.

The hint of a smile tugged at Reed's lips. "These two are gutsier and more talented than most anyone I've ever met. If anyone can single-handedly sink a fleet of ships, it's them."

Sefia worried the edge of the map. "I don't think I can do the whole fleet, Cap," she admitted. "That's why the outlaws would need to sail for Roku too. To support the Black Navy when the Alliance comes."

At her words, the outlaws erupted into disagreement.

"Three weeks," said someone. "The *Current* could make it, but what about the rest of us?"

"The *Current* could guide us."

"Let the kingdoms fight it out," said the captain with the scarred face. "It's no concern of ours."

"As you well know, Captain Bee, they've hunted us to the brink of annihilation," Dimarion said. "It's everyone's concern."

"Look who's gone all good and noble now!" Bee snapped. "You're a pirate and a slaver. Don't lecture *me* about *the good of all*."

"I admit to every one of my crimes, and I'm doing what I can to—"

"I say we look after our own hides," someone interrupted. "The land's for them that need it. The ocean's for the free."

Reed lifted an eyebrow. "You think the ocean will still be free if we let the Alliance win?"

Snatching up a rock in her wrinkled hand, Adeline banged it twice on the table. "Shut it, all of you," she said. "You have the facts. You have a proposal. These two kids are goin' to Braska to warn the sovereign the Alliance is comin'. They're gonna do what they can to prepare for the invasion. Question is: Are you gonna sail south, against centuries of tradition, to risk your lives to protect a kingdom from the greatest threat to the outlaws Kelanna's ever seen? Or are you gonna go your own way, as you've always done before? Talk to your crews and meet back here in an hour with your decisions."

226

Archer and Sefia returned with Scarza to the bloodletters, who had been helping to fish the dead out of the lagoon all morning. In the water, the wrecks of the outlaw ships were like a ruined city, burned and broken, half-submerged beneath the waves. Covered in white sheets, corpses were lined up in dozens of rows along the beach.

Archer began counting them while the bloodletters sat in the sand around him, debating their next course of action. He'd reached seventy before the bodies in the distance became too small for him to see anymore.

So many dead. Would this be his legacy too?

"Archer." Sefia touched his shoulder.

He blinked, fingering the piece of quartz at his throat. "I'm sorry, what?"

Frey's brow furrowed with concern. "I asked if you recognized anyone? When you were fighting the candidates?"

Archer closed his eyes. They all must have known boys who'd made it through the Cage in Jahara, boys who they'd thought were lost. But he couldn't tell if the candidates he'd seen yesterday had new faces or old faces or faces of the dead come back to haunt him. When he opened his eyes again, he shook his head.

"How many were there?" Scarza asked.

Archer squeezed the worry stone in his hand and looked away.

"Thirty? Sixty?" Sefia answered. "Maybe more."

In his mind, Archer saw them coming at him. He saw their scarred necks. He saw their red eyes.

No, they were alive. Only the dead, in his dreams, had red eyes. The candidates were alive, for now.

Unless he stopped them.

Unless he killed them.

The bloodletters were arguing. They could join Chief Kemura and the Gormani Resistance. They could go home, like they could've done months ago.

"What about the candidates?" Frey asked, turning her little book of trees in her hands. "They're our brothers."

"They're *not* bloodletters," Keon said.

"But they could've been." Aljan looked up from a roll of parchment, where he'd been sketching a map of Haven in exquisite detail. He rubbed his eyes, smearing the white paint at the corners of his brows, and continued in a softer voice, "Just like we could've been candidates."

Frey nodded. "We're the only ones who know what they've been through. We have a responsibility to them."

Another boy shook his head. "What are we going to do, make them bloodletters? They're not going to turn on the Alliance now."

"We can stop them." Frey glanced at the others. "Don't we owe them that?"

"*Owe* them?" Keon asked.

She shrugged. "If it were me, I'd want someone to stop me from hurting more people."

"But why us?" Keon tossed his sun-streaked hair from his forehead. "Haven't we done enough?"

Enough. The word was foreign to Archer. He'd started by wanting to do something good, to balance out the harm he'd done. He'd fought for it. He'd killed for it. He'd made mistakes, and his victims had come to haunt his dreams. And he wanted to make up for it. So he fought, he killed, and his victims came to haunt his dreams.

If he kept going this way, there would be no end to it. There would never be *enough*.

He didn't want to keep leaving bodies behind him. He didn't want the number of the dead who visited him in his dreams to grow and grow and grow, until they were lined up before him in never-ending columns, their red eyes aglow.

He didn't want to be the boy from the legends. He didn't want to lead an army. He didn't want to conquer the Five Islands. And, most of all, he didn't want to die.

He had to change his destiny.

And he could start now. By making a single choice.

"Archer?" Scarza asked gently. "What do you think?"

"I . . . You heard what happened to me yesterday on the *Black Beauty*?"

Frey and the boys nodded.

"I know the Guard has to be stopped. What's the best way to fight them? With my fists? With my weapons? With more"—tears splashed onto his fingers—"bloodshed? I could do it. I'd be good at it. A part of me wants nothing more than that. But after yesterday . . . I don't know if I should. I don't know if I can take all those lives . . . and still live with myself."

"Does this mean you're leaving us?" Griegi asked in a small voice. Keon quickly hugged the cook to his side.

Archer wiped his eyes, ashamed of giving up when he could still fight. Of not doing everything he could for what he knew in his heart was right.

And he was afraid. Because who was he, without violence?

"It's okay. You'll always be our chief." Griegi was the first person to throw his arms around Archer. Then Sefia. Then Frey and Aljan and whoever else was closest.

"Stop if you have to," Frey murmured. "No one will think less of you."

Scarza's voice was soft on Archer's shoulder: "Let us carry this for you for a while."

And Archer knew then who he was without violence, without killing, without destiny. He buried his face in Sefia's hair, crying softly—with grief, and with relief.

I'm a boy who lives.

CHAPTER 19

A Touch of Destiny

An hour later, Archer was sitting beside Sefia and Scarza on the steps of a collapsed gazebo, watching Adeline and Isabella pass Archer's revolver back and forth, the gold and ivory feathers on its grip glinting in the wintry light.

"So you found this in the Trove, huh?" said the Lady of Mercy, spinning the gun on her trigger finger. "Pretty. Well-balanced. Ain't yours, though, is it, my dear? I'd know your work anywhere."

Isabella laughed and shook her head. "It was made by some great-great-granddaddy of mine, I believe. He called it Lightning, after the extinct thunderbirds of Shaovinh Province."

"Lightning, huh?" Adeline said. She eyed Scarza, who'd been watching her, enraptured. "They tell me you're a good shot. What do you say—your rifle against Lightning? That is, if it's okay with you, Archer?"

Archer nodded, dumbfounded. The Lady of Mercy, using his weapon? He'd be honored.

Standing, Scarza smiled shyly. "My rifle's on the *Brother*, ma'am. But if you've got one lying around . . ."

"Do we have one 'lying around'?!" the gunsmith cried. "Addie, go fetch him the Long Arm of the Law."

With a little bow, the Lady of Mercy ducked away. When she returned, she had a beautiful rifle slung over her shoulder. She tossed it to Scarza, who caught it in his one hand. "Ready, boy?" she asked.

He grinned, dimpling the corners of his mouth.

While they shot targets against the burned hulk of the barn, Isabella regaled Archer and Sefia with stories from her younger days with Adeline, the only authority in the lawless territory at the tip of Liccaro, demanding order from pirates and slavers, dispensing justice with quick trigger fingers and a silver-and-ivory six-gun.

"It was a *life*, all right," she said happily, rubbing her bad leg. "I wish I could tell you everything before this old memory goes, but there just aren't enough hours in the day . . ."

"You could write it down. Or get someone to write it down for you," Scarza said, lifting the rifle to his shoulder and putting his last shot through the bullet hole Adeline had left in a fencepost.

The Lady of Mercy let out a whistle of approval. Squinting at the target, she fired, sending a bullet ricocheting off a dented trough and back through the bull's-eye. Archer, Sefia, and Scarza applauded as she gave them a little bow. Refilling Lightning's chambers, she spun it once more and extended it to Archer, grip first.

"You should have it," said Archer, offering it to Isabella. "If it belonged to your family."

Winking, she just patted his cheek. "I've got guns of my own, remember, boy?"

Leaning against the arm of Isabella's chair, Adeline pursed her lips thoughtfully. "I bet Meeks'd help us get down some of our stories."

"They're good stories." Isabella kissed the Lady's hand. "It was a good life."

"And it ain't over yet," Captain Reed declared, sauntering up to them. He tipped his hat to Scarza. "That was some good shootin', kid."

Ducking his head to hide his smile, Scarza plopped down next to Archer.

Slowly, the other outlaw captains filtered into the ruined garden until they were all gathered around the map and the makeshift table again.

"Well?" Adeline said, putting her hands on her hips. "Let's hear it."

Reed was the first to speak up. "The *Current*'s goin' south."

"Really." Dimarion raised an eyebrow. "Captain Reed, the quintessential outlaw, is going to risk his life, his crew, and the *Current of Faith* defending one of the Five Kingdoms. Are you sure?"

"Sure?" Reed laughed. "I was sure I'd never care for anyone but my own crew. I was sure the outlaws would never come together. I was sure I wanted to live more'n anything else in this whole blue world." He held out his hands, displaying the tattoos that marked his many adventures. "But I *have* lived, haven't I? Now I gotta look to the horizon, 'cause it's time for another adventure, a bigger adventure, one they'll never forget for thousands of years—leadin' the Resistance against a secret sorcerer society bent on world domination."

The pirate captain chuckled. "That does have a ring to it, doesn't it? The *Crux* will be with you."

Reed raised an eyebrow. "Quite a turn from your piratical ways."

"It's my own fault, for spending so much time with you."

"Count me and Bella in," said Adeline. "If you can use a couple old girls like us."

Dimarion bowed to her, low, like he was a vassal instead of one of the most feared outlaws on the Central Sea. But she was the Lady of Mercy. Archer supposed that was only her due.

• • •

After Sefia and Archer had packed their things and said their good-byes, the crews of the *Current*, the *Crux*, and the *Brother* gathered on the beach to see them off.

With his ruby-handled cane, Dimarion beckoned to two of his sailors, who brought forth a lacquered chest. Red tassels dangled from its handles. "A gift for the Rokuine sovereign," he said, lifting the lid with one of his large, bejeweled hands.

Sefia gasped. Inside, in a nest of crimson satin, was the biggest diamond she'd ever seen—bigger than a skull, shining in the morning light like a star—the diamond that used to sit in the hands of the *Crux*'s wooden figurehead. According to the stories, Dimarion had once been a captain in Roku's Black Navy, but he'd been obsessed with tales of dragons living in the littlest kingdom's volcanoes and the diamonds they collected, and when he'd gotten the chance, he'd killed Roku's last dragon, taken its largest diamond, earning his reputation for strength, savagery, and avarice, and been forever banished from the littlest kingdom's volcanic shores.

"Ain't you full of surprises," Reed murmured.

"You don't know the half of it," Dimarion said. Then, to Sefia: "Tell Ianai it's a token of good faith. If you present them with this, they might agree to hear what you have to say. After that, your survival's up to you."

"The sovereign's that tough, huh?" Sefia asked.

"*Tough* is an understatement."

Solemnly, Archer took the chest, balancing it against his hip.

"Thanks, Captain," Sefia said.

From his great height, Dimarion stared down at her, his face in shadow. "Thank me when I see you again, in the ruins of the Alliance fleet."

She smiled. Excising entire ships wouldn't be easy. But she had three weeks to learn. Three weeks to change the future.

"Now, speaking of surprises . . ." The captain of the *Crux* pivoted to Reed and, with a flourish, pulled a brass mallet from an inner pocket of his brocade coat. It was ancient looking, but through the crust of verdigris, Sefia thought she could see images of stormclouds.

Captain Reed stared at it a moment. "That what I think it is?"

"You didn't think I was going to leave *treasure* at the bottom of that maelstrom, did you?"

The maelstrom. That was where Reed had gotten the Thunder Gong six years ago. Where the water had told him how he was going to die. Where he decided he was going to sail for the edge of the world because no one had ever done it before.

Sefia blinked. Because of his time in the maelstrom, he'd gone to the place of the fleshless. He'd passed into the world of the dead and back out again.

The whole thing had a touch of destiny that made her shiver.

Reed snatched it out of Dimarion's hands, holding it to the light. "You bonesucker! You had it all this time?"

The pirate captain shrugged unapologetically. "It's hard to part a pirate from his treasure."

"Then we'd better get out of here," Sefia said.

"Ha!" Reed laughed. Dimarion looked dour.

She blinked. Gold light swirled across her vision as Archer clasped her waist. She skimmed the tides of gold, in search of their destination—in the deep south, across blue stretches of ocean, in the old lava tunnels on the side of a long-dormant volcano—the castle at Braska.

"I never get tired of seein' this," Reed said with anticipation.

She lifted her arms, parting the seas of light, and teleported her, Archer, and the chest through the currents—away from the beach, through the stone pillars outside Haven, over the ocean and past Roku's outer islands, black and volcanic, into the castle at the base of the volcano, its windows glinting like jewels.

Then they were through the walls, stumbling to the foot of

the dais where Ianai Blackfire Raganet, Sovereign of Roku, sat on their obsidian throne.

Immediately, the guards drew their black-and-gold spears, closing in around Sefia and Archer like a noose.

"The throne room?" he muttered.

"We wanted an audience, didn't we?" she said as they backed toward the windows. "Sovereign Ianai, I'm sorry for the interruption but—"

"You don't know what it's like to be sorry," Ianai replied, rising from the throne. "But you will."

Neither man nor woman, the sovereign was a younger person than Sefia had expected—Reed's age, minus a few years—and tall, almost as tall as Aljan, with short brown hair and cold eyes like pools of obsidian. Dressed in the black livery of a Rokuine soldier, they could only be distinguished from their guards by the crown of golden scales and the haughty expression on their high-cheekboned face.

"Please, Your Majesty, just lis—" Grabbing the chest from Archer, Sefia let out a cry as one of the guards prodded her in the shoulder with a spear, cutting her sleeve, drawing a thin line of blood.

Beside her, she felt Archer go for his weapons. She felt him tense for the jump.

"Don't fight," she whispered. "Fight, and they'll never listen."

"*Sorry,*" Ianai mocked her. "*Please.* You should've collected your manners *before* you appeared uninvited in my court." They nodded at the guards, who seized Sefia and Archer by the arms. Dimarion's chest fell to the floor, where its varnished lid cracked. "I don't know who you think you are, but you'll learn your place in my dungeons before you speak to me again."

But Sefia would not be silenced. "The Alliance is coming for you!" she shouted as the soldiers began to haul her away. Blinking, she summoned her magic and flipped the lid on Dimarion's chest. "They'll be here in three weeks! Look! We're your allies! We're telling you the truth!"

There was a collective gasp as the enormous diamond tumbled onto the polished black floor. Sefia felt the grip on her arms loosen, though the soldier did not let go.

Sovereign Ianai lifted an eyebrow. "You appear like enemies. You bear the gifts of friends. You're obviously a sorcerer, and you claim we're under attack. *Who are you?*"

Dimarion had been right—the diamond had at least gotten Ianai to listen. Now Sefia had to get them to believe.

"It's a long story, Your Majesty."

"Then start at the beginning, and make it quick," said the sovereign. "If you're right, we don't have time to lose."

Sefia couldn't help but smile. A story to save their lives and the lives of thousands of Rokuine citizens?

That was a story she could tell.

"Believe me or don't," she began, "but this is how it happened . . ."

CHAPTER 20

Red Hearts Can't Be Broken

On the journey through the Cloud Pillars and across the Oxscinian mainland, Ed, Lac, and Hobs encountered tides of other refugees fleeing from the coast. Over cups of tea brewed from scavenged bark, Ed heard stories of the Alliance punching through the Royal Navy defenses at the Bay of Batteram. In voices hoarse with smoke, the evacuees described fierce battles between flaming ships, circling one another on the whitecaps while Oxscini's onshore batteries emptied their cannons at the monstrous Alliance warships.

Delienean warships, Ed thought with a twinge of guilt. But then he'd remember the fleet he'd seen at Broken Crown and he'd tell himself, for the fifth, the twenty-first, the thirtieth time, that if Arcadimon hadn't joined the Alliance, the Delieneans would have been evacuating like these Oxscinians, sooner or later—uprooted, afraid, beaten.

Ed did what he could as they slogged through the Vesper

swamps toward Kelebrandt, the Forest Kingdom's capital, and Queen Heccata's protection. He organized foraging parties. He helped reconnect lost family members. He did his best to keep them fed and sheltered while, every few days, convincing Lac that they could not abandon the caravan to join the fight in Batteram. The trek through the bog wasn't a glorious battle, but it was where they were needed.

To keep Lac busy, Ed assigned him to the laundry, while Hobs scurried back and forth between sections of their caravan with messages, stories, and odd jokes. And whenever Ed felt his sadness creeping up on him like a cold tide, he took time out of his days to care for the horses. How he'd missed horses! And dogs! He loved spending time with the refugees' dogs, the cats, the goats and hogs and water buffalo.

But no matter how much he accomplished, no matter how exhausted he was by the trekking or the hauling water, at the end of the day, Ed never slipped easily into sleep. He'd stare up at the ceiling of the tent he shared with Lac and Hobs, his mind sifting through new ideas for helping the evacuees, until his eyes closed at last and he descended into fitful dreams.

Every time they found more refugees on the road, they asked for updates on the Red War.

Serakeen and the *Amalthea* had taken another Batteram fort, a woman said. The Alliance was pressing on toward the entrances to Tsumasai Bay like a tide crawling up a beach, and they could not be stopped.

"Tides always go out," Hobs said helpfully.

The woman shook her head. "Not this one."

Someone else reported that the Royal Navy was putting

up a good showing. No invaders had gotten past them before, and not even General Terezina and the *Barbaro* would get past them now.

This roused Lac from his despondency at not being able to rejoin the redcoats, and he led the two women from the village near Broken Crown in an upbeat rendition of an Oxscinian folk song, which the other evacuees picked up, their voices winding and flowing through the trees until the whole caravan was singing.

> *Oh my lady, lovely lady*
> *Who is weeping in the rain,*
> *Dry your tears, my lovely lady.*
> *Brighter days will come again.*

When they reached the outskirts of Kelebrandt, the refugees began dispersing, searching for housing, medical care, or missing relatives in the encampments Queen Heccata had established for them, until only Ed, Lac, and Hobs remained of their caravan.

"Well." Ed sighed as they walked into the city. "We made it."

"At last!" Lac declared. His brown curls were long now, pulled into a high knot and tied neatly with a piece of yarn. "I'm dying for a bath."

Ed sniffed. In fact, after a month in the jungle, they could all do with a wash. He wondered what Arc would have said, if he could have seen him now.

The thought sobered him. Arcadimon was in the north,

sending Delienean soldiers into the war. Arcadimon was almost certainly a Guardian. They'd probably never see each other again. And even if they did, they'd be enemies.

As if they could sense Ed's sadness creeping up on him, Lac and Hobs twined their arms in his, and they marched deeper into Kelebrandt together.

Soldiers were everywhere in their red-and-gold uniforms. Stevedores hauled kegs of powder and cases of bullets. Messengers in black armbands scurried in and out of the crowds, while war orphans gathered in groups and went scampering over the streets like herds of wild creatures. Everyone seemed to be abuzz with news.

And fear.

"What?" Ed asked someone as they ran past, pushing a handcart piled with sandbags. "What's going on?"

Lac went out at the knees when he heard. It was only Ed's quick reflexes that kept him from collapsing in the middle of the gravel street, his arm around his friend's waist.

Yesterday, the Alliance, led by the *Barbaro* and the *Amalthea*, had decimated the Oxscinian defenses at the Bay of Batteram. Joined by the Rokuine reinforcements sent by Sovereign Ianai, the Royal Navy had retreated to Tsumasai Bay and was preparing for siege.

"Siege?" Lac echoed as they wound their way through the city toward the Red Navy headquarters. "We should have made our way to Batteram when we had the chance."

"We wouldn't have made a difference," said Hobs helpfully. "We're two lowly soldiers and a boy with no last name."

242

"The Alliance won't make it into Tsumasai Bay." Ed tried to sound confident. "Kelebrandt is the best-protected capital in Kelanna."

Hobs glanced sideways at him. "How do you know?"

In truth, Ed had been to the other capitals—the dilapidated palaces in Umlari, the Liccarine capital; the districts of Braska arrayed on the shores of Roku's largest volcanic island; and, of course, Corabel, the city on a hill, overlooking the White Plains and the steep Delienean cliffs—but none of them were as well defended as Kelebrandt.

"I mean . . ." He swept out his hand, gesturing to the city laid out before them. "Just look at it."

Part city, part fortress, Kelebrandt had as many walls and turrets, parapets and battlements, as shops, promenades, gardens, and fountains. Great wooden bridges, spiked with thick stakes tipped with iron, straddled the massive river that wound down to the harbor in magnificent curves. There, right on the water, the castle at Kelebrandt stood: a gleaming hulk of Rokuine stone and black-lacquered Oxscinian hardwood, reinforced with steel. It was not as elegant, Ed thought, as the castle at Corabel, but it was resolute and formidable—a castle built for war.

Beyond it lay the span of Tsumasai Bay, where stone garrisons and fortified gun turrets were arranged along the waterline as far as the eye could see. On the waves, the crimson ships of the Oxscinian Navy were still streaming in from the east, forming into orderly rows as they entered the bay.

This was what stood between the Alliance and the heart of

the Forest Kingdom. Truthfully, the Oxscinian defenses were so impressive that Ed could hardly imagine them falling to even a force as large as the one he'd seen at Broken Crown.

But if they did fall, if the Alliance entered Tsumasai Bay and took Kelebrandt, it would not be long before the rest of Oxscini fell too, and the Alliance would have four of the Five Islands under its thumb.

As they made their way toward the Royal Navy headquarters, Ed, Lac, and Hobs were soon caught up in a rush of people streaming through the city. Pressed together, Ed could feel their nervous energy pulsating from one person to the next, moving away from the shoreline and up Kelebrandt's hills in a single sinuous mass.

Soon, the streets became barricaded, with makeshift wooden fences to keep pedestrians on the sidewalks and redcoats stationed along the barriers to keep people from jumping them. In the road, soldiers on stamping horses marched back and forth along the gravel. Soon, the press of people was so great, Ed, Lac, and Hobs could not move in any direction.

"We must have taken a wrong turn somewhere," Lac moaned.

Standing on his tiptoes, Ed could see that they were stranded on a hillside. On the downslope across the street, houses on stilts were built into the mountain, with the city and the bay stretched out below. Behind them, a forested hillside rose steeply on the other side of the guards and barricades.

"Maybe we're in line for a parade," Hobs suggested.

A young person beside them laughed, their merry blue eyes

twinkling with excitement. "The queen's making a public address! In the amphitheater." They nodded toward a wooded mountain overlooking the city, where the pale crescent of an amphitheater had been cut into the earth. "We're all waiting to get in."

Lac patted his stained, threadbare clothing uselessly. "We get to see the queen? The queen can't see me like this."

Ed tried to smile. He'd only met Heccata once before, when he was a child, and he remembered her like a flagship— imposing, powerful, glittering with danger. She'd reached for his chin, and he'd backed away at the touch of her cold fingers.

Raking him with a single glance, she'd said, "Don't cringe, boy. A monarch looks fear in the eye and does not flinch."

"Maybe we'll see her in her carriage as she passes by," said the person with a sigh, "but with this crowd, I don't think we're getting into the amphitheater today."

Lac looked crestfallen.

"Want to wait for the carriage anyway?" Ed asked, to cheer him up. "I don't think we'll make much headway if we try to leave now."

"For a chance to see the queen? Anything!"

The sun rose higher. Impatient, a few members of the crowd sneaked—some more successfully than others—past the soldiers and up the wooded hillside, where Ed saw them climbing the trees, only to appear moments later in the branches, their faces eager. One of them, a man in black, hopped the barricade and ducked behind a tree trunk, blending into the shadows as neatly as if he were nothing more than a shadow himself.

Ed inhaled deeply as the wind picked up. Over the scent of his own body odor, he could have sworn he smelled a strange metallic odor—copper, maybe.

After what seemed like an hour of waiting, excitement began to ripple through the crowd. "The queen! The queen!"

First came the foot soldiers, their crisp red uniforms eliciting an envious sigh from Lac, followed by the ones on horseback, bearing Oxscinian flags that snapped and waved in the breeze.

Lac craned his neck, straining to catch a glimpse of Queen Heccata through the crowd. Hobs peeked over the shoulders of the people nearest him.

Then the carriage came into view. Drawn by six white horses and flanked by a team of mounted soldiers, it was a splendor in black and gold, with the Oxscinian crest of a tree and crown emblazoned on the door and sheer white curtains drawn across the windows.

"The queen!" Lac whispered.

The redcoats on horseback rode in tight formation, their bodies and banners blocking much of the carriage from view.

But between the undulating flags, the horses tossing their heads, the soldiers' flashing gun grips, Ed saw a crowned silhouette inside the carriage lift its hand.

The crowd cheered.

"She's waving to us!" Lac cried.

Later, Ed would try to remember if he'd seen a puff of smoke from the treetops, if he'd heard the gunshot. If he could have done something to protect the queen. But no, it had been so fast, there had only been the royal wave, and then—

Blood, spattering the curtains like dozens of tiny red flowers. In the carriage, Queen Heccata collapsed.

Before anyone had time to react, there was an explosion on the opposite side of the street. Huge chunks of lumber and rock blew outward from the hillside. Smoke and powder clouded the air as the tottering houses collapsed and the edge of the mountain began to crumble.

Then came the screams.

The redcoats rushed to the queen's carriage. Others raced to the site of the explosion as the crowds trampled one another in their haste to escape.

"The queen is dead!" Lac cried, horrified. "Someone killed her, right in front of us!"

But Ed wasn't listening. He was watching the man in black climb down from his tree and turn nonchalantly up the hillside, but not before Ed caught a glimpse of a rifle beneath his long coat. In the chaos, no one else noticed as he slipped away.

"The queen!" Lac kept saying. "How could we let this happen?"

"Get ahold of yourself, sir." Hobs smacked him across the face. "We didn't let it happen."

"But we can stop who did it." Ed began to shove through the crowd. "Come on, before the assassin gets away."

"Assassin? Are you sure?" To his surprise, their new friend with the blue eyes was already behind him, all the merriment drained from their face. They drew a knife. "Which way?"

Lac and Hobs joined them as Ed leapt over the barrier, leading them into the forest.

"Assassin!" Lac shouted. Ed winced, knowing the man in black might have heard. "He went this way! Guards!"

They chased the assassin up the hill, between trees and over logs. At one point, the young person broke away from them, disappearing into the undergrowth.

They reappeared moments later, emerging from a crop of spiked leaves as they slashed at the man with their knife.

The man leapt back, drawing a curved, copper-colored sword in one smooth motion. Ed dashed forward—he'd gotten faster, stronger, in his three months at sea, on the road—his long legs pumping, closing the distance as he left Lac and Hobs behind.

The scent of iron wafted out from the blade as it nicked their new friend's throat. The blood on the weapon was quickly absorbed into the steel, but the rest of their blood spilled from them as they fell, clutching their neck.

"No!" Ed skidded to a stop by their side.

Their blue eyes were open, but they didn't see him. They were already dead.

There was a faint breeze as the man in black moved to strike again. But he paused, mid-swing, and Ed got his first good look at the assassin's face.

He was old—much older than Ed would have expected, given his agility, with lined eyes and sunken, sun-spotted cheeks.

For a moment, he stared at Ed. "So." The assassin's voice was like smoke, his words seeming to disappear almost as soon as they were spoken. "He lied to us."

He? Ed's mind whirled. *Us.*

Arcadimon . . . and the Guard.

The assassin knew who Ed was, knew he was alive—and that meant Arc was in danger. Ed grabbed the young person's knife from the ground beside their body.

But the man in black was so fast. The sword flashed.

Ed did not flinch.

But before the blade could reach him, a gunshot rent the air. The assassin hissed as a bullet struck him in the collarbone. The killing blow missed.

Ed glanced behind him. Lac was holding a smoking gun. Around him, a small army of redcoats was racing toward the man in black.

Ed lunged—probably a stupid move, he realized belatedly, something Lac would do—and the assassin's sword kissed his wrist, his thigh.

But the redcoats were too close. The man in black sheathed his blade and darted away, clutching his injury.

The soldiers streamed by them as Lac and Hobs knelt beside Ed. "You're bleeding!" Lac said, obviously.

Hobs began wrapping the injuries. "What did he mean, 'He lied to us'?" the boy asked, squinting at Ed. "Who's 'he'?"

Shaking his head, Ed didn't answer. Arc was in danger, and Ed was too far away to save him.

CHAPTER 21

The Power of the Scribes

Three weeks. That was all Sefia had to master excision, an extinct form of magic, with nothing to guide her but a Book she could not trust. Could she do it before the Book caught her in one of its snares, entangling her more deeply in her destiny? Could she do it before thousands died in the defense of Roku, and the Volcanic Kingdom fell to the Alliance?

She just had to be faster, smarter, stronger than the Book. She had to.

At night, she laid the Book in her lap and studied her father's progress with excision or practiced hand motions by her window while boats ferried back and forth between Braska and the outer islands. There were three entrances into Blackfire Bay—one to the east, one to the west, and a narrow channel to the north between two smaller islands. With the other entrances covered by the remains of the Black Navy, the north channel would be the most logical point of attack for the Alliance invasion fleet.

Sovereign Ianai had ordered the towns along the channel to be completely given over to the Black Navy and the volunteer militia, so nonessential citizens were being moved behind capital walls for safety.

Sefia pressed her forehead to the glass. Below her, the districts of Braska were separated by deep trenches that would channel mudflows when the volcanoes erupted, sending the blistering rivers of lava and rock safely into the bay. The stench of sulfur permeated the capital, muted only a little by the pans of sage and flowers that burned beneath the lampposts.

When she finally crawled into bed each night, she slept little, tossing and turning on the uncomfortably stuffed mattress. Every time she closed her eyes, she pictured the Illuminated world—bright and immense—trying to drown her.

After a few hours of fitful sleep, she'd pull on her cold-weather layers, take the Book, and leave the city before dawn, hiking up the cliffs that overlooked the capital to the high mountain plains, where geysers steamed and smoke from hidden volcanic vents went drifting over the brittle grasses and windswept trees.

Archer remained behind, hauling sandbags, stocking gun turrets, ushering evacuees to temporary housing, doing whatever Sovereign Ianai and the Black Navy required.

Alone in the dry cold, with the black cones of Roku's volcanoes in the distance, Sefia practiced what she learned of the Scribes' power.

To excise something without causing a ripple of consequences, you had to cut the threads of light that connected it to the rest of the world. A single stone could have dozens of

251

influences: the rocks it had chipped on its way downstream, the grasses it smothered, the insects and tiny rodents it sheltered, the miners it tripped as they stumbled home from the quarry.

In the Illuminated world, Sefia would sever the pulsing streams that linked the stone to these other things, so even if the stone disappeared, the chips, the smothered grasses, the stubbed toes remained. The insects and field mice survived. But there were gaps in their history—like the architectural wonders and technological innovations the Scribes left behind when they erased writing from the world, for though people could use them, no one could remember when or how they were created—and someone, taking off his boots at night, might wonder at a particular bruise on his foot, having no recollection of where he'd gotten it.

The days passed, but her progress was frustratingly slow. Again, she wished her father was actually with her, instead of just in the Book. Together, they could have conferred. Together, they could have made faster progress, more breakthroughs.

But every so often, instead of turning to the page she wished, the Book would remind her: Lon was in the place of the fleshless, beyond the dome of the living world, with Mareah and Nin. He was a specter of the person he used to be. Even if she could have talked to him, she wouldn't have recognized him.

"I *know*," she said once, snapping the covers shut. "But I need him. Show him to me."

When she opened the Book, it willingly parted to a scene of her father erasing skipping stones on the beach below the house. But she had to excise more than that. She had to excise *ships*. The people of Roku were depending on it.

On her.

She had to move faster.

With her father's progress to guide her, she began excising leaves from gnarled branches. She took boulders. Then entire trees.

When she returned to the city at dusk, the construction would still be under way. No matter how late the hour, people were at work on the walls and batteries, erecting watchtowers on the cliffs.

At the end of every day, Archer was exhausted but satisfied with the work.

Helping. But not fighting. Not killing. Though that didn't stop his nightmares.

"They're all counting on me," Sefia said, touching their window.

Archer came up behind her, smelling of sweat and dust and rain, though they hadn't seen rain in months. "I couldn't think of anyone better to count on."

"I'm scared. How many of them are going to die if I can't do this?"

"No one is going to die." He turned her around, away from the window. "I believe that because I believe in you. More than anything else in the world."

She let him enfold her in his embrace. "I hope you're right," she whispered.

One week turned into two. There was still no sign of the

outlaws, who just might make it in time, with the *Current* to guide them.

Had they been waylaid somehow? Had they run into the Alliance invasion fleet on their way to Roku?

As the days counted down, Sefia began excising weather-beaten shacks on lonely hills. She erased abandoned mine shafts. She removed a compound of buildings from the bottom of an old quarry.

Could she erase an entire ship?

Two?

Half a fleet of them?

The Alliance invasion fleet arrived at Roku three weeks after Sefia and Archer. It was a few hours before dawn, and the ships glittered along the horizon like a fearsome floating city, drawing ever closer.

The Rokuine defenses had been fortified. The cannons had been stocked with shot. The volunteer militia had been given armaments and been hastily trained. Boats were waiting to retrieve the wounded from the water. They were as ready as they could have been.

The steep ridges of the northern channel into Blackfire Bay had been evacuated and rigged with explosives that Archer found fascinating. You had to detonate the first by means of a wire, but if you placed them correctly, the others would be set off simply by the shocks, one after another, like a cascade. If Sefia failed, the explosives would be detonated, sending the mountainside crumbling into the water, taking out the edges of the Alliance fleet as it sailed into Blackfire Bay.

It was a destructive, desperate measure Sovereign Ianai hoped they wouldn't have to use, because if Sefia failed, it wouldn't take out enough ships to save them. But fewer Alliance ships might mean fewer Rokuine casualties.

It was in one of these abandoned cliff towns that Sefia and Archer stood, among the empty shells of houses, doors swinging in the chill winter wind. From there, the Alliance invasion fleet would sail close enough for her to reach it, excising half of their ships before they had the chance to fire a single broadside. In the south, Sefia could see Braska alight like a shining target.

Her gaze passed to the Alliance vessels, now beginning to take shape. She could almost pick out Alliance flags coiling and flapping in the moonlight like gold-blue serpents with forked tongues.

Archer stood by her, his body a shelter from the cold wind. Without a word, he placed a hand on her shoulder.

The warmth of his touch coursed through her.

She could do this.

She *would* do this.

Because he believed in her. And she wouldn't let him down.

She blinked. Light unfurled across her vision like a golden veil. In the Illuminated world, she could see all twenty-four ships of the Alliance fleet, and as they inched closer, she could see more—every rusted bolt at the portholes, every strand of rope in the rigging, every beating heart of every soldier.

She took a breath.

And when she exhaled, she felt her Sight expanding. The currents of light separated into filaments of time, into stories both close and distant. The fleet was a dense web of gold, more entangled than anything she'd ever seen, woven through with veins so bright they seemed to throb.

Lifting her hands, she began the work of excision. She sliced through the particles of light. She severed connections. She watched currents of gold go dark.

"Sefia?" Archer asked. "They're almost here."

She was running out of time.

She couldn't find all the connections, couldn't sever them neatly. She had to act now.

So she slashed. She shredded and tore. She could almost feel the story threads snapping in her fingers, until she held half the light of the Alliance fleet in her hands.

And she extinguished them. The timbers, the sails, the running lines, the anchors and anchor chains, all the history of all the ships dimmed, died, and disintegrated into nothing.

She'd done it.

She'd excised eight ships.

She'd saved hundreds—if not thousands—of lives. Her limbs felt watery with relief.

But then the screams reached her.

Sefia opened her eyes to . . . there was no better word for it than *horror*.

As expected, some of the Alliance ships had disappeared completely, their crews floundering, bewildered, in the black water. But three vessels had only been partially excised—their sails shredded, their cannons corroded as if by acid, their decks cratered with hundreds of holes.

The timbers of the nearest ship caught fire. Black smoke

billowed into the sky as flames licked at the cobweb-like rigging, the splintered masts.

But the ships weren't the only remnants of her failed magic.

In the light of the blaze, she could see sailors staggering across the listing decks—it was like they'd been half-erased, trailing blood and body parts attached only by raw tendons.

An explosion rocked the darkness as another ship went up in a ball of flame, so bright and hot, Sefia felt it on her tearstained cheeks.

As the small, flailing figures caught fire and fell, shrieking, into the water, she remembered the future the Book had laid out for her: *She would demolish her enemies with a wave of her hand. She would watch men burn on the sea.*

It had been written, and learning Alteration had not only failed to change it, doing so had *ensured* that it came to pass.

"What have I done?" she whispered.

Archer tried to take her hands. "Sefia, look at me. How do we fix this?"

Fix this. Yes. She had to fix this. She wrenched out of his grasp. Before he could say anything more, she was summoning the Sight, she was seeking stable landing among the wrecked ships, she was disappearing with a wave of her trembling arms.

Then she was among them.

The sounds struck her first: creaking ships being sucked under the water, crackling flames, the moans of the people she'd only partially excised, their screams and hoarse, pitiful cries.

They were missing arms, legs, fingers, eyes, chunks of their ribs. Some were already dead, and among the corpses she saw scooped-out skulls, black maws where chests should have been.

257

Some survivors were crawling toward her, gasping. One woman seemed to be missing her bones, her body going gelatinous, the dirty blond knot of her hair slipping from the top of her head as all her flesh collapsed under its own weight.

As Sefia hesitated, a man divested of his skin, like a peeled plum, staggered into her from behind, pleading for help.

Sefia felt the man's hot weeping muscles press against her back.

"Please." The skinless man could barely form the word with his bleeding lips.

Sefia nodded. She sobbed as she lifted her fingers . . . and snapped the man's neck.

She hadn't wanted this. The Alliance soldiers were dying in agony. Hundreds of them. They'd been her enemy, but they hadn't deserved this.

Blinking, Sefia drew one of her knives and lifted her shaking hands. The blade floated out of her fingers, hovering, for a moment, in midair, the firelight dancing along the steel edge.

The ship was sinking, shifting and groaning beneath her feet as the water claimed it. She didn't have much time.

In the Illuminated world, she found every person that could not survive after what she'd done, every tortured, half-erased soldier left on the ship, saw their pain in hot sparks of light, like signal flares.

"I'm sorry," she whispered, and flicked her fingers, sending the knife flying across the ship. One by one, she found them all—the sobbing, the screaming, the unconscious—and one by one, she killed them.

Her blade tore through the air, striking skulls, slitting throats.

She teleported to the next ship and the next, her knife swift and merciless—or was it merciful?—punctuating the end of every life with a quick cut. Some, the ones who might still make it, she left alive, hoping they'd survive long enough for the rescue boats to reach them.

When it was done, everything was silent but for the snapping and biting of the flames, the sounds of the sea swallowing the corpses. The rescue boats, bearing lanterns and doctors, had almost reached her.

Shivering, she teleported back to the cliff.

To the west, the remainder of the Alliance invasion fleet was retreating. The Black Navy ships were in pursuit.

And there were new sails on the northern horizon. War drums and battle cries.

The outlaws had arrived—the *Current*, the *Brother*, and the *Crux* leading the charge. They sailed in among the Alliance warships like a wedge into wood, making the blue vessels splinter off as they tried to escape from Blackfire Bay.

But the cliff was bare. Archer was nowhere to be seen.

"Archer!" Her voice was thin, stretched taut as a wire.

There was the scrabbling sound of falling rock.

"Sefia?"

She raced to the edge of the cliff, where she found Archer climbing down the jagged stones, his face drawn with worry.

But when he saw her, the fear drained from his eyes. He scrambled up, ignoring the cuts the rocks left on his hands and arms, and caught her as she fell to her knees in the dirt.

"I was going after you," he said, folding her into his arms.

Of course he was. She should have known. She squeezed her eyes shut, curling her fingers in his shirt.

"I'm sorry it didn't work."

"It did work. It just didn't work all the way."

"What do you mean, it worked? Was excision supposed to look . . . like that?"

"No, it didn't work on them . . . but it worked on the other ships."

"What other ships?"

"The ones I erased." She pulled away from him, frowning. "How many ships do you think were out there in the first place?"

He looked confused. "Nineteen."

"No. There were twenty-four. Don't you remember?" When he shook his head, she continued, "Where did you think those extra thousand soldiers in the water came from?"

"I don't know. I—" Archer passed a hand over his face, as if that would return the missing ships to his memory. "You really did it?"

Sefia swallowed. She had really done it. She'd rewritten the world. She'd changed the future. But there'd been a cost. One she would never pay again.

End of the Rope

With the knowledge that her illness was transmitted through the air she breathed, carried in the fine particles of blood she coughed out of her lungs, Mareah decided to turn her copper sword, which absorbed blood on contact, into three masks. The same blade she'd used to execute her parents would, she hoped, protect Lon and Sefia from contracting the same illness that was killing her.

So she unspooled the embossed leather of the grip, broke the wooden handle, and asked Nin to remake the steel into fine-gauge wire.

She cried as she wove the metal thread into a flexible mesh, her tears making her fingers so slippery she pricked herself again and again, her blood soaked up by the thin filaments that were all that remained of the weapon that had been at her side for decades. When she was done, she padded the masks with cotton and slipped one over her head.

Meanwhile, Lon did what he could to ease Mareah's symptoms and prolong her life.

In the mornings, while Nin watched Sefia in the

village below, Lon took to the kitchen, where he brewed draughts and potions, sparkling with magic. Wearing his mask, he'd bring them into the bedroom where Mareah lay, and she would drink them all down, grimacing at the taste, at the burn in her throat.

"I should have been an Administrator," he said. "Why was I studying books when I could've been studying the human body? What good are *books* when you can't save the ones you love?"

Mareah replaced her mask and squeezed his hand. "I believe in you." The corners of her eyes crinkled as she smiled a smile he couldn't see.

He continued to study the power of the Scribes, slowly mastering the magic required to erase Mareah's illness and rewrite her future.

Until one day, he learned that it would not be possible.

The Illuminated world was woven of filaments of shared history, individual threads—people, clouds, the turning of the seasons, tender green shoots, blistering changes deep in the earth, every creature, every pebble—all converging and diverging in an infinite web, a labyrinth, a sprawling story of the world.

Some of these strands were so important, so intertwined with other objects, other lives, other stories, that in the Illuminated world they blazed like fire, forming strong, bright connections that could not be severed without ripping away parts of everything they were connected to.

That was how it was with Mareah's illness. Lon couldn't remove the sickness from her lungs without shredding the rest of her body. And maybe his and Sefia's as well.

You see, excision was the simplest of the Scribes' powers, but it was also the cruelest. It was a hacksaw. It was a seam ripper. It could gouge out parts of the Illuminated world, but it could not heal the wounds it caused.

To do that, to fill in the cavities you'd left, to sew up the rifts you'd made, to stitch the raw edges of the world back together, you had to use the second half of the Scribes' powers—addition.

Addition allowed you to make adjustments to the Illuminated world. It allowed you to create, to build, to make the world anew. And, most relevant to Lon, it allowed you to excise even the brightest pieces of the Illuminated world without causing irreparable damage to the delicate fabric that surrounded it.

But when he turned to the Book to study the remainder of the Scribes' power, he found the pages missing. Every scrap.

Someone had taken them.

Through careful research, he learned that one of the Librarians had begun removing traces of the Scribes from the Book, starting with the highest tiers of their power, their best-guarded secrets, and placing them within a sealed chest inside the Library vault.

All those years with access to the greatest power in Kelanna, and Lon hadn't known.

The old Librarian had died before she could finish her task, but the damage to the Book had been done, the pages Lon needed now locked in the lair of his enemy.

The vault was a beautiful, complicated piece of work. Set deep into the unblemished stone of the mountain, its single five-spoke wheel was flanked by two keyholes. Lon remembered studying them with fascination when he was an Apprentice. The one on the left resembled a compass rose, embellished with a rising sun, a waxing moon, and fanciful images of flying creatures—an owl, a bat, a hawk, a lark—carved mid-flight around the edges. The one on the right was encircled by an engraving of a mythical thunderbird, its beak open, its wings spread, with lightning clutched in its talons. To open the door, you needed both keys and a complex sequence of twists and turns that only Librarians and Directors knew.

"We have the Librarian's key," Lon said. Nin had made them a copy eleven years ago, back when they thought they could steal the Book and escape the Guard without bloodshed, but their plans had changed at the last minute, and they'd never gotten the chance to use their copy. Since then, Lon had attached the key to a simple gold chain, which he twirled on his finger as he paced the bedroom, making the intricate bits and wards wink in the light from the window.

It was spring, and he'd filled the room with dozens of flowers—in vases by the bedside, on the dresser, on the sill—perfuming the room with the smells of the garden Mareah loved so much: earth, sprouts, sap, blooms.

In the bed, Mareah coughed. "We know the sequence. I couldn't forget it if I tried."

But to get the pages, they needed the second key.

And that key hung around the neck of the Director.

With a sigh, Lon caught the key in his fist. "We barely got out alive the first time." When they'd both been healthy.

And they hadn't had a little girl to protect.

Lon climbed onto the bed beside Mareah. She was getting so thin. Through his mask, he put his lips to her hair. "I'm sorry," he whispered.

When she spoke, her voice was muffled by her own mask: "It's okay," she said. "It was a lot to hope. After all, we already knew: *What is written comes to pass.*"

So he put the key in the back of the closet where they kept their coins and jewelry. And for the first time in his life, he gave up.

CHAPTER 22

Her Father's Daughter

Honoring the Rokuine victory over the Alliance in what the newsmen were calling the Battle of Blackfire Bay, the castle at Braska was hosting a celebratory feast. All day long, the castle staff had been busy making up the cavernous dining hall while the cooks prepared heaping platters of food for the outlaws, the bloodletters, and the officers of the Black Navy.

The *Black Beauty* and the candidates had escaped, along with ten other Alliance ships, but the rest of the nineteen—no, the *twenty-four*—had either been sunk or captured. All day, the Black Navy had been busy taking possession of the remaining Alliance vessels and their crews, while volunteers dredged the water for bodies and debris.

Curled on her side in her bed, Sefia had watched them—the black ships escorting the blue ones into the harbor, the prisoners disembarking, the outlaws and bloodletters being welcomed into the capital like heroes. She'd turned over. She'd slept.

If she'd had her way, she wouldn't have attended the feast either, but Sovereign Ianai had insisted. So she bathed in the volcanically heated pool adjoining her room. She may have slept again.

Archer was in and out. Sometimes he was lying beside her, his body curved around hers. Sometimes he was bringing her tea or plates of food she barely touched.

At some point, she donned the clothing that had appeared on the chair by the window: the silk blouse, the black corset and matching trousers with gold embellishments, the green velvet jacket. Once, Sefia looked up, into the mirror, and saw Frey standing behind her, gently combing the tangles out of her wet hair. The girl was dazzling in a floor-length cerulean gown that seemed to move about her ankles like water, the diamond bangle from the Trove sparkling at her wrist. She caught Sefia's eye in the mirror and smiled sadly. When Sefia looked again, Frey was gone.

Sefia stared at her reflection. These were the finest clothes she'd ever worn, but she hardly noticed the fine cloth, the dusting of gold Frey had left on her eyelids, or the ribbons Frey had woven into her hair. What she saw in the mirror were the dead arrayed behind her like an army: mutilated faces, missing jaws and noses and the caps of their skulls, the faces of people she'd flayed and tortured in dozens of unimaginable ways.

The daughter of an assassin and the most powerful sorcerer the world had seen in years, and she'd grow up to surpass them both in greatness.

But there'd be a cost.

There's always a cost.

She'd massacred over a hundred people in a single night. She must have taken more lives than even Archer now.

Had the Book wanted her to do this? Was it fate?

She would never attempt excision like that again. She looked down at her hands, the black-and-silver ring that had been her mother's glinting on one of her murderous fingers.

Never again.

"Sefia?"

She turned to find Archer standing there, awkwardly tugging at his cuffs, and for a moment, even through the haze of her guilt, she was struck by how well his tailored jacket fit every plane of his shoulders, how the gold piping of his suit accented the color of his eyes.

"Are you ready?" he asked.

She shook her head, and he crossed to her, taking her hands.

"We don't have to go," he said.

She looked up at him through her lashes. "You think the sovereign would be okay with that?"

He chuckled. "They'd probably send an armed guard to haul us down there."

"Yeah." In all her interactions with Ianai Blackfire Raganet, it had become clear that when the sovereign demanded your presence, you appeared, whether you wanted to or not. Sefia took Archer's arm with a sigh. "Let's get this over with."

O verhead, candles flared in the dining hall chandeliers, casting dancing waves of light over grand tables of Oxscinian hardwood piled high with food and drink.

Before they ate, Sovereign Ianai, crowned with a simple

circlet of diamonds, presented Sefia with a medal for her service to the kingdom. On one side, it was engraved with the Rokuine crest; on the other, a dragon, the sigil of the Raganet family.

Sefia bowed.

Everyone in the room applauded.

She didn't think most of them knew about the five ships she'd fully excised, but she wondered how many of them knew what had happened to the people who'd been half-erased by her magic. Some of them must have questioned the skinless, dismembered corpses they'd plucked out of the water. She wondered if they'd still be applauding if they knew the whole truth.

"You may not believe it," Ianai said as they put the medal around her neck, "but you did something incredible yesterday."

Sefia swallowed. "Do you know everything that I did?"

The sovereign nodded, and their hard black eyes softened slightly. "Archer told me."

"It doesn't feel incredible."

"Taking that many lives never should." They put their long, graceful hand on her shoulder in an unexpected display of compassion. "But you saved lives too—the lives of my people—and I'll be forever grateful for that."

With another bow, Sefia returned to her place, and the feast began. At the other tables, Aljan couldn't stop gazing at Frey long enough to eat, but Griegi picked apart every dish, pausing only to scribble notes in his recipe book or exclaim over choice morsels, which he offered to Keon at the end of his fork. Blinking in wonder at all the grand trappings of the castle hall, old Goro kept smoothing down his stubborn gray hair only to have it stick back up again moments later. At the head table, Reed was seated next to Sefia. He'd washed up, but he must not have had any finery to wear, because he was dressed in an outfit she'd seen him wear on the *Current* many times before. Compared to Dimarion, who sat across from them, decked out in silks and jewels, Captain Reed appeared a little grubby, though he didn't seem to care.

"Archer says you did it," he said, tapping each gold piece of cutlery before straightening one of his forks. "You magicked away five whole ships?"

She nodded.

"Five whole ships," he repeated, shaking his head. "And no one remembers they were even there in the first place?"

"Only me."

At the sound of her voice, his eyes softened with pity. "He also said you made mistakes."

Sudden tears flooded her vision. She nodded again.

"I'm sorry, kid."

A platter came by. She tried not to gag at the smell of charred meat.

Under the table, Archer squeezed her hand. "You're not back there anymore," he whispered. "You're safe."

Wiping her eyes, she squeezed back. "I don't know how to live with this. All those people . . ."

Reed looked from her to Archer and back. "I think it's a balance: forgive yourself so you don't get eaten alive by guilt, but never forget, unless you want to make the same mistakes again."

"I won't. Never again."

He took her chin between his callused fingers. "Listen, Sef. You messed up this time. But you still saved a kingdom. You still did some good, and you're still a force to be reckoned with." He kissed her on the forehead. "Don't give up on yourself."

As the feast continued around her, Sefia picked at her plate. She'd failed to save the dead she still saw when she closed her eyes. She'd failed to stop her own future from coming to pass. But she *had* succeeded in changing the future. She'd rewritten the world, excised five Alliance warships, so in everyone's memory but hers, the Alliance had sent an invasion fleet of nineteen instead of twenty-four. Not even the hundreds of sailors pulled out of Blackfire Bay knew how they'd gotten there.

Maybe the Book had tricked her into fulfilling part of her destiny, but she had changed something. Five ships might not have been enough to rewrite the future entirely, but it was something. She wasn't at the end of her rope yet. She could still fight.

Captain Reed was right. She couldn't give up. If she gave up, fate would claim her. And Archer.

She would have to try again, but not until she had the full power of the Scribes in her hands.

Her father hadn't had the resources to acquire the pages in the vault, but Sefia did. She could do what Lon hadn't been able to. Thanks to Mareah, who'd taught her the alphabet and sung her secret songs, she already had one of the tools she needed.

She'd recognized it the second she saw her father describe the vault's two keyholes, inscribed with birds and bats. To open the door, he'd said, you needed both keys and a complex

sequence of twists and turns that only Librarians and Directors knew.

Well, Sefia thought, *only Librarians, Directors, and my mother.*

The song Mareah had sung, night after night, had given Sefia
the series of rotations she needed to break into the vault.

Little hawk, little hawk, don't fly away.

Turn the left key to the engraving of the hawk.

For you're a mighty huntress with claws to catch your prey.

Turn the right key to the thunderbird's talons.

Sefia knew her father had discovered the alphabet blocks
Mareah had been using to teach her to read, but she wondered
if he'd known Mareah was also teaching her how to steal the
Guard's best-kept secrets when Mareah was too ill to do it
herself.

With the sequence already memorized, now Sefia only
needed the keys. A copy of the Librarian's key must be in the
house on the hill overlooking the sea, in the closet her father
had veiled with magic.

The Director's key, however, must be on King Darion
Stonegold, sailing aboard the *Barbaro* at the front of the war
in Oxscini's Bay of Batteram.

The key. The Director.

If she did this right, she could capture the single most important figure in the Red War and gain access to the second
half of the Scribes' powers in one fell swoop. Being a Politician,
Stonegold lacked the skill to teleport from a prison cell. She
could strip him of his magic after she'd stolen the pages from
the vault and mastered Alteration.

And in the meantime, the Alliance would be without a

leader. It would take time for even the Guard to recover from that. Time for Sefia to find, capture, and excise the powers from all the remaining Guardians.

The Alliance would disband. The Red War would grind to a halt.

And without a war to win, Archer would live.

She explained her plan to him the next morning, as the city was waking from its revelry. Below their window, people were staggering home along the steep streets, shuffling through used firecrackers and crumpled paper streamers.

"I've already done what I was supposed to do, though. I fulfilled my destiny. I killed"—Sefia swallowed—"all those people. There's only one thing I have to avoid now."

She'd already lost her parents. She had to make sure she didn't lose her friends, her allies, or the boy she loved.

Archer crossed his arms. "The legend also says you'll turn the tide of the war. You haven't done that."

"I changed the outcome of the Battle of Blackfire Bay." She shrugged into a coat. "Doesn't that count?"

"If it counts, then you only did what you were destined to do from the beginning." He sighed. "And if you excised those ships only because you were *supposed* to, then you didn't change anything at all. You can't have it both ways."

Sefia sat on the edge of the bed. He was right.

If excising the Alliance ships and changing the outcome of the battle was the event to which the legends referred, turning the tide in the deadliest war Kelanna had ever seen, then she'd done nothing but make her future come to pass.

But if that part of the legend was still to come, then she

could still change it. If that part of the legend still lay ahead of her, then so did hope . . . and danger.

And she would need the full power of the Scribes to overcome it.

"Did you see twenty-four ships out there?" she asked.

"No. Only sixteen and the three of them you . . ." His voice trailed off.

"Destroyed," she finished for him. Closing her eyes, she saw her victims—disfigured and dismembered, dying on the crumbling decks—and she vowed again that she wouldn't attempt excision until she'd mastered the entirety of Alteration.

"I fulfilled that part of my destiny because I only had half of the Scribes' power," she said, "but I still altered the future. If I learn the rest of Alteration, I think I can change both our fates . . . without casualties."

Archer was silent, running his thumb along the worry stone.

She held out her hand to him. "Are you with me?"

In answer, he put his arms around her waist. "Always."

She blinked and, with a wave of her arms, teleported them to the house on the hill overlooking the sea.

Snow covered the cliff, the steps. As Sefia opened the broken door, she saw drifts of it accumulating beneath the broken windows, powdering the decaying draperies and shards of pottery that littered the floor.

As Archer stood in the center of the room, turning slowly, Sefia made her way to the hidden closet, where she pulled open the door and dropped to her knees, pawing through the gold ingots, the scattered coins, the packets of seeds.

She found the key wedged between the floor and the baseboard near the back of the closet. Carefully, she rubbed her thumb over its surface, blowing on it to dislodge the years of dust and grime.

It was exquisite. Its bow had been formed in the shape of a thunderbird with rubies for eyes, and engravings of feathers cascaded down its shaft to the pin.

Nin had made this from a casting of Erastis's key.

Sefia had known Nin was a skilled locksmith, but she hadn't known Nin was an artist, with an unerring eye for beauty.

Slipping its chain over her head, Sefia could feel the key pressed against her chest, over her heart, and she wondered if the original was half as beautiful.

"Did you find it?" Archer called from behind her.

Sefia nodded. Sitting back on her heels, she accidentally set off a small landslide of seed packages—castor beans, crab's eyes, corn cockles, larkspur, moonflower, wolfsbane—and she paused for a second before pocketing a packet of strychnine seeds. If she was fighting the Guard, it could come in handy.

"This was your home," Archer said as she emerged from the closet.

She nodded again.

"It must have been nice."

"It was. Once."

They wandered through the house, Sefia pointing out the chair where Lon used to tell stories by the fire; the kitchen, where her mother had butchered chickens and filleted fish with sure, quick strokes of her knives; the basement bedroom, where Archer picked up a moldering toy in the shape of a crocodile.

At last, they ended up in the garden, blanketed with snow.

"If I can pull this off, we'll both be free," Sefia said, her breath smoking in the cold air. "But it feels like we've still got a long way to go."

"Steal the Director's key. Break into the Library. Learn a power no one's used for thousands of years." Archer listed the tasks on his fingers. "What could go wrong?"

She gave him a halfhearted smile, and he hugged her quickly to his side.

"I'll be with you," he said.

"It'll mean fighting again. Maybe killing." Her stomach churned at the thought. They'd both caused so much bloodshed.

"I won't do it, Sefia. Not unless I have to." His voice was heavy.

"I hope you won't have to." If all went according to plan, they'd beat fate without taking another life.

But fate, of course, had plans of its own. When they teleported back to the castle at Braska, Frey was waiting for them, still wearing her dress from the night before.

"Where have you been?" she demanded. "Everyone's been looking for you."

"What's wrong?" Sefia asked, glancing out the window. But there were no enemy ships in Blackfire Bay. The city appeared safe.

"A messenger ship arrived this morning," Frey said. "The Alliance has taken the Bay of Batteram. The Oxscinian capital is under siege."

CHAPTER 23

Strange, Beautiful, and Deadly

C annek Reed awoke to the sound of the water whispering, *Soon, soon, soon.*

He staggered from his quarters, pulling on his coat. In the frosty predawn, Horse and Doc were the only other two people above deck, sitting beneath a blanket in the crow's nest, watching the constellations disappear. Smoke curled from the galley stovepipes, smelling of cinnamon bread. The rest of the *Current* seemed to be asleep—the crew dreaming in their bunks, the timbers creaking and groaning like the breathing of some enormous slumbering beast. From above, Doc and Horse looked down at him, and the carpenter smiled one of his broad, encouraging grins, the kind that could light up the darkest of hearts. Tipping his hat to them, Reed gave the rail a quick pat and strode down the gangway.

As he reached the dock, he saw that the waves lapping at the hull were full of stars. *Soon, soon, soon.*

The outlaws and Ianai's war council had spent the previous day arguing. Would the remainder of the Black Navy sail to Oxscini to save their Rokuine brethren, trapped in Tsumasai Bay? Would the outlaws again risk their ships for the sake of a kingdom they had no stake in?

According to the messenger, King Darion Stonegold and his two generals, Braca Terezina III and Serakeen, had a fleet of over two hundred. Even if every outlaw vessel agreed to sail to Oxscini's aid, they'd still be outnumbered, fifteen to one.

What could they hope to achieve?

Reed's footsteps echoed on the wooden planks as he passed the *Crux* and the *One Bad Eye*, inhaling Braska's characteristic smells of sea, sage, and sulfur. Beneath his feet, the water still called to him. *Soon, soon, soon.*

At the other end of the harbor, where the civilian vessels were moored, he rented a skiff from a fisherman and set off across the still waters of Blackfire Bay.

Soon, the ocean murmured.

Nearly six years ago, it had promised him he'd die at sea. He'd get one last kiss from the lonely salt breeze. The Executioner would be in his hand. He'd see a white dandelion hovering above the decks.

Would it happen in Oxscini, if he took the *Current* into battle there? Even if it wasn't the season for dandelions?

Then the explosion?

The end of him? The end of his ship?

If it was going to happen in Oxscini, could he ask his crew to go?

Reed turned the skiff south, around the jagged shores of

Roku's largest island, leaving behind the smoke-smudged districts of the capital. Above him, the cliffs rose black and sharp.

Look to the horizon, he told himself. *That's where the adventures are.* If it was going to happen soon, he was going to see something he hadn't seen before.

Leaning over the side of the skiff, he touched the sea. It nuzzled his palm, cold and familiar.

"Bring me an adventure," he murmured.

And the water complied.

It brought him past the coastal mountains, so tall their heads were lost in the clouds, past the waterfalls diving headfirst into the ocean, past spikes of black stone jutting from the seafloor, until he reached the south side of one of Roku's most active volcanoes. Unlike the majestic cones you could see from the north side of the island, it was little more than a hill at this distance, scooped out on one side, with a coursing river of molten rock carving channels along a sprawling black plain, all the way to the sea. Along the coast, streams of fire seeped from the shore, dripping red-hot into the surf, where the breakers hissed and spat, exhaling clouds of steam.

Reed sat back in the skiff, lacing his hands behind his head. "Not bad," he said. "Not great, but not bad."

He watched gas pockets in the molten rock ignite as they spilled into the water, flaming brilliantly before being extinguished in the sea.

How many losses had the Oxscinian Royal Navy sustained trying to defend the Bay of Batteram? If they had enough ships, they might still be evenly matched against the Alliance . . . and sixteen outlaw ships might be enough to tip the scales.

Or they might all be gunned down before they reached Kelebrandt.

The capital was on the north side of Tsumasai Bay, which had four points of entry. The west entrance was so shallow, Stonegold's warships couldn't hope to make it through. The two east entrances were the widest and most difficult to defend; the Alliance would be concentrating their forces there.

The south entrance, though . . . it was the narrowest and farthest from Kelebrandt. A dozen ships were all that was needed to defend it from either side. More than twenty would be a waste.

If the outlaws attacked the Alliance forces at the south entrance, they could break the siege. The Oxscinians could circle back on the bulk of the Alliance fleet and attack on two fronts.

And sixteen outlaw ships would have made all the difference in the war.

But what would it cost?

Soon, the water murmured.

"Can you be a little more specific?" Reed drawled.

The water was silent.

Sighing, he touched the outline of the Resurrection Amulet between his shirt and his tattooed chest. There was a chance it would work without its missing piece, but he knew it wasn't likely. Without the last piece, it was just a hunk of treasure like any other. It couldn't save him.

He could go after the piece. He could leave now, for the Citadel of Historians in Corabel, in search of the Amulet's folklore, and hope to elude the Alliance patrols, somehow.

But could he leave Oxscini to fall? Could he leave his fellow outlaws, if they decided to go?

As he watched the burning shore, he saw something stir on the black cliffs—something *big*, and *fast*, with a dark, rough hide that camouflaged it among the rocks—crawling down the jagged stone and slipping into the water without so much as a splash.

What was it?

For a moment, he barely breathed.

Then a large, diamond-shaped head arose from the waves. Red lava dripped onto its forehead, hissing, and pearled off its scaled snout, dropping into the sea.

A dragon.

A real dragon. Reed had thought Dimarion killed the last of them.

Slowly, the creature swam toward him, its long body undulating through the waves like that of a crocodile. Its back and tail were armored in thick plates. It could snap the skiff in half like a twig. It could take one of his arms in a single bite.

But he was Captain Cannek Reed.

He lived for things like this.

He scrambled to the prow of the boat, leaning out over the water as the dragon approached. It paused a few feet from the skiff, peering up at him through slitted yellow eyes.

"I ain't gonna hurt you," Reed murmured.

In answer, the dragon let out a sound somewhere between a purr and a growl. Bubbles escaped from between its teeth. It rose from the waves—the wide, viper-like head, the elegant neck, the taloned forepaws flexing just beneath the surface. It smelled like the sea. It smelled like iron and earth. It seemed to study him for a moment, its head swaying from side to side.

Cautiously, Reed lifted his hand.

Hot breath, smelling of fish, wafted over him. It was like lifting the lid on a stew pot and being blasted with steam.

He waited.

Then the dragon pressed its nose to his palm. Its scales were almost too warm to touch, but he didn't draw back. From deep in its throat came that soft rumbling again, like the distant churning of rock.

After a moment, the creature slunk beneath the waves again, flicking its tail, and dove under the skiff on its way out to sea.

Reed watched it until he could no longer see its dark shape beneath the surface. Then he hoisted the sail.

The old ways weren't dead. The outlaws were still here, and there were still adventures to be found, uncharted waters to sail, strange and beautiful and deadly things to experience in this wonderful and terrible world.

If he was to have only one more story to add to his collection before he left the world, what did he want it to be? Did he want it to be in pursuit of something he might never find, gunned down on an ordinary day by an Alliance patrol somewhere off the coast of Deliene? Or did he want it to be fighting for the old ways, the wild ways, the ways of the free?

Because if Oxscini fell to the Alliance, it wouldn't be long before the rest of Kelanna did too . . . and the outlaws with it.

Would they tell stories of his last battle at the entrance to

Tsumasai Bay—an outlaw, a siege breaker, a hero, chasing impossible odds?

There were worse ways to die. Worse things to be remembered for.

Captain Cannek Reed was going to war.

CHAPTER 24

Traps Within Traps

On the night he returned from the far side of the island, Captain Reed outlined his plan to break the Alliance's siege at the southern entrance to Tsumasai Bay, giving the Royal Navy the chance to mount a two-pronged attack on their enemies.

He seemed so confident, in that bold, no-nonsense way of his, that the other captains quickly threw in their lot with him. As did the bloodletters. The *Black Beauty* and the candidates were still out there, and though they hadn't fought during the Battle of Blackfire Bay, the bloodletters' desire to stop them hadn't lessened.

They were taking their cue from Chief Kemura and the Gormani clans. They were forming the Resistance.

For days, while the outlaws prepared to go to war, Sefia and Archer argued over whether to use the Book to locate Stonegold.

They had agreed to capturing him and taking his vault key so Sefia could master the last of the Scribes' powers, but they could not seem to agree on *how*.

"The Book almost got Aljan killed because it didn't tell you about the nightmaker," Archer said.

"It got me to the bloodletters too," she replied, packing white paste made from strychnine seeds into the hidden compartment of her mother's ring. She didn't want to have to use it, but if she won this argument with Archer, she'd be facing the Book, and she wanted to be prepared for anything that might lay in store for them. "And it got us to Braska."

Archer ran his fingers through his hair. "But look what happened in Braska."

She closed the lid on the compartment, where the tiny spring-loaded blade would rest until she needed it, though she hoped she wouldn't need it. "You don't have to remind me," she said.

"Then why are you so eager to use the Book when we could just wait until we get to Oxscini and find the Director the old-fashioned way?"

"Because we're running out of time to stop the Guard before Oxscini falls. The Alliance could break through to the capital any day now."

Archer was silent, and Sefia knew she'd made a point he couldn't refute.

But he was right. The Book surely had traps in store for them. They might be able to evade some, but destiny always caught them, one way or another. Would getting Stonegold and the key be worth the consequences they couldn't foresee?

The key could end the war. The key could save Archer. Anything was worth that.

It wasn't until evening, as the outlaws and the bloodletters loaded their ships with the last of their provisions, that Archer spoke again.

"Okay," he told her. "Let's act now, before the Alliance grows any stronger. If we take Stonegold from them, they'll be leaderless. They might even be weak enough that the Royal Navy will be able to defeat them on their own."

Sefia nodded. "And the war might end."

Sighing, he took her hands. "Be careful. The Book will want to manipulate us into doing what it wants."

But using it could save thousands of people from battle. So she opened it. At that very moment, the Director was on the deck of the *Barbaro*, surrounded by Alliance soldiers, with General Terezina at his side.

She and Archer exchanged glances. They were good, but they didn't want to try fighting the Guard's Master Soldier. They needed to catch Stonegold when he was unguarded, for he was a Politician, less skilled in Illumination than other Guardians, and alone, he'd be no match against them.

They waited. They set sail for Oxscini aboard the *Brother*. When Sefia opened the Book next, it was nearing midnight, and King Darion Stonegold was in the *Barbaro*'s great cabin, alone.

She slid her knives into her belt. *Capture the Director,* she thought. *Take his key. Steal the pages from the Library vault.* She buckled her cuff of sleeping darts to her wrist.

Archer sharpened his sword and loaded Lightning with bullets.

End the war.

Archer lives.

Together, they teleported into danger.

The great cabin on the *Barbaro* was great indeed. Decked out in rugs of blue-and-gold silk, with wall-to-wall stained glass windows at the stern, it was brimming with portraits of lords and ladies, bronze busts on marble pedestals, sofas upholstered in the finest brocade. Porcelain urns flanked a siege door affixed with a hinged plank that would swing down, locking into a set of brackets to barricade the cabin in the event of an attack.

Dominating the center of the room was an enormous oak desk and, behind it, an equally enormous man. He had thinning blond hair, shrewd eyes, and wore a blue uniform adorned with medals and ribbons from his years fighting in Everica.

King Darion Stonegold, Director of the Guard and Leader of the Alliance.

"My traitor Apprentice is adjusting well to the drug," he was saying in an indolent tenor. "Ah . . . We've been expecting you."

Beside Sefia, Archer drew his sword.

Seated in a chair on the near side of the desk was a thin man in black with wrinkles and sun-spotted cheeks. He rose as Stonegold's voice trailed off, his eyes never leaving Sefia. "So this is my Apprentice's daughter," he said.

She knew that voice—dry, brittle, cold. She'd heard it only once before, the day Nin was taken. Cowering in the undergrowth, she hadn't seen his face, but she'd heard him. She'd *smelled* him, as she smelled him now, the scent of metal wafting from the scabbard that hung at his side.

The First. The Guard's Master Assassin. The man who'd taught her mother to kill. He wasn't supposed to be here. The Director was supposed to be alone.

The Book had tricked her again.

"How—" Her own voice sounded small, weak.

"You may have the Book," said Stonegold. "But we have the Librarian and, at his fingertips, the Library. He warned us of your murderous intent."

The Book hadn't warned her about the First, but Erastis had warned the Director of the attack. Did he know about the key too? Could she and Archer still get it? Catching his eye, she gestured to her neck. He nodded.

Everyone acted at once.

Archer leapt over one of the couches as the First kicked his chair aside. There was a flash of copper as the bloodsword emerged from its sheath.

Lifting her hands, Sefia barricaded the door. The reinforced plank slammed into its bracket just as the Alliance guards tried to burst in from outside.

Clang, clang. Across the cabin, Archer and the Assassin fought, their swords shearing off each other, their feet quick on the carpet.

Drawing a gold revolver from a side holster, Stonegold shot at her. With a flick of her wrist, Sefia sent the bullet spinning back at him. Not to kill him. She only wanted to slow him long enough for her to steal the key.

But before the bullet reached him, the threads of the Illuminated world warped. The bullet struck the wall to her right, splintering a portrait frame.

Out of the corner of her eye, Sefia saw the First's fingers come down. He was protecting his Director and fighting Archer at the same time. Stabbing, dodging, parrying, they were like dancers. A beautiful, complicated whirlwind of metal and blood.

Archer jumped back as the edge of the blade slit his trouser leg.

The Master Assassin was old, but he was fast. He might have even been faster than Archer.

Sefia hoped not.

She threw out her palms, shoving the heavy oak desk into Stonegold's stomach. A *whuff* of air went out of him as the massive piece of furniture scraped along the wooden floor, pinning him to the stained glass windows.

He grunted, fumbling for his second sidearm, as she grabbed at the air, trying to lift his necklace from inside the collar of his blue uniform.

But the First pushed the desk back at her, hurling it across the floor so fast she had to dive aside to avoid being crushed.

It slammed into the barred door behind her and she rolled to her feet as the Director drew his second revolver and began to fire. Bullets whizzed through the air as Sefia deflected them into the ceiling, the walls, the sofas and portraits and ornamental vases.

But she couldn't stop them all.

One caught her in the hand, ripping through the muscle of her palm.

She didn't even feel the pain at first. She narrowed her eyes, flinging Stonegold sideways into the wall. He fell to the floor like a sack of bricks.

Sefia started forward, flexing her hand as blood dripped down her wrist and arm. At least her fingers still worked.

But before she could reach Stonegold's unconscious form, a bronze bust flew past her, smashing into the wall at her right.

She turned in time to see Archer slice the First across the arm. She smiled. Archer was the best fighter she'd ever seen. He was fast and strong, and he could read a fight the same way she could read a paragraph.

But her smile faded from her lips as the Assassin parried his next slash and struck him in the face with the hilt of his bloodsword.

Archer staggered back, shaking his head. His eyes couldn't seem to focus.

Quick—too quick for Sefia to stop it—the Master Assassin pivoted, cutting Archer across the thigh. Raising his free hand, the First used Illumination to knock Archer off his feet.

Archer landed flat on his back, with the Assassin standing over him, blade raised to strike.

• • •

*N*ick his shins. *Get to your feet.* Somewhere in the back of his clouded mind, Archer knew how to stop the First from killing him. But he couldn't make his body obey.

Use your blade. It's still in your hand.

His fingers tightened on the grip of his sword as the First moved to attack.

But before either of them could strike, Archer was sliding across the floor, out of the First's reach.

Sefia.

Archer rolled onto his side in time to see the Assassin pull down the splintered portrait hanging above her. She sidestepped—right into the path of the bust the First hurled at her. It smashed into her thigh, making her fall to her knees.

Archer scrambled up as the Master Assassin advanced on her.

She pulled a couch between them.

He shoved it aside.

Archer drew Lightning from its holster. A quick shot to each leg, and he could stop the First right now. They just had to slow the Assassin long enough to get the key and get out of there.

Throwing out her hands, Sefia yanked the blue-and-gold rug out from under the First.

He jumped.

Archer fired.

With a flick of his fingers, the Master Assassin sent the bullet speeding toward Sefia, who barely managed to duck in time.

Archer was already running across the cabin when he saw the gunshot hit the wall behind Sefia's head.

He holstered his gun. *It'll be blades and fists, then.* Leaping into the air, he grabbed the hilt of his weapon with both hands and slashed downward.

The First countered, their blades meeting with such force that Archer was knocked back.

The Assassin was fast. Archer had never met anyone so fast. Both he and Sefia were injured, bruised and bleeding, but the First was as composed as he'd been when they entered.

The Master Assassin launched the broken side table at Sefia, who rolled out of the way.

Could they beat him?

Archer's gaze met Sefia's as she got to her feet.

She nodded.

They had to try. If they didn't, they might never get the key.

Archer slashed at the First, who parried and countered, cutting sideways. Ducking, Archer felt the bloodsword miss him by a hair. But the Assassin's face was exposed. Archer launched himself upward, striking the man in the jaw with his fist.

He felt the flesh crumple. He felt something crack.

Finally.

Wiping blood from his lip, the Master Assassin gave Archer an approving nod.

Then all three of them were at it again: Archer swinging, lunging, stabbing; Sefia pulling, wrenching; the First evading every attack, parrying every blow.

He broke Sefia's ribs.

He cut Archer in the side of the chest.

Crack, crack, crack. Their blades met again and again, and no matter how quick Archer was, no matter what Sefia threw across the room, the Master Assassin continued to outdo them, blocking and attacking, deflecting and feinting, until at last Archer ducked a slash, trying to strike upward the way he'd done before, and caught a knee in the face. He stumbled, lights popping in his vision as he saw the Assassin fling Sefia into the wall.

No.

Archer was a cage fighter whose skill in combat had made him a legend. Sefia was a sorcerer who'd massacred over a hundred people in a single night. But against the Master Assassin, they were outmatched.

And the longer they stayed, the more likely they were to be killed.

"Sefia, can you get to me?" Archer called as she got to her feet, holding her head with her bleeding hand.

She looked grim, but she nodded. "I can try."

The First said nothing—he merely reached for his empty scabbard.

Archer's eyes narrowed. *Was* it empty? The Assassin made a motion as if he were drawing a weapon, but Archer couldn't see anything in the man's closed hand.

His thoughts spun. The Assassins could make gloves that tripled the strength of a blow. They could make swords that drank blood. Could they make a blade disappear?

The First attacked, the bloodsword carving copper arcs through the air. Archer blocked the first strike, but something else, something invisible, cut him across the chest.

He stepped back, bleeding. "Sefia, can you see a second weapon?"

"Yes!" She raced past Stonegold's unconscious form, along the stained glass windows.

The Assassin pivoted, keeping his body between Sefia and Archer.

Archer's gaze skipped from one of the First's hands to the other. "Is it shorter or longer than the bloodsword?"

"Shorter. The length of his arm."

That would mean the point of the invisible blade was a little over two feet from the Master Assassin's closed fist.

Archer swung as Sefia reached out with her magic.

Ducking her grip, the First blocked Archer's attack and cut him across the leg with the invisible weapon.

Archer stumbled back, hissing.

Reaching their side of the cabin, Sefia flung a throwing knife. Whirling the bloodsword, the Assassin deflected it easily.

But Archer took advantage of the distraction. His sword cut through the air, striking the invisible blade. *There you are.* But when he swung again, he hit nothing but air.

The First countered, slicing Archer across the shoulder, but he was forced back as Sefia dragged a couch between them.

Now was their chance to escape.

Archer dashed for her. They'd almost made it to each other when the Assassin leapt over the sofa, his blades slicing through the air, driving them apart again.

Archer jumped back, but Sefia wasn't quick enough. The bloodsword cut her.

Once in the shoulder.

Once across the face.

She cried out, clutching her right eye. Blood ran between her fingers as she fell back.

Archer ran at the First, swinging. His sword sheared off the invisible blade. A slash, a cut, a step, and he was close enough to punch the man in the side.

The air went out of him, but the Master Assassin still spun the bloodsword, trying to stab Archer through the stomach. Archer twisted aside just in time and brought the hilt of his weapon crashing into the Assassin's face.

Archer slashed again.

But the First was too fast. His invisible weapon came up, flicking Archer's sword aside. He lost his grip on the weapon. It clattered to the floor.

Archer's front was unprotected.

The bloodsword was arcing through the air.

Pain seared through him as the blade sliced him deep across the chest. He fell backward into the couch as the First came at him again.

• • •

Through her bloodied vision, Sefia saw Archer's weapon fall. She saw the bloodsword carve him open. She saw the invisible sword, glittering in the Illuminated world, raised to deliver the killing blow.

And she couldn't let that happen.

She hadn't teleported before now out of fear that she'd leave Archer exposed. But Archer was already exposed.

Was she fast enough?

She had to be.

She pressed the latch on her silver ring and teleported.

She appeared in a crouch at the First's feet. As she expected, the Assassin sensed her coming. He turned the blow from the invisible sword aside, slicing her across the back.

But she felt the resistance of the fabric as her mother's ring cut his trouser leg.

Did it pierce his flesh?

She didn't have time to check. Flinging out her other hand, she rolled out of the way as she pulled Archer's sword from the floor.

It flew through the air, hilt smacking into his open palm.

Clang! Archer's blade met the First's. He parried and feinted, but the Master Assassin didn't move to counter. Something was wrong.

The muscles in the Assassin's neck went taut. His face twisted as he gasped for air.

Archer cut his wrist. The invisible sword fell. The First moved to catch it, but Sefia seized his fingers in her magical grip.

In the Illuminated world, she saw his bones pop.

Then, in a cold burst of wind, Tanin appeared in the center of the cabin. Like the Assassin, she was dressed in black, her silver-streaked hair pulled back into a knot at the base of her neck.

For a moment, Sefia was reminded of her mother.

But the illusion was gone in an instant.

Tanin was thinner than she'd been when Sefia saw her at Haven. Her jaw was mottled with greenish-yellow bruises. There were nicks and cuts on her hands and dark circles beneath her gray eyes.

What had the Guard done to her?

She moved differently now, sizing up the room, her gaze lingering briefly on the invisible sword. "Did you know they were coming?" she whispered. "Why wasn't I here?"

The Master Assassin cut her with a glance. "The Director didn't think you could do what had to be done."

Picking up the invisible weapon, she and the First came together, back to back. Bleeding, Archer fought them off as Sefia pulled at their arms and legs.

But the fight was quick, because the Master Assassin's face contorted. His back arched. The bloodsword dropped, landing on the floor as Tanin and Archer pivoted away, blades clashing.

"You—" His rasping voice was cut off as a convulsion seized him, bringing him to his knees, his fingers twitching.

Straightening, Sefia lifted her hand. Her mother's silver ring flashed. "Me," she said grimly.

Another kill. Another soul she was sending beyond the barrier to the world of the dead.

To her surprise, the First laughed. It sounded like the crackle of embers. "Do you know how the Apprentice Assassin becomes the Master?" he asked.

But Sefia wasn't listening. She was throwing Tanin aside and racing across the ruined cabin into Archer's bloodied arms. He was clutching her to him. She was sweeping her arms wide, searching the waves of the Illuminated world for a safe landing.

She teleported as another spasm wracked the Master Assassin's body. "By killing him," he whispered. "It should have been your mother, but I can't say I'm disappointed it was you."

CHAPTER 25

The Last Time

Reeling, Sefia collapsed in the *Brother*'s sick bay as Doc raced to close the deep gash the First had opened on Archer's chest. Her ribs throbbed. Her hand was still bleeding. She couldn't see out of her right eye; she didn't even know if she'd ever be able to use it again. But despite her injuries, she felt only shock.

Archer had almost died. She would've paid almost any price to stop the Guard, but not that. Not Archer.

The Book had almost taken him from her.

And at last she knew. Maybe she'd known it for months, and only now did she admit it.

She could not use the Book again.

"We failed," she said later as she sat by his bedside. Her wounds had been bandaged—"You're lucky the bullet missed every essential tendon in that hand," Doc had told her—and

298

her eye was covered with a patch. She'd still be able to see, when she healed, but, as Keon had pointed out, she'd always have a wicked-looking scar, fit for an outlaw.

Archer nodded. Under the blanket, the worst of his injuries weren't visible, but his face was swollen with bruises. They hadn't captured the Director. They hadn't gotten his key. They were no closer to stopping the Guard, and now they wouldn't be fit to try again for weeks.

"But we still know where Stonegold is," he said. "We're heading toward him right now. And when we see him next, the First won't be there to protect him."

Sefia looked down at Mareah's ring. Would her mother have been proud of her, for doing what Mareah was supposed to have done, if she'd remained in the Guard? For taking out one of their enemies so there were only nine left?

She hadn't known her mother well enough to say, and it was that thought that made her want to cry. She didn't even want Mareah's approval, really. She wanted to smell her smell of freshly tilled earth. She wanted to hear her say, "My little Sefia." She wanted her to wipe her cheeks with the curve of her finger.

But she couldn't have any of that.

And now, she couldn't even use the Book to see her.

Gingerly, Archer reached up and tucked her hair behind her ear. "We can still win, right?" he asked. "We can still beat fate?"

Beneath her bandages, Sefia felt her tears stinging her wounded eye. "Yes," she said, sniffing. "But not with the Book."

She'd never leaf through those pages again, never discover

new, surprising passages that took her breath away with their beauty, never see Nin or her parents again.

But Archer was still here, and giving up the Book was a small price to pay to keep him.

Archer cupped her face. "I'm sorry."

She squeezed her good eye shut, willing herself to stop crying. "Me too," she whispered.

The only constant in her life these past seven years could not be her constant anymore. Not when it had almost killed Archer.

Instead, they would sail with the bloodletters to Tsumasai Bay, which would give them time to heal. Once there, they'd sneak aboard the *Barbaro* the old-fashioned way to capture Stonegold and his key.

Sefia tugged at the frayed edge of the bandage on her hand. "There's something else," she said.

Something in her voice must have betrayed her, because Archer nodded like he already understood her. "The Library?" he asked.

She swallowed hard. "The Library."

Erastis had known they were coming. The Library was brimming with over a thousand years of stored information: Fragments copied directly from the Book, prophecies, conjectures. With that at his fingertips, he could foresee and foil any of Sefia and Archer's plans. It was the Guard's greatest repository of knowledge . . . and their greatest weapon.

If Sefia and Archer wanted to destroy the Guard, they'd have to destroy the Library too.

"We can use the Rokuine explosives," said Archer. He'd

learned enough watching the bomb teams before the Battle of Blackfire Bay. If he enlisted Keon's help, he was sure they could rig up something similar, and after Sefia retrieved the Scribes' pages from the vault, he could place the explosives throughout the Library.

Then . . . *poof.*

All those leather-bound codices, all those ancient works of history and science and philosophy, all those beautiful, deadly words would go up in smoke.

The thought pained her.

But it had to be done.

When Archer finally fell asleep, she tiptoed across the cabin to where her rucksack was hanging on the wall and lifted out the Book. It felt utterly familiar and utterly horrible in her arms.

Once she turned it over to Aljan, who had promised to keep it safe for her, she'd never lay eyes on it again.

When she'd learned to use the Book, it wasn't like she'd had her family back—she couldn't hold them or speak to them or be scolded by them—but seeing them again, there before her on the page, had been better than nothing.

Especially Mareah. Because of the Book, Sefia knew more about her mother than she ever had in life.

She'd watched her mother's funeral pyre get carried out to sea, but she'd never gotten to say good-bye to her father or Nin. They'd been taken too suddenly, too violently.

But she could say good-bye now, in a way, though she knew she shouldn't. But she wanted to say good-bye to the Book too, after all these years together.

So she sat in the pool of lamplight and ran her fingers along the edges of the cover, one last time.

She traced the ⊖, one last time.

She asked to see her family, one last time.

After this, she'd no longer get messages from the dead.

Nothing and Everything

Once Lon and Mareah gave up hope of trying to save her, they felt unexpectedly—wondrously—free. For the first time since they were fourteen, they weren't scheming or planning. They weren't running—Mareah couldn't run, in her deteriorating condition. They weren't grasping after greatness or power or control. They had no orders to obey, no higher purpose to which they were beholden. They were beholden to no one but themselves and their little family, with no other obligation than to love one another.

Without a doubt, Mareah was still dying, inexorably, painfully. She was often weak and exhausted; some days, she slept for hours without stirring to drink or eat or speak.

But she also lived.

She sat in her garden, her copper mask glinting in the sun, and picked strawberries, plump and red. She played with Sefia, arranging alphabet blocks while Lon was down in the village, and combed her hair, tying ribbons in it if Sefia, wiggling in her eagerness to check on the newborn lambs, would let her.

At nap time, Mareah counted her daughter's fingers and toes, touching her chubby knees and cheeks, sticky with last year's blackberry jam. She memorized the sounds of her daughter's tantrums as well as her laughter, like they were pieces of music played only once and never again.

She drank, if she felt like it, with Lon and Nin on the front step, after Sefia had gone to bed. She watched Nin's skillful fingers weave grass crowns and she leaned into Lon's shoulder, tugging one of his oversize sweaters closer about her bony frame. Together, they sipped from smooth glasses and watched the moonlight on the Central Sea and spoke of nothing and everything, as the tide spoke of nothing and everything, nothing and everything, with each breath of the waves on the cliffs.

On Sefia's fifth birthday, they threw a party. A small one. They decked the house with paper streamers and hung lanterns in the garden. They wore hats of foil and ate soft cakes with lemon curd centers and glazed blueberries like buttons on top. They played games and told stories, one for each year of Sefia's life.

That night, because she was tired, Mareah lay in bed against her patchwork pillows and watched Sefia and Lon through the window. They raced across the hillside, bearing handheld fireworks that threw off showers of sparks, which trailed behind them like the tails of shooting stars.

And silently, Mareah told herself other stories—
countless other stories—for the years of Sefia's life she
wouldn't live to see.

Sefia's first broken bone. Sefia's first kiss. Sefia's first
day sailing the open ocean, for in Kelanna, you've never
been home until you've been to sea.

Lying there, Mareah imagined Nin teaching Sefia
how to pick locks and Lon spinning stories to put her to
sleep. Mareah imagined Sefia's confusion when she began
to bleed and hoped her cramps wouldn't incapacitate
her. She wished Lon would live another fifty years, his
teardrop eyes growing less hungry but no less keen with
age, and she wished he'd know their daughter as she
became an adult. Mareah wondered what Sefia would like,
what she would hate, and whom she would love. Closing
her eyes, she imagined dozens of futures: Sefia would take
after Nin and become a locksmith, Sefia would take after
Nin and become a jewel thief, Sefia would be a mother,
an outlaw, a hermit, a hunter, a reprobate, a sheriff, and
she'd have hundreds of adventures and an equal amount
of peace. Mareah hoped Sefia would be passionate and
hopeful and fierce and happy and fulfilled. Most of all, she
hoped Sefia would have love, and that she'd live, like this,
wondrously and free.

A month later, Mareah was gone.

CHAPTER 26

One True King

Later, after the assassination of Queen Heccata, Ed found himself in an interrogation room somewhere inside the castle at Kelebrandt. Though he, Lac, and Hobs were witnesses, they were being treated as suspects. He wouldn't have expected anything less from the Royal Navy. The room was small, with moisture-slick walls and rust accumulating on the door's iron hinges. They were given rickety wooden chairs and made to wait while the narrow window in the door opened and closed, opened and closed, anonymous eyes peering in at them while hushed voices whispered outside.

The last time Ed was at the castle, he'd seen only the grand rooms appointed in crimson and gold, well-lit by crystal chandeliers dangling from the painted ceilings. It seemed so long ago now that he found it hard to believe he was the same wide-eyed boy wandering the carpeted halls.

Well, he thought, shifting on his creaking chair, *I suppose I'm not.*

He'd changed in the past few months. He'd put on more weight than he'd thought possible. He'd grown stubble. He'd begun to wear his hair long. When he saw his reflection these days, he looked more like an outlaw than a king.

But the transformation went deeper than that. He still had sad days, bleak with melancholy, but gone was the feeling that he was constantly drowning—cold, numb, gasping for a breath of lightness and air. And when he felt his sadness approaching, he now had ways to keep the worst of it at bay: listening to Lac and Hobs's simple, foolhardy chatter, tending to the animals he so dearly loved, finding ways to make himself useful. He may have lacked a crown, but he'd still found ways to serve and to lead, and when he lay down at night, he looked forward to waking. He *liked* being Ed, the boy without a family name.

But something was still missing.

After what seemed like half the day, a uniformed interrogation officer and court recorder entered the stone cell to begin the questioning.

How did you get to Kelebrandt? On which ship were you stationed when the Alliance attacked?

Lac and Hobs did most of the talking. They described the battle on the *Fire-Eater*, the loss of their friend Fox, the rescue by Captain Cannek Reed and the *Current of Faith*, the flight from Jahara on the *Hustle*, the voyage to Epidram and then to Broken Crown, the journey inland with the refugees.

They told the officer Ed was an Oxscinian who'd been living in Jahara until the day Deliene joined the Alliance.

Oxscinian? Ed touched his finger where he'd once worn the Corabelli signet ring. There was nothing left of that boy now, nothing to prove he'd ever been a Delienean or a king.

Why were you on the hillside where Queen Heccata was killed?

"My terrible sense of direction," Lac said.

With a rueful smile, Ed patted him on the shoulder. "Not one of his talents."

Who was the man in black?

"We don't know," said Hobs, "but he had an odd smell, didn't he, Ed? Kind of metallic."

"*I* shot him," Lac declared, preening.

"Yes." The interrogation officer exchanged a long-suffering glance with the recorder, who had been silently memorizing their every word. "You've told me. At least five times."

"Did you catch him?" Ed asked.

The officer said nothing.

Ed wanted to look around the room, searching for north, but he knew he wouldn't be able to tell in this cramped cell.

North was Deliene. North was Arc, who was surely in danger now.

After recognizing Ed on the slope, the man in black must have informed the Guard of Arcadimon's betrayal. Arcadimon Detano had let the Lonely King escape.

Eduoar Corabelli II was still alive.

Was he? Ed wondered. *Am I?*

He'd thought that part of himself had died that day beneath

308

Corabel. But maybe the king had just been slumbering deep inside him, like a maple in winter, waiting for spring.

Maybe now he was beginning to wake.

Ed didn't think the Guard would kill Arc now, when they still needed Deliene's support in the war, but it was only a matter of time before they found a way to replace him. And if they didn't need him, they wouldn't hesitate to eliminate him.

But what could Ed do to save him, at this distance?

At last, the interrogation officer seemed satisfied. She and the recorder left them. While they waited, Hobs proposed a game: he would hold up a certain number of fingers behind his back, and Lac would guess how many.

"Two!"

On Hobs's other side, Ed watched him uncurl his thumb and reveal his hand to Lac, three fingers spread.

"Let me try again!"

Smiling, Ed shook his head.

After thirty-three rounds of this, two riddles about sandwiches, and Lac repeating "I'm thirsty" twelve times, the interrogation officer returned. Their stories had been corroborated.

A few of the redcoats Ed had helped in Jahara had made their way to Kelebrandt. The refugees from Broken Crown and the Bay of Batteram had been found in the camps on the outskirts of the capital. Everyone they'd helped had vouched for them. Everyone maintained that Ed was one of them.

For their service and dedication, Lac and Hobs were to be given promotions, and Ed, despite his lack of military service, was to be offered a place in the Royal Navy. With the Alliance laying siege to the capital, they could use all the warm bodies they could get.

"Ed, it's perfect!" Lac said, leaping to his feet. "As a lowly seaman, you'll have to obey my every order, naturally, but—"

"Lac, no." Ed caught the boy's arm. "I can't."

"I don't understand." Lac's brow furrowed. "Don't you want to stay with us?"

"Of course I do, but . . ." His voice trailed off. *But I'm not a redcoat.* He wasn't a red-blooded, battle-loving Oxscinian. He couldn't be, not when his heart still longed for the White Plains, the Szythian Mountains, the Heartland, the snow-tipped spires of Gorman striking out of the icy sea.

"There's no guarantee you'll all be posted together," the officer added.

"What?" Lac's chiseled jaw dropped. "Whyever not?"

"You're redcoats. You'll go where your kingdom needs you."

My kingdom needs me home. The thought flickered to life inside Ed, and for the first time in months, he didn't try to snuff it out.

Deliene needed him. Arc needed him.

But they'd both made their choices, hadn't they? Arcadimon had thrown in his lot with the Guard and the Alliance. Ed had abandoned his kingdom and left Arc to contend with his enemies. He couldn't return to the Northern Kingdom to change anything now.

"Although, after all you did on your way here . . ." The interrogation officer bit her lip. "I suppose I could recommend that you all be stationed on the same ship. I'd hate to be the one to break up this merry band of misfits."

Lac beamed.

But Hobs looked solemn. "Lac and I need a third party, Ed. We don't work, him and I alone."

"Hobs!" Lac looked aghast.

"It's true, sir."

"You don't need to call him sir anymore," the officer said. "You're both midshipmen now."

Hobs shrugged. "I like calling him sir."

"Hobs is right," Lac said. "When we met you in Jahara, you were lost without us. Now, we're lost without you."

"Actually," Hobs said, "when we met him in Jahara, we still would've been lost without him."

Ed gave the two boys a fond smile.

He could no longer look back. He had to do what he could for the people who needed him here, now. He had new choices to make.

He could pledge his life to a foreign kingdom.

He could die, far from home.

But he'd do it fighting for what he knew was right. He'd do it standing for what he believed in.

Stopping the Alliance. Oxscini and the redcoats were the only ones who could do that now.

"I'm in," he said.

Soon, he, Lac, and Hobs were assigned to the *Thunderhead*, a warship of the Red Navy, posted in the center of Tsumasai Bay, in the event that the Alliance broke through the defenses in the east. As midshipmen, Lac and Hobs were assigned to the fighting tops—much to Lac's dismay—but Ed was a low-ranking seaman, and he was put on one of the gun crews, tasked with the firing and reloading of a great gun nicknamed "the Ripper."

As the winter rains slid into spring, they saw no action as the Alliance continued their siege of Tsumasai Bay and Kelebrandt. The Oxscinians mourned their dead queen for a day before her daughter took the throne, tightened the rationing, and imposed a curfew. Every day, there were reports of action in the east— rumors of the blue beasts of the Alliance chipping away at the Royal Navy line. Every day, the Alliance soldiers making their way overland through the swamps of Vesper Province gained a little more ground. Every day, there were more casualties.

People were afraid. But more than that, Ed could sense a seething undercurrent of anger passing from one person to another like a lightning strike in the water. He felt it too—a determination to fight, to resist, to die, if he had to, on his own two feet.

Then, one overcast morning when the flowers were just beginning to bud on the trees, while Ed was on watch aboard the *Thunderhead*, alarms began ringing all around the bay, calling civilians to their shelters and soldiers to their posts. On the coastline, battle flags went up on every fort and onshore battery.

The eastern defenses had been breached. If the Royal Navy could not push the Alliance back out of Tsumasai Bay, the capital would soon be under attack.

With so little space at the eastern entrances to Tsumasai Bay, however, too many ships would foul up the lines. So the *Thunderhead* did not depart immediately. They were the fifth line of defense and would be called up only if they were needed.

Grimly, Ed watched the growing cloud of smoke sweeping across the water like a black fog. He heard the sounds of the cannons coming ever closer.

Instinctively, he looked north. Toward Arc.

Toward home.

At noon, they got the signal. The *Thunderhead* was going to battle.

The captain began barking orders. The soldiers scrambled for their positions. Anchors were drawn up. Sails were loosed. Lac and Hobs went scurrying about their duties as Ed joined his gun crew at the Ripper, greasing the axles, laying out shot boxes, filling tubs with seawater.

As they neared the fighting, the smell of smoke grew stronger. The cannon fire grew louder.

Through the curls of smoke, Ed saw the Alliance ships, flying banners of blue, gold, and white. In the distance, he spied the *Barbaro*, General Braca Terezina III's prize flagship.

The blue beasts of the Alliance were sailing on Kelebrandt.

But to Ed, they were not beasts. To Ed, they weren't the enemy. Among the unfamiliar flags and figureheads, he recognized the *Eclipse*, the *Moonlight Run*, the *Red Hare* . . . They'd been repainted and outfitted with new flags, but Ed would have recognized them anywhere. They were the ships that had been stationed at Corabel since he was a boy.

"Cast off the tackles!" the gun captain shouted.

All around him, the redcoats scuttled for the Ripper, preparing to fire. The shot was loaded. The muzzle was raised.

But Ed didn't move.

He couldn't move.

313

Those were Delienean ships out there—*his* ships, at least a dozen of them within sight, and probably more battling in the chaos to the east—with captains and officers he'd known his entire life.

"Fire!" The command rang out.

The gun captain lit a match. He was lowering it toward the firing mechanism.

But Ed couldn't allow them to attack Delieneans. His Delieneans. "No!" Ed lunged forward.

"Hold!" the captain roared at the same moment.

Shocked, Ed whirled around.

"Hold!" the officers echoed.

The gun captain held. The match burned to nothing between his fingers as he and the other redcoats stared warily at Ed, who'd tried to stop them from firing on the enemy.

But Ed was watching the flag being run up their mast—black with a single white circle in the center—the worldwide signal for a cease-fire.

For a negotiation.

The new queen was inviting King Darion Stonegold to parley.

They waited for hours after the *Barbaro*, General Terezina's floating fortress, with King Darion Stonegold aboard, sailed past them toward the castle at Kelebrandt. Hours without word from the queen. Red and blue ships sat uneasily on the water of Tsumasai Bay, waiting for orders.

Ed sat against the gunwale with his head in his arms. He could feel the tension of the redcoats, their hands straying

314

to their weapons at sudden sounds, always looking over their shoulders at the enemy, lingering just within firing range.

Beside him sat Lac and Hobs, who, after fifteen minutes of cease-fire, had sneaked down from their own posts.

Hobs dabbed at his round head with a handkerchief. "What do you think they're talking about now?" he asked.

"They're probably still staring at each other from across the throne room," said Lac, "waiting to see who makes the first move."

Ed shook his head. "Stonegold is asking for her surrender," he said. "Surrender now and spare the capital the grief of a battle, or leave him no choice but to take Kelebrandt by force, sacrificing thousands of lives." He glanced at the Alliance line.

He couldn't fight them, if the battle resumed. He couldn't kill his own citizens. And they were his own citizens, he knew now, though he'd run from them, from his title, from his responsibilities.

He knew he'd be brigged for refusing to follow orders. In this time of war, he might even be shot for mutiny.

But he couldn't do it.

"The new queen would never give in to that bonesucker's demands," Lac declared loyally.

But by midafternoon, when the cease-fire flags came down, they were replaced by new ones—white as snow, white as surrender.

The new queen was surrendering.

Oxscini was surrendering.

The Alliance had won.

The captain of the *Thunderhead* didn't seem like he could

believe it. He glanced at the other ships of the Royal Navy line.

A few of them ran up the white flag . . . but not all of them. And every second they didn't, they could feel the increasing pressure of the Alliance guns on them.

"Orders, Captain?" asked one of the lieutenants.

The captain sighed. "Yes. Raise the—"

"No!" Lac cried, charging up the steps to the quarterdeck. "We can't just *give up*. We've barely done anything to stop them!"

Scrambling to their feet, Ed and Hobs dashed after their friend. They'd seen Lac defy orders before. It hadn't ended well for him.

"This isn't one of your stories, hero," the captain said. "We've done our duty. That's all we *can* do." He nodded at his first lieutenant, who opened her mouth to give the order.

No, Ed thought. If Oxscini fell to the Alliance, Roku would be the only free land left in Kelanna. No one would be left to fight. Even now, it seemed, there was no one left.

Except him.

But before he could speak, Hobs did something quite unexpected. And rather foolish.

He crept up behind the captain and hit him over the head with a belay pin. The captain's eyes rolled back in his head and he slumped to the floor.

Lac balked.

Hobs shrugged.

Guiltily, they turned to the lieutenants, who outranked and outnumbered them.

They could be shot for this.

But as the first lieutenant checked the captain's breathing, she looked up at them with a long sigh. "I hope you have a plan," she said, "because if we're not dead or victorious by the time he wakes up, we'll all face penalties for mutiny."

Lac gulped and looked to Hobs, who looked to Ed, who looked to the Delienean ships looming in front of them, still waiting for their surrender.

More and more white flags were going up on the Red Navy ships every second Ed wavered.

Could he do it? Could he be their king again without drowning in his sadness, like a man staked to a beach at high tide?

Yes. He could. He wasn't the Lonely King; he was not cursed. He was Ed, and with all that he'd learned about himself the past few months, all that he'd become, he could be Eduoar Corabelli II again.

Ed stepped forward. "I have a plan," he said.

He couldn't do it as a low-ranking seaman in the Royal Navy, but he wasn't that boy, really. He was Eduoar Corabelli II, rightful king of Deliene, and if he could signal the Delienean captains that he was alive, aboard the *Thunderhead*, and ready to take command of his ships and his kingdom, they *might* follow him.

They *might* be able to push the Alliance back out of Tsumasai Bay.

He just had to let them know he was here.

"I'm Delienean," he told the lieutenant.

"Shh!" Hobs said loudly.

Ignoring him, Ed continued, "I can get those White Navy ships to turn on the Alliance, if you'll continue to fight."

She eyed him suspiciously. "How?"

"Just give me a couple signal flags and a place at the bowsprit."

"Ed, what—" Lac began.

The first lieutenant stood. "Done."

Ed clasped Lac and Hobs by the shoulders. "Thank you, my friends, for everything you've done for me. Never have I met anyone more loyal or more brave."

"Brave?" Lac echoed.

Ed nodded. *"Brave."*

The rest of the crew raced back to their battle posts as Ed dug into the chest of signal flags until he found two that would suit his purposes: one in Delienean black-and-white, another with a gold crown, which would tell everyone they had royalty aboard. Asking Hobs to run them up the mast, he dashed to the prow of the *Thunderhead*, stripping off his crimson jacket, revealing a white shirt—thoroughly starched, thanks to Lac—and black trousers beneath.

He scrubbed his stubbled cheeks. Would his people recognize him?

They had to.

Before he reached the bowsprit, however, another of the Royal Navy ships let off a broadside. Cannonballs went soaring through the air, sinking into the hulls of the Alliance ships.

The crew cheered.

Bang! Bang! Bang! Their great guns rang out.

The battle began anew. It was chaos. No one seemed to know who was giving the orders. No one seemed to know whom to listen to.

There was the sound of distant cannon fire in the south. Someone at the southern entrance to Tsumasai Bay was fighting back too. They were all fighting back.

Ignoring the gunshots that whizzed back and forth between the riflemen and the enemy, Ed clambered along the bowsprit and stood, his tall form leaning over the water, visible to all.

Here I am, he thought, watching the Delienean ships. *Your king.*

CHAPTER 27

Not Today

Hunkered behind the islands at the southern tip of Oxscini, the outlaws peered around the shoreline to the southern entrance to Tsumasai Bay.

Thirteen Alliance ships were clustered in the deep water just out of range of the two stone forts flanking the mouth of the channel. Inside the narrow passage, the crimson ships of the Royal Navy stood guard. The air was strangely empty of the sounds of battle.

Because no one was fighting. Cease-fire flags flew from the onshore battlements and the front of the Alliance line. All was quiet.

"What in the blue world?" Reed muttered.

"Guess it isn't today after all," the mate said.

The captain tapped his belt buckle. *Once, twice* . . . He shook his head. He hadn't come all this way to turn back now. But before he reached the count of eight, a white flag went up on the nearest fort.

Surrender?

Captain Reed put away the spyglass. If the Forest Kingdom gave up now, the Alliance would control almost all of Kelanna. The Guard would have all but won.

Someone needed to do something. Someone had to show them that the world was still worth fighting for.

It might as well be an outlaw.

Pivoting to the rest of the crew, he called, *"All hands, to arms!"*

They cheered.

Killian ran up the battle flag as they loosed the sails. The outlaws surged toward the enemy line.

At the prow of the *Current*, the chase guns boomed. The sounds of gunfire were answered by the thunder of cannons in the north.

Reed grinned. At least someone in Tsumasai Bay hadn't given up the fight.

In the channel, one of the redcoat ships let off a broadside. Iron sank into the hull of the nearest Alliance vessel. The steep sides of the waterway echoed with the thunder of war drums.

The *Current of Faith* and the other outlaws sailed in, one after another, battering the Alliance ships like a wave upon the rocks, chewing out sections of the enemy line until they went crumbling into the sea.

The *Crux* punched through a gap between the Alliance warships, firing cannons from port and starboard. One after another, the outlaws rammed through the blue vessels until the Alliance line ruptured, enemy ships breaking off into scattered sections as the lighter, quicker outlaws closed in, sailing circles around the unwieldy Alliance vessels, taking out masts and puncturing hulls.

Reed loved it—the roar of the great guns! The wind in his hair! The quick spitting of firearms from the fighting tops!

The Red Navy ships began to emerge from the mouth of the channel, clearing a path for the *Brother*, which sailed past the battle and north into Tsumasai Bay.

Sefia and Archer were off to find Stonegold.

The Alliance warships were forming ranks again, battling back against the combined force of the outlaws and redcoats.

The *One Bad Eye* got raked by an enemy broadside.

The *Crux* lost a chunk of her stern.

And as the *Current* turned to let off another round of cannon fire, an Alliance vessel rammed them on the starboard side. The green hull splintered. The timbers groaned. The outlaws rushed to defend the rails as enemy soldiers flooded onto the *Current*. Cooky and Aly popped up from their places behind the gunwale, striking boarders with the butts of their rifles.

"Get us away from that ship, Jaunty!" Captain Reed shouted.

"We're stuck," the chief mate said.

At the same time, the helmsman answered, "No can do, Cap! The only way we get out of here is if they're not steerin' into us anymore."

The captain cursed. Trapped by the prow of the Alliance vessel, they were immobile in the water—an easy target for their enemies.

They had to get free. *He* had to get them free. And to do that, he needed to disable the Alliance rudder so they couldn't keep pushing into the *Current*.

"Meeks, you have the ship!" Reed cried, leaping down to the main deck.

There was a faint "Aye, Cap!" and a whoop of laughter.

Captain Reed raced to the prow of the enemy's ship, jammed against the *Current*'s green hull. He jumped onto the rail, kicking at an enemy soldier as he grabbed for the Alliance bowsprit.

Gunshots erupted around him, but he wasn't afraid. He wouldn't die dangling over his own decks.

He swung up onto the enemy ship and drew his guns—the Singer, blue and light, and the Executioner, cold as ice and heavy as lead. He was in Alliance territory now. Dozens of soldiers stood between him and the stern of the blue warship.

But that wouldn't stop him. He was Captain Cannek Reed.

Shooting, ducking, fighting, smoke drifting from the mouths of his revolvers, he made his way down the length of the Alliance ship. *One, two, three* . . . No one stopped him. *Nine, ten, eleven, twelve* people fell to his bullets. No one was fast enough.

But his cylinders were empty. He was out of ammunition.

A blue-uniformed soldier came at him with a boarding ax. Neatly, he stepped aside and heard the blade strike the rail, sinking deep into the wood.

Holstering the Singer, he drew a knife and rammed it into the woman's jawline as she struggled to free her weapon.

She dropped as Reed ducked behind a cannon and fished in his pockets for bullets, dropping them one by one into the chambers of his six-guns.

Then he was up again.

One of his shots found the helmsman. Another struck the ship's bell and ricocheted into the head of a lieutenant on the quarterdeck.

The Executioner was thirsty.

A round punctured the neck of an Alliance soldier, punching clean through to the skull of the woman behind him.

Reed's bullets found sailors, officers, gunners, topmen.

Until he reached the stern of the enemy vessel, where he clocked a rifleman over the head with the Singer and seized one of the miniature cannons they used as a chase gun.

Aiming for the rudder chain, he began counting. *One, two, three, four . . .*

. . . five, six, seven, eight. He fired.

The small cannonball snapped the rudder chain, which went rattling down into the sea.

The enemy ship was dead in the water. The *Current* was free.

He raced back across the Alliance decks just as his crew was disentangling their ship. The *Current* was sailing off. Holstering the Singer, Reed ran up the bowsprit and leapt, the Executioner still in his hand.

The sea surged below him. The air licked at his arms and legs.

He landed, rolling, on the deck, amid the cheers of the outlaws. Five of the Alliance ships were sinking or dead in the water. The others were turning tail and retreating to the east as the redcoats and the outlaws pushed them back from the entrance to Tsumasai Bay.

He didn't think the Royal Navy could still sail around to attack the Alliance on two fronts, but he and the outlaws had given them fewer ships to fight.

The redcoats joined the outlaw ships, forming a line of mixed colors—*The colors of the Resistance,* Reed thought—guarding the narrow channel.

Then he saw movement to the east.

The retreating Alliance vessels weren't retreating at all. They were joining up with another line of blue warships—at least twenty of them—led by an enormous ship even larger than the *Crux.*

She was blue instead of yellow now, but Reed recognized her figurehead—a white winged horse.

It was Serakeen's flagship, the *Amalthea,* and the man himself was at the prow, his burgundy coat flaring in the wind and a glint of metal at his wrist where his hand used to be.

Captain Reed bared his teeth and raised the Executioner.

One bullet, and the Scourge of the East would be dead.

He just had to get in range.

"Let's do it, Cap," Meeks said.

Reed nodded.

Meeks gave the order. The *Current* and the other outlaws sped toward the enemy. The Royal Navy ships joined them.

Reed began to count.

One.

Two.

Three.

He had to get to eight.

Eight, and he wouldn't miss.

Six.

Seven.

But before he could pull the trigger, the chase gunners at the bow of the *Amalthea* unveiled a set of weapons the likes of which Reed had never seen. There were three of them, each the length of his arm, with six barrels strapped together and a belt of bullets feeding into the cylinders. Beside each gun stood a soldier, grasping the handle of a crank.

Captain Reed figured it out a second before it happened. A second before the chase gunners began to turn their cranks.

"Take cover!" he cried, throwing himself to the deck.

The bullets came at them fast as hail, pitting the hull, peppering the rails as the crew crouched behind them—fast, faster, faster than Reed could aim or breathe or blink.

He heard the screams of his sailors as they fell, saw the bursts of blood as the hot beads of metal hit them. Jaunty went down, still clutching the helm. One of Theo's legs was shot out, and he collapsed, spectacles cracked, as his red lory huddled in the curve of his neck, nuzzling his chin. Horse was plugged with bullets as he flung his massive body in front of Doc, shielding her from the onslaught even as she screamed and struggled to move him out of harm's way. Reed's hat was knocked from his head as splinters spiked his ear and the side of his neck.

What kind of gun is that?

He had the answer in the faces of his crew—bloody, ashen, petrified, dead. Old Goro had been too slow, and now Marmalade was curled behind his inert body, using it for cover, her pale face freckled with his blood.

No human could outshoot a gun like that, not him, not even Adeline. It was unnatural, impersonal, and against it, they could not win.

Not today. Not ever.

CHAPTER 28

The Third Adventure of Haldon Lac

Embarrassingly, Midshipman Haldon Lac had a bad case of the hiccups. On this, the most important battle of his entire life! If he hadn't been so preoccupied with the fight, he'd feel affronted by the indignity of it.

Oxscini had surrendered, but much of the Royal Navy had refused to give up. Disobeying orders, they continued to battle the blue beasts of the Alliance, their ships churning the seas, their cannons filling the air with smoke. They were rebels against their own kingdom now—rebel redcoats.

Could Lac even consider himself a redcoat anymore?

Shot soared over his head and slammed into the sea, drenching him with spray, which successfully shocked him out of his . . . shock.

He grabbed Hobs's hand. "What's Ed"—Lac hiccuped— "doing? We have to get him down from there!"

On top of everything, their best friend in the whole world was standing on the *Thunderhead*'s bowsprit, an easy target. The swift reports of gunfire echoed across the water.

"He looks like he's posing for a portrait!" Hobs cried as they dashed across the ship.

Ed *did* look handsome up there, Lac had to admit, and quite heroic, with the black waves of his hair rippling in the breeze, his long, lean form poised above the waves as if he were about to dive.

But looking good didn't make him any less likely to be killed.

The blue warships of the Alliance were sailing ever closer, turning their guns on the *Thunderhead*.

But not all of them, Lac realized. The closest ship, with a red rabbit for a figurehead, was lowering its Alliance flags and raising a new one—a white poppy on a black field studded with stars.

The Delienean flag.

They were chanting too, their voices rising in the smoke-riddled air: *The king lives! Delieneans, to the king!*

In fact, all along the enemy line, ships were sending up the Delienean flag. They were turning their great guns on the other blue ships. They were firing.

Lac's head spun. The Delieneans were defecting from the Alliance. They were joining the rebel redcoats in the defense of Tsumasai Bay.

But why?

A cannonball struck the *Thunderhead*, throwing Lac and Hobs to the decks as broken bits of wood and shrapnel flew through the air. The lieutenants were shouting. The gun crews were firing. Parts of the deck caught fire, the blaze sweeping across the timbers as sailors tried to beat out the flames.

Lac got to his knees. Something sharp pained his shoulder, but he ignored it. "Ed!" he shouted. "Get—*hic*—down from there!"

"Sir!" Hobs dragged him under cover as an explosion of scrap shot struck the ship. "You're bleeding!"

Sparks flew past them as Haldon Lac batted his hands away, still hiccuping. "I'm not your ranking officer anymore, Hobs!" He didn't know if he even *had* a rank anymore. Did traitors to the crown get ranks? He shoved down his nausea.

He was a *traitor*. Traitors didn't *deserve* ranks.

On their hands and knees, Lac and Hobs continued to crawl toward the bowsprit. "Ed!"

Hearing his name, Ed glanced over his shoulder. Their gazes met. And for a split second, the boy Lac had met in Jahara looked like a stranger. He seemed taller somehow, more stately in his bearing, wiser and braver and . . . ready.

Ready for what?

Haldon Lac didn't have time to wonder, however, because as he leapt to his feet again, an enemy broadside shook the hull. The masts toppled. The ship cracked and groaned. There was a deafening explosion as a rapidly expanding blossom of heat caught him in the back, pitching him and Hobs and Ed into the air.

They all hit the sea as the *Thunderhead* went up in a conflagration of flame and splintered beams.

It was cold in the water! Lac's shoulder hurt. And he was

still hiccuping. But he kicked and fought, searching the turgid waters for his friends.

"Hobs! Ed!"

Broken powder kegs and dirty swabs drifted past him. Gasping sailors scrabbled for floating bits of debris. But he couldn't find Hobs or Ed.

Finally, Hobs burst from the waves beside him, spitting seawater. "Sir!"

"Don't call me that, Hobs! Are you all right? Where's Ed?"

"There, sir!"

Their friend was facedown on the surface, his white shirt appearing almost gauzy in the dark sea. *No!* Lac swam for him, his well-toned arms and legs carrying him easily through the waves. He turned the boy in his arms, hoping for the flicker of his eyelids, for breath.

Ed coughed.

Haldon Lac let out a sound that was part gasp of relief, part hiccup. "I've got you. I'm not letting go."

Ed patted his arm.

Lac hiccuped again.

"Try holding your breath, sir," Hobs volunteered as he swam up to them.

"You can't hold your—*hic*—breath while you're swimming! And stop calling me sir!" Lac gagged as salt water splashed into his mouth.

The bay was in chaos. Rebel redcoats were rushing the enemy line. Warships flying the Delienean flag were firing on the blue beasts that had, moments ago, been their allies. Haldon Lac didn't understand what was going on, but he knew enough to clutch Ed tighter when an enormous blue vessel drew up beside him.

But the soldiers staring down at them from the rails didn't fire.

"It's okay," Ed murmured. "Don't worry."

Rope ladders struck the water around them, and the strangers scrambled down the side of their ship.

The first woman to reach them hesitated, an extra length of rope dangling from her hand. Then she bowed her head and said, "Your Majesty."

For a moment, Lac was confused. His family had no royal blood . . . that he knew of. But maybe . . . ?

The woman looped the rope under Ed's arms as he grasped for the rungs of the ladder. Other people helped him find hand-holds as he began climbing out of the water.

"We thought you were dead," she said.

"So did I," Ed replied.

The soldiers helped Hobs and Lac, still bewildered, onto the rope ladders. Shot soared through the air around them as they climbed over the rail. The gun crews were still at it. The powder monkeys were rushing across the decks as the officers shouted orders and rifles popped in the fighting tops overhead.

But amid the frenzy of battle, the captain was kneeling, head bowed, before Ed's dripping form.

Haldon Lac's eyes widened as he finally understood.

Ed was a *king*.

And his name wasn't Ed—it was Eduoar Corabelli II, the one true king of Deliene.

"Come on, Captain," Ed—the king—said. "We've got a battle to fight."

Immediately, the captain rose. He snapped his fingers at a pair of soldiers, who came forward with thick wool blankets, which they offered first to Ed, who took one with a nod, and then to Lac and Hobs.

Grabbing a blanket, Hobs immediately swung it around his shoulders. But Lac let his dangle limply from his hand as he stared at Ed. The hiccups, it seemed, had been shocked right out of him. "You—" he began, ducking as the cannons fired again.

Ed nodded. "Me."

"Since when—"

The boy smiled sheepishly. "Since always."

"But you—" Lac whirled on Hobs. "Are *you* one too?"

"Royalty? Don't think so." Hobs shrugged. "But stranger things have happened."

Haldon Lac moaned. All these months he'd been with the Lonely King? All those unwashed months? He'd smelled so bad! In front of a *king*! For a moment, he wanted to faint.

But there was no time to faint, he reminded himself. There was still a battle to fight.

"Your Majesty." Despite the rocking of the ship, he managed a respectably deep bow. "We are at your service."

Beside him, Hobs bowed too.

It all made sense now: the grace, the courtly manners, the complete ignorance of common chores. Ed was a king. Even if they'd been the same age, Lac never would've stood a chance. Not as a partner.

But as a friend?

"Just Ed to you." Ed put his hands on both their shoulders, making them stand again. "To both of you."

Lac beamed. He was friends with a king!

Then the king was whisked to the quarterdeck with the officers, leaving Lac and Hobs in the care of the Delienean soldiers. The ship that had picked them up was called the *Red Hare*, and soon it was flying a second flag beneath the Delienean black-and-white—a gold crown.

In the midst of the battle, the Delieneans rallied to their king. Explosions rent the air. Ships splintered. The whitecaps turned red with blood as bodies were thrown into the sea. Lac and Hobs joined the riflemen at the prow of the *Red Hare*, firing at enemy gun crews as they tried to load their cannons. For a time, it seemed that the combined might of the rebel red-coats and the Delienean defectors would turn the tide of battle against the Alliance.

If they won, Lac might be allowed back into the Royal Navy. He might be Midshipman Haldon Lac again.

But the enemy still had more ships. They still had superior weaponry. They still had the upper hand. Slowly, they began to drive the resisters together, circling them like sharks.

"This doesn't look good, sir," Hobs said.

"Don't call me sir." Lac squinted through the rail. A red ship with white markings on its prow was sailing at them from the west, flying the flag of a boy with bowed head and crossed arms. It didn't belong to any navy Lac recognized. Had it come from the capital? Was it a civilian vessel? No, it couldn't be, not with those great guns on its decks.

An outlaw. Where had an *outlaw* come from?

Haldon Lac popped up from under cover and fired at the nearest Alliance ship. "Ed—I mean, Your Majes—I mean, Ed!" he called, pointing.

On the quarterdeck, the king nodded. He spoke to the captain, who put a spyglass to his eye.

The strange outlaw ship was coming closer. On its decks were boys, alternately waving frantically at the *Red Hare* and pointing south.

Even to Lac, their meaning was clear: *Follow us.*

They wanted the resisters to retreat to the south. Had the southern entrance of Tsumasai Bay been cleared? By *outlaws*? That would be their only way of escape now.

The red outlaw ship sailed straight up behind one of the blue beasts of the Alliance and let loose a broadside that raked the giant warship fore and aft, shattering glass and timbers. The enemy line faltered.

The *Red Hare* seized its chance. It broke away from the rest of the resisters, sailing past the Alliance. The outlaw ship turned, heading south out of Tsumasai Bay. The rebel redcoats and the Delienean defectors followed.

The enemy ships began the pursuit.

Haldon Lac spared one last glance for Oxscini's disappearing shoreline—the stone forts, the forested hills, the wooden houses on stilts at the edge of the water. He'd betrayed his orders. He'd betrayed his queen. He was leaving his beloved kingdom behind. He didn't know if he'd ever see it again . . . or if he deserved to.

CHAPTER 29

The Promise Keeper

Since the assassination of Queen Heccata, Tanin had made herself indispensable to the cause.

First, she'd suggested Arcadimon Detano's punishment: a drug that, once taken, would make the body entirely dependent on it for survival. As long as Detano remained loyal to the Guard, the Apprentice Administrator would deliver a dose to Corabel each morning, and he would live another day. If he stepped out of line, however, if he tried to contact his little king, the drug would be withdrawn, and he would die before noon the next day.

Then she became the Master Assassin's shadow. She followed him everywhere in his search for Detano's missing king—combing the hillside for clues, locating witnesses, questioning bystanders.

When she wasn't searching, she was training. She endured sparring sessions that left her hands covered in cuts and her body covered in bruises. She submitted herself to hours of mental torment. At the First's insistence, she killed all manner of creatures—stray dogs, infant rodents that hadn't yet opened their eyes, war orphans from the camps ringing the capital—in all manner of ways. And if her face showed a single glimmer of emotion—dismay, pity, even rage—she was beaten.

Mareah had never talked about her training. Now Tanin knew why.

It was torture. But it was effective. Assassins weren't human, after all. They were living weapons.

Tanin answered to "Assassin" or "Second." She waited, unnoticed, in the shadows while her Master conferred with Stonegold or the Soldiers. She held her tongue. She bided her time.

Stonegold may have forgotten the humiliation he'd put her through. But Tanin had sworn he'd die by her hand, and she kept her promises.

By the time the First was killed, she'd perfected the art of inconspicuousness as well as the art of patience.

While Stonegold sat on one of the overstuffed sofas, nursing his aching head, she examined the First's corpse.

Strychnine. As a former Administrator, she would have recognized the signs anywhere. She found the nick on his shin where the poison had entered his system. The cut matched the blade on Mareah's silver ring.

"This could have been you, Director," she whispered. "They probably thought that killing you would end the war."

"Then they'll try again." He pointed a thick finger in her direction. "And next time, you'll stop them."

Tanin bowed. Her face was impassive now, but if she'd been

the same woman she was nearly four months ago, she would have been smiling.

Stonegold called off the search for the missing king. He needed a guard dog, and Tanin—who had become the Master Assassin by default—would do.

Now, clad in black with the old First's weapons sheathed at her side, she accompanied Stonegold everywhere. She slept on a pallet on the floor of his cabin. She waited outside the door while he emptied his bowels. She listened in on conversations with the other Guardians, who hardly seemed to notice her in the shadows, and waited, silently, for her opportunity.

During the attack on Tsumasai Bay, she followed Stonegold everywhere. She was on deck with him when they broke through the Royal Navy defenses. She was at his side when he sailed to the castle at Kelebrandt, when he entered the throne room with its stone floors and floor-to-ceiling windows. One side of the hall overlooked the capital's harbor and the amassed navies beyond. The other had views of the courtyard, gardens, walls, and the city sprawled over the forested hills.

She witnessed the young Oxscinian queen's surrender and, minutes later, the rebellion on the bay, when a slew of redcoats refused to yield and dozens of Delieneans defected from the Alliance.

Detano's little king must have resurfaced at last.

But Stonegold appeared unfazed. Tanin supposed it was easy to remain collected when your forces so greatly outnumbered the opposition. He ordered the Oxscinian queen to send her reserve ships to intercede between the rebels and the Alliance, and the candidates escorted her out of the throne room so she could obey.

Tanin was left alone with Stonegold.

He stood at the windows, watching the reserve Royal Navy ships leave the harbor. It wouldn't be long before the Alliance subdued the resisters. She was certain he wanted to see the moment the waters of Tsumasai Bay calmed at last, and he had four of the Five Islands in the palm of his hand.

Tanin stood by the room's main entrance, a set of double doors that led to an empty antechamber and the guarded corridor beyond. Unlike Stonegold, whose gaze was fixed on the battle, she could see both the action on the bay and the view of the castle grounds. Which meant she was watching when Sefia and Archer appeared on the outermost ramparts.

Even now, Tanin didn't allow herself the satisfaction of a smile. Smiling was for victors, and she'd had victory snatched from her grasp too many times to believe it would come easily to her now.

But she'd been waiting for this moment. She'd known Sefia and Archer would return to finish their assassination of the Master Politician.

She just had to make sure that this time, they succeeded.

Together, they raced across the castle walls and disappeared into a tower.

"Director," Tanin whispered, "if I may be excused?"

"Now?"

"The queen has been gone a long time. I think I should check on her."

He didn't bother turning around. "Go, and be quick about it."

Tanin left through the antechamber, passing the candidates on guard in the hall.

With Stonegold dead, the Directorship would be vacant, and since she'd shadowed his every move since the death of the First and was privy to every scheme, there would be no one more suited to take his place than Tanin.

She'd already had opportunities to kill him, of course, but if the rest of the Guard was to accept her as Director, her innocence had to be out of the question, her alibi inviolate even to the Sight. If there was a single shred of doubt, their Master Soldier, Braca, would seize control of the organization and have her executed for treachery.

No, she'd had to wait. She had to lay the blame elsewhere. She had to retain the loyalty of every division: the Soldiers, the Librarians, the Administrators. As their military leader, Braca would assume command of the Alliance.

She would be the public face of the first union of all Five Kingdoms, and Tanin, the Director of the Guard, would control her from the shadows.

It would be as it should have been before Stonegold usurped Tanin's place.

Tanin stalked the corridors. She peered into empty chambers. She slunk through the kitchens, the courtyards, the halls.

She heard them before she saw them, whispering in one of the stairwells. She paused on the landing above, listening.

Sefia's voice drifted up to her: "Where do you think he is?"

He. Stonegold. Tanin had been correct—they were going to try to kill him again.

Except she'd vowed that he would die at *her* hand.

"Would he be in the council room?" Archer asked.

In the tense silence, Tanin peered around the curve of the stairwell. Wearing an eye patch to cover the injury she'd received when fighting the First, Sefia was staring through the windows at the battle on the bay. The resisters were fleeing south, pursued by the Alliance's swift scouts.

Archer stood beside her. As before, he had two weapons: a revolver and a sword.

Perfect. The sword was what she needed.

"If I know Stonegold," she said softly, stepping around the corner, "and I think I do, he'll be in the throne room, gloating."

The attack came, predictably: a burst of magic, a knife flung through the air.

With reflexes honed by her training with the First, Tanin ducked, redirecting the knife into the curved wall, where it pinged off the stones and went flying back at Sefia.

Archer went to push her out of the way, exposing the hilt of his sword.

That was all the opening Tanin needed. She teleported, appearing on his other side. Swiftly, she grabbed his blade from its scabbard and darted away.

She led them into the servants' passages that wound throughout the castle, up and down tight stairwells, until she was certain they were close enough to the throne room to make it on their own.

Then, when they were behind a corner, she waved her arms, reappearing in the empty antechamber.

Amid the sliding paper screens and hand-carved chairs of Oxscinian hardwood, Tanin slipped on a pair of gloves and plucked a tin, no bigger than a case of powder, from her vest. Inside was a sponge soaked in a transparent poison.

She'd gotten the idea from Detano, of all people. To save his little king, he'd needed to conceal a murder, and to do that, he'd needed a poison that would distort a corpse until all its distinguishing marks were unrecognizable, even to Illuminators.

She would do the same to Stonegold.

Tanin ran the sponge along the weapon's cutting edges and returned the sponge to its case. Then she removed her gloves, turning them inside out to avoid contact with the poison, and clipped the case closed.

Taking Archer's sword from the chair, she opened the double doors and strode into the throne room.

Stonegold hadn't moved from his place at the windows. Out on the bay, the resisters had disappeared from sight. The remaining Royal Navy vessels were being boarded, their captains relieved of their command. In the evening light, the smoke-filled sky was a red haze, silhouetting his girth.

King of Everica. Master Politician. Director of the Guard.

But not for much longer.

Quietly, Tanin locked and barred the doors.

At the slight sound, Stonegold turned, his expression pinched with irritation. "Took you long enough. Where is she?"

That lazy voice. That condescending tone.

She'd never have to hear it again.

In an instant, she'd teleported across the room. She was quick, as her Master had taught her. Archer's sword sank hilt-deep into Stonegold's broad chest.

At Detano's swearing-in ceremony, she'd promised herself that this was how Stonegold would die. It gave her no small satisfaction to know she was a woman who kept her promises.

Immediately, she stepped back, checking her clothing for spots of blood.

Stonegold looked down, his eyes widening as he saw the sword.

The old Tanin would have gloated.

But the new Tanin merely watched as Stonegold opened his mouth as if to speak, though no words came out. The poison was fast, eating away at his clothing, his skin, his fat, his muscles and bones.

He screamed and fell back, Archer's sword protruding from his rapidly deteriorating corpse.

There was a ruckus beyond the antechamber. The candidates had heard Stonegold's cry.

With a smile, Tanin lifted her arms and teleported away.

CHAPTER 30

Close to the End

The scream was followed by a hammering sound—*bang, bang, bang*—like a battering ram.

Sefia and Archer raced toward the noise, through the winding servants' passageways, until they burst into a hall of glass and polished stone. At one end stood a throne; at the other, a set of great barricaded doors that strained their hinges with every blow from the other side.

Bang! Bang!

One bank of windows overlooked the harbor, where the Alliance soldiers were disembarking from their blue ships, marching into the capital waving their flags.

By the windows lay a body. It wore a gold crown set with five blue jewels.

Stonegold. Director of the Guard.

As Sefia approached, she could see that much of his torso was gone, eaten away as if by acid, with winking gold buttons here and there among the sizzling flesh and deteriorating bones, and Archer's sword tilting out of the corpse like a broken mast.

Archer pulled out his blade, examining the steel for traces of poison.

"She framed us," Sefia said, kneeling. They could still get what they came for. Gingerly, she began picking through the king's pockets—or what remained of them—searching for the vault key.

Her hands were going for Stonegold's neck, where a gold chain was visible through a part in his collar, when Tanin burst into the throne room with a squad of soldiers in tow.

No, not soldiers. They had scarred necks. *Candidates.*

Sefia's fingers closed around the chain and she gave it a tug as she stood. The links parted, and a little key came loose from the remnants of the king's ruined uniform. Quickly, she spooled it into her palm, hoping Tanin hadn't noticed.

But Tanin's silver eyes were on the sword in Archer's hand. "You killed the Director," she rasped.

Before either Sefia or Archer could protest, the candidates came rushing toward them, quick and agile. Bullets sped through the air. Tanin disappeared and reappeared between them in an instant, the First's bloodsword in her hands.

Archer's blade clashed against Tanin's as he and Sefia were driven apart. Summoning her magic, Sefia pushed Tanin away from him, deflected bullets, wrenched candidates aside.

At last, the woman turned on Sefia. While the candidates flooded toward Archer, Tanin advanced, bloodsword extended.

Sefia expected the woman to speak—to taunt her, to say *something*. But Tanin was silent as her copper blade, tinted with red in the last light of the sunset. She attacked. Sefia dodged, still pulling candidates away from Archer.

But they kept slipping her magic. They swarmed Archer, swords flashing. He backed toward the throne, parrying and countering, his blade finding wrists and exposed legs, his bullets finding shoulders and sides.

But he wasn't killing anyone.

A bullet grazed his shoulder. He faltered.

Thrusting Tanin aside, Sefia teleported to him. She landed, shakily, on the steps to the throne, with the candidates closing in.

Archer's arms went around her.

Oxscini might have been lost. Four kingdoms might have fallen to the Guard. But now she and Archer had the key to the vault.

They could strike back.

The streams of the Illuminated world ran before her like a flood, and with a wave of her arms, she teleported them away.

• • •

Once they'd retrieved the explosives from their cabin aboard the *Brother*, they appeared with a soft *thud* beside a bronze statue, its face stern. All around him, Archer could smell the odor of varnished wood, tanned leather, ancient paper. From the stained glass ceiling, dusky light filtered through the tall shelves, casting shadows like prison bars along the elaborately patterned floor.

So this was the Library.

Tentatively, Archer reached out to touch the spine of a book on one of the lower shelves. The leather felt warm and supple to the touch, almost as if it were alive.

Between the books, he could see a gold light at the other end of the room. Perhaps one of those electric lamps Sefia had told him about?

There was the creak of wood, followed by the soft *swoosh* of velvet on stone.

They weren't alone here.

Erastis, Sefia mouthed, pointing.

Archer nodded. She'd told him the Master Librarian frequented the Library at night. He'd just hoped they'd be lucky.

Sefia tapped her brow, above her eye patch. *I have an idea.* She pointed at him, then at the marble floor. *Stay here.*

Cocking his head, he touched his temple, asking for her plan.

Sefia motioned with her arms. She was going to disappear, and when she returned, she'd have something to neutralize the Librarian.

Quickly, he mimed planting the bombs nestled in his pack.

Putting her finger to her lips, she nodded. *As long as you do it quietly.*

Archer reached for his pack as Sefia teleported away, leaving only a puff of air in her wake. He backed into the shadows, away from the golden light, and, pacing up and down the aisles, he found darkened corners to hide the explosives he and Keon had made: canisters of gunpowder and blackrock dust linked to firing mechanisms he'd stripped from revolvers. After planting each bomb, he very carefully pulled back the hammers, listening to them *click* into place.

One good jolt and the hammers would hit the firing pins,

detonating the explosives and sending the whole vaulted annex up in flames.

He hoped.

There were only two bombs left in his pack when a voice made him halt in the shadows: "Who's there?"

Stashing his pack among the shelves, Archer ducked as the lantern light flared. Crouching, he peeked through a set of blue-bound books. Erastis was only twenty feet away, squinting into the shadows.

He was old, with skin as brown and wrinkled as a walnut. His hand shook as he held the lantern, making the light flicker and jump over his long velvet robes.

"Is that you, Tolem?" the Master Librarian called. "Your Master won't appreciate you snooping around here."

Tolem? The Apprentice Administrator that had attacked them at the messengers' post in Jahara. Archer remembered round spectacles and an unruly crop of dark curls.

Erastis shuffled forward, forcing Archer to retreat around a shelf, toward a set of carpeted steps.

He couldn't see the Librarian anymore, but he could hear him stalking slowly along the aisles. "Or perhaps you're not Tolem at all," Erastis said. "Perhaps you're someone with more malicious intent."

Silently, Archer backed up to the stairs. Even here, the walls were lined with books. Enough books for Sefia to read for the rest of her life and never run out of new passages to discover.

He felt a twinge of regret.

Through the stone banister that edged the steps, Archer could see the light of Erastis's lantern bobbing through the Library. He just had to evade him long enough for Sefia to return.

But as Archer reached the upper landing, the Master Librarian appeared at the bottom of the steps. Archer tried to duck out of sight, but before he could move, an invisible force gripped him tight and flung him sideways over the stone railing.

He felt the air rushing past him.

He felt his body strike the marble floor.

Wincing, he pulled himself into a crouch.

But then he froze. He couldn't move. Erastis had caught him again.

Archer struggled as the Master Librarian approached, unhurried, with a wary look in his eyes. "Who are you?" His gaze flicked to Archer's throat. "Not one of ours?"

When Archer said nothing, Erastis tilted his head curiously. "Archer?" There was a pause. "Sefia . . . is she here too?"

Still, Archer refused to speak.

The Master Librarian padded forward until Archer could see every cloud in his rheumy eyes. "Where is she?" When Archer didn't reply, Erastis sighed. "Never mind."

Wearily, the old man sat down in a wooden chair, which creaked under his weight as he set the lantern on the floor beside him. "I'd hoped to never meet you," he said finally.

After everything Sefia had told him about the Librarian, Archer should have guessed that Erastis would say something unexpected, but still, the words caught him off guard. "Why?" he asked.

"Because I knew if I met you, we'd end up here, as adversaries." The Master Librarian sighed. "And I'd hoped you'd run instead of fight."

"We tried to run. It didn't work."

"You could have disappeared at any time in the last four months. Sefia could have teleported you back to Deliene or any of the hideaways from her days with the Locksmith. The two of you would have been alone, but you would have been free of your destiny. Instead, you're here. The Red War is coming to an end. And so is your time in this world. But I suppose that's how destiny works."

Archer swallowed. "I don't have an army. I can't win any wars. And if I don't do that, I can't be the boy from the legends."

"You'll find a way, I'm sure."

"Out of it?"

"Into it." Erastis smiled sadly. "What are you doing here, Archer? There must be a better place for you to be right now, so close to the end."

Archer was about to say that it wasn't the end. But then he realized it didn't matter. End, middle, beginning. Wherever he was in his own story, all that mattered was that he was with Sefia.

Reaching for a tasseled rope on the other side of the room, Erastis used his magic to give it a pull. Nothing happened. Was it attached to a bell somewhere in the depths of the mountain? Whom had he summoned? "Now tell me," the Librarian continued. "What were you planning?"

CHAPTER 31

Past the Edges of the Stars

Rucksack in hand, Sefia landed on all fours in the center of the Administrator's Office. With her was the Book, which she'd retrieved from Aljan's quarters after leaving Archer in the Library.

Dim lights flickered along the curved walls, illuminating two chairs and a single wooden table in the center of the room. She shivered as the cold of the mountain seemed to press in around her.

She hoped her plan would work. Erastis was, by all accounts, the most powerful Illuminator the Guard had. In a fight, she didn't think she could beat him without hurting him.

And she didn't want to hurt him.

Tightening her hands on the straps of her rucksack, she headed for the laboratories. The chill corridors were silent as she passed room after room of specimens floating in jars, metal tables and glass beakers, cases of instruments, walls filled with wide drawers.

There was no sign of either Dotan, the Master Administrator, or his Apprentice.

At last, she found what she was looking for: the apothecary. In the center stood a table laden with weights and a scale, and beside it sat a large iron sphere, almost as high as her waist, with a strange glass contraption inside. Two of the apothecary's walls were crammed, floor to ceiling, with tiny, neatly categorized drawers: *aconite, arnica . . . byronia . . . chamomile . . .* Along the other two walls were glass cabinets that held neatly ordered bottles, all their labels facing out.

Quietly, Sefia opened the cabinet doors, searching for the compound she needed.

Nightmaker—the poison Tanin had slathered on Frey's and Aljan's locks, the poison that had stripped Sefia of her powers for weeks.

Had Dotan finished brewing it?

Yes. There it was, with a new, bright-white label among the yellowed ones. She snatched the bottle from the shelf. Pulling the Book from her pack, she took a step backward, accidentally knocking into the strange iron sphere by the apothecary table.

It rocked, the glass contraption inside shattering. Bits of glass collapsed, tinkling, inside the metal ball.

She winced, wondering if anyone had heard the noise. It was so delicate. What could it be for?

Laying the Book on the table, Sefia put her hands to the

sphere, stilling it. For a moment, she waited, listening for footsteps in the corridor.

No one came.

Breathing a sigh of relief, she straightened and removed the Book's leather casing. She hadn't seen it in weeks, since she'd given it to Aljan, and the sight of it now was like seeing an old friend she'd thought she'd never see again.

As if of their own accord, her fingers traced the ⊖ on the cover.

Answers. Redemption. Revenge.

The symbol had changed her entire life . . . and Archer's. The symbol was the reason she'd found him, the reason they were together, the reason he was destined to die.

Carefully, she uncapped the bottle of nightmaker and poured it onto the covers. The clear fluid was almost syrup-like in its consistency, a long, slender thread of poison trailing between the mouth of the bottle and the Book's surface.

Taking care not to touch it, Sefia took a scoop from the tabletop and smeared the liquid across the cover until it became a thin sheen. Then she flipped the Book and applied the poison to the back cover as well.

As she was rewrapping the Book in its waterproof covering, she heard a noise in the doorway.

She didn't stop to think. In the lair of the enemy, she didn't have time to think.

She reacted.

She teleported . . . and appeared in the doorway, one of her knives embedded in the boy's chest.

A boy?

Just a boy.

Tolem staggered back, his eyes wide behind his spectacles, his dark hair seeming to wave in a nonexistent breeze.

His brown skin was going ashen. His white shirt was going crimson. He opened his mouth, but no words came out.

Then he fell facedown on the apothecary floor, and he didn't stir again.

It took another second before Sefia realized what she'd done.

The boy wouldn't have been a threat. She could have subdued him another way. She could have let him live.

He could have lived.

She backed away, stumbling against the iron sphere, making the broken glass contraption shift and crunch inside. She was running out of time: the longer she lingered, the greater the chance she'd be discovered . . . again. And she shuddered to think what the Master Administrator would do if he caught her.

Swaddling the Book carefully in its leather casing, Sefia took one last look at the boy on the ground and summoned her magic, teleporting back to the Library.

The light had shifted. That was the first thing she noticed. The second was the soft drift of voices, echoing slightly under the domed ceiling.

"You love her like her mother loved her father," Erastis was saying. "Their love was so great, they destroyed an institution that had lasted for thousands of years."

Archer had been caught. Sefia hefted the Book in her arms as she dashed through the aisles of books.

"The Guard hasn't been destroyed," Archer said.

There was a pause before the Master Librarian asked, "Hasn't it?"

Stonegold. Sefia recounted the dead. The First. The Apprentice Administrator, dead on the apothecary floor. Once a society of eleven readers, the Guard now numbered only seven.

"Their love was the beginning of the end for us," Erastis continued. "What will you and Sefia destroy in your love for each other?"

Before Archer could reply, Sefia found them by the steps. Archer's pack was nowhere to be seen. Had he already planted all the explosives? She skidded to a stop with the Book extended in her arms. "Please," she said, "let him go."

The Librarian's eyes widened as he recognized the shape of the Book within the folds of its waterproof wrapping.

"You know who he is," she continued as Erastis got to his feet, his gaze never leaving the Book. "Help me save him. If there's a way, you'll find it. You can have the Book. Just help me, please."

The Master Librarian didn't stop to think. If he had, he might have wondered where she'd been while he was catching Archer in the Library. He might have wondered if it was a trap. He might have wondered what her real motives were.

But Erastis could think of nothing but the Book, which her father had stolen from him so many years ago.

He'd taken it from her in an instant, flinging the protective casing aside, his old, gnarled hands trembling as he caressed the leather covers, tracing the cracks, the spirals of long-lost gems and their delicate gold settings. His hunger for the Book was so great he seemed not to notice the tackiness of the poison. Even if he had, it would've been too late—he'd already touched it.

In his enthrallment, he let his grip on Archer slip away.

Archer ducked in among the bookshelves while the Librarian pressed his lips to the gilt-edged pages and opened the covers.

She was reminded of what Erastis had said to her father the first time Lon was left alone with the Book: *I like to think of the Book as an old friend. Faithful, with a good heart.*

While Archer backed toward the shelves, the Master Librarian skimmed the page. His lips moved.

What was he reading?

What was the Book telling him?

"Fire will visit the Library three times," he murmured, almost too softly for her to hear.

Her stomach dropped. The Book was warning him.

"Sefia." When he looked up, his eyes were filmed with tears. "How could you?"

But as he thrust out his hand to seize her, his magic failed. The poison was already at work. He stared at his fingers, aghast, as Archer reappeared with the bombs.

"Nightmaker," the Librarian whispered as Sefia used the leather wrapping to take the Book from him. "No, Sefia. Please."

"We have to move quickly," Archer said, binding Erastis's hands. "I think he called for someone, but I don't know who."

They walked him to the center of the Library and the curved tables where Sefia had begun her study of Transformation.

"Think of what you're doing," Erastis said. "This is the only bastion of literacy left in Kelanna. This is where history lives. Where poetry and literature and philosophy reside. If you take this from us, we'll be lost."

He continued to plead as she drew Nin's copy of the Librarian's key from her pocket and tossed Stonegold's key to Archer, who set a bomb on one of the tables in the center of the hall and tied Erastis to one of the chairs.

"Darion," the Librarian whispered, his gaze on the little key in Sefia's hand. "Is he dead?"

Sefia traced the image of the thunderbird, which surrounded one of the vault keyholes. "Yes," she said, "but not because of us."

That was at least one death that wasn't on her hands.

As one, she and Archer inserted the keys into the locks and began to turn. The markings etched into the vault were their guide.

Little hawk, little hawk, don't fly away. Archer turned his key to the image of the hawk, flying at the top of the keyhole.

For you're a mighty huntress with claws to catch your prey. Sefia turned hers to the thunderbird's claws.

The pins in the locks clicked as they turned to the lark, the beak, the owl, the thunderbird's right and left wings . . . until at last there was a heavy *clank*.

The vault door cracked open.

Sefia hesitated. Inside were the pages she needed to rewrite the future. Inside was hope. And hope could be snatched away.

Archer nodded at her. "Go," he said.

With a deep breath, she took the last bomb with her into the vault.

Inside, the air was cool and surprisingly fresh. On pedestals were tarnished objects inscribed with incantations: a shield, a silver quill with a sharp blade instead of a feather, a bottle of ink that had long since gone dry. Along the walls were dozens of pages suspended in glass frames, and in the center of the vault was an empty crystal case that must have been for the Book.

Lifting the lid, she set the explosive on the crushed velvet and pulled back the hammer. Then, with her magic, she began breaking sealed chests, cracking them open and riffling through them, searching for the pages she needed, the ones that would allow her to rewrite Archer's future.

At last she found them. Kneeling, she gathered them in her arms.

When she looked up, she spied the poem—nothing grand, just twenty-four lines—mounted on the wall. The paper was burned—it must have been caught in one of the Library's previous fires—but the words were still legible.

THIS IS A BOOK, AND A BOOK IS A WORLD,
AND WORDS ARE THE SEEDS IN WHICH MEANINGS ARE CURLED.
PAGES OF OCEANS AND MARGINS OF LAND
ARE CIVILIZATIONS YOU HOLD IN THE PALM OF YOUR HAND.

BUT LOOK AT YOUR WORLD AND YOUR LIFE SEEMS TO SHRINK
TO CITIES OF PAPER AND SEAS MADE OF INK.
DO YOU KNOW WHO YOU ARE, OR HAVE YOU BEEN MISLED?
ARE YOU THE READER, OR ARE YOU THE READ?

This is a word, and a word is a spell—
a promise to keep or a secret to tell.
Controlling the word means the power to frame
how the ages of history remember your name.

Are you hero or villain? A savior or spy?
Some titles are lovely. Some titles are lies.
You can claim who you are, now that you've found
    your voice.
But those who are chosen will not have a choice.

This is a story as vast as the sea,
but on its waters, you'll never be free.
No matter your course, your future is set,
and destiny laughs as she tightens the net.

Words to Kelannans are breath on a glass,
but if it is written, it will come to pass.
Is your sight growing clearer, the closer you look?
The Book is a world, for the world is a book.

As Sefia read the words, something stirred within her, some
deep realization, splitting her open as a beam of light splits the
dark.

Reading was the interpretation of signs, her father had said,
and the world was full of them. Scars, scratches, footprints. If you
could tap into the Illuminated world, you could read the history
of each mark as clearly as you could read a sentence from a book.

This is.

She remembered the first time she'd seen the Illuminated world in all its magnificence, all the little golden currents, a million of them and a trillion motes of light, all perfect and exact and brimming with meaning. It made her feel like she was peering past the edges of the stars into whatever lay beyond.

This is. This is. This is this is this is this— She'd written it so many times before. How had she not understood what she was really writing?

"We're all in the Book," she'd told Captain Reed once. "All of history. All knowledge. Everything."

The Book is a world . . .

She glanced down at the pages in her hands, then back up at the poem.

. . . for the world is a book.

The world.

This is a book. A book. A book.

Sefia blinked, and the Illuminated world sprang to life before her—a never-ending sea of light, twined with bright webs of gold so brilliant they could not be untangled.

She looked closer, not at the streams of light but at the sparkling particles that comprised them. She looked deeper.

She saw more.

The particles were not mere specks of light.

They were sentences.

They were phrases.

They were words.

They were letters and punctuation marks so infinitesimally small it was no wonder she'd never noticed them before.

The world was a book. She was living in a book. She was in a book.

And all books were written by someone.

Maybe someone was reading her right now, and if she looked up, she would see their eyes staring down at her, following her every move. Maybe someone was reading the reader.

Sefia looked up then, past the stone ceiling of the vault, through the mountain air, between the stars.

And beyond . . .

There was me, looking back at her, telling you her story.

CHAPTER 32

The Storyteller

You see, I've been here since the beginning, watching, telling the story as it unfolds before me, and I'll be here when it ends. (For it does end, now. When she first touched the Resurrection Amulet, Sefia forever altered the course of the story . . . and now it ends with victory . . . and loss . . . and darkness.)

It's been so long since anyone saw me—since the Scribes, who knew what kind of world they were in.

Sefia's eyes widen, just once, and I know she knows I'm here. She knows what I am, and she knows that against me, she cannot win.

But I can only read what is written, and what is written cannot be changed—not even by me, a mere narrator in this tale of ink and gold.

What is written is what *is*.

And there are bombs to detonate. Conflagrations to spark. Destruction to wreak.

Words to burn.

When Sefia hurries from the vault, clutching the precious pages to her chest, she doesn't look up once. I watch the top of her head, willing her to look up again, to see me, to acknowledge that I'm here.

That I have to stand by and watch . . . all of this.

That I am a reader, a bystander, a witness, as much as you are, and the only power I have is in the details—the quality of the light in Sefia's eyes as she places the pages in her pack beside the Book, safely wrapped in its leather casing, the way she takes Archer's hand, the descriptions, the turns of phrase, the carefully chosen words.

Did you get any of my messages?

Did she?

I tried to warn her, when I could. Before she met the bartender in Epidram. When Harison died on the *Current of Faith*. Before she left Archer on that cliff in Deliene. And after.

I would warn her now, but she couldn't hear me. I can't speak to her except through the Book . . . or in the Illuminated world.

So I watch. I watch as they usher the Master Librarian into the greenhouse—he's crying now, weeping, like he's watching the death of a loved one, which I suppose he is—and I want to tell him I'm sorry.

I'm sorry. I knew this would happen from the beginning.

Fire would always visit the Library three times: once

under Morgun's watch, and twice under Erastis's, when Mareah set fire to the shelves the day she and Lon stole the Book . . . and now, as Sefia and Archer and the Librarian stand in the greenhouse.

Outside, the beginnings of spring are upon the mountains, and flowers are poking their heads through the last of the melting snow.

Sefia blinks and lifts her fingers, finding the hammer on the only explosive she can see, on one of the curved tables where Erastis and June taught her Transformation.

She doesn't look away when she brings her hand down.

The hammer falls.

The firing pin strikes.

The gunpowder ignites, and the blackrock dust burns—burns—*burns*—exploding outward from its canister in a dozen whirlwinds of heat and fire.

The explosion shakes the nearest bombs, secreted all throughout the Library, and they, too, detonate.

Shelves burst into pieces. Stone crumbles. Statues fall. Inside the vault, the glass frame of the poem shatters, and the page is consumed by flame.

The blast catches the Fragments, painstakingly copied, and the Commentaries, the volumes of poetry, the histories, the scientific treatises, throwing them outward in an inferno of blazing paper.

Archer shields his eyes. Does he regret?

Yes, of course he does.

The fire climbs the carpeted steps, gnawing at the bookshelves, the bindings, the leather covers.

The fire eats the curved tables, the quills. It's so hot, the gum erasers melt. The inkwells shatter.

Erastis, in a sudden fit of strength and desperation, wrenches out of Archer's grasp. He's fast, faster than he should be, considering his great age, but he's watching something he loves die, and that gives him speed.

Archer chases after him, but when the heat stops the boy at the threshold of the Library, the old man marches on, into the flames.

Sefia tries to sweep aside the blaze, but it's too strong, even for her, and the Master Librarian will not be stopped.

The ropes at his wrists burn.

The velvet robes too.

And still that doesn't stop him.

He reaches for the nearest shelf.

The room no longer smells like old books. It smells like scorched stone and smoke, and the volumes he pulls from the fire blister his wrinkled skin.

At last, through the insulation of his grief, the pain reaches him.

He shrieks as he presses the books to his chest.

As they consumed him in life, now they consume him in death.

Oh, Erastis.

I've had almost a century with him. Almost a century to watch and know and love him. He wasn't the kind I had to learn to love. I've loved him since the beginning.

Lon would have cried, if he'd been here, as Sefia is crying now.

As the Librarian falls, there is movement on the other side of the Library. Sefia sees it through her tears, through the smoke and the haze of heat.

Sees her—June—her limp brown hair pulled into a messy bun, her pinched face smudged with ash.

June watches her Master die.

I watch her watch her Master die.

I'm sorry, June. For that. And for this.

Her gaze meets Sefia's across the Library, and she teleports.

Sefia lets her come. She's already taken a life tonight. She doesn't want to take another.

But she doesn't have to, does she?

Archer is there.

And someone is coming for the girl he loves.

He doesn't have time to think before he reacts. As June appears in the greenhouse, carrying with her a cloud of heat and sparks, Archer draws Lightning.

He shoots her, and the light in her eyes dies.

Erastis was right. Lon and Mareah's love was the beginning of the end, and now, with the destruction of the Library and the killing of three Guardians, Sefia and Archer's love will soon bring the Guard—and this story—to a close.

Part of the mountain begins to crumble.

Dotan, the Master Administrator, is in the Main Branch somewhere, but he isn't going to die here now. No, he and the four remaining Guardians survive this night.

Shakily, Archer steps closer to Sefia. Puts his arm around her, as much to comfort himself as to comfort her. *Born killer.* The words haunt him.

He won't be able to escape his nightmares tonight.

And neither will Sefia, though her nightmares will be of a different kind. For she can't unsee what she's seen, can't unknow what she knows.

"Let's go," Archer whispers to her. "The others might need us."

She nods. She has no words. Not now.

But she will have them later. With me.

She summons her sense of the Illuminated world, and through the charging waves of light, she finally looks up . . . at me.

Though one of her eyes is concealed by her eye patch, her gaze is venomous—filled with such resentment and malice and hatred that it could kill.

But I cannot be killed, by looks or mortal weapons. I've been here since the beginning, and I'll be here when it ends.

They disappear.

Somewhere on the southern side of the world, they reappear on the deck of a red ship with white markings, among their friends.

But here, as the Library burns, there's a disturbance in the greenhouse shadows. A slender, well-dressed figure. It's Dotan, and he's wearing that same look of resentment and malice and hatred on his nearly symmetrical features.

Oh, Sefia. I wish you could have seen him.

I wish you could have stopped him here.

But it wasn't written.

CHAPTER 33

Now Is All You Have

For all they'd done—stealing the power of the Scribes, destroying the Library—Sefia and Archer were too late to stop the Guard.

Oxscini had fallen to the Alliance. The Guard, diminished as they were, controlled four of the Five Islands, and as soon as they recuperated, they would come for Roku, the Volcanic Kingdom.

But the Resistance had grown too.

Of the seventeen ships that sailed in to break the siege of Tsumasai Bay, fourteen sailed out again, including the *Brother*, the *Current*, and the *Crux*, and they were accompanied by triple their number in allies: rebel redcoats who'd disobeyed their queen's order to surrender and Delienean defectors who'd rallied to their king when he emerged from the battle to reclaim his throne.

All told, there were fifty-eight ships fleeing from the Alliance forces in Oxscini when Sefia and Archer appeared on the deck of the *Brother*, smelling of smoke.

Sefia was silent while Scarza told them the Resistance was retreating to Roku. She barely stirred when Archer told him that Stonegold and three more Guardians were dead, that the Library was burning even as they spoke.

She allowed Aljan to take the poisoned Book from her custody without protest. For she'd seen the truth of their world, and it had rendered her speechless.

That night, while Archer thrashed in his sleep, she sat by the lantern and pored over the pages she'd taken from the vault, hoping to find answers.

Everyone in the Guard knew the Book was a record of the world, but only the Scribes had known the world itself was a book.

She was in a book, and the end had already been written.

No wonder all of her plans to beat the Book had failed. You couldn't change the story if you were trapped inside it.

To use Alteration, the Scribes had cut passages from the Illuminated world, rearranged words, revised history, but even their power had limits.

They could make some changes, as Sefia had done in the Rokuine highlands. They could erase pebbles and plant entire forests on barren hillsides. They could invent weapons, alter the courses of rivers, massacre wave after wave of people.

But they could not change the outcome of the story without destroying the world and everyone in it.

The story would always end the same way.

Shoving the pages back into her pack, Sefia crept from the cabin, up onto the main deck, and climbed out onto the *Brother*'s bowsprit, with the water racing beneath her and the cold wind fast around her body. There, she summoned her magic.

The world, once dark, blazed to life before her eyes. Past. Present.

Future.

She flipped ahead to the ending—to a world without color, shape, or shadow. To the world of the dead.

For years, for endless years, they would be suspended in the void, unable to tell if they were fixed or moving because there would be no landmarks for them to recognize. There would be nothing to tell them where they'd been or where they were going. They would be alone.

But, at last, they would hear the call. Someone was summoning the dead from the black edge of the world.

They would rise, shooting upward through the darkness like bolts of light.

They would return—to the deep blue, the world just below the surface, the white flashing underside of the sky.

They would remember. The unforgiving blue. The wind. The sound. The people.

Sefia gasped. Someone was going to use the Resurrection Amulet, she realized, but it wouldn't save them. It wouldn't keep anyone from dying. It would summon the dead.

As the rivers of light cascaded past her, Sefia caught words in her hands, pulling them from their streaming sentences, and put them together again.

And for the first time in ages—in thousands of pages—I answered: YES.

She looked up.

And again, she found me.

"Who are you?" she whispered.

I'M THE STORYTELLER.

I don't have a voice the way you do. I don't have a tongue or lungs or a heart. I spoke to her in light, taking the threads of the Illuminated world and twisting them into shapes—letters—punctuation—explanations—apologies.

"Have you been here the whole time?" she asked.

YES.

Since the first sentence—*Once there was, and one day there will be*—I have been here.

I KNEW YOUR FATHER, I told her.

AND YOUR MOTHER.

AND THE LOCKSMITH.

Sefia's fingers tightened on the running lines. I suspect she wanted to keep from crying. Mareah had died nearly twelve years ago, and the grief was still so fresh.

"Can you bring them back?"

No. If I'd had a voice, it would have broken.

"Why not?"

IMAGINE THERE IS A WALL BETWEEN THE WORLD OF THE LIVING AND THE WORLD OF THE DEAD, AND IN THIS WALL, THERE IS ONE GATE.

"The sun," she said. "Captain Reed and the *Current of Faith* passed through it."

FOR THE DEAD, **WHO** SO LONG TO RETURN, THE GATE OPENS IN ONLY ONE DIRECTION.

"What about the Resurrection Amulet?"

Don't you know by now? I wanted to ask. *Haven't I said it enough?*

Some stories are lovely. Some stories are lies.

I told her the Resurrection Amulet was never supposed to keep a person from dying. It was supposed to bring one soul— and only one soul—back from the dead.

"'To tether his love to the living world,'" Sefia murmured.

The blacksmith who created the Amulet wanted to restore life to someone who was already dead. When he wore it, he would summon her soul from the place of the fleshless, and to keep her here, he would give her some of his own life force.

But he didn't know that you can't come back from the dead . . . not really.

She was a phantom, like the ones Captain Reed had encountered beyond the edge of the world. He couldn't touch her without her draining his warmth and breath. He didn't even know if she was really herself or some amalgam of his own memories of her.

So he sent her back to the world of the dead, severing their connection, and split the Amulet in two, burying it where he hoped no one would ever find it, so no one would be tempted to use it again.

Sefia shuddered.

DO YOU REMEMBER WHAT ERASTIS TOLD YOU HE LEARNED FROM YOUR PARENTS? I asked.

She closed her eyes, dismissing her magic—dismissing me—

and when she opened them again, the night was dark and the sea was black.

"'Love what's in front of you, right now,'" she said, "'because now is all you have.'"

But she didn't return to her cabin right away. Instead, she teleported from the *Brother's* bowsprit to the *Current of Faith*. The green ship was battered after the battle in Tsumasai Bay— rails shattered, hull pitted with bullets, chunks of Cooky's galley and Horse's workshop missing. As she crossed the splintered decks, the chief mate found her in the dark.

"You made it," he said.

She nodded. "What happened here?"

"Serakeen." His lip curled as he spoke the name. "He has new guns."

"Is everyone all right?"

"No."

Old Goro was dead. Others were gravely injured. Horse was barely hanging on, while Doc watched over him in the sick bay.

"I'm sorry." Sefia looked down at her feet, where a bloodstain hadn't been completely scrubbed out.

"Something else troubling you, girl?" the chief mate asked. With one thick finger, he tilted her chin up.

Tears sprang to her eyes.

Everything was wrong. The burning of the Library. The deaths of June and Erastis and Tolem and Goro. And Archer . . . no, she couldn't even think it. The *world* was wrong. Unfair . . . and unbeatable.

Roughly, the mate patted her shoulder with one callused palm and waited for her to stop crying. "There," he said when her tears had dried up, "now that you've stopped your blubbering, go see the captain." Holding her at arm's length, he gave her shoulders a reassuring squeeze. "I suspect it'll do you both some good to talk."

Then he put his hands behind his back and paced across the broken ship, into the dark.

Sefia found Captain Reed in the great cabin. The back windows had been boarded up, and bullet holes riddled the walls. Shards of the glass cases littered the floor, the treasures inside tilted on their stands. One of the rubies was chipped. The Thunder Gong and the mallet Dimarion had gifted to Reed lay together on the floor.

Reed was sitting at the long table, counting his tattoos in the lamplight. "You get what you wanted?" he asked as she sank onto the bench across from him.

Wiping her eyes, she told him how Archer had been framed for Stonegold's death, how she'd killed the Apprentice Administrator, how the Library had burned and the Librarians with it. And she told him about the storyteller, the world, the Book.

"Well . . . shit."

She laughed. Or sobbed. Some combination of the two. "Yeah," she said.

"You know, though . . ." Reed rubbed his jaw. "That explains a lot."

"How do you figure?"

He turned his palms up, exposing the tattoos on the undersides of his arms. "I've been lucky, haven't I? To have done all this. Only a main character coulda racked up stories like these."

Sefia tried to smile, but it faltered on her lips. Archer was important too. But he wouldn't get the chance to have half as many adventures.

Which reminded her why she'd come. To tell Reed the truth about the Amulet.

As she spoke, the captain pulled the Resurrection Amulet from inside his shirt. "You mean I've been wearin' this ugly hunk of metal for months, and it don't even do what I thought it did?"

She shrugged.

"Why'd Tan lie?"

"Maybe she didn't know the truth."

"You remember the fuss you kicked up about this thing? How you were so sure fate wanted Archer to have it so he could fulfill his destiny?"

In the light, the red stones winked like dozens of little eyes.

Sefia reached out, the tips of her fingers almost brushing the dull metal. "Maybe fate wanted *me* to have it, so I . . ." So she could call him back from the world of the dead when he died. But there were so many other people she wanted to see too.

Her father.

Her mother.

Nin.

She missed them so keenly she'd do anything to see them again.

But the Resurrection Amulet would summon only one soul from the black world beyond. Not three.

"It doesn't matter," she said, drawing back her hand. "It won't work if it's incomplete."

Reed touched his chest, where the location of the missing

piece had been buried beneath years of ink. "I gave up on findin' that," he said.

"Why?"

He began tapping each of his tattoos again, one after another. "Because it happens soon." The water had told him, he said. He thought it might have been in Tsumasai Bay, but since he'd survived it, he suspected it would be at Roku, whenever the Alliance came for them.

"You and the outlaws could still run," Sefia said, though she couldn't quite bring herself to believe it. They were in too deep to leave now. "We could all run."

"We threw in our lot against the Alliance the day we set sail for Oxscini. There's nowhere left to run now, and no one left to stand against them . . . except the Resistance."

She watched him trace the lines of ink that covered his skin like letters covering a page. "I think . . . ," she began quietly, "I think I could find the last piece."

He stopped, mid-count, staring at her with his sea-blue eyes. "How?"

"With magic." She'd done it before, hadn't she? Removing strains of mold from a page. She could remove strands of ink from flesh. "I think I could take all your other tattoos, except that one. The first one. Although . . . I think it might hurt."

Captain Reed looked down at his arms. He flexed his fingers, studying the images inked onto his knuckles. All his adventures. All the stories he'd worked so hard to collect.

She could take them. If she did, she'd be able to find the last piece of the Amulet and make it whole. Make it work.

"I didn't want to die," he said finally, "but if I was gonna die, if my heart was gonna stop beatin' and my body was gonna turn to ash, I wanted to be remembered, because that was the only way I could live forever. And I was gonna live a life so big, so fast, so bold that I'd never be forgotten."

Removing the Amulet, he placed it on the table between them. "You think I accomplished that? You think I did good with the time I had?"

She nodded. "Better than anyone, Cap."

With a sigh, he stood and crossed the cabin, placing the metal disc in one of the broken glass cases. "Then I'll keep what I have," he said. "And you should too, while you have it."

CHAPTER 34

Those Who Will Die

Archer was dreaming again, and in his dreams the Library was still burning. Smoke billowed from the broken stained glass windows and gaps in the crumbling stone as pages flew, blazing, into the sky like firebirds, trailing sparks.

He was standing in the greenhouse again, but it was Kaito with him and not Sefia. The boy's skin was dark—*with ash?*—and in the light of the flames, his eyes seemed to glow red.

As if he could sense Archer watching him, Kaito looked over, rolling his neck at an unnatural angle. Under his scarlet eyes, he wore a hang-jawed smile, his teeth eerily white.

But before Archer had the chance to recoil, Kaito had moved. He was quick as lightning. He was standing in front of Archer now. He was crouching over the Apprentice Librarian, withdrawing his blade from her chest.

He was still smiling.

Archer gasped. Did he speak? *She was just a kid. She was innocent! What's the matter with you?*

Kaito only shrugged. "We kill people and we get people killed," he said, though his voice wasn't his own. "You better come to terms with that now if you're going to lead us."

Then he was dissolving, his edges melting into the shadows, the red light dying in his eyes, leaving only the echo of his words:

. . . *if you're going to lead us.*

. . . *you're going to lead us.*

. . . *lead us.*

Archer woke with a start, still feeling the heat of the fire on his face, still smelling the smoke.

But he wasn't back there anymore. Dawn glinted in the portholes, glancing off the tops of the waves as the *Brother* and the Resistance ships raced south toward Roku. Archer reached for the worry stone at his throat. He was safe.

And Sefia was there, sitting at the other end of the bunk, with the pages from the vault crinkled in her lap. "Archer," she said softly, "there's something I have to tell you."

He listened as she told him the truth. What their world really was. How the ending had already been written. How they were approaching it even now. As she spoke, he traced the facets of the crystal hanging around his neck.

You're safe, he tried to tell himself. *You're safe.*

But he wasn't. He never had been.

All the things that had happened to him. All the things he'd done and become. All the beatings, the fights, the kills, the *suffering* . . . it had all been planned. Orchestrated. Intended.

Written.

It didn't make sense.

Someone had done this to him? Someone had wanted this to happen? Who?

Tears slipped from the corners of his eyes.

How could someone be so cruel?

If he'd written this story, he would have eliminated every hardship, every illness, every conflict. He would have written it with kind, loving people, and he would have made it so not a single one of them died.

If he'd written this story, everyone would have lived.

Happily.

Ever after.

"I'm so sorry," Sefia said.

Archer swallowed. His throat had gone dry. "Do you know how I—" He swallowed again.

She shook her head.

It would take the Guard some time to establish their hold on the Forest Kingdom, but after that, they'd come for Sovereign Ianai and the Black Navy, they'd come for the outlaws and the rebel redcoats and the Delienean defectors, and, one way or another, the Red War would come to an end.

Would Archer take command of an army during that time?

Would he be victorious?

It didn't make sense.

Was the Resistance supposed to prevail? Was he supposed to lead them? Or was he supposed to turn on them in the space of a few weeks? Months, at most?

Is that all the time I have left?

Shoving the papers aside, Sefia climbed across the bunk to him as he began to cry. She held him while he wept, while his shoulders trembled and his tears bled through her shirt.

"I don't want to die," he whispered.

But he was *going* to die. Soon. *After his last campaign . . . alone.*

"You won't." Sefia gripped him tight. "I won't let you. I'm going to fight this, and so are you."

"How?"

"You know who said it was impossible to save you? That we should stop trying?" Reaching out, she grabbed the discarded pages in her fist. "The Book. The Book that *wants* you to die. You know what that means?"

He sat up, sniffing.

Once, somewhere in the depths of the Oxscinian jungle, Sefia had asked him what he would do if he knew how he was going to die.

Now he had to decide. Would he run toward it? Run from it? Or do something entirely different?

"It means we should do the opposite," he said.

She wiped his cheeks. "Yes. We should do the opposite. The power of the Scribes changed the *geography* of the world. It's got to be able to save the life of one boy." She lifted her first two fingers, crossing one over the other. "The boy I love."

Taking a deep breath, he clasped her hand.

He was a boy who was loved. And the girl who loved him would never give up on him.

S o they continued to fight.

After the funerals, when they said good-bye to old Goro and the others who had fallen in battle, Archer asked Scarza to begin working with the bloodletters again. As they sailed toward Roku, they drilled and sparred on the deck of the *Brother*, their breath clouding the frigid air.

He instructed them. He guided them. He demonstrated if he had to, though with the bloodletters, who had coalesced under Scarza's command, more disciplined, more of a team than they'd ever been under Archer's, he rarely had to.

The last battle was coming, and a lot of people were going to die.

Archer couldn't lead them, but he wanted them to be ready. He wanted to keep them alive, however he could. As long as he could.

And that meant getting them ready to fight.

While they skirmished, Sefia studied the power of the Scribes in the *Current*'s sick bay. She had to hurry—Horse was dying, his great big body too damaged to repair itself, even with Doc's skillful attendance.

For the first time since Archer had known her, the surgeon had lost the steady quiet he knew her for, pacing the tiny cabin, obsessively arranging the bottles of ointment on the shelves, dabbing Horse's feverish brow with a damp cloth.

But even when Sefia had finished reading and rereading the pages, she hesitated. "What if I make the same mistakes I made at Blackfire Bay?" she asked. "What if I excise his lungs instead of healing them? What if I erase part of the ship, or you, or—"

Doc grabbed her roughly by the shoulders, her strong dark fingers curling in Sefia's shirt. "Stop," the surgeon said firmly. "If he could, Horse would tell you he believes in you. As do I. Do not doubt."

Archer watched Sefia take a steadying breath. Bowing her head, she removed her eye patch. A diagonal scar cleaved her brow and cheek, but her eye was bright as ever, blazing with focus, determination, daring. And then . . . she healed Horse's bullet-ridden organs. She closed the holes in his flesh. He sat up, wide-eyed, as Doc flung herself into his massive arms with a sob of relief.

Cradling the surgeon's head with one massive hand, Horse met Sefia's gaze with a teary smile that, more than the newly mended patches of skin or the health returning to his pallor, made Archer realize she'd done it. She'd mastered the power of the Scribes. She was the most powerful sorcerer the world had seen in centuries.

She'd rewritten Horse's future. Could she rewrite Archer's?

Later, while she walked the pitted decks with the chief mate, cataloguing the necessary repairs, Archer wandered to the bowsprit, where Captain Reed was standing in the branches that spiraled out over the water.

"Hey, kid," Reed said as Archer approached. "How're you holdin' up?"

Archer climbed onto the bowsprit, closing his eyes as the spray kissed his cheeks. Sefia had already told the captain everything, and it was a relief not to have to go over it all again. Not to have to admit the truth.

"Sometimes I'm okay," he said, leaning back against one of the tree limbs. "Sometimes I'm barely holding it together."

In the shadow of his wide-brimmed hat, the corner of Reed's mouth twitched. "Sounds about right."

Death may have been coming for all of the Resistance, but only Archer and Captain Reed knew without a doubt that it wanted to take them.

Soon. After his last campaign. Alone.

Archer reached for the worry stone. "Sefia said you're not going to run," he said.

The captain nodded.

"Why not?"

"Same reason as you, I reckon. Couldn't live with myself if I did." With one finger, Reed tipped up the brim of his hat, giving Archer a once-over with his piercing blue gaze. "And 'cause I have hope."

"Hope that you'll make it?"

"Hope that if I go out this way, I'll be leavin' a better world behind. Can't ask for a better legacy than that, can I?"

Looking down, Archer watched a pod of dolphins join them, leaping and cavorting in the waves as the *Current* carved through the water. They clicked and squealed, their shining backs arcing out of the sea.

"What's my legacy?" he wondered aloud.

A string of murders? A count of his victims?

The bloodletters?

"What do you want it to be?" Reed asked. "Now's the time to make what you want to leave behind."

What *was* he leaving behind? Besides his weapons, he had no real possessions of his own.

But he had a family, back in Jocoxa, the little village on the northwestern tip of Oxscini.

He had a family here, on the *Current* and the *Brother*.

He had Sefia.

Captain Reed had returned to watching the water, and he didn't seem to notice when Archer climbed back onto the main deck.

He might survive the end of the war. But if he didn't . . . He wanted to make something to leave behind, just in case. And he wanted it to be made of paper and ink.

S oon, Sefia was visiting all the fleeing ships to make repairs, her mastery of Alteration growing stronger each day. Dangling over the side of the hull, she excised bullet holes, repaired broken rails, plugged fissures left by cannon fire.

And wherever she went, Archer went too.

They found Haldon Lac and Olly Hobs on the first vessel they teleported to. Archer flung his arms around them, crying, "I wasn't sure if you made it out of Jahara!"

Lac laughed. "We did!" Archer hadn't thought it possible, but the boy seemed even more handsome than before—his hair more wild, his appearance more rugged, his nose, which must have been broken at some point over the past few months, adding character to his otherwise symmetrical features.

"We had help from a *king*!" Hobs added.

"You what?"

"Are those really the bloodletters on your ship?" Lac asked, peering over Archer's shoulder at the *Brother*, where Frey and the boys were sparring. "Who's the handsome one with the silver hair?"

"That's Scarza. He—"

"Is it true you're giving combat lessons?" Hobs asked.

Before Archer could get a word in edgewise, Lac interrupted, "Are you doing that for all of the Resistance? I mean, Royal Navy training is nothing to turn up your nose at, but . . . well, from what we've heard, no one is as good as you."

"Will you teach us?" Hobs added. "Please?"

"Or maybe that handsome silver-haired boy could do it?" Lac asked. "Scarza?"

With minimal wheedling, they managed to convince their commanding officer to allow Archer to train the redcoats.

They weren't as skilled as the bloodletters, but who could have been? Led by Lac and Hobs, who were enthusiastic enough to make up for their lack of ability, the redcoats practiced counters and takedowns, pausing only to marvel at Sefia as she smoothed out the splinters in the decks and sealed leaks in the hull.

Somehow, word of his identity reached the other Resistance ships. He was the boy from the legends. He was a born killer. He was Archer, chief of the bloodletters.

Former chief, he kept correcting them.

They didn't care. They'd heard he was training fighters. They wanted his help.

And, with Scarza and the bloodletters to help him, Archer obliged.

Is this my army? he wondered. *Am I building it right now?*

No. He would train them. He would hope they survived. But he would not lead them. Not even the bloodletters.

A few days later, Archer and Sefia were given an audience with the Delienean king, Eduoar Corabelli II.

Lac and Hobs had told them how the king, who they'd kept calling "Ed," had sneaked them out of Jahara, kept them alive on the *Hustle*, helped the refugees from Broken Crown, and joined the Royal Navy as a boy with no last name.

"And you had no idea he was the King of Deliene?" Sefia had asked.

"No clue!" Lac had declared.

She smirked. "What a surprise."

Now she and Archer sat across from the Lonely King himself, in the great cabin aboard the *Red Hare*. He was tall and well-built, with skin a little darker than Sefia's and black hair pulled back in a high knot. To Archer's surprise, he didn't wear a crown.

But what did Archer know? Maybe monarchs didn't always wear crowns.

He had such sad eyes, Archer noticed, dark but clear, like if his eyes caught the light in just the right way, you'd be able to see the shapes of his sadness deep inside him, like formations in a cavern.

The king thanked Archer for showing the Delienean soldiers "a thing or two" and he thanked Sefia for repairing the *Red Hare*.

But, if she didn't mind, he had another request. He wasn't sure if she could do it, but he'd heard some pretty remarkable things about her—about them both—and he thought if anyone could do it, she could.

Before they left the *Red Hare* that evening, Sefia lowered herself off the edge of the bow, right beside the figurehead. She flicked out a knife and, furrowing her brow, she began to carve into the blue-painted timbers.

Archer didn't know what she'd written, but when she was finished, the hull turned white. Dazzlingly white. White as the snow that capped the Szythian Mountains.

She'd given them back their colors.

B y the time they reached Roku, three weeks since fleeing from Tsumasai Bay, all fifty-eight ships had been repaired. Using Transformation, Sefia had altered the paint on all of Eduoar's vessels, changing them from Alliance blue to Delienean white. She'd even begun augmenting some of the Resistance ships, starting with the *Brother* and the *Current*, carving words into their prows to imbue them with speed and strength.

When they sailed into Blackfire Bay, with the glittering spread of Braska laid out before them, Sovereign Ianai was waiting on the dock, flanked by Adeline, Isabella, and the Black Navy generals.

There was much work to be done.

Archer and Sefia were offered their old room in the castle, but they chose instead to remain in the harbor on the *Brother*.

In the mornings, Sefia was whisked away to fortify walls and ships with magic, and Archer stole off to work with Aljan on their books.

But the afternoons Archer and Sefia claimed for themselves.

No one even tried to refuse them. They spent their hours hiking the Rokuine highlands, peering into steaming geysers of the most vibrant colors Archer had seen in his life, skipping over dry volcanic mudflows, watching mountain buffalo go wandering over the plains.

They spent their hours talking.

They spent their hours in bed.

They spent their hours with the bloodletters and the crew of the *Current* and Adeline and Isabella, who had begun dictating stories to Meeks to put in the book of their lives.

Often, their friends could be found writing in the books Keon could not churn out fast enough. Aljan was recording the exploits of the bloodletters, though he had little time for it because the others continually approached him with questions about their own books, which he answered without wavering in his patience, no matter how frequently they interrupted him. Meeks was writing the saga of Captain Reed and the *Current of Faith*. To her book of trees, Frey was adding mangroves she'd seen as they sailed toward the siege of Tsumasai Bay. Griegi was still scribbling in his book of recipes.

And Archer had work of his own. For every long hour that Sefia was occupied with the Resistance, he and Aljan sat together—Archer speaking, Aljan transcribing—in the lantern light, until Archer's voice grew hoarse and Aljan's cramped fingers were stained with ink.

Then, after dinner, Archer and Sefia attended the evening council meetings. They answered questions about the Guard. They helped plan for the defense of the kingdom.

When they retired to their cabin, sometimes long past

midnight, Sefia continued her study of Alteration. She got quicker. She got stronger. And while she practiced, Archer watched her for as long as he could keep his eyes open, thinking of all the things he still wanted to say to her.

Then, one day, almost three months since the fall of Oxscini, a single ship appeared on the western horizon, bearing flags of blue, gold, white, and a new stripe of Royal Navy red.

The Alliance had sent a messenger.

Sovereign Ianai and Roku were to yield to the Alliance. The so-called Delienean king was to renounce his claim to the throne and declare Arcadimon Detano the rightful leader of the Northern Kingdom. The Alliance would mete out just consequences for the Delieneans who had defected and the redcoats who had disobeyed their queen. To everyone else, the Alliance would be merciful.

If these terms were refused, however, the Alliance would strike the Volcanic Kingdom with the combined might of the four larger islands, and they would give no quarter.

Surrender or perish.

The messenger reported that the Alliance forces were six days from Roku. The Resistance had six days to decide.

Sovereign Ianai called an emergency council meeting, where the leaders from the outlaws, the bloodletters, the Delieneans, the redcoats, and the Black Navy argued back and forth for a day.

Some believed they should submit.

Others—like Reed and all of the outlaws—wanted to fight.

Someone suggested they use the boy from the legends. Put him at the head of an army, and destiny would do the rest.

Someone else claimed they put stock in guns and ships, not in *stories*. The Alliance had hundreds of fighting vessels at their disposal. No matter who led them, the Resistance was outnumbered.

Another said, legend or no, they weren't going to hand over their soldiers to a child.

Some wanted to use Sefia. She was a sorcerer.

Archer knew, however, what the Resistance leaders would decide long before they came to a unanimous conclusion.

The Red War had to have a last battle.

It had been written.

The Resistance would fight, and they would hope.

The next day, the fifth day before the Alliance's arrival, against the advice of the war council, who warned their sovereign to give Sefia a wide berth when she was wielding magic, Ianai escorted both Sefia and Archer to the cliff where they had stood during the Battle of Blackfire Bay, so Sefia could use Illumination to alter the Rokuine defenses.

It was too dangerous, the royal advisers said. You know what happened the last time she attempted such powerful magic.

"It's my kingdom," Ianai snapped. "I want to see this for myself."

So the sovereign, in a black traveling cloak and a crown of scales, and Archer were the only witnesses when Sefia raised a mountain range from the depths of the ocean. At the base of the cliff, the breakers thrashed. The rocks groaned. It took her until long after sundown, standing there in the wind without food or water or rest, her hands weaving through the air—tugging and grasping, sweeping and interlacing—but by the time she was done, there was a long spine of stone blocking the northern entrance to Blackfire Bay.

Ianai's dark gaze shone with admiration. "It's a shame you weren't born royalty, Sefia. You would've made a formidable queen."

In the starlight, the ridge's faces were slick and black, jagged and sharp. It seemed . . . unfinished. New and unrefined. But it would do what they needed. Not only would it stop the ships, but it would also stop an army. No soldiers could cross those steep sides.

Sefia collapsed, exhausted, as Archer ran to catch her.

"You did it," he said.

Like the Scribes before her, she'd changed the geography of the Five Islands. Now there were only two ways for the Alliance to attack Braska: from the west, and through a much narrower channel to the east.

She slept through the fourth day.

Archer spent the entire time working with Aljan on his book.

On the third day, while Sefia was off carving spells onto the Black Navy vessels, King Eduoar Corabelli II came to see Archer aboard the *Brother*.

At the sight of the Lonely King, Archer bowed. "Your Majesty."

Eduoar sighed. "You don't need to do that."

"But you're a king."

"I am." The king smiled faintly. "But I'm not just a king anymore."

Out in the bay, the ships of the Resistance were arrayed in a multicolored ribbon—the alabaster Delienean vessels, the rebel redcoats from Oxscini, the Rokuine Black Navy, the fourteen outlaws, led by the green *Current* and the golden *Crux*.

"I wanted to talk about curses," Eduoar said, idly touching his middle finger. "I suppose you know mine."

Archer nodded. Everyone in Kelanna had heard of the Corabelli Curse. It had claimed everyone in the king's family, and anyone his family had ever loved.

"But curses don't always work the way you think they will."

"I'm not cursed," Archer said.

The Lonely King cocked his head. "Isn't that why you're not fighting with us?"

Cursed. Prophesied. Archer supposed there wasn't much difference.

"I'd always believed that to break my curse," Eduoar continued, "I'd have to lose everything—my kingdom, my castle, my life—and I did, in the end . . . just not the way I thought."

Archer reached for the worry stone. "You want me to be with you when the Alliance arrives. You want me to fight."

The king's sad eyes gleamed. "Yes. Both the outlaws and the bloodletters say you're unparalleled in battle. We could use someone exceptional out there."

"But if I fight, I die." It had been written. He'd do what he could to avoid it, but it might come for him all the same.

"Could you stand there and watch everyone else die?" Eduoar asked.

Archer was silent.

"Your curse may not be broken the way you think it will be," the king said. "Mine wasn't."

"But you're a king," said Archer. "I'm just a boy from a small town in Oxscini."

Eduoar gripped his shoulder. "I think we know you're much more than that."

CHAPTER 35

Who Controls the Story?

As the days counted down to the arrival of the Alliance, Sefia grew more and more desperate. Her skill with Alteration was growing, but not quick enough for her to rewrite Archer's destiny. In fact, the more she understood about the Illuminated world, the more frustrated she became.

She couldn't excise his scars. She couldn't resurrect his victims. She couldn't keep them together, that day on the cliff, when she left for the Guard and he left for Oxscini.

If you want to save him, the Book had told her, *you can't keep him.*

At her lowest point, she even tried eliminating the day they met each other. She'd excise the ⊖ branded onto the sides of his crate. The impressors would pass beneath her as she lay in her hammock, studying the Book. She'd never rescue him. He'd end up a candidate. But he wouldn't be destined to die.

Except he was.

The threads of his life were too bright to erase without taking the rest of the world too.

Even with the power of the Scribes, she couldn't change her world from inside it.

So while the rest of the Resistance stocked ammunition for their cannons and rifles, while the Rokuine merchant ships and fishing vessels were converted into rescue boats, while the volunteer militia joined the city guard on Braska's walls, Sefia turned to the storyteller.

She teleported to the high plains where she'd trained for the first Battle of Blackfire Bay, and there, alone in the wind, she tried to figure out other ways to save the boy she loved.

"Tell me about the ending," she said once, wandering along the western slopes of Roku's main island.

It's happening soon, I told her. In ninety pages.

"But *how* does it end?"

In darkness. Beyond that, I can't tell you.

"You *can't* tell me or you *won't*?"

I can't narrate what I can't see.

"I looked into the future," Sefia said, kicking at a stone, "the night we destroyed the Library, and I saw the dead returning. Is that because of the Resurrection Amulet?"

Yes.

"But you said it could only recall one soul from the world of the dead."

Yes.

She glanced up. "Can I use it to save Archer, then? Is there a way to transform it so he doesn't turn into one of those . . . things?"

IT's THE ONLY OBJECT THAT **CONTROLS** THE LAWS OF THE DEAD.

"That's not an answer," she snapped.

Neither was this: I CAN SEE THEM—IN THE DARKNESS BEYOND THE EDGE OF THE WORLD, WASHING UP AGAINST THE BARRIER BE-TWEEN THE LIVING AND THE DEAD LIKE A WAVE AGAINST A GLASS GLOBE.

"Why can't you just tell me? What am I supposed to do?"

BECAUSE YOU'RE SUPPOSED TO CHOOSE, I said. CANNEK REED HAS ALREADY TOLD YOU HE DOESN'T WANT THE LAST PIECE OF **THE** AMULET. WILL YOU FORCE HIM TO GIVE UP ITS LOCATION, TO GIVE UP ALL THOSE STORIES HE'S WORKED SO HARD FOR, IF IT MEANS YOU MIGHT BE ABLE TO SAVE ARCHER?

"Might?" she said.

MIGHT, I agreed.

But she didn't trust me. Why would she? She and her family had all been manipulated into this. She could only trust her power, her instincts, her intelligence.

She wished she could read the Book. But it was in Aljan's safekeeping, and she knew it would only seek to thrust her toward destiny if she opened it now.

She wished she could ask Nin and her parents for guidance.

But even with the Book, they wouldn't be with her, not really, in the way that she wanted. She might see passages from their lives, but that wouldn't be the same as if they were here to listen to her and advise her and hug her.

The dead were gone, no matter how much you wanted them with you.

With two days left before the arrival of the Alliance, Sefia came to see me at dawn. She teleported to a gravel beach she and Archer had seen on their explorations of the main island, with distant cliffs and misty spires rising out of the water, and she begged me to save Archer's life.

I CAN'T, I said.

"Why not?" she demanded. Her will to fight blazed so hot inside her, she could have burst into flames and I wouldn't have been surprised. "You're in control of this whole thing, aren't you?" She swept her arms wide, encompassing the gray pebbles beneath her feet, the smoking mountains to the east, the world itself.

NO, I'M NOT.

She flung her hands outward, seizing a sun-bleached log from the gravel and throwing it into the waves, where it cracked in half. She was desperate and frightened and furious and she didn't know how to be all three at once. "You're the one telling the story, aren't you? The one writing all of this? Archer's grand destiny? His *death*?"

There are times when I wish I had arms, and this was one of them. I wanted to wrap her up. I wanted to tell her it was all right. I wanted to give her . . . *something*.

But all I had—all I have—all I am—are words.

I NARRATE THE TURN OF EVERY SEASON, EVERY MOVEMENT IN KELANNA, GREAT AND SMALL, BUT I DIDN'T WRITE THIS **STORY**. I DON'T CONTROL THE EVENTS OF THIS WORLD OR THE ACTIONS OF ITS PEOPLE. I WATCH. I TELL. THAT'S ALL.

"*Someone* planned this."

BUT SHE'S GONE.

Sefia fell to her knees, her legs a W beneath her and her arms limp at her sides. "Why," she mumbled. She had started crying, but she didn't seem to notice. "How could she do this to us?"

Because she was hurt and broken and confused. Because people die and they don't come back. Because you don't get messages from the dead.

In truth, I didn't know, so I didn't answer.

To some questions, there are no answers.

Sefia dug her hands into the gravel. She looked like something had been cut from her and she was never going to get it back.

"Is there no hope, then?" she asked quietly.

THERE IS HOPE, I replied, IN CHOICE.

"What choice?" she asked bitterly. And that was the last thing she said to me before she teleported away.

The day before the Alliance arrived, Sefia and Archer reported to the watchtower where they would spend the last battle. From this vantage point on the cliff, they could see the walled capital of Braska to the east, the entirety of the Resistance arrayed in Blackfire Bay, and the Alliance approaching from the west, and they and a small squad of soldiers would raise and lower signal flags to allow the various parts of the Resistance to communicate with one another.

They did another tour of the watchtower—the single door at its base, the winding staircase, the square stone roof where the Black Navy soldiers were stationed.

And then, taking each other's hands, they disappeared.

Sefia brought them back to Oxscini, to the cave overlooking

the waterfall. The jungle was crowded with the buzz of insects and the chirping of birds flitting through the canopy, but to Sefia it felt like the first time they'd been alone in months.

"Do you remember this place?" she asked, looking up at the tree that covered the cave's entrance.

Archer answered her with a smile.

It had been her birthday. He'd given her a green feather. Then she'd shown him the Book and asked him to follow her.

That was almost a year ago now. In eight days, she would turn seventeen.

They climbed up the collapsed rock pillars to the cave, which seemed smaller now as they lay down shoulder to shoulder, peering at the waterfall.

That seemed smaller now, too, coursing through the forest below them into a vivid blue pool.

So much had changed in a year. The feather was gone. The Book had betrayed her. She'd learned more than she ever wanted to know about her parents and her enemies and the truth of her world.

But Archer was still with her.

In all the ways that mattered.

"Leave with me," she said, turning onto her side. "We can disappear. We can go anywhere and no one will be able to track us."

All they had to do was run.

If they ran, he'd live.

On his face, a sad smile formed and failed and formed again. He nuzzled her shoulder. "You know I can't . . . and neither can you."

Their friends needed them. The world needed them.

Nodding, she began to cry.

She knew.

Leaning over, Archer kissed the tears from the corners of her eyes, gathering them with his lips as if they were drops of sweet wine.

A deep ache flowered inside her, dark and damp and urgent, and she grasped the back of his neck, pulling his mouth to hers. They undressed, awkwardly, banging their heads and elbows in the cramped space, laughing and coming together again, tongues and hands. Then—

Opening, gasping.

The sweltering heat making their skin slick with sweat.

Hair clinging to her neck. Words, barely intelligible, caught somewhere between whisper and longing. The arching of spines. And a sudden glimpse of the sky through the mouth of the cave—blue. Startlingly, dizzyingly, *vastly* blue—Sefia blinked, eyes widening, lips parting—it was the bluest she'd ever seen—the blue of the sea, the blue of the waves, crested with spray, the blue of the tides rushing in and back out, again and again and again.

Later, they bathed in the pool at the base of the waterfall, washing the sweat from their skin and hair, with the stones slick under their bare feet. They dried and dressed. Archer tucked her hair behind her ear and clipped it back with the emerald pin.

"Ready to go?" he asked.

"Where?"

His smile was full of secrets. "The *Current*," he said.

It was a party.

He'd thrown her a party. Everyone had—the bloodletters and the crew of the *Current*, Adeline and Isabella, Lac and Hobs. Garlands of flowers cascaded from the rigging between glowing globe lanterns, hovering over tables heaped with so many treats, it was as if Cooky and Griegi had been trying to outdo each other: glazed duck, salads of summer greens speckled with pink and purple flowers, berry tarts, swirled bowls of chocolate and cream, four different kinds of herbed butter to slather on rolls and sizzling cuts of beef, spicy skewers of pork and sweet onion, and, her favorite, little white buns with sugary decorations and sour lemon curd centers.

Theo, whose injured leg had been replaced with a wooden one, played lively tunes on his fiddle while his red lory sang sweetly along. Beside him, Marmalade strummed Jules's old mandolin, her fingers expertly finding their way up and down the frets.

"Surprise!" Lac declared, embracing her. He was dressed smartly in his redcoat uniform, so smart, in fact, that it was hard to look away. "It's a birthday party!"

"My birthday's not for over a week," she said, turning to Archer, who grinned at her unapologetically.

"That's why it's a surprise," explained Hobs, who'd also shown up in uniform, as, he later told her, it was a fancy occasion.

"No, I get it. I just . . ." She took a shaky breath. "I've never had a party like this before."

Taking her hand, Archer kissed the top of her head.

They made their way among the party guests, stopping every

so often to grab bites of roast pigeon or drunken cherries and to refill their glasses with liquor the chief mate had dug out from his special stores. Griegi dogged Cooky across the deck, asking if it was crab or lobster stock in this broth, true cinnamon or cassia in this chocolate sauce, jotting each gruff response down in his book.

Every so often, someone cleared their throat and raised their glass and, after a bit of stamping or shouting to get everyone's attention, they'd tell a story.

First was Captain Reed, who leapt onto the rail. "The first time I met this kid, she was a scrawny little thing that smelled like the bilge, but in the time I've known her, she's . . . well, she's still scrawny, but at least she don't smell no more."

There was a chorus of laughter as Sefia blushed.

He shook his head, grinning down at her. "Nah, this kid . . . this kid brought me adventures I never thought I'd have." He gave them a play-by-play of the fight with the Administrators in Jahara—the magic, the enforcers, the vial of poison flying through the air, the way she'd teleported them to safety. "I always thought the world was big and full of wonders, and I was more'n happy to go my own way, doin' what was right for me and my crew. But this kid showed me the world's got more wonders than I ever dreamed, and it ain't so big that people don't need each other to survive it." He tipped his hat to her. "Happy birthday, Sef. You're my crew, now and always."

The others whooped and hollered as he hopped down and Sefia rushed into his arms, hugging him tight.

Later, Meeks told a tale of the discovery of the Trove.

Frey talked about the first time she caught Archer in Sefia's cot. There was a chorus of whistles and catcalls. Sefia could feel her face burning. Archer took a bow.

Aljan described how Sefia had taught him to write, giving him a voice to express himself after what the impressors had done to him.

Archer told the last story, his voice quiet and sure, describing the night she rescued him from the impressors—the crack of light, the sound of her voice, the way she'd saved him, over and over, in more ways than one.

Lifting herself up on tiptoe, she kissed him.

"And that's seventeen!" Reed declared. "Seventeen stories for seventeen years in this world—"

"And many more to go!" the others cried.

Sefia turned to them, beaming so brightly she was sure she was crying again. "Thank you," she said, hugging her own arms like if she didn't she'd burst open with joy. "I always wished for a big family, and you've given me the biggest, wildest family I could have ever imagined. I love you all."

There was a round of applause, and Marmalade and Theo, with Harison's red lory perched on his shoulder, struck up the music again, the notes so bright they seemed to shiver in the air.

Grabbing Griegi's hands, Keon dragged him into the center of the deck for a dance, quickly followed by Frey and Aljan, who swayed, forehead to forehead, as if the songs were slow and tender as romances, while Killian and Horse and Doc, Archer and Sefia, hauling Scarza along behind her, whirled around them like petals in a sudden wind. From their seats, Adeline and Isabella laughed and clapped.

Even Jaunty, normally so taciturn, took to the dance floor, jigging and hopping and clicking his heels as everyone else whooped and cheered him on.

Haldon Lac wanted to dance with everyone, taking turns with Frey and Keon and Scarza and Doc. He even tried dancing with the chief mate, who crossed his arms and stood, unmoving, at the edge of the dance floor while Lac spun and kicked up his feet, completely oblivious or completely unconcerned.

Late into the night, they danced and talked and sang, until at last they all crowded the rails, where Keon, who had placed a flower crown in his sun-streaked hair, had stashed crates of fireworks for them to launch into the air—exploding into the shapes of chrysanthemums and stars, sparks raining down on the water of Blackfire Bay in dazzling showers of light.

But morning was coming, and eventually, they had to retire. The crew of the *Current* began to clear away the remains of the party while the others stumbled down the gangway, some wearing leftover flower garlands like scarves, mumbling sleepy farewells.

Back on the *Brother*, Sefia and Archer collapsed in a tangled heap on their bunk, where they halfheartedly shucked off their shoes and clothes, crawling under the blankets as the darkness softly closed about them.

Sefia was already half-asleep when she felt Archer curl up against her. "Stay with me," he murmured, laying his head on her chest.

Protectively, her arm went around him. "Always," she whispered.

At dawn the next day, they reported to the watchtower. To the east, the sun was rising over Braska, the light descending over the black volcanic slope, flashing on the windows of the castle, the slanted rooftops, the walls, the soldiers in the harbor. Below, the Resistance was arrayed on the water: the rebel redcoats, with Lac and Hobs among them, beside the Lonely King's White Navy; the ebony Rokuine ships; and the outlaws, speckled every color of the rainbow, from the red of the *Brother* to the gold of the *Crux*.

And on the western horizon—the Alliance. Fleet after fleet, they came. There didn't seem to be an end to them.

Sefia squeezed Archer's hand. Even with all the preparations the Resistance had made, she didn't know how they could possibly withstand the united force of the four larger kingdoms.

On the flagpole in the center of the tower, the Black Navy soldiers raised a flag. *The Alliance is coming.*

Beneath it, they raised two more to communicate the number of blue ships and their distance from shore.

All along Blackfire Bay, the Resistance signaled their understanding.

That they were gravely outnumbered.

That they might die.

Sefia shivered in the morning wind. She may have been the child of an assassin and the most powerful sorcerer the world had seen in years. She may have been deadly. She may have been formidable.

But she was also just a girl who loved a boy, and she was frightened.

After Nin died, she'd closed herself off. She told herself

she'd done it to protect other people from getting hurt, but now she knew she'd done it to protect herself.

If you don't love anyone, you don't get hurt when they're taken from you.

But Archer had changed her. Archer had cracked her armor, and now she loved so, so many people.

She loved Captain Reed and the chief mate and Meeks and the crew of the *Current*.

She loved Scarza and the bloodletters.

She loved Adeline and Isabella.

Some of them were going to die that day, and she didn't think she could endure any more loss.

So she looked up—at you, the reader—and she begged.

Please, she thought, *stop reading. If you stop now, the battle doesn't begin. If you stop now, the war doesn't end. If you stop now, fate doesn't get him.*

He can live, if you let him.

Watch. I'll even finish the story for you, right now.

Gently, the reader closed the book, and they all lived out their days together—thousands of moments of joy and rage and heartache. They had years—no, decades—of arguments, meals, songs, and adventures beneath the revolving skies. They weren't always happy, because who is? They had their problems, like anyone else. But they loved each other, and they had a lifetime to learn what that meant.

You don't see how it ends. Because it doesn't end. The story goes on and on and on, forever, and they live. They all live.

As long as you don't turn the page.

CHAPTER 36

Through the Storm

C aptain Reed was awake before the sun. On the main deck, Jaunty was already in place at the helm, while Cooky and Aly bustled about in the galley, clattering pans and stoking the cast-iron stove. In the workshop, Doc and Horse leaned against his workbench, his broad hands tenderly cradling her face as she kissed him.

Reed climbed out onto the bowsprit. He stood there for a moment, listening to the swells knocking softly against the *Current*'s green hull.

They would be at the front of the battle, the Resistance's first line of defense, arrayed at the western entrance of Black-fire Bay with a curious combination of allies: white Delienean vessels, rebel redcoats, the Rokuine Navy, and outlaws of every stripe and color.

Behind him, on the eastern horizon, the sun was emerging

from the sea as if from a crucible of molten gold. In the dawn light, Roku's volcanic slopes were dotted with white.

The end of dandelion season.

Today, the water murmured. *Today, today, today . . .*

He chewed his lip and blinked tears from his eyes.

So this was it—the last day he'd ever see, the last battle he'd ever fight, the last adventure of Cannek Reed. He'd do it for freedom and the outlaw way. He'd do it for his crew. For Archer. And the promise of adventures to come . . . for someone else, if not for him.

The crew began to stir, grabbing bowls of breakfast and mugs of coffee from Cooky and Aly. Sitting atop the empty pigpen, Marmalade plucked out a tune on Jules's mandolin. It was an old melody, familiar to outlaws everywhere, though now she played it slow and in a minor key, like an unrequited love. Beside her, Theo adjusted his spectacles and began to hum in his lovely, haunting baritone. One by one, the others began to hum along.

Reed knew the words, though no one was singing. He felt them in his bones.

> *In the past, we were forced to abide by the rules,*
> > *But the law ain't a life, so we struck out on our own.*
> *Free as the wind, with the salt on our skin,*
> > *We answer to the sea and to the sea alone.*

> *No kings! That's the outlaw way.*
> *No land! We struck out on our own.*
> *We answer to the sea and to the sea alone.*

They said, "This is your home, so you bow to the throne,"
And they said we'd be safe if we fell in line.
But the line tied us down, so we broke from the crown.
Now each day is full of danger and that suits us fine.

No kings! That's the outlaw way.
No land! We struck out on our own.
We answer to the sea and to the sea alone.

We're sailin' through the storm.
We're ridin' every wave.
We're livin' for today.
'Cause that's the outlaw way.
'Cause that's the outlaw way.

"Will they live?" the captain asked.

And the water replied: *They live, they live* . . .

"All of them?"

The water was silent.

"Too much to hope for, I reckon." He sighed. "Do me a favor, will you? Protect them? When I'm gone?"

The sea slapped the hull of the *Current*, misting him with spray, and faintly, he heard the answer: *I will.*

Captain Reed tipped his hat to the water that had been his home, his guardian, his love, and jumped down from the bowsprit.

He joined the chief mate where he stood alone, fondly patting the rail.

The mate's dead gray eyes flicked toward him. "Is it today?" he asked.

Reed nodded.

Only the slight shifting of the mate's deeply chiseled features betrayed his dismay. They both knew: Reed would die with the Executioner in his hand as the ship exploded beneath him.

"You want me off the *Current*?" Reed asked.

The chief mate's face went impassive again. "Don't be stupid." Giving the rail a last tap, he clasped Reed's hand. "And don't take the rest of us down with you."

"I won't."

The mate gave him a grizzled smile. "I know."

As they parted, there was a cry from one of the fighting tops: "Flags on the watchtower!"

Reed glanced up. On the nearest cliff, where Sefia and Archer would be watching the battle, the soldiers had raised three flags.

One to tell them the Alliance was in sight.

A second to tell them how many ships the Alliance had brought.

A third to tell them how far away they were.

On the captain's orders, the crew leapt into action, preparing the *Current of Faith* for war. The chief mate stood, still as a pillar, in the center of the ship as the outlaws swirled around him like currents in a maelstrom. Meeks, however, was in constant motion, running this way, shouting, tying down a cannon before springing up again and cracking a joke. From belowdecks came the hammering of Horse and his assistants as they reinforced the shutters. Along the rails, Cooky and Aly checked the rifle racks while Theo and Marmalade's strong voices led the sailors in hoisting up the anchors.

The Alliance was drawing closer. The sun was climbing

higher. And the water was turning that fierce blue Reed loved so dearly.

It was a good day to go.

On the watchtower, they raised another flag—emerald green, for the *Current of Faith.*

Go.

Now.

Seeing the signal, the crew of the *Current*—his crew— looked to him. If he were another captain, he might have made a speech. But he was Cannek Reed, and his strength was in deeds, not in words. So he looked from one to another—the mate and Meeks and Horse and Doc and Jaunty, Cooky and Aly and Theo and Marmalade and Killian and all the dozens of other sailors under his care and command.

And he said, "We ain't all gonna make it to sundown, so those of us who live, remember the ones who don't. And those who die . . . make your last day worth remembering."

They let out a roar. A final call—*We were here.*

Then the *Current of Faith* set sail—a lone green leaf on the blue water, leaving the rest of the Resistance line behind, the multicolored ships shrinking as the wall of the Alliance loomed larger and larger before them.

When they were almost in range, Jaunty cried, "Wind's right!"

The mate nodded at Aly, who went scampering into the great cabin, reappearing with the Thunder Gong clutched in one hand and Dimarion's mallet in the other. She skidded to a stop in front of Reed, her braids falling over her shoulders.

They were going to summon a storm. The high winds and

rough waters would stop some of the Alliance before they reached Roku, culling their numbers so the Resistance would have a better chance.

They hoped.

"Think it'll work, Cap?" Aly asked as he took the ancient instrument.

Ahead, he could see the Alliance gun crews loading their cannons.

"Probably shoulda given this a test run, huh?" he said with a nervous laugh. "Oh well. Too late for regrets."

"Hard to starboard!" Jaunty cried suddenly. On his signal, he and Killian threw themselves against the helm.

The captain began to count: *One, two, three, four* . . .

The ship groaned. The masts swayed.

. . . *five, six, seven* . . .

The *Current of Faith* turned to run.

"Eight," Reed whispered. He raised the gong, his gaze traveling over the verdigris, rough under his hands . . . and he struck it with the mallet Dimarion had fished out of that maelstrom over six years ago.

The sound was a crash, a roar, a drumming of war.

As the *Current* began to race back to the safety of the Resistance line, a storm gathered overhead.

The air went chill and dark.

At the wheel, Jaunty cast a glance over his shoulder, laughing madly as clouds coiled out of the sky like black knots, twisting and churning, laced with lightning.

Thunder clashed overhead.

"Been nice knowin' you all!" Reed whooped as the storm closed in around them like curtains drawing on a performance.

The wind tore at their rails. The waves heaved. Torrents of water rained from the sky, drenching them all in seconds. Lightning flashed over and over, illuminating the green ship, the turgid sea, the warships behind.

The rest of the Resistance was little more than a smudge in front of them as the crew of the *Current* fought the storm— Jaunty at the helm and the sailors on the yards, tying and lashing, trying to harness the screaming wind.

Behind them, lightning speared an Alliance battleship, cracking it like an egg. Strikes caught two more ships, flames devouring their masts and drenched sails.

Reed clung to the rail, cackling, as they charged out of the storm, leaving it roiling behind them, and rejoined the Resistance. Wrestling the helm with all his stringy strength, Jaunty spun the ship again, and they came about to face the distant clouds, hovering just out of range, a curling black wall with lightning flashing in its depths.

But out here, only a faint breeze and the rumble of thunder reached them.

"It worked!" Dimarion bellowed from the deck of the *Crux*. "All those years of enmity, and look what havoc we could have been wreaking together!"

Laughing, Reed waved his hat at him. The crew of the *Current* cheered.

Then there was a growl of thunder, like a warning, and the blue beasts of the Alliance began to emerge from the storm, trailing black clouds like smoke.

There were gaps in the enemy line. As planned, the storm had taken some of them.

But not enough.

Iron began raining down around the *Current*. Cannonballs screamed through the air, making geysers of water erupt all around them.

And at the front of the charge was Serakeen's flagship, the *Amalthea*, with her three cycling guns—fast and relentless.

Bullets peppered the *Current* as Reed and his crew took cover behind their reinforced bulkheads. Splinters showered them. But the timbers held.

Shielding his eyes, Reed found his steward crouched behind the gunwale. "Aly!" he cried. "Think you can take out the crank on one of those guns?"

She glanced at the cook beside her. They touched knuckles in their special handshake. "On it, Cap." There was the *click* of a rifle.

A second's pause as Serakeen's guns continued to bury them in fire.

Then Cooky broke out from behind the rail, offering Aly covering fire.

With breathtaking accuracy, she stood, sighted, shot.

Aboard the *Amalthea*, one of the cycling guns shuddered and stopped.

"Good *shot*, Aly!" Cooky crowed as they ducked down again.

"Gun crews, ready!" Reed shouted.

They scrambled to their posts.

"Aim!"

But they were forced to take cover again as the second of the

Amalthea's cycling guns let loose, spattering them with bullets.

Gritting his teeth, Cooky popped up from behind the bulkhead and loosed two shots, taking out the soldiers on the second gun. The light flashed on his earrings. He grinned.

The *Current*'s gun crews sprang into action again.

But before Reed could give the order to fire, there was a sharp *crack*.

Cooky fell, his rifle trapped beneath him.

Bloodied lips and unseeing eyes.

Crying out, Aly dropped to her knees, her fingers feeling for a pulse.

Reed watched them for a moment, and when he looked up, he stared down the oncoming *Amalthea* with cold rage.

"Fire," he said.

"Fire!" Meeks shouted.

The deck shuddered as the cannons roared. In the smoke, Reed knelt beside Aly. He closed the cook's eyes.

And as the *Amalthea*'s cycling guns started up again, the rest of the Alliance assault began pouring around the edges of the storm.

CHAPTER 37

The Story of a Traitor

With a trembling hand, Arcadimon Detano lifted the single-dose vial to his lips. The tiny glass bottle held little more than a thimbleful of thin indigo liquid, and it was waiting for him every morning on the lacquered ebony desk in the Guard's office in the tunnels beneath Corabel.

"Insurance," his Master, King Darion Stonegold, had explained over four months ago as he watched Arcadimon drink the first dose. "From now on, you'll need to take this drug once a day, every day, at dawn, or withdrawal will kill you before noon the next day."

Inwardly, Arc had shuddered, but he'd affected nonchalance. "And I suppose the only way I get my doses is from you?" he'd asked.

"Tolem will deliver it to the Corabelli Branch each morning in time for your draught. But if you step out of line again . . ."

Darion's voice had trailed off, for he didn't need to finish the threat.

Each morning, the Apprentice Administrator delivered the drug.

After Tolem was killed, the Master Administrator delivered it himself, sometimes waiting until Arc drank it to slink back to the ruined Main Branch.

Each morning, Arcadimon dosed himself.

He'd been forbidden from leaving Deliene until the Gormani Resistance in the north was quashed. "Kill their children if you have to," his Master had ordered, "but end the Resistance before we're done in Kelebrandt, or I'll cancel your daily deliveries."

For a time, Arc had obeyed. The Gormani Resistance had faltered.

But deep down, he knew that he'd face death sooner rather than later anyway. Darion had warned him once, after all: *Sentiment will compromise the mission, and it will get you killed—if not by your rivals, then by me.*

By letting Ed live, Arcadimon Detano had already proven himself disloyal. Once the Guard found a way to replace him in Deliene, he would be disposed of.

So when Eduoar Corabelli II had revealed himself on the last day of the siege of Oxscini, Arc knew what he had to do. With the reappearance of their king, the Gormani Resistance had gained renewed strength, but Arcadimon had paid them little heed. All he cared about now was seeing Ed one last time.

He should have done it as soon as the First reported he was alive.

Arc was a traitor.

A traitor to the Guard, letting the Lonely King escape.

A traitor to Eduoar, over and over, killing his cousin, seizing his kingdom, sending his people to fight and die in a war they might have escaped.

A traitor to himself, choosing to pursue the mission instead of his heart. Ever since he'd watched Ed disappear into the sunset, Arc had been regretting it.

He should have escaped with his king.

He should have followed his friend.

He should have believed in them.

And now, too late, his chance had come.

Today, the last battle in the Red War would begin. Eduoar would be there, and Arcadimon had one last chance to see him before the end.

The drug went down smooth, as it always did.

There.

Even if he died tomorrow, without the drug, he would survive the day. That was all he needed.

One more day to follow his heart.

One more day to change, after a lifetime of mistakes.

He'd already left word with his messengers and his newsmen, who would spread the announcement throughout the Northern Kingdom: Arcadimon Detano was renouncing the title of regent. He was giving Deliene back to the Lonely King, from whom he never should have taken it in the first place.

As he left the Guard's office beneath Corabel, Arc checked the pocket of his blue wool jacket for Eduoar's signet ring, which Arcadimon had lifted from the castle's portrait gallery, where it had been kept under glass for six months. He hadn't been able to get himself an Alliance uniform—he didn't have access to that—but in the heat of battle, he hoped no one would notice.

Though he was afraid, his heart gave a little leap as he opened the door to the portal room. As a Politician, whose training emphasized statecraft over magic, he wasn't a skilled enough Illuminator to teleport—he'd barely achieved Manipulation. But Guardians had been using the mirror-like portals to get around Kelanna for ages, and he had them at his disposal now.

He slipped through the portal to the Main Branch and the room of black and green marble, lit by electric lamps.

Four full-length mirrors lined the walls. The one framed by silver waves led to Tanin's—the Director's—ship, the *Black Beauty*. The one with metal flags flying from intricately carved parapets led to Darion's old chambers in the Everican capital. The one Arc had just left depicted Corabel's lighthouses. And the last was bordered by great golden waves, seeming to flood over the portal's reflective surface.

It led to Braca's flagship, the *Barbaro*, where it must have been engaged in the last battle.

Arcadimon was going to see Ed again.

My king.

My friend.

My love.

Arc crossed the patterned marble floor and slipped through the gold portal with barely a shiver.

On the other side, the summer light through the portholes was bright and the noise was deafening: the swift *ratatat* of gunfire, the explosions of cannons, orders barked crisp and clear in the cacophony of battle.

He was in a ship's cabin, roomier than most and the very definition of *shipshape*—the blankets neatly tucked, every scrap of clothing stowed in the chests and built-in wardrobes. In fact, there were no signs that anyone lived here at all, save for the glass cases of medals and velvet ribbons bolted to the walls. A Master Soldier's achievements.

He was in Braca's quarters.

Instinctively, Arcadimon checked his pockets, where he'd stashed three vials of sleeping powder beside the signet ring. He was a poor Illuminator, a terrible shot, and absolute rubbish with a sword, so the powders were all he had to defend himself if he were caught.

At the cabin door, Arc paused for a moment to straighten his jacket.

"Here we go," he muttered.

While the battle raged on overhead, he sneaked through the *Barbaro*'s corridors, popping up in a hatchway, the top of his head barely visible over the lip of the deck.

He was just below the quarterdeck, near the mast. And he could see Braca, leader of the Alliance forces.

She was standing at her war table with her lieutenants, small but fearsome with her aggressively short hair and her cold, merciless eyes, accented by her blue suede coat. At her sides hung her gold-tipped guns.

When she gave an order, it was followed, immediately, precisely. Her lieutenants obeyed her as if they were extensions of her own body, and their soldiers obeyed them with similar urgency. Flags went up on the masts, directing every movement of the Alliance invasion.

Braca had been trained for this.

No, *forged* for this. She was a Master Soldier in her element.

Beyond the rails, the battle was in full swing. Rebel redcoats and Black Navy warships were going down in great explosions of flame and timber. From the onshore batteries, the Rokuine defenses shot cannonballs into the Alliance line. In watchtowers on the cliffs, signal flags flapped in the wind, sending communications between the city of Braska and the Resistance ships on the bay. Outlaws swooped through the chaos, quick on the water, but they were no match for the heavy artillery of the Alliance, which riddled them with gunfire every time they got too close.

Under Braca's direction, the Alliance mowed down the Resistance fighters, shredding their sails, splintering their masts, pitting their hulls with holes and pelting them with cycling-gun fire.

The Resistance was breaking. The first line had already collapsed, the myriad of ships falling back to secondary positions as the *Barbaro* sailed through the western entrance of the bay like a conqueror.

Arcadimon wasn't a military tactician, but nearly a decade studying games of power had given him a sharp eye, and he could see that no matter how hard the Resistance fought, no matter how much courage they mustered, they were simply too few.

The Alliance was going to crush them.

The Resistance must have known before they even began

that this was a losing enterprise. They could have had no hope of winning.

For a moment, Arc admired their stupid bravery.

He'd never been brave in his life. But maybe today that would change.

As he strained to catch a glimpse of the White Delienean Navy, someone grabbed him by the collar, hauling him half out of the hatchway.

"Get to your post!" the soldier snarled, his breath stinking of fish. The man's eyes widened as Arcadimon reached into his pocket, popping the cork on one of the vials. "Hey, you're not Allian—"

Arc flung the powder directly into the soldier's face and held his breath as the man toppled facedown into the hatchway, unconscious.

That left Arcadimon with two vials of sleeping powder and the answer to a different problem.

He stripped the soldier of his uniform, bound and gagged him, and left him in one of Braca's wardrobes. The man would sleep for half the day, if Arc was lucky.

Enough time to find Ed, he hoped.

He took a glance at his reflection in the mirrored portal. The blue uniform was a little loose, but he still thought himself quite the picture of an Alliance soldier.

He sneaked back to the main deck and ducked into the throng of soldiers scurrying across the *Barbaro*, searching for Eduoar's ships.

There, to the southeast. They'd been repainted white, and they were flying the poppy flags of Deliene.

Arcadimon's heart sank. They were so far. He wouldn't be able to swim, or even row, with the water choked with corpses, debris, and rescue boats. Could he cut the *Barbaro*'s rudder chain and hope the king's ship would reach them in the chaos? Could he fix the sails?

Arc took a deep breath. *I'll find you, Ed.* Somehow.

CHAPTER 38

The Fourth Adventure of Haldon Lac

It may have been an exaggeration to say Haldon Lac was stationed aboard the biggest warship he'd ever seen, but he was never one to shy away from a little hyperbole. The *Fury of the Queen* was immense—once, she'd been the pride of the Royal Navy, her three gun decks brimming with cannons, her four towering masts flying stiff white sails, her full complement of well-trained redcoats thirsty for battle.

Well, he admitted, not *redcoats*. They still wore the uniforms. But they were not members of the Oxscinian Royal Navy anymore. He didn't know if there *was* an Oxscinian Royal Navy anymore, or if it was just the Alliance now.

The Resistance needed a last line of defense between the battle on Blackfire Bay and the capital, where the civilians were huddled in shelters, so many of the biggest ships, including the *Fury*, dropped anchor at the mouth of Braska's harbor, forming a chain of floating fortresses that would protect Rokuine shores.

If all went well and the rest of the Resistance battled back the Alliance, she wouldn't even see combat.

But all did not go well.

The morning of the last battle, Lac and Hobs climbed the mainmast to the fighting top, where they and the other topmen watched Captain Reed's storm spread across the western horizon, flickering with lightning. They cheered when the Resistance vessels sailed out, multicolored flags flying, to meet the blue beasts of the Alliance beyond the entrance to Blackfire Bay.

But as the hours wore on, the Alliance pushed them back. The Resistance defenders were forced to retreat.

The *Fury of the Queen* could not move from the harbor entrance without risking the safety of the city, so Lac and Hobs could do little but watch as the enemy attacked the islands on the north side of the bay, capturing forts and watchtowers, commandeering gun turrets and firing back on the Resistance.

Flaming ships floundered in the waves, trailing thick clouds of smoke that obscured patches of the midsummer sky. Even with Sefia's magical reinforcements, the Resistance ships were still tar and timber. Under enough cannon fire, they still broke. They still burned.

Haldon Lac's topmen were nervous. He could feel their fear spiking as they watched sailors who had been thrown into the sea swim for floating bits of debris. But he didn't know how to help them. He didn't even know how to help himself.

"There were six sister sand witches," he muttered, "and six sandwiches: two tuna sandwiches cut in two, a sandy sandwich which slipped from the hands of the sixth sand witch, and a tuna sandwich which Witch One had bit into. Witch Two wished for—"

"What are you mumbling about?" one of the topmen asked, gripping the stock of her gun.

"It's a riddle," Lac said.

"I've been working on it for months," Hobs added proudly.

Speeding out of the harbor, unarmed rescue boats sailed into the confusion, running over the corpses of enemies and allies alike. But they were at the mercy of the battle. Doctors went down under stray gunfire. Cannonballs went wide of the Resistance fighters, sinking the small rescue ships instead.

"Well, keep going," said another of the topmen. "What's the rest of the riddle?"

Hobs beamed. "Okay, so, Witch Two wished for a tuna sandwich which Witch One had skipped while sampling sandwiches"—he continued rattling off his riddle while the other topmen huddled around, needing a distraction—"and would willingly switch sandwiches with any sand witch that wasn't Witch One. The sixth witch switched with Witch Four, which for Witch Four was a sinister sandwich switch, so Witch Four granted Witch Two's wish and switched her sandwich with her sister sand witch—"

Out on the water, there was a great *crack* as an Alliance warship crashed into a rescue vessel, smashing the smaller boat into pieces. Lac thought he saw bodies crushed beneath the enemy's enormous blue hull.

"Don't stop," said one of the topmen.

Lac turned back to them, swallowing. "Which sand witch ate which sandwich?" he asked.

The topmen conferred.

"Witch One ate Witch Two's sandwich, so . . ."

"Which one had a tuna sandwich again?"

"No, Witch One had *half* a tuna sandwich, but Witch Two . . ."

On Blackfire Bay, the whitecaps turned red.

The Alliance kept gaining. The Resistance kept retreating.

From the entrance to the harbor, Haldon Lac could no longer see the *Red Hare*, the White Navy ship on which Ed—the king—was sailing, or the *Current*, lost somewhere in the chaos. But he kept catching glimpses of the *Barbaro* and the *Amalthea*, which seemed to be everywhere, firing their great guns, taking down everyone from outlaws to rebel redcoats.

On the western cliff above the city, Sefia and Archer's watchtower was still flying message flags. The Alliance didn't seem to have attacked the fortifications of the main island yet. Lac hoped it would stay that way.

It was midday when the Alliance drew into range of the *Fury*'s cannons. They were a blue serpent with black spines, one massive warship following another in a long, sinuous line.

Were any of them Royal Navy vessels? Under their new coats of paint, it was hard to tell.

On the fighting top, the topmen had agreed Witch Two had ended up with the sandy sandwich, but they hadn't decided which other witches had eaten which sandwiches.

And they wouldn't, now that the Alliance had come for them.

Below, the rebel redcoats worked the great guns, raining iron down upon the enemy. Blossoms of flame erupted from the mouths of the cannons. Black smoke drifted into the fighting tops.

One after another, the Resistance line took out the invaders. They cracked hulls. They demolished masts. They wounded officers and soldiers.

But the Alliance was relentless, sailing in from the northwest, firing broadsides, and sailing back out again. Red and orange lights flowered in the smoke as the decks of the *Fury* were shot to pieces. From above, Lac could see his fellow redcoats falling. Dying. One of the other midshipmen, posted on the main deck, went down with a spar of timber through the neck.

Closer and closer came the blue beasts of the Alliance . . . until at last they were in range of Lac, Hobs, and their topmen.

They fired across the water, taking out soldiers in the enemy fighting tops.

Were they Oxscinians beneath those blue uniforms? Former comrades? Friends?

But they couldn't stop the Alliance. There were simply too many of them.

One enemy ship, smaller than the *Fury*, sailed in from the northwest, but instead of firing a broadside and retreating again, it charged in toward the Resistance line.

"They're trying to board!" the captain of the *Fury* cried, his voice carrying up to the fighting tops.

Below, the gun crews let off one last broadside. A cannonball struck the Alliance mast. Another took out a piece of their stern. But the enemy was still coming.

Gesturing to his topmen, Lac ordered them to prepare for boarding. They grabbed chests of grenades or climbed out onto the yardarms, preparing to drop powder kegs on the enemy boarders.

Hobs touched Lac's elbow. "You scared, Lac?"

Lac gulped. "Yes."

Of death, capture, and drowning. Of being impaled by shrapnel. Of falling. Of fighting his own. Of his friends not making it to sundown.

"Me too."

On the gun decks, the crews loaded their cannons with scrap shot, and as the Alliance ship drew up alongside them, the *Fury* let loose her last volley of fire. Lead barbs, nails, and other sharp bits of metal went flying from the cannons, studding the enemy hull. Blue-uniformed soldiers went down with hundreds of tiny wounds.

But they didn't stop coming.

There was a great *crunch* as the bow of the blue ship crashed into the *Fury*. From the yardarms, the topmen lit powder kegs and sent them plummeting onto the enemy decks, where they exploded, burning boarders wielding revolvers and axes.

Lac and Hobs began hurling grenades as the Alliance soldiers leapt from their ship onto the *Fury of the Queen*. Some didn't make it. One man misjudged the distance, striking the redcoats' rail with his chin.

As the enemy swarmed the *Fury*'s decks, the rebel redcoats detonated powder chests strapped to their bulwarks, sending up bursts of fire. The leading Alliance soldiers were blown back, but they were replaced by others, leaping through the flames, firing their sidearms as they landed among the resisters.

It was a bloody business. Soldiers on both sides were slashed

430

and stabbed, their faces blown off, their guts spilled. Below, the decks turned crimson.

In the fighting top, Lac threw himself onto his belly and began firing his rifle. *Bang. Bang. Bang.* Beside him, Hobs and the other topmen did the same.

But soon he heard the useless clicking of the hammer. "I'm out of ammunition!"

"I've got it!" Hobs got to his knees. But before he could move toward the case of bullets, his whole body jerked back.

Blood spattered Lac's face as he turned to see Hobs, clutching his shoulder, fall from the fighting top.

"Hobs!"

He kept seeing Fox making the leap across the deck of the *Fire-Eater*. The nauseating drop. He kept seeing Fox going limp in his hands.

Not Hobs too.

Bullets struck the fighting top as Lac crawled to the edge of the platform, searching for his friend.

Hobs was dangling twenty feet below him, tangled in the rigging. Looking up, he gave a wide grin.

Fox had grinned too, right before she was shot.

And Hobs was an easy target, hanging over the melee below. Gunshots shredded the ropes around him. On the main deck, the enemy set fire to the rigging.

At the stern, a blue-uniformed soldier seized one of the chase guns and turned it on the fighting top. A fist-size ball of iron slammed into the platform, scattering the redcoats.

Ignoring the height, Lac scrambled off the platform and after Hobs, who was struggling with the ropes now, the flames

431

climbing swiftly toward him. Lac had almost made it to him when the rigging frayed.

Midshipman Haldon Lac felt his stomach rise into his throat as he and Hobs were dropped onto the decks.

A sharp pain lanced through Lac's ankle as he landed. An Alliance soldier raced toward him, boarding ax raised to strike.

Lac fumbled for his sidearm.

He was too slow. He was too clumsy. He'd never get his gun out in time.

But he had Hobs. As the enemy reached them, Hobs shot him in the chest.

The boarder collapsed on top of Lac, who yelped. He tried to squeeze out from under the body, but the decks were hot and slippery. It was so loud! There was a dead man on his chest! People all around him were fighting and shouting and dying.

Cradling his wounded shoulder, Hobs helped push the soldier's body off of Lac and, leaning on each other, they got up again, shooting, slashing.

They cut. They stabbed and punched and dodged, always coming back together in the battle, driving off the Alliance soldiers that came at them, swinging.

Dimly, Haldon Lac wondered if all that practice with Archer had made them better fighters. Certainly, they weren't doing too poorly, injured as they were.

But they were being driven toward the rail. The enemy was overwhelming the *Fury*.

Lac ran out of bullets first. He struck someone with the butt of his pistol as he heard the *click click* of Hobs's empty sidearm.

They were pinned against the gunwale with nothing but their swords. There was nowhere left to retreat to.

Blue-uniformed soldiers closed in around them, raising their weapons.

Smoke and flame shot from the barrels of the Alliance guns.

"Hobs!" Lac flung himself at his friend, taking them both over the edge of the ship as the bullets passed through the air.

As the three gun decks flashed past them, Lac wrapped his arms around Hobs, who hugged him back, and they plunged into the cold water together.

CHAPTER 39

The Few or the Many

From the watchtower, Sefia could see the whole stretch of water, witness the whole carnage of the battle. The Alliance had captured most of the onshore batteries on the north side of the bay. The *Barbaro* was leading the charge on Braska's harbor while Serakeen and the *Amalthea* cornered the remnants of the outlaws and the Black Navy in the east.

In the fire and smoke, she'd lost track of both the *Brother* and the *Current*. Tanin's ship, the *Black Beauty*, was nowhere to be seen.

A few more hours, and it would be over.

"We have to get down there," Archer said, checking Lightning's cylinders as he strode toward the tower steps.

Sefia grabbed him by the arm, pulling him back from the stairs. "You'll *die*."

"Our *friends* are dying." His golden eyes were wide and frightened.

"There's nothing you can do. We'd need an army to—"

For a second, an idea flickered to life in her mind.

They didn't just need an army. They needed an unstoppable army. They needed—

"What about the power of the Scribes?" Archer interrupted.

She hesitated. The last time she'd tried to influence a battle— here, on Blackfire Bay—she'd mutilated hundreds of people. She'd massacred them. "I don't think . . ."

"You know more than you did then. You won't make the same mistakes. Come on. We have to do *something*."

He was right.

She was better than she used to be. She was stronger and more skilled. She couldn't stand by and do nothing.

Taking a breath, Sefia summoned the Sight, and the Illuminated world flooded across the bay. Cascades of gold drenched the islands, the ships, the flames.

But she knew it was hopeless even before the tide of gold had finished coming in.

The bands of light connecting the ships and the embattled soldiers were too bright. They connected the Alliance, the Resistance, the city, winding up the black cliff to the watchtower like climbing vines, piercing her own heart—and Archer's.

"I can't," she said, blinking as her eyes filled with desperate, frustrated tears. "Even if I tried, it's all too connected. I'd end up taking our friends with our enemies. I'd end up taking you. All of us would be erased or half-gone."

Archer cursed and lashed out with his sword, shearing one of the flagpoles on the ramparts.

"We're too late," Sefia whispered.

Too late to intervene.

Too late to save anyone except themselves.

They'd chosen the few over the many, and this was the cost.

Would it have made any difference if Archer had agreed to fight? What were they supposed to have done? Why had the storyteller pushed her toward the Resurrection Amulet if it was never going to help them anyway?

The Resurrection Amulet was never supposed to keep a person from dying. It was supposed to bring one soul—and only one soul—*back from the dead.*

A shadow of the person you knew in life.

A phantom, deprived of warmth and breath and memory, unable to get it except by draining the living.

No one could break the laws of the dead.

Kelanna was a world rife with magic, *inconsistencies, exceptions.*

Sefia looked up suddenly. Maybe there *was* a way to help their friends. Maybe there *was* a way to save them all.

And, a little voice inside her said, *maybe I can see my family again.*

"I have to go," she said.

"Where? Why?"

"The Amulet. I think I can change it. I think I can get us the army we need."

"How?"

It would cost her, she knew. It might cost her own life, if whoever summoned the phantoms was the one who died at the end of the war.

But still . . . she had hope. She was rewriting the world. She was changing fate. Anything could happen.

She pulled Archer into an abrupt, clumsy kiss, his lips surprised and soft on hers. "I think I can save you," she whispered, and before he could reply, she teleported out from his embrace to the deck of the *Current of Faith*.

All around her were the sounds of cannons, gunfire, shouting. The decks were slick with blood and spiked with shrapnel.

Captain Reed looked surprised to see her. He was crouched behind the gunwale, his upper arm and thigh neatly bandaged. In his smoke-smudged face, his blue eyes sparkled. "Hey, kid!" he cried, grinning. "What are you—?"

But before he could finish, she grabbed him, and in the blink of an eye, they were gone.

They reappeared in the great cabin, where Reed stumbled away from her. "In case you hadn't noticed, we're in the middle of a . . ." His voice trailed off as he saw her grim expression. "Sef?"

"I need the Amulet," she said, almost choking on the words. "*All* of it."

The captain's hand went to his chest. His tattoos. She'd have to extract all of his tattoos but one. The first one. "I thought we agreed—"

"We did. But something's changed." She paused as he took a step back, his hand poised over his holster. "I'll take them, if I have to."

"You can try."

For a moment, they stared at each other, and Sefia saw their friendship strung out between them like a bridge: the story she told to earn a place on his ship, the name she scrawled on a scrap of canvas, the battles they'd fought together, the treasures they'd found, the home he'd given her after years of wandering.

She flung out her hand.

He went for his gun.

If he hadn't hesitated, he might've shot her. But they were friends, weren't they? He hadn't wanted to hurt her. And Sefia had been counting on it.

She pinned him against the glass cases, flicking the lock on the door and barricading it with the heavy oak table where Doc had stitched up Archer their first night on the ship.

Captain Reed fought her grasp, but he couldn't buck loose.

"This is the way we save everyone," she said.

By taking his stories.

By betraying him.

By breaking their friendship.

She hoped he'd forgive her, one day. But she didn't think he would. Not after this.

In one swift movement, she ripped off his shirt, exposing his wounded arm—which began bleeding freely, dripping off the point of his elbow—and the tattoos he'd spent a lifetime collecting.

"Sef," he said in a voice she'd never heard from him, a voice laced with fear. "Sefia, don't. *Don't.*"

She focused her Sight on the tattoos, finding each layer of ink in his skin like bands of color in sandstone.

"Don't take this from me, kid. Not today."

She lifted her other hand, feeling the webs of light tickling her fingertips.

"I'm sorry," she said. "This is going to hurt."

And she took his tattoos: the sea monsters, the winged fish, the man with the black gun. She siphoned them from the pores of his skin like she was extracting mold from a paper page.

He tried to resist. He squirmed in her grasp.

But as she took the stories of the Lady of Mercy, the Rescue at Dead Man's Rock, his love affair with Lady Delune, he began to beg.

"No. Stop. Please. Sefia. No. *No!*"

Every word was a wound, a cut, a punch in the chest.

But she didn't stop.

"Cap?" Someone began pounding on the door, but it held fast. "Cap!"

She took Captain Cat and her cannibal crew. She took the floating island. She took new stories about her and Archer and the Trove of the King.

Until at last she laid bare the first tattoos he'd ever gotten, the tattoos her parents had given him, the tattoos that told her where she'd find the last piece of the Resurrection Amulet. Had they known she'd need it? Or had they simply done it because the Book had told them to?

She memorized them quickly and let him fall, gasping, to the floor. Tears squeezed from the corners of his eyes.

She almost asked for his forgiveness. But she knew she didn't *deserve* his forgiveness.

Breaking one of the glass cases, she summoned the Amulet to her. It flew across the room and landed, cold, in her palm.

"Get off my ship," Reed growled.

Sefia cringed at his words. For a moment, she wanted to say good-bye, wanted to say thank you for all he'd done for her, wanted to say she loved him. In case destiny caught her.

"Go!" He drew the Executioner.

She'd known the day he holstered that weapon in front of her that if he drew it on her again, he'd kill her.

With one last glance at him, she lifted her arms . . . and teleported away.

After the uproar of the battle, the clearing was so quiet, it seemed almost deafening.

So peaceful, it seemed almost dead.

Trembling, Sefia looked out through the treetops. She was at the peak of a mountain, with a blue channel and a large landmass to the north, its sides carpeted by verdant jungle.

She was in Oxscini, somewhere in the southern cluster of islands they'd passed on their way to Tsumasai Bay.

She'd been so close to the last piece of the Amulet, and she hadn't known.

Turning away from the view, she faced the five stones arranged at the other end of the clearing, creating a neat sitting area where you could admire the view.

The palest of the stones was just left of center, overgrown at the base with moss and ferns. In fact, when she looked closer, it hardly seemed like a stone at all, almost perfectly round, as if it had been made by human hands.

Summoning her magic, Sefia split it neatly down the center with a swift *crack*.

There, nestled inside, was a ring of strange metal. Picking it up, she fitted it inside the Amulet, where it locked into place with a *click*.

She could read the symbols, now that the Resurrection Amulet was whole:

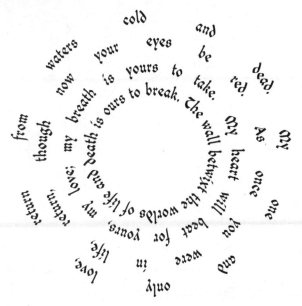

But she couldn't use it yet. If she put on the Amulet now, she could only summon one soul from the world of the dead.

And she needed more.

She needed an army.

Flexing her fingers, she allowed herself to sink into the deeper seeing of the Scribes. She never would have been able to modify the Amulet with Transformation alone. She needed Alteration to erase some words of the spell and to add her own, changing its purpose . . . and rewriting the future.

She would control the story.

And she would save Archer.

When she was done, she blinked. Most of the inscription was untouched, but not all of it. Not the most important parts of it.

She would get her army. The Alliance would fall. Archer would live.

She hoped the first souls she saw would be her mother and father and Nin. After all this time, she was going to see them again. She was going to tell them she was sorry. She loved them. She hoped they'd be proud of her.

Tucking the Resurrection Amulet into her pocket, she swept her arms wide and teleported back to the watchtower.

No sooner had she landed than Archer swept her up in an embrace.

For a moment, she closed her eyes, savoring the sound of his heartbeat beneath her cheek—strong, solid, magnificently alive.

I'm going to save you, she thought. *I'm going to save everyone.*

But as he released her, she caught sight of something silver flashing in his palm—no, over his head.

She checked her pocket.

But the Resurrection Amulet wasn't there.

It was around Archer's neck, hanging just over his heart. He gave her a small, sad smile. "I'm sorry. I couldn't let you do it," he said.

And his eyes, his beautiful golden eyes, went red.

CHAPTER 40

We Were Dead, but Now We Rise

S efia tried to grab the Resurrection Amulet from him, but Archer staggered back, shaking his head. He hadn't known how or why, but as soon as she mentioned the Amulet, he'd known she would try to use it herself.

Now, against his chest, the metal disc burned cold, like ice, eating through his shirt to the flesh beneath, where it latched on to him—a dozen pointed talons digging deep into his skin.

From the metal, there came a low humming, dark as an ocean and deep as a sky. The sound filled the spaces in his bones until he could feel it thrumming—or was it keening? moaning?—in his marrow.

Dimly, he thought he heard voices—or glaciers cleaving, cliffs crumbling to dust—whispering, chittering, mad.

Gasping.

The last gasp of Oriyah, before Hatchet put a bullet through his skull, of Argo, of countless others, and of Kaito—sounds that haunted Archer in the late hours of the night when the darkness shuttered him in and the cold crept in through the cracks.

Then Sefia's voice reached him, like a warm breeze, smelling of salt and sweetgrass: "Archer, the Amulet."

He looked down at his chest. In their settings, the stones seemed to glow—no, to pulse—brighter and dimmer and brighter again, like the beacon of a lighthouse.

When he looked up again, there were tears in Sefia's eyes. "I wanted to do it," she whispered. "So you wouldn't have to."

"I know." Archer touched the Amulet. "But whoever uses this might die. And I didn't want it to be you."

Sefia bit her lip. "This means you'll have to kill again."

His heart felt heavy in his chest. "And if I—when I . . . after all this is over, that's something I'll have to figure out how to live with."

She blinked back tears as he traced her scarred brow. "We'll figure it out together. After you help our friends and send the dead back where they came from."

"I'm scared, Sefia."

"I'll be with you the whole time."

He kissed her then, as sweet as the first time—amid the wind and the black water with the stars wheeling overhead—and every kiss since, every touch, every look, every word.

"Tell me you love me," he whispered.

"I love you." She nestled her cheek against his palm.

He'd already memorized the words, already fastened them to his heart. But hearing them again made him dizzy and breathless with desire.

For her. For life. For all of it.

"Tell me we'll make it," he said.

Her lashes were starred with tears. "We'll make it," she whispered.

And Archer chose to believe her, even if the fear in her eyes told him she couldn't believe it herself.

He kissed her again. Like it was the last time.

Like it was the first.

Darkness appeared on the western horizon, spreading through the water like spilled ink. Archer could feel it approaching, drawn to the Resurrection Amulet—to *him*.

He thought he saw red lights winking in the deep.

Then the darkness hit the base of the cliffs and surged upward, spiraling through the air like wisps of smoke. The soldiers on the watchtower cried out in fear.

Instinctively, Archer pushed Sefia aside as the darkness reached him, spearing directly through the Amulet fused to his chest.

He gasped.

"Archer!" Sefia cried. But he could hear her only faintly, as if he were at the end of a long black tunnel. He seemed only partly in his own body, barely seeing, though his eyes were open, barely feeling the tower stones under his feet.

Instead, he felt them all—all the dead, every one—pass through him like bullets, each taking a little of his warmth, a little of his life, a little of whatever essential substance made him *Archer*—the boy from the lighthouse, the boy in the crate, the victim, the killer, the chief, the friend, the lover, the—

"Brother," someone said, in a voice that resembled his own, in a voice that almost sounded like . . .

Archer turned. "Kaito," he murmured.

The boy—or the shadow of the boy—stood at Archer's side, like he'd done so many times before.

And behind him stood Versil, tall and slender, looking almost like his twin, Aljan, without the white patches at the corners of his eyes and mouth that he'd had when he was alive. All around the roof of the watchtower were the dead Archer had known: Hatchet, Redbeard, Oriyah, Gregor and Haku from the Cage—he'd suspected they were dead, yes, but now he knew for sure—the First Assassin, Erastis, a sick girl from back home in Jocoxa, people he might have seen only once or twice in the street, his father . . . looking the same age he was when he died, though Archer had aged thirteen years.

All the dead he'd ever known were here.

"I told you to run, girl," one of them said, shouldering her way past the others. She was short and wide, like a small mountain. Most of her features were hazy, but her hands were well-defined, wrinkled and scarred and strong. "I'm proud that you didn't."

Choking back a sob, Sefia started forward. "Aunt Nin."

The phantom held up a hand to stop her. "Don't cry. You've got work to do."

Sefia nodded. "Yes, ma'am."

Except that wasn't Nin, not really. That wasn't his father, beaming at him from the tower stairs. That wasn't Kaito from the north. They were shades—less than flesh, more than smoke—and they were a part of him.

Archer could feel every one of their spectral limbs, see himself through each of their crimson eyes.

"We're with you, brother." And Archer wasn't sure if it was Kaito speaking or his memory of Kaito—the voice melding with dozens of other voices and with his own.

"Literally," Versil added in the same blend of voices. "I think we *are* you. Or you . . . are us?"

"Both, I think," Sefia said. "Until Archer sends you back."

"Hey, sorcerer." Versil's spectral face shivered, his features blurring. Then he grinned.

She managed a strangled smile. "Hey."

"Is that brother of mine still with Frey?"

"Yeah," she murmured.

"Eh, she's too good for him." He laughed. "But I'm glad."

"We're here to save them, aren't we?" Kaito asked, looking out over the bay, where the battle was still raging on. "We're here for one more fight?"

Archer nodded. "Just one more."

"All right, then, brother. Lead the way."

Archer wanted to embrace him, but wasn't sure if he could. "I'm sorry," he said softly.

Kaito's expression went hazy for a moment, but then he was back again, smiling sadly. "I know," he replied in the voice that was not his voice. "I am too."

Arrayed across the tower roof and the cliff below, the dead looked to Archer. He looked so small through their glowing eyes, but in this battle, they would obey his every thought.

They were his.

His army.

"Take care of him, sorcerer," Kaito said.

She swallowed, hard. "I will."

447

Archer looked to her, and he saw her not just through his own eyes but through the eyes of all the dead. He'd always known she was beautiful, but for some reason, with the breeze in her hair and the top button of her shirt undone and the glistening in her dark eyes, he couldn't remember her ever being more beautiful than this.

Fool, he chided himself. She was this beautiful the first time he saw her, a slender silhouette against the firelight as he crawled out of his crate. She was this beautiful in the Trove, sleeping in the crook of his arm. Every time he looked, she was this beautiful.

"I love you," he told her. *"We'll make it."*

She nodded.

As the phantoms began their march down the cliff, Archer knew he was more *them* than *him* now. He was more aware of their limbs of smoke than his own body, more aware of the waves splashing at his many ankles, the breeze cascading from his many shoulders.

Ahead of them—ahead of him—the battle waited. The *Barbaro* and the bulk of the Alliance fleet storming the harbor. Serakeen and the *Amalthea* cornering the rest in the northeast.

Only faintly did he sense Sefia taking up a stance beside him, watching over him, protecting him. The way she always did.

CHAPTER 41

The Fracturing of the World

As the Resistance crumbles—

As the dead walk across the surface of Blackfire Bay—

As Archer and Sefia make their stand on the watchtower—

Somewhere across the ocean, at the western edge of the world, where the place of the fleshless and the place of the living nearly touch, something happens that I did not expect.

The Resurrection Amulet was only ever supposed to summon one soul from the world of the dead.

When Archer put it on, he summoned hundreds.

Hundreds of ghosts rammed into the invisible barrier between the living and the dead, surging back into this wonderful and terrible world, this world rife with contradictions and inconsistencies and magic, and where they came through, the barrier cracks.

It's a fine break—a bone that doesn't need setting; a paper cut so clean, at first it doesn't even bleed.

But it's a break, and slowly, the souls of everyone who has ever died—every single one—begin to reenter Kelanna.

They leak through the fracture like ink in water.

Like smoke in a white sky.

They spill across the pages of this world—more and more of them, faster and faster. The crack splits, spiderwebbing, as if in glass or a sheet of ice.

Unlike Archer's phantoms, which have been given life and form by his beating heart, his living body, these ghosts form and re-form like wisps of fog—there and not, here and gone.

It's a slender figure that finally shatters the barrier between the worlds of the living and the dead. She's strong and desperate and determined, scrambling through the break until at last the divide splinters into millions of fragments, and the dead pour from the black place beyond the edge of the world.

She pauses while they flood past her. She looks over her shoulder, and her shadowy hair is pulled into a knot at the base of her neck.

Is it Mareah?

And there, behind her, is it Lon? The darkness flowing about him like oversize robes?

They take each other's hands, as much as they can with their ghostly fingers.

And they leave the place of the fleshless behind.

They come to the deep blue, where the whales sing their sad songs and starving sharks swim for miles in search of prey. They stream by squid, sea turtles, clouds of shrimp, schools of shimmering fish, and enter the vivid turquoise world just below

450

the surface. The white flashing underside of the sky and the sun striking the water.

Like spears they burst into the air. They remember how bright the world is, how the waves sparkle, how the sky is so unforgivingly blue.

And as they dissipate, burning away like mist in the sun, they remember.

This world.

This wonderful and terrible world of water and ships and magic.

And their daughter.

They have returned.

CHAPTER 42

Of Heroes and Kings

There had always been little hope for the Resistance, but now that they were down to their last defenses, Eduoar could not help but wonder if they should have surrendered. Many would have been killed—the rebel redcoats for mutiny, the Delieneans for defection, certainly his own life would have been forfeit—but so many more would have lived.

When the *Barbaro* and the Alliance fleet began attacking the harbor defenses, Eduoar and the *Red Hare* led the remainder of the White Navy to their aid. But they were no match for the blue beasts of the Alliance. Many of the Resistance warships had gone down under fire. Others had been boarded and captured.

Lac and Hobs had been on one of those ships. Ed still didn't know if they'd made it.

Now the resisters were scattered. Some had been corralled by Serakeen and the *Amalthea* in the east. Others, like Eduoar and the *Hare*, were making their last stand in the harbor while blue-uniformed soldiers began storming the city walls. On the ramparts, Ed could see Adeline, the Lady of Mercy, firing into the Alliance ranks, taking out enemy after enemy with the quick, clean shots that had made her a legend. Beside her, another old woman, with curly, graying hair, reloaded weapons faster than anyone Eduoar had ever seen and tossed them to Adeline, who caught them in midair and continued shooting.

But they were all being overwhelmed. Reaching the top of the wall, an Alliance soldier struck the second woman in the head with the hilt of his sword. She crumpled. The Lady of Mercy whirled on him, but she, too, was knocked aside.

The *Barbaro* cornered the *Red Hare* against the eastern arm of the harbor, pummeling them with broadside after broadside, filling the air with smoke and the screams of men.

This was the end.

Instinctively, Ed looked to the north. Toward Corabel. Toward Arc. Toward home.

He wished he could have seen them all, one last time.

But as he turned back to face the enemy, he spotted men— no, not men, *shadows*, hundreds of them—marching across the bay, their footfalls sinking only a few inches before the water buoyed them up again.

As they reached the nearest Alliance ships, they began crawling up the blue hulls, swarming the decks. From this distance, Eduoar couldn't see what was happening, but over the din of cannon fire, he could hear shrieking.

And the silence that followed.

Abruptly, the *Barbaro*'s assault halted. Her guns went quiet.

Beside Ed, the captain of the *Red Hare* held a glass to his eye. "What in the blue world is happening?"

Ignoring the Resistance fighters, the phantoms moved on to other Alliance vessels. Blue-uniformed soldiers began pitching themselves into the sea to escape them.

Eduoar shook his head. "I don't know. But whatever those things are, I think they're on our side."

The captain clapped him on the back. "Then let's take advantage of them. Come on, Your Majesty, it's time for your first boarding." To his crew, he roared, "Ready the grapples! Boarding parties, to arms!"

There was a flurry of activity as the helmsman brought the *Red Hare* around, Delienean soldiers stuffing their belts with axes and extra bullets. The wind filled the sails as they turned, coming alongside General Terezina's flagship.

Across the harbor, the phantoms amassed on another Alliance vessel.

The *Barbaro* loosed a broadside. Chunks of the *Red Hare* exploded. Shards of wood soared through the air, striking Delieneans as they dove for cover.

The shadow soldiers may have been an unwelcome surprise, but General Terezina would not go down easy. From the fighting tops, riflemen peppered the resisters with gunfire. Powder kegs dropped and exploded in blazing spheres of heat. Ed and the crew of the *Red Hare* were pinned to their own deck. None of them could get near the Alliance ship.

Until the phantoms appeared over the rails of the *Barbaro*.

Bullets, swords, cannon fire, all passed through them as if

454

through fog. With arms of smoke, they seized enemy soldiers, who shrieked and flailed, their faces going slack with shock and fear, until their voices lapsed into muted whispers and their bodies went limp and lifeless.

With a roar, the Delieneans charged over the rails. Ed launched himself onto the deck of the *Barbaro*, wielding a boarding ax, same as the rest of them. It was chaos. The shadow soldiers were relentless, ducking and moving as if the battle were a complicated, deadly dance.

Ed blinked. He knew those moves, didn't he? He'd been taught them with the rest of the Resistance as they fled from Oxscini two months ago . . .

The phantoms caught hold of the Alliance soldiers, who could not fight an enemy they could not touch nor hurt nor kill.

An unstoppable army.

These were Archer's fighters.

Where was Archer?

But as Eduoar scanned the melee, he thought he spied someone else, the last person, really, he expected to see.

Arc?

Ed had to look twice.

Arcadimon Detano, on a battleship? In a blue Alliance uniform, his face smudged with smoke, his hair mussed, blood and grease on his hands?

But Eduoar would have known him anywhere, no matter what disguise he wore, no matter how many days or decades had passed between them.

As if he could sense Eduoar watching him, Arc looked up.

His perfect lips parted in surprise, relief and joy suffusing his features like the scent of a sea breeze through a newly opened window.

Ed nearly choked on his own laughter.

Arc. *Here.*

Eduoar started forward. But while Arcadimon watched him, distracted, one of the phantoms reared up behind him and grasped him by the throat.

Ed lunged forward before he even knew what he was doing, ducking blades and striking enemies, dodging shadow soldiers as they swept across the deck, killing blue-uniformed fighters.

Arc's face was losing color, his bright blue eyes going dull.

The phantom's wraithlike fingers tightened.

Shoving Arcadimon out of its grasp, Eduoar immediately felt its hands pass through him.

He gasped.

He knew that feeling. It was his life draining out of him.

For a second, he thought of the white room in the castle at Corabel where he'd found his father's body, the white room where he'd tried to take his own life.

Then the phantom released him. It spoke: "Your Majesty?"

Ed recognized that voice, though it was distorted—it was Archer's voice, entwined with hundreds of other voices he'd never heard before.

"You did it," Eduoar said softly. "But how—?"

"Sefia." The shadow soldier's face flickered and blurred. "You were right. We couldn't stand there and watch every- one die."

As they spoke, there was an explosion to the northeast,

where Serakeen and the *Amalthea* were hunting down the out-laws that were left.

The phantom wavered.

"Go," said Eduoar. "And thank you."

All around him, the shadow soldiers began to crawl over the rails and back down to the water, leaving what little fighting that remained aboard the *Barbaro* to the Delieneans.

As Ed reached down, Arcadimon caught his hand, callused from months of hard work, and slipped the signet ring onto his finger. "My king," Arc whispered.

But Eduoar couldn't care less about the ring right now. He hauled Arcadimon to his feet. "What are you doing here?" Ed's gaze passed over Arc's face as if the answer would be there, on his brow, his cheeks, his dimples.

"I had to find you." Arcadimon's voice was shakier than Ed had ever heard it. "I had to tell you—"

But Eduoar didn't want to hear what Arc had to say—and in truth, he didn't know if he could trust him. So before Arcadimon could finish speaking, Ed took him by the back of the neck, ignoring—loving—the shock on Arc's handsome features, and pulled him in for a kiss. Rough lips and a few teeth.

Arc let out a soft moan, full of longing.

Despite himself, Eduoar felt his heart flutter at the sound.

A shot broke them apart, searing Ed's shoulder as he and Arcadimon sprang back.

Above them on the fighting top stood Braca Terezina III, the most feared commander in the Alliance. She must have retreated there when Archer's phantom army arrived, but now she swung down to the deck, her blue suede coat flaring out behind her, brandishing one of her gold-tipped guns. Her boots, cuffs, and scarred face were spattered with blood, though she wasn't bleeding.

"Traitor," she spat at Arcadimon.

Ed half-expected Arc to come back with a witty reply.

He didn't expect Arcadimon to lash out with his hand, sending a wave of invisible force at the general.

Arc really was a sorcerer, Eduoar thought, bemused.

Not a great one, though. Braca barely rocked back on her heels as the magic hit her. Calmly, she drew her cutlass from its scabbard.

Arcadimon grabbed his hand. "Run!"

Together, they dashed around cannons and fallen bodies. Bullets struck the rails around them as the Alliance general followed, taunting them.

When they reached the steps to the quarterdeck, Ed spared a glance behind him. Braca was advancing slowly, almost leisurely, stalking through the chaos, cutting down Delieneans with careless grace, hitting targets without even seeming to aim.

"Come *on!*" Arc hauled him up the stairs, where they scrambled onto the quarterdeck.

They'd barely made it past the steps when General Terezina materialized in front of them.

She could teleport, like Sefia. Ed and Arc could run the length of the decks and dive into the sea, and they'd never be able to escape her. Unless . . .

"Arc." He grabbed Arcadimon's arm. "Can you teleport too?"

"I wish!" Arc thrust him aside as Braca shot at them. With a flick of his wrist, he tried shoving her back.

She dodged easily, and one of the lanterns at the stern of the ship shattered. "What were you hoping to do here, Apprentice?" she asked. "You couldn't have hoped to match me."

"I came to see you lose," Arcadimon said, putting Eduoar behind him as he began to back up the way they'd come.

"You're one of us," Braca snapped. "Or did you think your little king would forget that, even if you live past midday tomorrow?"

Her cruel words made Ed pause. "What's she talking about?"

"That's one of the things I wanted to tell you—" Arc began, but a gunshot stopped him. His leg went out from under him.

Eduoar grabbed for him, but they fell in a heap at the top of the stairs.

"He's been poisoned." Braca laughed. "By coming here, he forfeited his right to the only cure."

Arcadimon struggled to his feet. Even in his ill-fitting Alliance uniform, bleeding from the knee, he still looked heroic. "I'd rather die at Ed's side than live on yours," he said.

Such a gallant thing to say. Eduoar almost smiled as he stood beside him.

But the general was unamused. "Done," she said, drawing her second gold-tipped revolver. The barrels flashed.

In that second, just before they died, Ed looked to Arcadimon.

The boy who'd betrayed him.

The boy who'd saved him.

The boy he'd been in love with since he was old enough to recognize it.

As Braca pulled back the hammer, Arc gave him one of those irresistible grins of his.

Ed didn't close his eyes. He wanted to look as long as he could.

But instead of a gunshot, there was an explosion. The general's eyes bulged. Her mouth twisted. And she pitched forward, her blue coat torn open at the back, exposing flesh and shrapnel and broken bones.

Eduoar gasped.

Then he reached for Arc's hand.

"Ed!" someone cried.

At the stern of the *Barbaro*, beside the broken lantern, Lac and Hobs were perched, their crimson uniforms dripping seawater. Between them sat a smoking swivel gun.

The fighting aboard Braca's flagship was done. On the main deck, the Alliance soldiers, having seen their commander fall, were surrendering.

Dragging Arcadimon behind him, Ed ran for his friends. "I thought your ship was captured!"

"It was," Hobs said, hopping off the rail, his boots squelching. "But we weren't."

Haldon Lac was staring, openmouthed, at Arc. Eduoar didn't blame him. In any light, Arcadimon Detano was stunning.

"What's the matter?" Arc clapped the redcoat on the shoulder, as at ease here on the deck of the *Barbaro*, in the middle of a war, as he'd ever been in a Delienean council room. "Never saved a king before?"

"Oh no," said Hobs, "but he's saved us loads of times."

"Actually," Ed interjected, throwing his arms around both redcoats, "these boys are heroes. I never would've made it without them."

Lac's green eyes filled with tears. "Heroes," he whispered.

CHAPTER 43

Captain Cannek Reed

The dead were unstoppable—reaching through shuttered gun ports, bursting through hulls, emerging from below-decks to grasp Alliance soldiers by the ankles and siphon the life out of them.

Still, the Alliance kept fighting. Shot after shot, their cannonballs whistled through the phantoms' spectral forms only to batter into the scattered Resistance ships. Through it all, the *Current of Faith* sailed in and out of the broken enemy line, letting off one devastating broadside after another.

Across the water, the *Crux* let off a round of fire that shook the very timbers of the *Current*. Flames bloomed on one of the Alliance vessels, climbing the masts and devouring the sails, which fell in smoking tatters to the tarred decks.

As the shadowy figures spread north, killing any enemies that stood in their path, the flaming Alliance ship drifted behind the *Current*, where it crashed into another enemy vessel, setting its rigging on fire. The two burning ships came to a stop, dead in the water, while their soldiers dove over the rails to escape the blaze.

On the quarterdeck of the *Current*, Captain Reed could feel the heat on his back as he watched the phantoms through the smoke.

The dead were turning the tide of the battle.

He pressed a palm to his stinging chest. Sefia may have taken his tattoos, but in doing so, she'd saved them all.

If he ever got the chance, he'd tell her he was sorry. For being so selfish.

When it had come down to it, she'd been better than him.

As the burning wrecks crackled behind him, he opened his mouth to order Jaunty to take them north, into the remnants of the battle.

But before he could speak, the *Amalthea* appeared out of the smoke before him like a blue dragon, spewing flame.

"Take cover!" Captain Reed roared as the cycling guns began spitting bullets. Diving forward, he yanked Meeks down beside him as they covered their heads.

Cannon fire rocked them, taking bites of the rails and chunks of the hull.

Over the din, the chief mate was cursing. Reed glanced around, searching for escape.

But the *Current* was pinned between the blazing wrecks and Serakeen's flagship. She may have been the quickest ship in the west, but she had nowhere to run, and with the phantoms amassing on the enemies to the north, she had no one to rescue her.

Mind racing, Reed peered over the bulkhead. His ship and his crew would be blown to bits if he didn't do something.

Between the iron teeth of Serakeen's artillery, he spied a stack of powder kegs and shot boxes, overflowing with cartridges for the cycling guns, poised at the edge of the *Amalthea*'s main hatchway, waiting to be distributed to the gunners.

And he knew.

All along the rails, he counted powder cases—explosive traps ready to be sprung upon unwary boarders. If he could split them open, then . . . He thought of Lac's retelling of the death of the *Fire-Eater*: *an explosion so bright it was like the ocean itself was aflame.*

He knew how it would happen.

A black gun. A white dandelion.

He could save the *Current*.

Amid the gunfire, Reed clasped Meeks's hand. "The ship is yours," he said. "If I make it, get the *Current* as far away as you can."

The second mate—no, the new captain—blinked at him. "Cap, what—"

All of a sudden, Reed wished he had more time. There were so many things he wanted to say about the legacy of the *Current*, about goodness and freedom and curiosity and wonder and loyalty to your crew. But he said the only words he could find: "Look to the horizon. That's where the adventures are."

Leaving Meeks by the bulkhead, Reed dashed toward the

main deck, narrowly avoiding chain shot as it whirred past his head, and grabbed a boarding ax from a weapons chest. Ducking, he slid a handful of bullets into his pocket.

"Cap?" Jaunty's rough voice reached him from the helm.

Reed stuffed the ax into his belt. "Can you get me onto the *Amalthea* without gettin' the *Current* gutted?"

The helmsman narrowed his eyes, the hesitation plain on his stubbled, weatherworn face. Could he see Reed's plan in his eyes the same way he could read the weather and the water?

As was his way, Jaunty didn't question or protest or even say good-bye. He just nodded, once, and hauled on the wheel.

As the *Current* turned, Reed climbed into the rigging, up above the *Amalthea*'s relentless gunfire.

Grabbing one of the running lines, he paused on the yardarm.

One.

Below, Meeks and the chief mate were ordering the gun crews into position while the riflemen began popping up from their positions to take aim at Serakeen's soldiers.

Two.

Doc was racing among the injured, her black bag in hand, her clothes stained with blood.

Three.

Horse must have been belowdecks, plugging holes. Reed wished he could've seen the big carpenter's smile one last time. It would've given him courage, now, when he needed it most.

Four.

The water thrashed below him. Closer and closer, it carried him toward the *Amalthea*.

Five.

Theo's strong baritone reached him, calling, "Fire!" The *Current*'s cannons spewed thunder.

Six.

The waves plunged the *Current* down into the troughs and back up again.

Seven.

Serakeen's flagship loomed huge and menacing before him—a monster of war.

Eight.

Reed leapt from the yard, swinging toward the deck of the *Current* and arcing out—breathless—over the water, over the cycling guns, until he was above the bow of the *Amalthea.*

But as he was about to drop, there was a shot. Fire tore through his side as his grip on the rope loosened. His quick eyes found the enemy, there, by the prow's chase guns.

He fell, hitting the deck of the *Amalthea*, where he rolled once and came up shooting. The blue-uniformed soldier collapsed with a bullet between the eyes.

Pulling the boarding ax, Reed ran toward the other end of the ship, ducking, swerving, each of his shots finding its target, his ax carving open any enemy who got too close.

He had to be fast, before Serakeen figured out what was happening and came to stop him.

Reaching a couple powder kegs, Reed kicked them onto their sides and sent them rattling down the deck, where they burst open, spilling powder.

Good.

He tried skidding after them, but a volley of gunfire made him jump back. A bullet cut him across the cheek.

One of the gun crews was firing on him, pinning him behind a chase gun.

Beyond them lay the powder kegs, unattended by the main hatch as the rest of the gunners launched volley after volley of fire and iron at the *Current of Faith*.

Dumping the empty casings, Reed reloaded the Singer. The graze on his cheek bled down his chin, but the wound in his side was making it hard to breathe. It must have struck something important.

Flicking the cylinder of his revolver closed, he leapt to his feet, ready to charge across the ship, when there was the report of a rifle.

One of the Alliance soldiers dropped. And another.

The others scrambled for cover.

Reed spared one glance at the *Current*. Aly was at the rail, rifle to her shoulder, braids undone. Then a flash of copper hair as Marmalade sprang up beside her, taking out another pirate and pausing briefly to wave at Reed.

"Go get 'em, Cap!"

He grinned.

Then he sprinted across the deck, making for the powder cases at the rails. Reaching the first, he pried it open with his ax, pausing only to fire the Singer in the face of an Alliance soldier, and tipped the powder toward the main hatchway.

Someone cut him in the calf.

They paid with their life.

But his leg wasn't working quite right anymore. He had to half-hop, half-drag himself to the next powder traps, forcing them open, hiding behind cannons as the enemy tried to stop him.

Again and again, his bullets struck home.

Ten, nine, eight left . . .

It was getting harder to breathe. He ducked as covering fire from the *Current* flew over his head. He was bleeding in more places than he could count now.

But he was almost there.

Reed holstered the Singer as her chambers emptied. Flipping the ax into his other hand, he drew the Executioner.

He'd almost reached the stack of kegs and shot cases when a blow caught him in the side of the head.

Pain exploded in his skull. His vision spun. He reeled, lashing out with his ax as he fell.

Someone *tsk*ed. On his hands and knees, Reed caught sight of an aubergine coat and a gleaming metal hand.

Serakeen.

Reed shot.

He missed.

Five bullets left.

Serakeen kicked him in the stomach, sending him rolling into the stash of powder and ammunition.

Blood ran into Reed's eyes as he staggered up.

"Captain Reed," Serakeen said. His eyes were blue, like Reed's, but pale as ice. "What are you doing here? Did you think you could kill me all by yourself?"

Reed swayed. He'd lost so much blood. "I'm Cannek Reed." He shrugged. "I've done dumber things than this."

"Not after today," Serakeen replied. He flung out his hand—a wave of magic hit Reed in the chest, sending him crashing into the powder kegs.

The barrels toppled, cracking open. Black dust went trickling over him, down the hatchway in a glittering ribbon.

Reed smiled as he pushed himself to his knees. The Executioner spat fire.

Serakeen dodged, but the shot still struck him in the ribs.

Four bullets left.

Reed danced away, toward the last powder case on the rail.

Three. Two. He took out a couple Alliance soldiers by the bulkhead and began hacking at the wooden box with his boarding ax, splitting it open.

He felt slow. Clumsy. His injuries were catching up to him.

The powder spilled across the deck as Serakeen straightened, holding his wounded side, and flung his magic at Reed like a hammer.

Reed sidestepped. Barely.

Whirling, he leveled the Executioner at the pile of broken kegs by the main hatch.

His stomach sank.

Most of the gunpowder and ammunition hadn't made it down the hatchway. It lay in a mound on the deck, among the splintered boards and iron hoops.

He had to get back there. He had to dump it belowdecks to the magazine.

But Serakeen stood between him and the hatch. He flung the boarding ax. He fired his revolver.

The pirate easily swept both aside.

One bullet left.

Reed's mind whirled. Maybe enough powder had trickled into the hatchway. Maybe the plan would still work.

Maybe it wouldn't. And if it didn't, the *Current* and all his crew were as good as dead.

He'd have to dive past Serakeen and shove the powder down there himself. All it'd take was one good leap.

But he was injured.

And Serakeen had magic.

Reed readied himself for the lunge.

But before he could move, he heard the water calling: *Wait . . . wait . . .*

He paused.

Now.

A wave struck them. The *Amalthea* heaved. Loose shot clattered toward the stern as the deck tilted, and the pile of ammunition and gunpowder slid into the hatchway, leaving only broken bits of wood and iron behind.

The corner of Reed's mouth twitched. He inhaled deeply, taking one last breath of salty wet air.

"Thank you," he murmured.

With a final glance at the *Current of Faith*, her green hull, her tree-like figurehead, her curves and cannons and battered bulwarks, he raised the black gun.

Serakeen closed his fist. Reed felt the magic tightening around him like a net.

But he was the quickest draw in the Central Sea.

He pulled the trigger before the magic paralyzed him.

The bullet sped across the ship, past Serakeen, past the gun crews and their cannons, straight into one of the powder kegs' broken iron hoops.

There was a spark, flashing like a white dandelion above the deck.

The gunpowder caught fire.

And the timbers of the *Amalthea* burst apart in a flash of heat and light that consumed Serakeen's aubergine coat, his outstretched hand, the cannons, all the cycling guns, the soldiers, and flung Reed from the deck.

Shrapnel pierced him through the chest, through the only tattoo he had left.

The *Current* was saved. His crew would live. Reed smiled.

And as he hit the water, the Executioner flew from his fingers. It sank into the depths, never to curse another soul again. The sea reached up around Reed's bleeding body, cradling him in its cold arms as he closed his eyes . . . and let the water take him.

Long after the battle, as the dead washed up on the black Rokuine shores, the surviving outlaws searched for him. They combed the breakers and the beaches, wanting to give him a proper burning, wanting to send him off with the singing and storytelling befitting a legend.

But they didn't find him.

Some said he'd been washed out to sea by the tide, with the rest of the bodies still unaccounted for.

But some, like Meeks, who saw Reed go into the waves, said he'd been claimed by the ocean, that the waters he'd so loved had given him the one thing he desired most.

He'd become one with the sea, and the sea had no ending and no beginning. The sea had always been and always would be.

And now, so would Captain Cannek Reed.

Decades—centuries—after, they continued to tell stories of a man with eyes as blue as the water on a clear day. They told of his bravery, his dedication to his crew, his adventures chasing the wind.

Some sailors claimed he rescued them from hurricanes and washed them up on sandy shores.

Some said he drowned those who were unworthy of the outlaw name.

Others said he sent their ships toward floating islands and magical sea creatures rising from the deep, bringing currents to carry them to miraculous undiscovered places and adventures beyond their wildest dreams.

"It was Captain Reed," said the survivors, said the treasure hunters and the thrill seekers as they huddled around tavern tables, whispering in hushed reverent tones. "The legends are true."

Captain Reed lives.

CHAPTER 44

Destiny

Out on the bay, the battle was almost over, and Sefia watched the Alliance warships, one by one, fall to the army of the dead. In the harbor, she could see the *Red Hare*—the Lonely King's ship—through the smoke, but the *Current* was somewhere in the northeast, and she hadn't seen the *Brother* in over an hour.

Were they okay?

Had she and Archer acted in time to save them?

Archer stood beside her, motionless except for the flickering of his eerie red eyes. Though they weren't touching, she could feel the cold coming off him, as if the phantoms had brought the winter and darkness with them from the edge of the world.

"Sorcerer," one of the tower soldiers called. "Look."

Sefia turned. To the south, over the last rise of the hill leading to the watchtower, was Tanin. She'd abandoned her Assassin's garb for a black vest and white blouse, and her dark hair billowed out behind her in the wind. All around her, dozens of candidates were marching on the cliff—blue coats, scarred throats, eyes blazing with the light of battle.

No wonder Sefia hadn't seen the *Black Beauty* on the water. Tanin must have sneaked around the south side of the peninsula while Sefia and Archer were watching the bay.

Did Tanin know she'd already lost?

"You know why Archer has that scar around his neck?" Sefia asked the Rokuine soldiers, who nodded. "Those boys are like him, only they didn't escape. And now they fight for the enemy. Her. Their sorcerer."

"Can she do what you do?" someone asked.

Sefia nodded. "I'll take care of her. Just don't let any of them near Archer."

The Black Navy soldiers took up positions on the ramparts. They readied their cannons. They waited for Tanin and the candidates to march into range.

"Archer," Sefia said, hoping he could still hear her while his mind was out with the phantoms on the bay. "Tanin's coming with the candidates. They'll be in range in minutes."

For a moment, nothing happened.

Then, slowly, his head turned. His lips parted.

"Sefia?" His voice sounded thin, as if it were coming from a great distance.

She let out a relieved breath. "Call some of them back," she said, gesturing to the dead swarming the Alliance battleships in the northeast. "The tower guards will fight, but I'm afraid they're no match for the candidates. And I—I'm afraid I'm no match for Tanin."

Archer shook his head. "The dead are too far." His voice wavered. "They won't make it in time."

"Send them back to the edge of the world so you can fight."

He closed his eyes. His hands went to the Resurrection Amulet, still latched to his chest. But when he looked up again, he looked stricken. "I can't," he said. "I think they need to come back to me first."

They'd have to cross the whole stretch of Blackfire Bay. Would they make it to the watchtower before Tanin and the candidates?

Behind the red glow of his eyes, he looked scared, like the boy she'd found in the crate a year ago, crouched in the moonlight.

Around them, the tower cannons went off. The candidates must have been in range.

She held his cold hands and kissed his cold lips. When they parted, her breath was smoking.

"We've done the impossible before," she said. "We'll do it again."

He smiled a smile to break her heart. "Together, we can do anything."

The first bullets pinged off the stones as she ran to the battlements, summoning her magic. With one hand, she deflected gunfire back at the candidates, who took cover behind jagged boulders, halting their advance. With the other, she ripped the ground out from under Tanin's feet, pulling it up and over the woman like a wave of earth and dune grass. Tanin winked out and appeared again at the top of the crest, flinging out her hand.

A chunk of parapet broke off and flew backward. Sefia leapt aside as it crashed into one of the tower cannons.

Even at this distance, she could feel Tanin's smirk.

"Just wait till you see what Archer's done to your Alliance," Sefia muttered.

She threw stones, redirected bullets, ducked and dodged and wrenched rifles from the candidates' hands. Tanin took out their second cannon with a gust of magic. Beside Sefia, the Black Navy soldiers fired and fell to well-placed shots as Tanin and the candidates advanced.

A stray bullet nicked Archer in the arm.

He didn't even flinch. His shadow soldiers were halfway across Blackfire Bay now, converging slowly on the cliff.

But they wouldn't get here in time. The candidates were too close.

Desperately, Sefia cast about for a way—*any* way—to stop them.

And as her gaze raked the bleak terrain, she saw him— Scarza, his silver hair glinting white in the sun—charge over the hillside. Behind him came Frey, Aljan, Griegi, Keon, all of them. The bloodletters! They broke over the candidates' rear guard, hacking, slashing, all steel and gunpowder.

They must have followed the *Black Beauty*.

Instantly, the candidates re-formed their ranks and began to fight back.

It was beautiful and painful to watch: blades and bullets and boys all leaping and feinting and calling for blood.

Blinking to dispel the Sight, she ran to Archer, where he still stood facing the bay. The graze on his arm had already stopped bleeding.

He was fine.

She allowed herself a smile.

He was *fine*.

"The bloodletters are here," she told him. "Your bloodletters."

There was a cry from below, and she rushed back to the ramparts. Griegi was on his knees in front of the tower door, blood matting his curls, as Keon stood valiantly over him, fighting off candidates, blades spinning so fast they were like two discs flashing in the light.

Other candidates were hurling grapples onto the parapets, the remaining tower soldiers racing to cut their ropes before the enemy could climb up.

Sefia blinked, preparing to sweep the attackers aside, but as the Illuminated world flooded her vision, the streams suddenly coiled, bunched, and exploded in a burst of light.

Tanin appeared on the ramparts.

Her silver eyes widened at the sight of the decimation on the bay. And narrowed again as she saw Archer, standing with his back to her.

She lashed out, sending a wave of magic in his direction.

Sefia dashed in front of him, taking the full force of Tanin's blow, which sent her crashing to the ground.

Wiping dust from her cheek, Sefia struck out again, catching Tanin by the shins, and flung a knife from her sleeve.

Tanin twisted as the blade raked her thigh and threw a fistful of powder in Sefia's face.

White filled her vision. She couldn't use Illumination if she couldn't see. Around her, she could hear the tower soldiers grunting and falling. Staggering back, she felt for Archer.

He was still standing. She could still feel the cold through his clothing as she bumped into him.

"Where is it?" Tanin's raspy voice came from somewhere to Sefia's left.

It? *The Book?* It was safe in Aljan's bunk on the *Brother*. After all this, Tanin still wanted the Book? Sefia pivoted, trying to keep her body between Archer and Tanin. "It's over," she said. "The Alliance is no more. You only have a handful of Guardians left. Give up. Just give up and leave us alone."

But when the Guard lost the Book, Tanin had hunted Sefia's parents for fifteen years. Even now, on the brink of defeat, she still wanted it. When she'd lost her position, she'd waited and planned, and when the moment came, she'd killed one of her own so she could be Director again.

When had Tanin ever given up?

"I may not live to see it," she said, "but the Guard can rebuild. How do you think we survived all these generations? By rebuilding, even when we were at our most broken."

Sefia swiveled again as her vision began to clear. She swiped at a hazy figure to her left, but there was a rush of air, and Tanin spoke again from her right: "And for that, I need the Book."

Sefia's vision sharpened as Tanin raised her arm. She saw the threads of the Illuminated world pull back.

"No!" she cried.

Then there was a burst of blood at Tanin's wrist.

She cursed and drew her injured arm back to her chest, pulling out the switchblade embedded in her flesh.

Frey leapt up the tower steps, pistols blazing.

Sefia almost laughed with relief as the girl dashed to Archer's side. "Took you long enough to get up here!"

"Sorry." Frey made a sour face. "We can't all wave our arms and poof around like you."

Sefia really did laugh at that.

Aljan and Scarza raced up to them, and together, the four of them turned on Tanin, who teleported in and out, pushing them back, freezing them in place, swiping aside their bullets. But good as she was, she wasn't good enough to beat all of them together.

She disappeared as the candidates emerged from the tower steps. The bloodletters raced to push them back.

Sefia rushed to Archer's side. "It's almost done," she said, sending a candidate flying from the ramparts with a flick of her wrist.

He managed a faint smile. "Almost free."

They were going to win.

They were going to live.

But as she surveyed the smoldering remains of the battle on the bay, the ruined harbor, the smoke rising from Braska's damaged walls, she spied movement on a nearby cliff, high above the city. A thin figure was crouched over a large iron sphere, tipping in materials from glass vials and clay jars.

No.

"Dotan," Sefia whispered. The Guard's master of poisons. The sphere had been in the apothecary the night she and Archer destroyed the Library. She'd wondered what it was for, at the time, but now . . . Curls of smoke began to seep from openings in the metal, winding along the ground, finding the low places in the earth.

Was he going to poison all of Braska? All the children, the ailing, the elderly? Adeline and Isabella were down there, on the ramparts. Sovereign Ianai was down there, directing the battle from the castle.

And no one but Sefia could reach Dotan in time.

"What's wrong?" Archer asked. On the bay, the dead had almost reached the base of the cliff.

Quickly, she explained what the Master Administrator was doing above the city, and she watched the hope bleed from Archer's expression.

"Go. Before it's too late." He swallowed. "I'll be here when you get back."

Nodding, Sefia staggered backward. As she summoned her magic, she saw him cross his first two fingers, one over the other. Gold swirled up the back of his hand, over his knuckles, and in the light of the Illuminated world, their sign blazed like a million stars.

I'm with you.

A declaration. A promise.

"Always," she whispered.

And with that, she waved her arms . . . and disappeared, and was on the cliff, where the Master Administrator's poison was already beginning to roll downhill in slow, undulating coils.

Dotan regarded her with his mismatched eyes. "Your parents took my first Apprentice from me. Now you've taken another."

"Then fight *me*. Punish *me*. Not the people down there."

A wisp of a smile crossed his dark face. "I am."

Cold gripped her as she turned back to the watchtower.

Amid the fighting, Tanin had appeared behind Archer.

She spun him around.

She reached for his chest.

With a flick of her fingers, Sefia snapped Dotan's neck. She kicked the iron sphere away from the cliff and the city below. She could hear it rattling and clattering down the opposite slope, streaming poisonous mist, as she teleported back to Archer.

CHAPTER 45

The Resurrection Amulet

As Tanin's fingers closed around the Resurrection Amulet, she felt a grim sense of satisfaction.

Ever since she found out about Mareah's death, she'd wanted the Amulet for herself. That was why she'd sent Reed and Dimarion after it in the first place.

She'd wanted to ask Mareah why. Why their oaths had meant so little to her. Why *Tanin* had meant so little to her that she was able to turn her back and walk away.

But now that she saw what it could really do, well, when she rebuilt the Guard, controlling Kelanna would be easier with an unstoppable army at her command. With an unstoppable army, not even Sefia could prevent her from getting the Book back.

Archer's red eyes flicked to her as she stood before him, gripping the Amulet. "Please," he said, in a voice that wasn't quite his own.

And for less than a second, Tanin hesitated.

She could let him go.

She could accept defeat with grace.

She could give Sefia the happy ending Lon and Mareah had always wanted for her.

But why should Sefia get what Tanin had never had?

Archer's shadow soldiers were climbing over the tower walls now, their faces hungry . . . and some of them familiar—the First, Stonegold, Erastis, the Locksmith.

She began to pull.

As the metal hooks ripped one by one from his skin, there was a hot searing pain as a gunshot tore through her chest. Whirling, she saw the silver-haired boy by the stairs sling a smoking rifle over his shoulder. Around his neck was a mottled scar. On his lips was the shadow of a smile.

Flicking her wrist, she sent a blast of magic at him. His head struck stone, his rifle falling from his hand, and he crumpled like a rag doll.

Archer was collapsing, the red glow fading from his eyes. The dead on the ramparts were dissipating like trails of smoke from hundreds of candles that had been suddenly snuffed out.

Tanin gasped. She tasted blood in the back of her throat.

She was bleeding.

No.

She was dying. The bloodletter had killed her. The Resurrection Amulet slipped from her fingers, landing with a *crack* on the stone.

She fell to her knees, and the last thing she saw before her world went dark forever was Sefia, teleporting in, catching Archer just before he hit the ground.

Chapter 46

Gone

She hit the ground just as the shadow soldiers were evaporating.

"No!" The word fell from her lips before she even registered what she was seeing. "No, no, no—"

Archer's body going limp, arms and legs buckling under him, wounds visible on his chest where the Amulet had been.

She caught him, gathering him up in her arms. "No, no, no, *no.*"

His head, his hands falling back again as she tried to cradle him to her chest, tried to hold him, tried to bring him back with the force of her denial.

"No, no, no—"

Until, at last, words failed her.

Until her grief bubbled up from her like a spring, hot and endless, spilling from her chin and onto Archer's upturned face.

Her tears struck his cheeks, each one a letter, a word, a plea.

I love you.

I need you.

Come back.

The unanswered language of grief.

She kissed his forehead, his brows, his lips, desperately hoping that some of the stories were true, that her love would bring him back to her.

It didn't.

"Sefia," Frey whispered, touching Sefia's shoulder. "He's gone."

All around her, the candidates were surrendering to the bloodletters. Tanin was dead, shot through the chest, her gray eyes sightless.

But Archer was dead too.

On the water, there were a few last bursts of cannon fire, but those petered out quickly, like the last drops of a sudden rainfall.

He's gone. Faintly, the words trickled down to Sefia. *Gone . . . gone . . . gone . . .*

"The Amulet," she said suddenly, casting about for the metal disc. The Resurrection Amulet would bring him back to her. She'd take a shadow of him. She'd take anything.

Anything.

But Aljan knelt beside her, shaking his head. In his hands, he held the shattered pieces of the Amulet.

Gone.

Sefia hugged Archer's body tighter. "Come back," she whispered. "Don't leave me. Don't be dead. Come back. Come back. Please, Archer, come back."

But he didn't.

The war had been won.

His last campaign was over.

And, just as foretold, Archer had died alone.

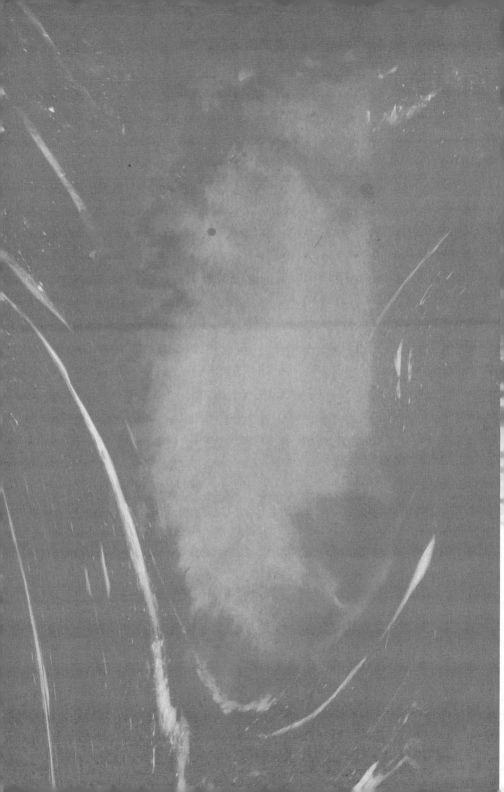

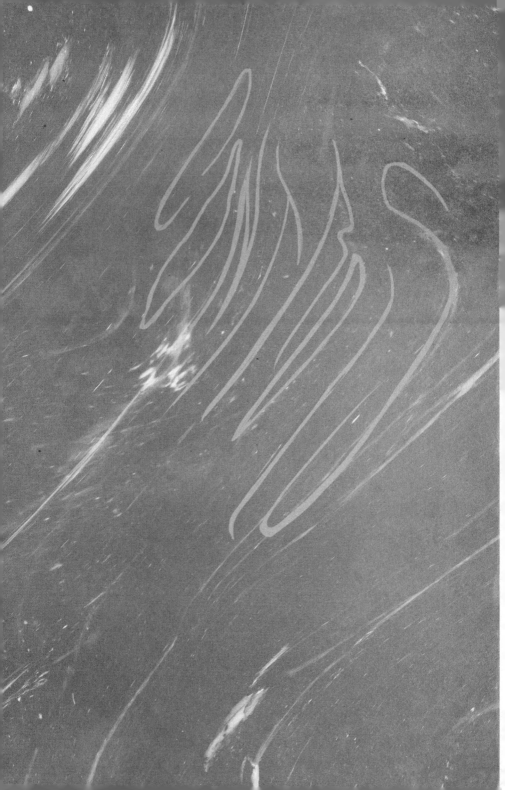

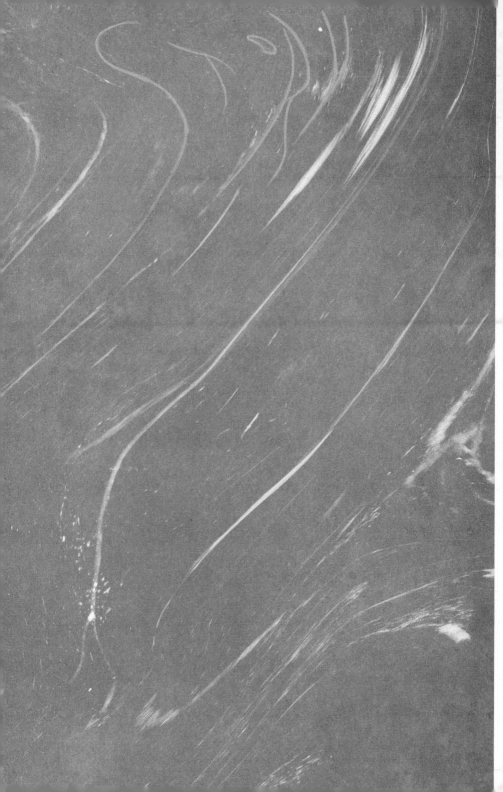

The End?

No, a beginning.

I always thought it would end in darkness. I thought it would end with grief and unanswered questions and the unbearable emptiness of staring down the rest of your days, knowing you'll have to endure them without the one person who should have been there to share them with you.

But I should have known—some people are too strong, too resilient, too clever, too resolute to be constrained by something as trivial as *fate*. Their stories are wild and changeable, like new rivers, carving channels on their way to the sea, altering the very geography from which they first sprang.

Sefia and Archer didn't beat the Book.

They broke the world.

They shattered the barrier between life and death, and now Kelanna is *filled* with the souls of the departed, full of ghosts and calming spirits that walk by your side after your friend or your sister or your father has died.

The living don't know it yet, but they will, soon enough. The dead are all around—on the air and in the water; in reflections, half-seen, by candlelight. They're frequenting the places they used to love; haunting the people who did them wrong; whispering through trees and dune grasses; bringing good fortune, or ruin, to the ones they left behind.

When the Kelannans finally figure it out, I suspect customs will change. Maybe one day, when you die, they'll mark your resting place with a stone. Maybe every year, on the anniversary of your death, they'll visit you there, bearing overflowing bunches of white flowers, and they'll speak to your grave, because they'll believe you'll hear them.

Maybe one day, to send you to rest, they'll burn stacks of paper inked with your fondest memories like a long, true bedtime story.

Maybe one day, they'll get messages from the dead.

Who knows? It's a new world, with new rules.

Once there was a world called Kelanna, a wonderful and terrible world of grief and magic and ghosts . . .

All the Things He'd Never
Get a Chance to Say

S efia didn't know how long she remained on the watchtower, holding Archer's body, but when she looked up again, the sky was ribboned with fire—scarlet and tangerine and gold in the light of the sunset.

The tower was mostly empty now. The flags no longer flew.

The defeated candidates were gone. Tanin was gone, only a bloodstain marking where she'd died. The Black Navy soldiers who'd defended the ramparts were gone.

Only Sefia and the bloodletters remained.

Scarza was there, sitting beside Sefia with his chin on his knees, his gaze never leaving Archer's body. Frey and Aljan were there, perched on the parapets, her head on his shoulder. Many of the others were there, on the watchtower, talking or crying quietly.

But not all of them had made it. They'd been nineteen in number. Now Sefia counted only fourteen.

Among the missing was Keon.

She remembered seeing him by the tower door, defending Griegi, crumpling under the candidates' onslaught like a sapling under an avalanche.

She didn't ask what happened to him. She didn't think she could handle hearing it.

Not now.

Not after this.

Not after Archer.

In the hours since his death, he'd gone stiff and cold in her arms, so he didn't even feel like Archer anymore. But if she laid him down, if she let him go, she knew she'd never have the chance to hold him again.

Scarza touched her shoulder. "Are you ready, sorcerer? We should take his body soon, before it gets dark."

At his words, the grief doubled her over again, fresh and painful. Her hair, which had come loose from its clip during the battle, fell across her face. Tears spilled from her eyes. "I'll never be ready," she said.

Scarza said nothing.

In the silence, a breath of wind, smelling of dust and thundershowers, brushed a stray lock of hair from her forehead.

The movement was so familiar it made her shiver.

She lifted her head, looking for someone she knew wasn't there.

Because he was in her arms.

Because he was dead.

But as she searched the damaged battlements, the stricken faces of the bloodletters, the colors fading from the sky, she felt something else.

A kiss—tender and strong—that echoed her first kiss, under cloud-swept skies, with the moonlight skittering across the waves.

A kiss for all the things he felt for her.

For all the things he'd never get a chance to say.

"Archer?" she whispered.

There was no answer.

But he was there, somehow, against everything she knew to be true, against all the laws of life and death. She'd never touch him again, not really, never see the light in his golden eyes or hear him speak her name. But he was *there*, somehow.

With her.

In the only way he could be.

Wiping her tears, she kissed his forehead one last time and, folding her first two fingers, one over the other, laid her warm hand over his. "Always," she said.

As if responding to some unspoken signal, the bloodletters— the ones who had survived—gathered around them. Kneeling, they bowed their heads and crossed their tattooed forearms, and, in broken voices, they murmured, "We were dead, but now we rise."

The Survivor King

When the shadow soldiers withdrew and the Alliance finally surrendered, there was much work to be done.

There was Captain Reed's storm, roaring off the coast of Roku, to dispel with the Thunder Gong. There were prisoners to take. Ed tied Arcadimon's hands and escorted him into the custody of the Black Navy. "I'm sorry," Eduoar said. "I have to."

Arc squeezed his fingers and attempted one of his winning smiles as the Rokuine soldiers took him toward the castle dungeons. "I know."

There were wounded to treat, like Lac and Hobs, who seemed to take great pleasure in showing off their injuries and retelling the story of their heroic rescue of the Delienean king.

And there were casualties to be counted as the dead were pulled off the black beaches and plucked from the tides. Volunteers brought back body after body—Evericans, Oxscinians, outlaws, Delieneans, Rokuine and Liccarine soldiers—and took them through the winding streets of Braska to the crypts inside the cliffs, where they would be prepared for burning.

Though he was heavy with grief, Eduoar moved with more confidence than he'd ever felt, conferring with Resistance leaders, directing rescue efforts, planning for the funerals, which would take place three days hence. Little by little, he heard stories from the battle—Captain Reed destroying the *Amalthea*, Archer summoning the phantoms, the assault on the watchtower by the Director of the Guard and dozens of branded boys who had been taken and trained by the impressors.

Someone told him the bloodletters had returned to the watchtower to fight by Archer's side. They'd killed the Director and taken her soldiers captive. But they hadn't been able to save their old chief.

Ed dashed tears from his eyes. He'd been wrong. Sometimes a curse was just a curse. Sometimes death was just death—cold and permanent.

That night, from a cell in Sovereign Ianai's dungeons, Eduoar and two court recorders heard Arcadimon's confession. Sitting behind a set of iron bars, his blue Alliance uniform rumpled, Arc told them his story, insisting he start from the beginning: from his induction at age fourteen to his knowledge of the Guard's plans, all their grand ideals of creating a more stable Kelanna, the things he'd done for those ideals—bribery, blackmail, threats, murder—and the pride he'd taken in doing it.

Because he'd liked being a part of something greater than himself.

Because he'd been good at it.

"But . . ." He inhaled deeply, his blue eyes never leaving

Ed's. "That all changed when I killed Roco. I didn't do it with my own hand, but it was I who ordered the poison to be put into his drink."

Through the prison bars, Eduoar watched him sadly. The longer Ed had been gone from Deliene, the longer he'd been out of Arc's intoxicating presence, the more he'd begun to suspect that the boy he loved was responsible for killing his cousin, their childhood companion, who used to dog their heels as they capered across the castle grounds.

But now Eduoar knew for sure.

He shouldn't love a traitor and a murderer.

But he did, and that felt like a betrayal of its own—a betrayal of the Resistance, of everyone they'd lost in the battle against the Alliance, of Archer and Sefia, of Roco.

How could Ed hold all these things inside him at once? Guilt, love, loathing, duty? The desire to kiss Arcadimon through the bars, the desire to set him free, the desire to see him imprisoned for the rest of his days.

But, Eduoar soon learned, that wouldn't be a problem. It was well into the night when Arc finally revealed the nature of the poison General Terezina had mentioned. Only the Administrators knew exactly what it was and how to use it, he said, and now that they were dead . . . withdrawal would kill him by noon.

And that, at last, would be the end of the Guard.

"I'm sorry," Arcadimon said. He was weeping now. "I'm so sorry. I don't expect you to forgive me. But I wanted to tell you. I've hidden half of my life from you, whom I love most, and in the end, I wanted there to be no more secrets between us."

Eduoar was on his feet before Arc finished.

His hands were on the bars.

He didn't want Arcadimon to die. Not like this, in a Rokuine cell, so far from Deliene. Not like this, when they'd just found each other again.

"There's still one person who might be able to save you," Ed said.

E duoar found Sefia aboard the *Brother*, which had been sailed into the harbor beside the other ravaged outlaw ships. Scarza, the chief of the bloodletters, was on watch and, even knowing who Ed was, refused to let him see Sefia until he'd explained why he wanted her.

As Eduoar told him about Arcadimon, Scarza watched him with serious gray eyes. Then he leaned in and, in a low voice that brooked no protest, even from his own sovereign, said, "This better be the last thing you ask of her, King. She gave up everything to save the Resistance. We don't deserve more from her."

"And if you try anything," added one of the other bloodletters on watch, who looked remarkably like she could have been Sefia's taller sister, "you'll have us to answer to."

Eduoar waited on the main deck, twisting the signet ring on his finger. He'd worn it every hour of every day for twelve years, after his father died, but this was the first time it felt like it fit.

It seemed to take hours for Sefia to appear, as the sky lightened to a charcoal gray and the seconds Arcadimon had left trickled away like sand through Ed's hands.

When Sefia finally appeared in the hatchway, the stars were beginning to go out. Silently, she accompanied Eduoar to the dungeons, where she stood before Arcadimon's cell, fidgeting with the piece of rutilated quartz she now wore around her neck.

"So you're the Apprentice Politician," she said dully.

"Not anymore." Arc's gaze met Eduoar's. "And never again."

Sefia nodded at Ed. "He wants me to save you."

"Can you do that?"

"Maybe." She paused. "But I don't know if I'll try."

Eduoar took a step toward her. "Sefia, please—"

"Why do *you* get to live? Why do you get to live when so many others had to die? Is it because you love him?" She pointed at Eduoar. "Is it because he loves you? Because that isn't enough. Love isn't enough. I loved him, and he loved me, and *he still died.*"

Her shoulders were shaking. Clenched at her sides, her fists trembled.

"I do love him," Ed murmured, "but that's not the only reason I want him to live. I want him to stand trial, back in Deliene. I don't want the Guard's poisons to punish him. It's my people who deserve to do that."

Sefia glared at him as tears spilled down her cheeks.

Then she turned away. "Be quiet," she said. "And let me work."

She stood across from Arc, watching him while, through the high and narrow window, daylight touched the far wall of the cell.

Dawn.

If Sefia couldn't cure him, he had only a few hours left.

But she simply stared at him. Reading him. Examining the events of his life like scenes in a play.

Judging him, Ed thought.

Then Arcadimon began to sweat and shake, his breath coming faster and faster in his chest, like he couldn't get enough air, no matter how hard his lungs worked. Ed glanced at Sefia.

Her pupils were like pinpoints of darkness in her brown irises.

Her hands moved through the air, her fingers twining in the invisible substance she and Arc called the Illuminated world.

Arcadimon slid from his chair. His eyes rolled back in his head.

"Arc!" Eduoar cried, rushing to the bars. He fumbled with the keys. He didn't know what Arcadimon was to him, if he could ever forgive him, if they could ever be together, after all that had transpired between them. But he knew he wanted to be with him, if this was the end.

Before he could make it into the cell, however, Sefia lowered her hands. Arcadimon stopped shivering. His breath came deeply and evenly.

"You're welcome," she said.

Flinging open the cell door, Eduoar raced to Arc's side, cradling his head in his lap. "Thank you."

"Archer would have wanted me to save him," she said flatly.

For the next two days, Ed was busier than he'd ever been in his life. The political structure of Kelanna was in shreds.

The kingdoms of Everica and Liccaro were without leaders. With the Gormani Resistance, Deliene had been through a civil war. There was so much to do, so much to repair and rebuild, as he and the other Resistance leaders began to imagine what the world could look like without the Guard, without the Alliance, without war.

There were council meetings to attend. Messengers to dispatch. Ships to repair. Defensive walls to tear down.

And to Eduoar's surprise, he was good at it. What was more, with the horse stalls to muck out when he needed to clear his head, and a new litter of puppies in the royal kennels to visit when his melancholia threatened to overwhelm him, he felt energized. Was this the king he could have been without the curse? Without Arcadimon's poison inhibiting him all these years?

No, that was an unfair question, to himself and to Arc.

This was the king he was *now*. And for all he was frightened of becoming the Lonely King again when he returned to Corabel, he'd come so far since he'd left, he wouldn't let a little fear stop him from being the king Deliene deserved. The king he knew himself to be.

To fill the gaps left by the dead, promotions were given. Medals were awarded. Haldon Lac and Olly Hobs were made lieutenants of the Royal Navy.

For saving his life, Eduoar awarded each of them the White Star of Valor, the highest honor he could bestow upon those who were not his own citizens.

True to form, Lac had the audacity and pettiness to complain that it clashed with the gold bar of his new rank.

"I can take it back, if you want," said Eduoar, reaching for the pin.

"I didn't say that!" Lac cried, hastily batting him away.

Hobs laughed.

They spent what time they could together, when Lac and Hobs weren't helping with the construction in the harbor and Ed wasn't in some meeting or another.

They told him stories they'd heard on the docks. People were feeling sudden chills or waves of peace when they remembered those they had lost. Objects of sentimental value were going missing and turning up in unexpected places. Since Archer had summoned the dead, something was different in the world, and the Kelannans were just beginning to learn what it was.

"Has anyone seen Sefia?" Hobs asked one day. "Is she all right?"

From the top of the wall, Eduoar looked out over the city— the smudges of sage being burned on the street corners, the doors draped in white curtains. "No," he said. "I don't think she is."

You Miss a Man So Much

When Sefia returned to the *Brother* after saving the Apprentice Politician's life, she found a book lying on her bunk. It was a slim black volume, with gold tooling she recognized as Keon's, and a note clipped to the first page.

Sorcerer—

We started work on this after you returned from the Library. ~~We hoped you wouldn't need it, but~~ We knew how much you wanted to hear from Him and your parents again, and ~~in case he~~ he didn't want you to wonder.

—Aljan

Her vision blurred as she turned the page. Beautiful black lettering spiraled across the paper—Aljan's handwriting; Archer's words.

Memories from his childhood in Jocoxa.

Lists of his favorite colors, foods, festivals.

Adventures he'd hoped to have.

Catalogues of regrets.

Letters to his mother, his grandfather, his aunt and uncle, his little cousin Riki, to Annabel, to Scarza and Griegi and Aljan and the bloodletters.

But most of all, letters to Sefia.

Ruminations, meanderings, random thoughts. Things he might have said to her while they were washing pots, or conversations they might have had during the early-morning watches, staring out to sea.

Sefia—

Did I ever tell you the moment I knew I loved you? It was that day on the Current, after Meeks told us about the Red War. You were sitting on the edge of the quarterdeck, reading, with the wind in your hair.

You were so beautiful.

Then a lock of hair flew into your face,

and I went to brush it away. I felt so brave,
and so scared, so sure you'd pull away.

But you didn't.

And as I slid your hair back around
your ear, you smiled.

I couldn't remember wanting anything
so badly as I wanted to kiss you then.
It was like I'd never really wanted
anything before then, and now this wanting
was blazing inside me like a lamp, bright
as a beam from a lighthouse.

That was the moment I knew.

I love you.

—Archer

She leafed through the pages, trying to avoid staining them
with her tears. This was what he had been working on while
she repaired ships and fortified turrets. She could have been
spending that time with him. She could have had more time
with him. But she'd squandered it. She'd always assumed
they'd have more time.

But Archer had known. You have only a short time in this
world, such a short time, before you're gone, and he'd wanted
to leave her something before he went.

Messages from the dead.

When the funerals finally began, it was a gray morning, and the sea was a chipped shield, glinting in the fragile sun.

Mourners lined the road from the crypt to the beach, tossing bouquets of tiny white flowers, brittle as matchsticks, beneath the wheels of the funeral carts.

Body after body arrived on the beach, where they were loaded onto barges and sent flaming onto the sea.

Everyone paid tribute to the dead in their own way. Delieneans lit sticks of incense, perfuming the salty air with trailing vines of smoke. Oxscinians brought offerings of folded paper, pleated into the shapes of flowers and fantastic sea creatures. Evericans left palm-size stones on the beach, one for each of the dead, creating eerie sentinels of rock at the edge of the water. Outlaws on the beach fired their six-guns. Outlaws on the water fired their cannons.

But it was those from Roku who bid farewell in the most spectacular fashion.

After the stories—

After the songs—

After the lists of names—

After the barges were set ablaze and carried off by the tide, the Rokuines raised handheld fireworks and loosed long jets of flame into the sky. Sparks showered the beach like rain.

Somewhere on those barges were Tanin, Dotan, and Braca. Serakeen's body still hadn't been found.

The candidates who had fallen in battle were sent off by the bloodletters, who saluted them like brothers—heads bowed, forearms crossed.

On the cliffs above the beach, Sefia watched. She heard the words of mourning.

You miss a man so much.

She didn't repeat them.

She was a specter, a shadow, there and not there, with the breeze tangling in her hair, tugging at her clothes.

And Archer's book in her arms.

The next day, the funerals continued—enemies, allies, friends. The skies darkened with ash.

The bloodletters bid farewell to Keon and the other boys who'd died at the watchtower. Face streaked with tears, Griegi laid a small parcel of Keon's favorite foods beside him on the bier.

The crew of the *Current* said good-bye to Cooky and Killian and half a dozen other sailors.

With the red lory on his shoulder, the only speck of color among the mourning white, Theo sang in his aching baritone, with Marmalade plucking out a few plaintive notes on Jules's old mandolin.

Sefia should have gone down there, she knew. She should have joined the crew in their grief.

She didn't. She couldn't.

But that didn't stop her from regretting it later.

There was no floating pyre for Cannek Reed, but Captain Meeks recited his name among those the *Current* had lost.

Sefia clenched her jaw and dug her palms into the corners of Archer's book.

There was a tapping sound behind her, and she turned as the chief mate, led by Aly, came slowly up the path to the cliff top.

His head was bandaged; his arm in a sling.

But he was *here*, on land, using a cane to navigate over the rough ground, the metal tip clicking softly against rocks and dips in the path.

He'd left the ship.

For Reed? she wondered.

But she knew. *For me.*

She was silent as Aly paused beside her—there was a glimmer of silver along the curve of her ear: Cooky's earrings. Patting the chief mate on the hand, she released his arm and embraced Sefia quickly before retreating a little ways down the trail, leaving Sefia and the mate alone on the cliff.

They stood together for a moment, as Sefia imagined what the chief mate had come all this way to say to her.

To accuse her. To blame her. To tell her she'd made a mistake, taking Reed's tattoos.

To tell her she'd done the right thing.

But he said nothing, and after a moment, he drew her into a hug so quick and hard that for a second Sefia wasn't sure if it was a blow or an embrace or some combination of the two.

She tensed.

But when he didn't let her go, she felt herself turn watery, felt her sorrow and her anger and her guilt boiling up inside her again.

Down on the beach, Meeks was telling the story of Reed's single-handed assault on the *Amalthea*.

Tears ran down Sefia's face. "I'm sorry," she blurted out. "I'm sorry I betrayed him."

The mate rubbed her arm roughly. "You didn't."

"He hated me for it."

"No, girl." The chief mate clicked his tongue, chiding her with unexpected gentleness. "He loved you like you were his own."

"I should've told him I was sorry."

"He knew. And he was sorry too, in the end."

With a sob, she buried her face in the crook of his shoulder, and he held tight to her as she cried and cried and cried and the bodies of her friends floated out to sea.

On the third day, there was only one funeral—Archer's. The capital was quiet. There was no sawing or hammering from the harbor. There was no conversation from the deserted market. Over closed doors and empty gardens, white banners snapped and cracked in the wind.

The road from the crypt was so full of flowers that, from a distance, it appeared to be covered in snow.

Clouds of mourners flocked from the city—Oxscinians, Delieneans, Rokuines, outlaws—settling on the hills, overlooking the road, on the cliffs opposite Sefia, on the pebbled beach. Everyone had turned out to pay their respects to the boy with the scar.

The boy who'd saved them.

The boy she loved.

But they left Sefia alone on her cliff, as if she were untouchable in her grief.

Below, the remaining bloodletters and the sparse crew of the *Current* gathered around the floating bier.

Maybe there was a song or two, one of those old battle tunes from the frozen north.

. . . Through the waves, we ride.

To our deaths, we ride.

Our foes will not forget how we fight . . .

Maybe there was a story.

"It's the same with stories as it is with people: they get better as they get older. But not every story is remembered, and not all people grow old."

Maybe there was more, but she couldn't remember.

What she remembered was the size of Archer's body, swathed in those layers of white cloth. Small. Too small for the boy who had climbed out of the fighting pit in the Cage. Too small for the boy who'd leaned her back on a cot while the snow came down outside. Too small for the boy silhouetted against the stars with the whole red desert laid bare before him.

What she remembered were his white-wrapped hands. Still. Too still for the boy marching out of the jungle, snapping necks, throwing swords. Too still for the boy rubbing a piece of quartz in the firelight. Too still for the boy who'd ridden across the Heartland on a chestnut horse.

Every so often, the others—Scarza and Frey and Aljan, Meeks and Horse and Marmalade—would look up at her, where she stood on the edge of the cliff, as if offering her a chance to speak.

But what could she say?

I left him.

I let him die.

I killed him.

One by one, they turned away again.

There were offerings of rubies and river stones, paper flowers and sticks of incense. Aljan tucked a letter among the kindling. Frey left one of her switchblades. Scarza retired his rifle. Everyone who wanted to give something for the boy who'd sacrificed himself for them placed their gifts at the edge of the water, beside the floating bier.

Sefia kept thinking she'd get some sign from him, some signal that he was there, that he was with her. The smell of rain and lightning. A phantom touch on the elbow. A whisper of her name on the wind.

But there was nothing. For hours, as the mourners came and retreated again like a tide, there was nothing.

And at last it was time to return him to the water.

Aly and Doc loosed the mooring lines.

Scarza lifted the torch, the light playing across his handsome, grief-stricken features. His hand shook, and Jaunty, the taciturn helmsman who'd shared long hours of silence with Archer, before he could speak, stepped forward to steady him.

And then, with a wave of her arms, Sefia was down there, teleporting in among them, crying, "Don't. Don't. Not yet."

She climbed onto the bier with Archer, burying her face in his swaddled arms.

"I'm sorry," she whispered. "I'm sorry I wasn't there. I'm sorry I wasted the time we had. I should have shown you every day, every hour, every breath, how much I loved you. I love you, Archer. You were so, so loved."

She choked on the words.

"How do I go on without you?" she asked, rubbing her cheek against the coarse linen, damp with her tears. "How can anything ever be the same as it was? How do I survive this?"

Somehow, the others helped her from the funeral bier, clasping Archer's book to her chest. She remembered collapsing into someone's arms as they set fire to Archer's body and sent him burning onto the waves.

The Rokuine candles flared.

The cannons of the *Crux* and all the remaining outlaw ships went off in salute.

Reaching for her neck, Sefia grasped the worry stone so hard its point dug into her palm, drawing blood.

On the water, Archer burned.

Paths Alight with Gold

Weeks passed. In Braska, the work went on. One by one, the Resistance repaired their broken ships and departed—the navies to their home islands, the outlaws in search of new adventures. In their place came delegations from every kingdom and province in Kelanna: from the Gorman Islands in Deliene to Umlaan in the Liccarine desert; from the Vesper swamps in Oxscini to Chaigon, the island off the hidden coast of Everica. The outlaws sent their own representatives as well: Captain Meeks, Adeline and Isabella, and Captain Dimarion, who was dedicating his life to Reed's legacy of outrageous heroics and assorted do-goodery.

People were calling it the Rebuilding. Everyone had lost so much because of the Guard that it would take a cooperative effort to make up for it.

The Five Islands, brought together for one purpose—to

establish stability and peace for all the citizens of Kelanna. The war really had united them, though not in the way anyone had expected.

Sefia had been invited to take part, of course, but she dismissed the messengers who brought her dispatches. She skipped more meetings than she attended. And when she was present, she was usually silent, absently rubbing the worry stone.

More often, she could be found on the funeral beach, staring out to sea.

Or reading. She carried two books with her now: the Book, which she'd asked Aljan to return to her, and Archer's messages. Sometimes she searched the Book. She'd made it to the end of the story—she didn't have anything to fear from it now. She read about Nin and her parents. Sometimes, inexplicably, she felt as if Lon and Mareah were peering over her shoulder, scanning the lines just as she was.

She read Archer's messages. She read them so many times she knew them by heart.

Some days, on her way back from the beach, she dropped in on Aljan's classes in the castle, sitting in the back of the room while he chalked letters on a large slate wall. At Sovereign Ianai's request, he had begun teaching reading and writing to the delegations, their recorders, their historians.

Frey wanted to return to Deliene, where she would travel to Shinjai Province to give her brothers the first edition of her book of trees before she departed again to create an illustrated taxonomy of all Kelanna's plants and their various uses.

The Lonely King had offered both her and Aljan permanent

positions at the Citadel of the Historians, where hundreds of record keepers lived and worked. It was the place Aljan's twin, Versil, might have gone, if his time with the impressors hadn't affected his memory.

If he'd lived.

"Versil would have been proud," Sefia told Aljan.

"He is," said Frey, who was convinced they'd heard Versil's laughter on the wind, once or twice.

In Corabel, Aljan and Frey would give literacy back to Kelanna. To the messengers, the architects and engineers, the shopkeepers, the smiths and newsmen and traveling bards. Their idea was that everyone would have the chance to learn, to take back what the Guard had stolen from them centuries ago.

They'd build a library there, and the first volumes would be *The Chronicles of Captain Reed and the* Current of Faith, compiled by Captain Meeks, and *Death and Resurrection: The Story of the Bloodletters*, by Aljan Ferramo and Archer Aurontas.

Eduoar offered Sefia a job too, if she wanted one. Eventually, sorcerers would begin to emerge. They'd need new training programs, new laws, new occupations. They could use someone powerful to help them.

She didn't give him an answer. She couldn't, not when thinking beyond the next day was still agony, a sudden spiral of grief, reaching up to yank her down, gasping, into its depths.

When the Rebuilding councils finally dispersed to their separate corners of the world, each kingdom's delegation bearing one of the Guard's old portals to facilitate access and communication between the islands, the Lonely King and

Arcadimon left for the Northern Kingdom, where the last Guardian would stand trial for his crimes.

It was Deliene he'd hurt most, and it was Deliene that would judge him.

The *Current*, with Sefia aboard, was one of the last ships to leave the harbor.

Many of the bloodletters joined them, filling in the gaps left by those who were gone. Griegi took over Cooky's old position. Scarza became the new second mate. They were like broken bones, knitting together, becoming whole again after being shattered.

They set sail for Zhuelin Bay, on the southern coast of Everica. A hundred years ago, the bay had been the bustling center of commerce, art, and politics in the Stone Kingdom, but during one of their wars, Oxscini had used the Gong in an attack, summoning a storm that would last until the Gong dismissed it.

Now, as a gesture of goodwill, the *Current of Faith* charged into the rains, the winds, the rough waters, and rang the Gong once more.

The downpour ceased. The clouds rolled back, revealing waterlogged ruins along the shore, swamps where deserts used to be, great swaths of exposed earth where entire mountainsides had slid away in the hundred-year storm.

It looked the way Sefia felt inside—wrecked—so transformed by disaster that any landmarks that might have shown her where she was or where to go were utterly unrecognizable.

But the disaster had passed.

And now they—she—could rebuild.

The *Current* turned west, for Oxscini—for Jocoxa, Archer's hometown—to tell them what he'd done, who he'd become.

And to bring them his messages.

One evening, poised on the deck of the *Current of Faith*, Sefia watched the sun sink into the waves. Night spread across the sky like spilled ink, dripping into the golden sea below.

While the songs and conversations of the crew arose from belowdecks, Captain Meeks crept up beside her. "Look to the horizon, remember?" he said. "That's where the adventures are."

She was glad of the company, though she didn't take her eyes off the water. "I've had enough adventure to last the rest of my life. I don't need any more."

He shook his head, making the shells and beads in his dreadlocks clink together—small sounds like raindrops. "There's all sorts of adventures, Sef," he said.

The light in the water dimmed, all the gold overwhelmed by the black. In the east, the constellation of the great whale was rising out of the ocean, spangled with stars.

"You had to let him go," Meeks said.

"Did I?" Her voice cracked.

He put a hand on her shoulder. "It was supposed to happen from the beginning, wasn't it?" His warm brown eyes sought hers in the darkness. "Because it was written?"

"I thought I could rewrite his future," she whispered, and the words felt strange on her lips, as if she'd wanted to say something else, though she couldn't imagine what else she would have said. "I thought I could save him."

With a sigh, the captain let his hand fall. Leaning down, he planted his elbows on the rail and put his chin on his fists. "He always said you did save him . . . in all the ways that mattered."

"I felt him. I swear I felt him with me on that watchtower, after he died."

Meeks nodded. "I believe you. Just like I believe Captain Reed's still out there, watchin' over us. Something's changed in Kelanna, Sef. Something so big we can't even imagine it yet . . ."

The warm glow of the sun disappeared, and soon they were awash in the cool light of the stars, twinkling distantly overhead.

For a long time after, Meeks remained beside her, uncharacteristically silent, watching the horizon.

Late that night, she climbed out onto the bowsprit. Some of the branches had been snapped, but the ones that remained seemed to cradle her. She almost felt like she was back in the Oxscinian treetops, except for the water hissing and rushing below.

The Book lay in her arms, more cracked and stained than it had been when she'd found it, the covers dimpled with dents and crescent marks from her fingernails, bookmarks peeking from the gilded edges of the pages like light through blinds.

What would she do with it, now that there were no more answers to find? No redemption to be had? No revenge to seek?

Captain Meeks had offered her one of the glass cases in the great cabin, where she could easily retrieve it if her longing for all the people she'd lost grew too great and she needed to dive back into the infinite pages like a diver into a wreck, searching the passages for relics of her loved ones.

Aljan had suggested she bring it to the Citadel of the Historians and use it to teach.

In the past, the Book had caused so much grief, so much bloodshed. If the world knew where to find it, would they want it for the things it could teach them about history and magic and power?

Sea spray flecked the cover, dotting the leather with water marks.

It was so vulnerable.

To fire.

To the damp.

To the passage of time.

And to theft.

It would be easy to destroy it. To fling it into the waves and let the water leach the ink from its pages. To set it on a pyre of blackrock and let the flames consume every last letter. To protect the world from its contents in a way the Guard had never been brave enough to do.

As she stared at the Book, she felt Archer's presence, almost as if he were curled around her, in the branches of the bowsprit. She closed her eyes as tears dampened her lashes. She should have felt grateful that he was there at all, and she felt guilty for wanting more. For wanting him back. For wanting him to not be dead.

But he was gone.

And she was still here.

And she had a decision to make.

When she opened her eyes again, she could see her choices before her in the Illuminated world, almost as if they were paths alight with gold, from which there would be no turning back.

Keep it. Share it. Destroy it.

Tracing the ⊜ on the cover, Sefia took a deep breath. She knew what she had to do.

One Day

What comes after the end of a book?

Hope.

And possibility.

For thousands of years, the people of Kelanna were beholden to destiny, all their births and deaths and loves and failures spelled out, indelibly, in fine black ink. For thousands of years, I knew every parting, every period, every ending.

But thanks to Sefia and Archer, all the endings have finally come and gone, and now, for the first time in my existence, I'm looking forward into the empty expanse of paper ahead, not knowing what happens next.

It's exciting, isn't it? The not-knowing?

For the new world is a blank page—the word, still to be written—and the people of Kelanna are going to fill it with millions of stories.

Stories of their own making.

Stories with less suffering and more joy.

Stories that end happily, or don't end at all.

I've been here since the beginning, and I'll be here beyond the end, collecting tales from this wonderful and terrible world of water and ships and magic and ghosts.

And if you'd like to hear another story, I'll have so many to tell you . . . one day.

Acknowledgments

W hat comes after the end of a book?

Gratitude.

Sefia, Archer, and Reed have been in my head since 2008. Now, ten years, a bajillion drafts, and three books later, their story exists in the world. What a gift that is! What a gift to be here—after the struggle and the doubt and the tears and the soaring moments of joy—with all the people who have come together to bring this series to life. I am so honored and so grateful to have taken this journey with you.

Thank you to Barbara Poelle, agent-warrior extraordinaire, for your enthusiasm, your advocacy, and your ferocity. You told me in our very first conversation that you go to work every Monday with joy in your heart because you "get to do books!" Thank you for doing books with me. It has been a true joy. Many additional thanks to Maggie Kane and the team at I.G.L.A.—I am still so grateful to be one of your authors.

Thank you to Stacey Barney, my inimitable editor, for all the things you do, both on the page and behind the scenes. You challenge me. You support me. You make me a better writer. Working with you these past three years has been both a pleasure and a privilege—thank you from the bottom of my heart for every second of it.

To Cindy Howle and Chandra Wohleber, who have combed through these books so many times with such thoroughness, I am grateful for all of your questions regarding the number of ships, the colors of each flag, the optimum usage of every comma and pronoun. Thank you for making sure I didn't fall from the high-wire act of writing a trilogy.

For making the dream of these books into a reality, I have so much awe and gratitude for Cecilia Yung, Marikka Tamura, and David Kopka. Your design work has brought the story to life in ways I never could have imagined, from every fingerprint and bookmark to every faded sentence and hidden message. Thank you for giving so much of your talent and your time.

To Deborah Kaplan, Kristin Smith, and Yohey Horishita, thank you for your vision. I could never have imagined how incredible these books could look on a shelf. They are gorgeous and eye-catching and perfect, and now they are complete!

Thank you to everyone on the preposterously excellent team at Putnam and Penguin: Jen Loja, Jen Klonsky, David Briggs, Emily Rodriguez, Elizabeth Lunn, Wendy Pitts, Carmela Iaria, Alexis Watts, Venessa Carson, Rachel Wease, Bri Lockhart, Kara Brammer, Felicity Vallence, Elora Sullivan, Christina Colangelo, Caitlin Whalen, Courtney Gilfillian, Marisa Russell, and the rest of the good people who have made the Penguin family such a welcoming place these past three years. My additional gratitude to the hardworking team at Listening Library and PRH Audio for telling this story the way they'd tell it in Kelanna.

Thank you to Heather Baror-Shapiro for taking *The Reader*, *The Speaker*, and *The Storyteller* to so many new places, and thank you to my foreign publishers for bringing this series to so many new readers.

Thank you to my critique partners and readers, without whom this book never would have made it off the ground. To Emily Skrutskie and Jessica Cluess, thank you for helping me whip the first act into shape. One day, I'll figure out how to get a plot moving on my own, but until then, I am grateful for your expertise. To Christian McKay Heidicker and Parker Peevyhouse, thank you for helping me work through all sorts of mind-bending meta-level acrobatics and off-the-wall ideas about narrators and blacked-out pages. I couldn't have made it through the twistiest parts of this labyrinth without you. Thanks also to Ben "Books" Schwartz, Mark O'Brien, Mey Valdivia Rude, and K. A. Reynolds for coming through in the clutch with your incredible speed and insight! I feel honored to keep learning from all of you.

More thanks than I can possibly express to my friends and family. Thank you to Tara Sim, who's been on this journey with me since Pitch Wars. Maybe I almost killed you with cashews one time, but you're my dear friend and one day I'll prove it to you by staring deep into your eyes for an uncomfortably long minute. Thank you to Meg RK for caring about the Easter eggs even more than I do. You're a dream reader, and you remind me to believe in myself. Thank you to Kerri Maniscalco for sharing your wisdom and your experiences and your laughter (and really good takeout!). I treasure your friendship and can't wait to share many more stories and food adventures with you. Thank you to Mom, Auntie Kats, and my Bay Area and hometown communities. You nurture my creativity. You encourage my dreams. You inspire me with your own accomplishments, your work ethic, your kindness, your selflessness. Thank you all so much for your love and support. To Cole, thank you for your cooking, your fight choreography, your vacuuming, your incomparable talents at finding plot holes, and most of all, for your love.

Finally—ultimately—my undying thanks to you, dear reader, for following me here, to the end. Thank you for shouting about these books on the internet, for handselling them, for gifting them to your friends and family, for checking them out at the library, for showing up to events and creating fan art and loving this series, these characters, this world as much as I do. Thank you, thank you, thank you a thousand times for sharing this with me.